NIGHT CALLER

Baaaringngngng.

Now what inconsiderate son of a bitch would be ringing a doorbell this time of night?

Stauer picked up a pistol from atop a bookcase and, after pulling the slide, and letting it slam forward to ensure the pistol was loaded, walked to the front door muttering foul imprecations the whole way.

"Dirty, miserable, ill-mannered bastard! Who the fuck calls on someone at three in the fucking morning?" Wes made sure that his muttering wasn't so low that whichever rotten SOB was at the door wouldn't be sure to hear it.

He continued cursing while fumbling with the door chain. If there was someone at the door with criminal intent, he didn't want a narrowly opened door restricting his field of fire. No, he wanted a clear path to shoot the son of a bitch.

Wes flung open the door and stuck the muzzle right against the nose of . . .

COUNTDOWN
★ THE LIBERATORS ★

★ ★ ★

TOM KRATMAN

BAEN

COUNTDOWN: THE LIBERATORS

Copyright © 2011 by Tom Kratman

A Baen Books Original

Baen Publishing Enterprises

www.baen.com

ISBN 13: 978-1-4391-3402-3

Cover art by Kurt Miller

First printing, February 2011

Distributed by Simon & Schuster
1230 Avenue of the Americas
New York, NY 10020

Printed in the United States of America

10 9 8 7 6 5 4 3 2 1

★★★

For my mother, Agnes Quinn, nee Henchey
8 January, 1936, Boston, MA
10 October, 2008, Radford, VA

★★★

COUNTDOWN

★ THE LIBERATORS ★

★PROLOGUE★

When you're wounded and left on Afghanistan's plains
And the women come out to cut up what remains . . .
—Kipling, *The Young British Soldier*

D-815, Kandahar Province, Afghanistan

No one had intended it as a joint op, let alone a combined one, but the nearest support to the beleaguered SEAL team had been a team of Army Special Forces, under a captain named Welch. Because of that, once they were committed, the next echelon in had been the green beanie's boss, one Colonel Wes Stauer. And Stauer had come with a company of Afghan commandos, trained by his own people and paid for directly by the United States.

The valley was high and the air thin. The passengers on the Blackhawks could *feel* the rotors straining to keep the things in the air. They could look up and still see mountains. But they could also look down and still see clouds.

It was a relief, then, to almost all concerned, when the

1

choppers, nine of them, touched down in staggered trail formation along either side of a dirt trail running between two ridges. It was a relief even though the air around the landing zone went from still and clear to a thick, choking cloud of dust in half a second.

First off was Stauer, though the ninety-odd Afghans accompanying him weren't far behind. The latter bolted for the ridges, to relieve the American Special Forces currently providing a thin guard.

He was a big man, Stauer, six-two, graying but still with all his hair. Framed by deep crow's feet, his eyes were a pale blue that both saw too much and had seen too much. He was widely considered to be a son of a bitch. Most of those he worked for were of that opinion; though only a smaller percentage of those who worked for him shared it. And even they were more often than not of the "but he's *our* son of a bitch" persuasion.

This was his straight third year in Afghanistan, *this* time. He'd had four year-long tours previously, unusual in special operations. But why not? No wife, no kids; Stauer was married to the Army and had been since graduating Notre Dame ROTC thirty plus years before.

Stauer didn't think they were going to win the war. He hadn't thought so in a long time. Oh, the troops did well. Washington's influence he found baleful. Sometimes he wished it were over. *But what else do I know how to do?*

He stepped off the chopper into the dust and ran, bent over, to a point outside the sweep of the rotors. Though he had a pistol in a shoulder harness, he also carried a rifle in one hand. He didn't wear any armor. Up this high, in air this thin, the protection the armor gave just came at too high a cost, protecting the enemy as much as the wearer, or perhaps even more so.

Stauer's beanie was stuffed into a pocket against the chance of it being sucked into one of the Blackhawks' engines. He wouldn't put it on until either the helicopters left or he was *well* out of range.

A SEAL with a recruiting poster jaw met Stauer about fifty meters past the rotors. If Stauer was big, the SEAL was effing *huge*. "They've got my lieutenant and one of my SEALs," the SEAL told him. Stauer read the swabbie's nametag, "Thornton," and thought, *So this is Biggus Dickus, himself. Gotta help a man with that kind of rep.*

Thornton pointed at the adobe and scrap rock village down below and added, "And none of these people will tell me shit. I want my people back, sir." Thornton's voice was plaintive, remarkably so for a man who exuded as much strength as he did.

Thornton was a senior chief, the rank equivalent of a master sergeant in the Army. Enlisted from a Midwestern town so far from the sea he'd never actually seen it before joining the Navy as a young man, he'd started real life as a Navy corpsman, a very thoroughly trained medic, supporting the Marines, before switching over to SEALs. He probably had more decorations than Stauer and, given that the Navy was cheap with medals and that the Army overly generous, especially with officers, that was saying something.

"What's your case that they know where your men are?" Stauer asked.

"We watched 'em drag our people through the town, leading 'em by ropes around their necks," Biggus said. "They sure acted like they knew each other, the Muj and the townsfolk. Sir, you *know* what's going to happen to my people if we don't get them back *quick*."

Stauer nodded and said, "Yeah, I know. Lemme think for a minute."

"Okay, sir," Thornton replied, as all but one of the Blackhawks began taking off again, raising a still more enormous cloud of dust as they left.

It had been a long war, and a hard one . . . and, so it increasingly appeared, a losing one. After all the years, all the treasure, all the blood and pain, the tide of victory was receding. First Russia had cut off reliable transport through it or its satellites; though they still occasionally let some things through when they needed some concession or other. Then Pakistan had openly and officially granted the enemy safe asylum across the convoluted, mountainous border. This, naturally enough, had caused the United States forces – though not generally NATO allies—to treat the border with no more respect than the enemy did. Indeed, once Pakistan effectively ceded sovereignty, it could hardly claim to still have it. Nonetheless, the U.S. incursions had had the unfortunate effect of bringing down the Pakistani government and seeing installed one still more firmly committed to helping the Taliban and Al Qaeda. Of course, the Pakis had also cut off surface transportation. Worse still, they used some of their own special operations forces, by no means contemptible, to support the enemy, just as they sometimes had against the Russians, decades before.

Now the war was being waged purely on the aerial resupply ticket. And it wasn't enough. Five divisions were needed to win, at least five. They had the equivalent of, and could barely support, three, one of these a mixed NATO formation that sucked up logistics but added little or nothing to the war effort. (There were feelings, among Americans, Brits, and Canadians, that, but for the latter two, the non-U.S. NATO contribution represented a net minus.) It was a formula for eventual defeat.

And everyone who mattered, not least the enemy, knew it.

These were not the first Americans Stauer knew of who had been captured. What had happened to the others, except in the rare case where a timely rescue had been possible, was horrible beyond belief. And frustrating, as the entire war had been frustrating. As the idiocy emanating from Washington had been frustrating. As the refined idiocy coming from Kabul had been frustrating.

Seven years of war can do odd things to a man. Thinking about the fate in store for his countrymen, Stauer felt something give inside him. It might have been his sense of restraint.

Pacing, Stauer clasped his hands behind his back. *Never mind that you wanted stars, Wes. If that's your most important value you don't deserve to have them, just like most of the motherfuckers wearing them. So skip that. Even if what you have to do costs you stars; you haven't lost anything you could have saved.*

He looked down at the villagers, the men from Welch's team surrounding them in the village center. One man alone, Welch's medic, was watching the women and children, who were kept separate.

And what's the worst case if all this gets out? Again, forget prison. If you're afraid of that you're also not worthy of stars. What's the worst case to the war effort?

He snorted softly but with profound derision. *What difference? Since Jesus Christ in his second coming occupied the White House, we've been losing anyway. About the only good news is we've kept the Pakistanis out of the country, if not officially out of the war. But every troop that can be spared is holding the passes, now, leaving not a lot to clean out the guerillas. Now it's so far gone I doubt we even can win, not without carving a chunk out of Pakistan. Silly, arrogant, slick-talking bastards have micromanaged us all the way to defeat.*

Stauer considered some of the stars sitting in Kabul and thought, *Not that they didn't have some help, silliness and arrogance-wise.*

Okay, forget all that, too, for now. What about the rights and wrong of the thing? Again he snorted. *Wrong to lose a war, terrible, morally execrable, in fact. And wrong to let your men be led off and butchered.*

"Captain Welch!"

"Sir!" answered the bright-eyed team commander. Terry Welch was not so tall as Stauer, nor so broad in the shoulders as Biggus Dickus Thornton. He was, however, an intensely strong West Pointer, and former captain of their weight lifting team.

"Back me up in this. You and your men aren't going to like it."

"Whatever you call, sir, however you call it."

"Major Mosuma?"

"Sah?" the Afghan commander replied. He, too, knew

the war was being lost, that he'd backed the wrong side, and that his life, in the medium term, was forfeit. He spent every cent he made supporting his extended family, now in India.

Stauer handed the Afghan his rifle. "These people your tribe? The tribe of any of your men?"

"No, sir. None of us."

"Stand by to translate, then."

Without another word, Stauer glanced around at the three score or so adult male villagers assembled. One, in particular, caught his eye for the arrogance and confidence the Afghan showed under what should have been very frightening conditions.

Stauer drew his .45. Special Forces, never liking the Italian 9mm forced on the rest of an unwilling army, had had its own order of .45s specially made by Heckler and Koch. He walked to the arrogant looking Afghan and crouched down in front of him. The Afghan sneered until, in a single, smooth motion Stauer placed the pistol almost on the bridge of the Afghan's nose and pulled the trigger. Just before that moment the sneer had disappeared as the eyes widened in shock.

Of late, Special Forces also tended to ignore the rule against frangible ammunition. Given the size of the bullet and the fact that just about all of its energy was suddenly dumped inside the Afghan's brain, his head exploded like a melon, the wide eyes popping out, breaking their optic nerves, and bouncing off Stauer's chest.

Welch's Special Forces people stirred. The Afghan commandos took it in stride. Better than Americans, they understood that sometimes the medium *is* the message.

"Major Mosuma?"

"Sir?"

"Translate now please. Tell these people that I have seventy-one rounds in my ammunition pouches and in my pistol. Inform them that one of two things is going to happen. Either we get my people back, alive and well, or every male in this village old enough to sprout a beard will be killed and the women and children will be sent to market in Kabul and sold as slaves."

Stauer had to change magazines, just once, before the information was forthcoming.

D-814, Kandahar Province, Afghanistan

What the mixed team of SEALs, SF, and Commandos brought in the next day didn't resemble anything too very human. After they were cornered in a small complex of caves, and when it was obvious there was no escape, the guerillas had soaked their bound captives down with gasoline and applied a match. After that, whatever they'd done to the captive SEALs beforehand was impossible to tell.

And, of course, there were no guerilla prisoners taken so they weren't going to say anything about it.

Stauer walked over to the first of the stretchers and pulled back the poncho that had concealed the remains. These were curled into a fetal position, and charred beyond all recognition, except for blackened metal dog tags and chains with bits of burnt flesh stuck to them. Stauer said nothing, but walked to the next stretcher and did the same. He didn't want to even think about what these men had suffered. When he'd finished inspecting he called, "Major Mosuma?"

"Sir!"

"I'm a man of my word. Kill all the men. The women and children belong to you and yours."

Then Stauer boarded a helicopter and winged back to Kabul to turn himself in. He wept the entire way back.

Seven years of war will do odd things to a man.

D-803, Kabul, Afghanistan

An air conditioner whined in the office window. The office was outfitted with the kind of furniture that looked good but didn't last. It was expensive, though, and still more expensive for having been shipped by air, at government expense. Nobody much cared about expense to the government, but everyone who wore or aspired to stars cared about image. And, it had to be admitted, while it would last the furniture gave the right image.

"Why won't the son of a bitch just resign and go away?" whined the commander of all special operations forces in Afghanistan, Major General Jeff McPherson, a tall, confident-looking redhead, careful touch of distinguished gray at his temples, who harbored a deep suspicion that unauthorized persons had been test driving his young and lovely wife. The not-entirely-unfounded suspicion tended to cloud his judgment, especially his moral judgment. Still, to be fair, for ordinary purposes, when he wasn't doing stupid things like having his subordinates, though tasked to blend in with bearded locals, shave, or salute in the field, or any number of other things that set his troops' heads to shaking, he could be competent. And no one had ever questioned his physical courage.

The problem, from the general's point of view, was that while one could court-martial lower ranking officers, noncoms, and junior enlisted, court-martialing a senior officer indicated a flaw in the system. From the Army's point of view, this was highly suboptimal. People, as individuals, could be flawed but to admit to a systemic problem? No, no; that was just unthinkable unless the blame could be pinned on some outside, malevolent, foreign agency. The KGB had once been good for that.

And since colonels had been promoted five times, and gone through numerous other checks, to include what amounted to a Department of the Army Inspector General witch hunt, court-martialing one indicated a systemic problem, indeed. Why, the Army had been known to promote a colonel to brigadier general, after discovering that the man was guilty as sin of forcing a subordinate to commit an act of forgery and fraud, to get him to resign. Anything but publically admit to a systemic problem. And a general officer who let a systemic problem out into public view? No more stars for him.

"Because he *wants* a court-martial," answered the one-starred Val—for Valerius—Pettigrew, tall, slender, and café au lait. "He told me, when I talked to him, that a court-martial is the only way he's ever going to be able to rake—and I quote—'those miserable, incompetent, son-of-a-bitch, anti-Christ, pseudo-messiahs in Washington and Kabul over the coals as they so richly deserve,' unquote."

"But doesn't he understand what this will do to the Army? To the war effort? To himself?"

"He says the war is lost anyway, that it was lost, and again, I quote—"

"Spare me," said McPherson, holding up one halting palm. "So what do we do, Val? What do we do when the press gets wind of this?"

"I don't think they will, sir," Pettigrew answered. "Everybody in the village is either dead or dispersed to various well-guarded harems, or slaving in a factory somewhere in Pakistan or, maybe, India by now. The Afghans won't talk; they made a good profit off the sales and probably got their dicks wet as an added benefit. The SEALs and Welch's A-Team aren't going to say shit. Look up the word 'reticence' sometime. Any decent dictionary will show a picture of an SF operative, or a SEAL, or a Ranger, or even a Marine, seated on a witness stand, with his mouth thoroughly closed."

Pettigrew's face grew soberly amused. "Besides which, sir, do you realize we haven't had a lick of trouble anywhere within fifty miles of that village since the . . . ummm . . . incident. In an area that used to see firefights two or three times a day. The people there are scared shitless of supporting the other side now. 'Course, that will change as soon as word gets out that Stauer's on trial."

"There'll be no trial," McPherson insisted. He went quiet then, thinking hard.

"Go back to what you said before," McPherson ordered, rolling his hand in a backwards circle over his desk.

"We haven't had a lick—"

"No, not that. Before that."

Pettigrew thought hard for a moment. "You mean about reticence and our people, SEALs, Rangers and Marines?"

"Yeah . . . those." McPherson's face lit with a wicked grin. "So he wants a court-martial, does he? I wonder if he wants all those others, people just like the ones he committed mass murder for, court-martialed, too."

Man, you really do *have shitty moral judgment*, thought Pettigrew. *Makes me glad I boffed your wife.*

"And that's the deal, Wes," Pettigrew told him later that afternoon. "You retire, without prejudice, or Welch and his team, and Thornton and his team, get tried as accessories. Moreover, the red-headed bastard is going to turn your man, Mosuma, over to the Afghan authorities. They'll hang him, no drop."

"What a piece of shit," Stauer said with a sneer. "Almost makes me wish I'd fucked his wife."

"You mean you didn't?"

Stauer looked at Pettigrew with great suspicion. "You don't mean you did?"

"Well, what was I supposed to do? I gave her a ride home from the O club, where she'd been drinking, oh, to excess. Next thing I knew, her head's over my lap, and my brain is being sucked southward. Right on Riley Road. I fucked her in the post stables."

Stauer was about to chew out his long-time friend, viciously. But then, what's the point?

He laughed. "How was she?"

Pettigrew sighed. "Words can't describe, Wes. Words just can't describe."

★ ★ ★

"He'll do it, sir," Pettigrew told McPherson. "But there's a little problem."

"I see no problems."

"Well . . . both Biggus Dickus Thornton, Terry Welch, and the entire teams of both of them are punching out, too. That's Wes' condition; we have to let them go if we want to get rid of him and if they want out."

"Fair enough," said McPherson, relieved that the problem was going to go away. "Do they?"

"To a man, sir. Every one of them said the war is lost and it just isn't worth it. *They said other things, too, but you don't want to hear those.*

★★★

PART I

★★★

★CHAPTER ONE★

How dull it is to pause, to make an end,
To rust unburnish'd, not to shine in use!
—Tennyson, *Ulysses*

D—127, San Antonio, Texas

Like watching fish in a tank, Wes Stauer thought, looking at the thin traffic making its way along East Evans Road and down Bulverde. No, that's not quite right. It's like watching paint dry. *Not even enough cars on the road to provide the hope of a decent accident.*

He watched one of two identical two-seat cars pass the other anemically and sneered, *Battle Song of the Proletariat Specials. Painted "Green," of course.*

He shook his head. He could afford a decent, which these days meant an imported, car. Most couldn't anymore, after the bite tax took. Indeed, most who could afford any kind of personal transport these days could only support one of the designed-by-committees-of-special-interests things, like those two seat jobs asthmatically chugging up the road in front of Stauer's house.

Stauer didn't really care that much about the tax

17

rates, personally. His home was held by a corporation masquerading as a religious organization he'd set up in Lebanon once upon a time. He paid the corporation, which is to say, himself, a very modest rent. The rent just matched depreciation and expenses, so there was no tax burden there. Likewise most of his money was overseas where Uncle's sticky fingers couldn't get at it. Oh, yes, the Internal Revenue Service took a whopping bite out of his retired pay, but that, in relation to his overall finances, was "mere."

Unpatriotic? Stauer mused. *It's never unpatriotic to keep your government from wasting your money on things that shouldn't be done anyway.*

Not that he was necessarily all that illiberal in every particular. He wasn't really, at least as far as domestic issues went. Student aid, for example, to send someone to school to learn to be an engineer? Or a doctor. Or, just as good, a machinist or plumber or farmer? Those kinds of things he was fine with, though he was rather finer with them if there was some price involved; teaching poor kids or providing health care in Appalachia, for example. Or military service, of course.

To take a master's on the public ticket in resistingbadevilhonkywickednaughtydeadwhitemaleop pressionandrepressionlittleEichmannismbadbadbadidnes s? I'm not precisely enthusiastic about that.

And he had the strong sense that the money collected to help the poor and even out the playing field was, in fact, mostly being spent on upper middle class drones with sociology degrees, *Who sow not; neither do they reap*, and construction contracts for the very well connected.

Case in point, he mused, *that program to pay schoolgirls not to get pregnant. They pay a hundred thousand inner city girls a thousand or so dollars a year, each, and ten thousand social workers ninety thousand a year, each, to administer it, and half the girls end up getting knocked up anyway. Case in point, the senatrix from California whose husband somehow just managed to land a three-billion dollar contract to build wind farms in a place with no wind, because, unfortunately, the Senator from Massachusetts has a vacation home overlooking the place where there really is wind. Case in point . . . ah, what the hell's the use?*

And it's not entirely fair to blame the President for this, either. It was building up for years, since the nineties, anyway. Maybe the eighties. And maybe President Wangai made it worse; but maybe he didn't, either. Nobody was going to make it a lot better. You drink enough; you get a hangover. You spend enough; you get broke. Maybe we could have spent our way back to prosperity. I doubt it, but maybe. But, if so, we'd have to have spent on the right things. We haven't.

At least it's a little better here in Texas. A little.

Stauer'd thought he knew why he'd retired to San Antonio. *To use the PX and commissary, to have Brooke Army Medical Center nearby when the time came for that. That's what I thought I was doing.*

It wasn't those things, though. Or, at least, it wasn't entirely those. *What the hell did I want? The facilities—*he mentally shrugged—*yeah, okay, sure. But I wanted the facilities someplace where I wouldn't be reminded of what I was missing. No sharp young troopers, fit as a fiddle and* *ready to fight. No listening in the morning air for the distant cadence I can't join in any more.*

I do miss the Army.

And I didn't want to be in a purely Air Force town. And at least my arthritis isn't too bad here. And home . . . well, it hasn't been "home" in a very long time.

"It sure sucks to get old," Stauer muttered, "and I'm not convinced that the alternative is worse." He sighed, looking down toward his feet. Briefly, his eyes rested on his stomach. "Two years ago, you miserable bastard, you were flat." Traveling further downward, he scowled and said, "And don't you even *think* about getting old. At least *you* still have a purpose."

From inside the residence he heard the purpose's plaintive call, "Honey, come to bed."

Philomena Potter—Phillie, for short—stirred in the big bed, reaching for the man who should have been there but who now stood on the balcony. Her questing hands coming up empty, she awakened and sat up. Immediately she called out, "Honey, come to bed."

Phillie, ER nurse, aged twenty-seven, five feet, ten inches, thirty-five, twenty-three, thirty-six, was a quarter-English, eighth-German, eighth-Irish, half-Mexican self-propelled monument to mixed marriages. She had short blond hair that had not come out of a bottle, large emerald green eyes, and skin that was essentially white but tanned really, really well. Long legs were a given. She was quite pretty without being painfully so, having a regular, straight nose, full lips that were almost pouting, high cheekbones and a rather endearingly delicate chin.

She was also one of those not entirely rare human females predisposed toward older men. Perhaps "hard-wired" would be more accurate. Indeed, Phillie was so hard-wired for older men that she'd hung on to her virginity—technically, anyway—until well after turning seventeen, precisely so she'd be legal for the class of men that interested her. At the time, the minimum age for that had been thirty-five. She'd added a year and a half, on average, every year since. Her current lover—Wes Stauer, presumably sitting on the balcony watching life crawl by— was a little young by those standards. If young, he was also a soldier, had been, anyway, for about thirty years. That had the effect of making him look older. It was also the other area in which Phillie was hard-wired: *Soldiers; yum.*

Oh, she'd tried doctors, naturally enough, being an RN and all. Leaving aside the potential problems at work, she'd decided they were, on average, a bunch of arrogant pricks, and especially the specialists. She'd also tried Air Force types. The student pilots from Randolph AFB were interesting, but they were mostly arrogant pricks, too. And she tended to be taller than them, which was awkward and operated against the third area of her genetic predispositions. *At six-two Wes is just about right. Why won't the bastard come back to bed?*

The Special Forces medics, training at Fort Sam, downtown, had been her most enjoyable group. She'd even thought about marrying one of them. Then he'd been killed in Afghanistan and a colonel had come to tell her how very sorry he was and all, and how much the country appreciated . . . and that colonel had led to another colonel and that colonel . . .

★ ★ ★

"I'll be there in a few," Stauer called back. *No I won't. Not tired, not horny, not even lonely. Just miserable.* "Go back to sleep."

Nice girl, though, he thought. *And, unlike most women that age, I can't say she has neither the charm of innocence nor the skill and grace of broad experience. And she's not even immature. She'd be a good match for an old fart like me. If I wanted a match. Family? I put all that off—"married to the Army"—and never missed it. And now I've no Army and no family. She says she wants kids. I just don't know if I'm up to it. Or if I'd be a decent father. And why the hell am I even thinking about this? I don't want to get married. Christ, I'll "be stone dead in a moment."*

A car was pulling into the complex's parking lot as Stauer stood up. He ignored it. Walking inside and gently closing the sliding glass door behind him, Stauer padded quietly on stocking feet to the bedroom he'd set aside as an office. The hardwood floor underfoot didn't so much as creak.

Which is just as well. Phillie will put up with my staying on the balcony. She's good about leaving me space. But if I've come inside and not to her she's likely to get a little testy.

Instead of returning to bed, then, Stauer went into the office and closed that door even more gently and quietly than he'd closed the glass one. Only then did he flick on the light.

Even after two years of living here, most of his books were still packed up in boxes in the upstairs bedroom. Thus, the fifteen book cases were half empty. They'd have been even emptier if Phillie hadn't brought down, unpacked, and shelved about a thousand volumes. The walls were marked, too, with little holes, the only remaining traces of the various nick-knacks he'd picked up in service. He'd put them up when he'd first moved in. After a year or so he'd discovered they depressed him more than anything. Fortunately, there were the empty boxes from Phillie's unpacking of books. The plaques, awards, certificates, commendations . . . they'd all gone into the empty boxes and up to the upstairs bedroom, there to await the judgment day or the auction that would surely follow Stauer's eventual death.

He'd left some things out, still up on the walls, or in cases, or on stands. These were his weapons: forty-seven odd bayonets, knives and daggers, two dozen swords, including a matched fifteenth century daisho that had set him back forty thousand dollars, two crossbows, one modern, one medieval, sixteen rifles of various calibers and capabilities, nine pistols, one morning star . . .

Man without a family ought to have a hobby, at least.

He sat down, as lightly as he'd closed the doors and then cat-footed across the apartment.

Maybe I actually should have taken a job, Stauer thought. *But what was there available? Office work? Being a bodyguard for some State Department maggot? Supervising guard details on a gate in Iraq or Afghanistan for seven hundred bucks a day? That shit got old when I was eighteen. And if I'd wanted to do direct action the options were not only limited, I'd have been reporting to some ex-SEAL who inherited a pile of money. Maybe I should have gone with that Ph.D. from King's College*

London . . . but what would have been the point? It's not like I need the money. Military pay isn't extravagant, but when you don't have a family to support, and have no moral qualms about keeping Uncle's fingers off your money, you can invest yourself to a not inconsiderable wealth. Toss in the retired pay and it comes to quite a sum.

But I'm just so bored . . .

And it isn't just me.

Stauer flicked on the computer monitor, a twenty-inch flat screen, and pulled up his e-mail. He tried to keep in touch with old comrades, such as wanted to keep in touch. And the refrain from them was so common as to be stereotypical. "I'd give up a year's pay for just one day back in the jungle . . . I am bored out of my gourd, boss . . . What the hell was I thinking when I punched out? . . . There's no work, sir, not for people like me. Not that isn't government make-work . . . "

Guys, if I knew how to help, I would, Stauer sighed. *Maybe we should all get together sometime. But . . . nah . . . when it's over; it's over.*

Alone in the bed, Phillie lay on her back, hands behind her head and fingers interlaced. *I've never felt this way,* she mused, *and I don't just mean horny. He looks right, acts right, smells right. Everything's right. I'd be proud to be his wife and bear his children. And I think he cares for me. Loves me? I wish I knew. But if he doesn't, it isn't for anything I've failed to do. He loves history so I enrolled in a couple of history courses at UTSA so we could discuss it. That helped some, but would have helped more if he hadn't*

*thought all the profs but one were idjits. Rollin, Wes said,
knows what he's talking about. But then Professor Rollin
left for greener pastures, so . . .*

*And, of course, I can't talk to him much about my job.
"Phillie, honey, most of us are quite content to go through
life without thinking of ourselves as animated bags of skin
filled with obscene glop." He won't even admit he stole
that line from that antiwar science fiction writer.*

*Besides, since the government introduced medical
rationing, I've come to hate my job. Why should I talk
about something I hate?*

*Still, we have good times together. We have enough in
common to make a go of things. He's met my mom, so he
knows I'm going to age really well. We could—*

Baaaringngngng.

*Now what inconsiderate son of a bitch would be ringing
a doorbell this time of night?*

"I'll get it, Phillie," Stauer shouted from the office. He
picked up a pistol from atop a bookcase standing against
one wall and, after checking the magazine well, pulling
the slide, and letting it slam forward to ensure the pistol
was loaded, walked to the front door muttering foul
imprecations the whole way. The federal government,
quite despite some recent rulings from the Supreme
Court, was being difficult about personal arms, but Texas
and a number of other southern and Midwestern states
were being equally difficult right back. It was a bad sign,
really; everyone said so.

"Dirty, miserable, ill-mannered bastard! Who the fuck
calls on someone at three in the fucking morning?" Wes

made sure that his muttering wasn't so low that whichever rotten SOB was at the door wouldn't be sure hear it.

He continued cursing while fumbling with the door chain. If there was someone at the door with criminal intent, he didn't want a narrowly opened door restricting his field of fire. No, he wanted a clear path to shoot the son of a bitch, quite despite that the Feds were likely to prosecute these days on civil rights grounds no matter what the local Castle Doctrine laws said.

Chain unhooked, hand grasped around his pistol, Wes flung open the door and stuck the muzzle right against the nose of—

The muzzle didn't waver. Rather, Stauer's head rocked from side to side, as if to bring a jumbled memory to the surface. The scars on his face seemed familiar. The medium tall, slightly pudgy black man slowly and carefully raising his hands over his head looked like . . . *but no . . . it's been freakin'* years.

"Wahab?" Stauer asked.

The pudgy black face rocked, the nose moving the muzzle up and down with it. "Yes, Wes," the man said in a clipped, almost British accent, "it's Wahab. And I need help."

★ CHAPTER TWO ★

God preserve us from our friends.
—Lenin

D-165, Commonwealth Avenue, Boston

Rain came down in a steady drizzle, filling the low points in the streets and soaking everyone in a cold, wet misery. From the left, headlights dimmed by the thin, half-frozen deluge, an automobile came. Ignoring pedestrians, the car passed through a muddy puddle, casting up the filth therein onto sidewalk and foot traveler alike. Overhead, icicles were beginning to form on the trees that lined the broad green strip that divided the street.

"God, this weather is shitty," said one of the party, a black man, tall and thin but with refined, almost Arab features.

"Shitty it is, Gheddi," agreed an older man, likewise black, "but at least it isn't California."

"What's the matter with California, Labaan?"

"Californians," the older man, Labaan, replied. Though he often, even usually, wore a smile, Labaan lost

27

it every time the subject of California or Californians came up. And he would never say why.

The car reached them, splashing filthy water from the street onto their coats and trousers.

"*Sharmutaada ayaa ku dhashay was!*" Gheddi shouted. He shook his fist as he swore at the splashing car. *Fuck the whore that bore you.* When the car ignored him, continuing on its way without a backward glance, he began to reach under his coat.

"Easy, Gheddi," said Labaan. It was said gently but was an iron-bound order nonetheless. The older man placed a hand on Gheddi's wrist, advising, "We have other business this evening. And we don't need trouble from the local authorities."

Gheddi seemed inclined to argue the point, at first. At least his hand continued to attempt to move under his long woolen coat. After a few moments of vain struggle, he gave it up, returning his hand to his pocket for warmth. "You're right, of course, Cousin," Gheddi admitted. "God will have to avenge me on the ill-mannered pig."

"God will do as He will do," answered the cousin, Labaan, leader of the little family group and the only really fluent English speaker among them. Gray-haired, desert- and war-worn, Labaan spoke calmly. He alone knew this city, having studied here as a young man. Indeed, Labaan had studied at the same school as the group's target. That, however, had been many years and several wars in the past. Now, studies abandoned as useless in the violent, anarchic world he inhabited, Labaan led a small team in the service of his clan. And why not? It wasn't as if he had a country anymore.

No, all I've got left is blood. The whole nation thing turned out to be a lie, and the whole international thing turned out to be worse than a lie. In the end, only blood matters, only blood counts, only blood lasts. Everything else is illusion. Everything but blood is a fraud.

Labaan's was not a high-tech team. They had Bluetooth equipped cell phones, recently purchased at a Wal-Mart. They had pistols; this was what Gheddi had been reaching for, of course. They had a rental van, currently idling a few blocks away on Gardner Street under the control of the fifth member of the group, Asad, the lion. The van was GPS equipped, and there was also a hand-held device, which would be used to find the ship that would take them home. They also had tape to secure their target, the tape likewise courtesy of Wal-Mart. Lastly, for the delicate time between confronting their target and getting him on the ship, they had two surplus atropine injectors, the atropine having been removed and replaced with a cocktail of various drugs that the clan's chief chemist—*Come to think of it, Tahir the pharmacist studied here, too. Wonderful city, Boston! Well . . . except for the weather*—had assured them would render the boy half insensate but calm and cooperative in a brief instant.

"He should be coming out soon," Labaan said. "Abdi, you and I are the only ones who can identify the boy. You and Delmar go past the entrance to his apartment building. Wait. If you take the boy, I'll call for Asad. If he turns toward us, you call."

"*Haa*, Labaan," Abdi agreed. Like his cousins, he was tall and slender, with café au lait skin, and delicate of feature. He and Delmar walked briskly to the public transportation stop, a partially Plexiglas enclosed and fully covered shelter from Boston's execrable weather. In theory, the thing had radiant heaters. In practice, these helped little if at all. The two men shivered in a night far colder and infinitely wetter than the worst their barren country had had to offer since sometime around the last ice age. The shelter reeked of piss despite the cold.

"And Gheddi? You get that hostile look off your face. Now."

The air shimmered around the closing door, the result of the overheated air of the apartment meeting the frigid air of the second floor landing. Adam Khalid Hodan, twenty years of age and son and designated successor to his father, Khalid, chief of the clan of Marehan and leader of the Federation of Sharia Courts, shivered in his coat as he locked the door behind him.

Khalid was approximately as religious as Richard Dawkins, but he knew how to mouth the right phrases. Adam, the son, was considerably more religious, though he wanted nothing whatsoever to do with some of the more extreme elements in his father's domain. For that matter, he avoided the big mosque on Prospect Street precisely because it seemed to him to be dominated by the nuts.

And besides, as the boy often thought, there's no requirement to have any man interpose himself between oneself and God.

The apartment was on the second floor, of five, in the converted townhome. Whatever heat there might have been outside of the twenty small apartments of the building had risen to the upper floors.

"God," whispered Adam, "grant that spring come soon to this frozen place."

Physically, Adam, too, was a near match for the men outside who sought him. Perhaps he was a bit darker, as coming from a more southerly province. About them, of their existence or their mission, he had not a valid clue. His father had sent him here—ordered him, really, and much against his will—to further his education for the day he would lead the clan. If his father had thought there was any danger to the boy, he'd neglected to mention it.

Steeling himself against the coming wet and cold, Adam turned toward the door and began to walk the tiled landing to the steps that led down and out. His father could be very touchy about allowances if grades were not maintained. Adam had business at his school's library, across the river.

"Warya, Adam," someone called out before Adam's feet touched the glistening street. He looked and saw someone he'd met, very briefly, in the restaurant down in Roxbury, a countryman, though of a different clan. Odd it was, how clan lines blurred in this foreign place.

"We define ourselves by what we are not," one of Adam's professors had said once, in lecture. He'd found that true, once he'd thought on it. For that matter, what passed for a girlfriend here, Maryam, was not even of his own country, but of a neighbor. Though she'd hardly lived at all in the Dark Continent, she, too, defined herself as "not American, but African," and so she, too, seemed close kin here in Boston.

Pretty and to spare, Maryam was pleasant to be around, except of course when she started speaking politics.

Some of what she said, what she had learned from her UN father and his progressive friends, Adam agreed with. But she was depressed, so often, by things beyond her control, and let that depression bleed over to things that were, that the boy wasn't sure their relationship was going anywhere.

Who, after all, wants to live with a steady diet of "brain drain," "rule of law," "reparations," "colonialism," "aid," or "Bob Geldof"?

"Warya . . . Labaan," Adam returned, raising a hand in polite greeting. He'd had to search his mind for the name, which had, at least, taken his mind off Maryam's obsessions.

Abdi saw that the target had turned toward Labaan. He immediately pushed the dial button on the cell phone hidden in his pocket.

"I hear you," Asad answered, from the rental van idling not far away.

"Come," Abdi said. "Labaan has the target close at hand. We are moving in."

"Two minutes," Asad answered.

Adam consulted his watch. Sighing, as if with sincere regret, he told Labaan, "I've a girl waiting for me, friend, at the library. I really must be going."

Maryam was not waiting, however. She had nothing to do with his desire to leave the area. Instead, it was the look in the eyes of the one accompanying Labaan, the one introduced as "Gheddi." He looked hostile, however much he tried to hide it. He seemed a lion, about to spring.

Waving farewell, Adam turned toward the trolley stop. He wasn't looking forward to the urine stench, but at least it would be out of the rain, now falling steadily. As he turned he discovered two men standing right in his path. Neither of them so much as attempted to hide the hostility in their eyes.

Adam opened his mouth to call out for help. The cry never came. Instead, he felt a fierce stabbing pain in his right buttock, followed by a feeling of complete weakness and confusion. Distantly, he was aware of his arms being pulled over the shoulders of the two men who had blocked the path behind him. He barely felt or heard the scraping of his toes being dragged across the concrete of the sidewalk and the asphalt of the street. Of being stuffed into the back of a van, of the clammy feel of the rubberized sheet between him and the corrugated metal floor, Adam had no knowledge whatsoever.

D-165, Constitution Marina, Charleston, Massachusetts

It was useful, Labaan had reasoned, to change jurisdictions in case anyone had witnessed Adam's kidnapping and called the police. Given the place, Labaan had thought this unlikely. Still, *any advantage that can be squeezed out, should be*. And the extra time could mean the difference between spiriting Adam away to the ship and being caught red-handed. It also allowed them to take the more circuitous route across the river along Massachusetts Avenue and through Cambridge.

Thus, wipers pounding a steady beat, the party had driven across the Charles River, along Memorial Drive, across the Gilmore Bridge, and finally to the marina.

There, on the dock, next to a small boat that had been bought on the team's behalf, stood a lesser functionary of the big mosque on Prospect Street. Neither the mosque nor the functionary much cared about the mission. They'd gotten a request, a check to cover expenses and then some, and had, as dutiful members of the *Umma*, the Family of Islam, cooperated. The functionary, who had met only Labaan, simply handed over the keys to the boat and left for his own vehicle. He never even saw Adam, still laid out in the back of the van.

Labaan watched as the unnamed functionary drove off, cold, muddy water spraying to either side. He sighed. *Mouth the right words, utter a few pious phrases, and a devout Muslim will just assume you're on the business of the faith. Idiots. What I am about has nothing to do with Islam, and everything to do with the position of my clan.* When he was convinced the man had truly gone—*no sense in having an unnecessary witness*—he ordered, "Put him in the boat and get our bags."

Abdi and Gheddi hastened to comply, opening the van doors, wrapping Adam carefully and fully in the rubber sheet, and carrying him to the waiting boat. Gheddi looped all five bags, including one Labaan had filled with necessities for their captive, over one shoulder. As he hefted the last bag, Gheddi thought, *What a waste to be so solicitous of an enemy's welfare. Labaan's softheartedness will be his ruin.*

Rain running down his face, Labaan walked around the van and stared intently into Asad's eyes, demanding, "Tell me again what you do from here."

Asad sighed. Labaan could be so anal about things.

Even so, the driver answered, "From here I take the van back to our hotel and clean the thing with a lice comb. Then I put the seats back in place. After that, I check us out from the hotel. I return the van to the rental yard by the airport, before it opens. My flight to Amsterdam is tomorrow, KLM 8526, departing at twelve fifty-five in the afternoon."

"Off with you then," Labaan ordered, slapping his hand to the van's driver's door. "And God be with you."

The van began pulling away as Labaan turned his attention back to the small boat. He saw Gheddi pulling at the starter rope. Even from this distance he could sense the frustration growing in his younger comrade. *You should have cut lawns here for some extra spending money, Cousin,* Labaan thought. *Then a little outboard would not vex you so.*

By the time Labaan reached the boat he could see, more than just sense, that the younger cousin was about ready to kick the outboard overboard and use the oars that lay in the small boat's bottom, half concealed by the rubber sheeting surrounding Adam.

Carefully descending the few wet wooden rungs of the ladder and stepping into the boat, Labaan bent over and checked to ensure the tank vent was open. There was no time for tact. He pushed Gheddi aside and tilted the propeller into the cold salt water. He then set the gearshift for neutral. After adjusting the choke, Labaan took the handle of the starter rope. He gave the thing a smooth pull. Nothing. Another pull likewise produced nothing. On the third, the engine coughed but did not start. With the fourth, it did catch, spewing out a cloud of noxious fumes. Labaan nodded sagely, then called, "Cast off the rope."

★ ★ ★

The stars were hidden behind the clouds, the half-frozen rain, and the sheen of the city glancing off them. The moon was no more help if, indeed, it was even risen. Labaan couldn't actually tell. Instead, they had a good GPS with an integral compass, a Magellan Meridian Platinum, in fact. It hadn't even been all that expensive. This Labaan held in his left hand while his right controlled the motor.

"Call the boat," Labaan said. "They are waiting."

Gheddi did, likewise relaying their position. "On your current course we're about three kilometers, dead ahead," the boat answered. "On our port side you'll find we've lowered a boat. Put your cargo in it, then board yourselves. Dump your outboard and drag your own boat in after you. We can raise the whole mess. We'll dump the boat at sea, after we prepare it.

"We'll show a series of lights, red-green-red, to guide you."

D-164, Bandar Qassim, Ophir

The walls of the inner room were hung in banners of green, the sacred color of Islam. It would be stretching things to say that the people in the room were all that devout. In a place this arid, and with most of what wasn't dry being salty seacoast, hence mostly devoid of plant life, it wasn't hard to understand why here, as in Saudi Arabia, green was something between pleasing and divine.

Because the local people shared considerable affinity—culture and blood, both—with the Arabs on the other side of the Red Sea, the floors were covered in carpets and cushions, with the dominant color of the former being red. Between the red and the green, and the gold of some of the cushions, the overall effect was not displeasing to the local eye, though a westerner might have found it garish, even Christmassy.

Few or none of the locals, of course, celebrated Christmas. This close to Mecca and Medina, Christians were few and far between. Of those few, the bulk were slaves. Nonetheless, the ambient mood in the room was as joyous as any western Christmas.

"We've got the little bastard," exulted Gutaale, chief of the Habar Afaan and ruler of this little experiment in anarchy. His ample belly, so unusual among his people, shook with unrestrained mirth. "Let Khalid, that Marehan boy buggerer"—a charge even Gutaale knew was false—"balk us now!"

Despite the back slapping, the laughter, the cheers, one of Gutaale's advisors seemed very subdued. Old, thin to the point of emaciation, nearly bald, and gray where hair remained, Taban, one of the senior of the sept chiefs, just made a frown while staring at the red carpet and rubbing his hands together, worriedly.

"What's the matter, Taban, old friend?" Gutaale asked.

"Precedent, Chief," Taban replied. "I'm worried about precedent."

"Well, I'm not," Gutaale said. "I'm more concerned with stopping the endless war among us while getting our people their just due."

"Nonetheless, you *have* set a precedent," Taban said.

★ CHAPTER THREE ★

A dream, too, is from God.
—Homer, the *Iliad*

D-126, San Antonio, Texas

Neither the sun nor the chickens were quite up by the time Wahab had almost finished his story. Traffic had picked up a bit though; so much Stauer could hear from the streets and the nearby intersection. Even then, the traffic was much lighter than it would have been even a few years prior.

"So they have your chief's son," Stauer shrugged. "So what?"

"Not just his son, Wes," Wahab corrected. "His *only* son and his heir. They've got him—my chief, I mean—by the balls. We just don't *do* these kinds of things back home. At least decent people don't. That someone has is frightening."

"And you've no idea where the boy is being held?"

Wahab shook his head, sadly. "We don't even know for a fact what continent he's on; Africa, Europe, even maybe

38

still here. And none of the governments that are friendly to our faction have been able to find a trace. We asked for help. They all said the same thing: 'Tell us where he is and we'll be glad to help you retrieve him.' Oh, yeah, *that* was a big help."

Stauer stood up from the leather couch on which he'd been seated and walked across the room to the bar. There he poured himself another drink and held the bottle up in query of Wahab's desire for another.

"No thanks, Wes," the black said, holding up one hand defensively. "I'm a bad enough Moslem already and another would be pushing the willingness of the Almighty to forgive. Besides, it's a little *early*, isn't it?"

Stauer shrugged off the question and returned the bottle to its place on the bar counter. He said, "I don't see where I could be a 'big help' either. I mean, sure, if I knew where the boy was—this is what you were getting at, right?—I could probably assemble a team out of personal friends to get him back. But if I knew that it would be because you knew that. And if you knew that, any of a dozen countries with first class special operations forces would be willing to help. Maybe even for free." *Provided one doesn't attach a monetary value to influence, anyway.*

"Money wouldn't be . . . wouldn't have *been* a problem," Wahab assured his friend. "I mean, this is my chief's *only* son. Despite having four wives and a dozen concubines, all he throws are girls, except for this one. For that one, Adam, all he has to give . . . "

"All he has to give," Stauer answered, "is still apparently not enough to find the whereabouts of his son. Get that and you can retrieve the boy."

"Would you be willing to come to help organize the intelligence effort?" Wahab asked. "We'd make it worth your while."

Unheard and unseen by either, just behind a corner, Phillie listened attentively as she had since shortly after hearing the doorbell ring.

She felt sick to her stomach. *Please, God, don't let him go. We've just really gotten comfortable together. I mean, this might really be a match good for both of us. I don't ask for much, God, but this one little thing . . .*

"I don't need money," Stauer answered, shaking his head. "Haven't in years. And the amount I could *really* use would be beyond your chief's means, I suspect. I mean, maybe Mobutu could have funded my wildest dreams. But your guy? Nah."

Stauer laughed at the absurdity of his own "wildest dreams."

"You might be surprised," Wahab answered, chewing at the inside of a cheek. That was all he'd say on the subject, however. Whether that was because of a negotiating stance he'd been told to take, embarrassment at his clan's poverty, if they were truly poor, or even simple ignorance, Stauer didn't know and wouldn't guess.

"It's all academic, anyway, since I can't do a thing without knowing the boy's—Adam, you said his name was?—Adam's whereabouts. I can maybe give you the name of a really good intel guy or two . . . ummm, three, if that's any help."

★ ★ ★

Thank you, God, Phillie thought, turning green eyes ceilingward. *Special prayers and candles. Promise. Also much fornication so I'll have something worthwhile to confess.*

Phillie's theology was not necessarily sound, however sincerely held.

As quietly as she'd gotten out of bed and walked the hallway to eavesdrop still more so did she turn and slip off back to bed.

"Why me, anyway?" Stauer asked. "I'm nobody special."

"Exactly what I told my chief," Wahab agreed. "'This American neocolonialist bastard is nothing special,' I said, 'except that he seems to believe nothing is impossible and I have never seen anyone his equal for making the impossible possible.' My chief, of course, scoffed. Do but note, however, that he sent me here anyway."

"Not a total loss, that," Stauer said. "It's good to see you, and that's the truth. Will you be in town for a few days?"

"At least that," Wahab answered, "or my chief will not believe I truly tried."

"Where are you staying?"

"I've a reservation at the airport Marriott."

"Nonsense." Stauer was adamant. "You're staying here. Where's your bag, by the way?"

Wahab grinned despite his overall disappointment. "I seem to recall leaving it on the landing when some rude barbarian asshole stuck a pistol in my face."

When Wes laid himself down next to Phillie, after showing Wahab to his room, she sensed such a weight bearing down upon him that she didn't even think about offering sex. Instead she just asked, voice full of concern, "What's the matter, hon?"

He told her a truncated version of the story, not that she needed it, having already eavesdropped on virtually every word.

"And you're disappointed about having to turn down an old friend?"

"That, yes," he admitted. "But more than that, for just a brief moment I had the sense that my youth was in my hands, to spend again as I wish. I thought I sensed purpose again. But . . . no."

This was not precisely what Phillie wanted to hear, since she rather hoped to become a purpose for him, full and entire in herself. Still, she clucked sympathetically and sidled over to lay her head on his chest.

"Sleep," she said. "And you're not useless. And you're most emphatically not old, that you would need some fountain of youth. And if you don't believe me . . . " Her hand wandered down to where he had the means of proof that he was not yet so very old.

Gently he moved her hand aside. "Not tonight, Phillie, because tonight I feel old and useless."

He felt her head nodding on his chest and wrapped one arm around her. In moments they were both asleep.

The lack of sleep, the starvation, and the stress of U.S. Army Ranger School affected different people different ways. Many of these ways were lasting. Many of them were adverse. Stauer's souvenirs from the course included bad knees, a weak back, and the almost complete inability to either dream, except for nightmares, or to remember any dream that wasn't a nightmare if he happened to have one. And it had been nearly three decades since he'd attended ranger school.

It had cost him one girlfriend, in fact, years prior. His nightly, sweat-pouring, terrorized awakening, his suddenly sitting bolt upright and shouting out, "I wasn't sleeping, Sergeant," had been simply too unnerving.

Still, sometimes . . .

The magnets came in all shapes and sizes, large bars, small bars, discs, rods, and horseshoes. Rather, they came in all sizes relative to each other. Compared to his own tiny dream self they were huge and threatening, every one. Indeed, they didn't just threaten; they struck; they bounced; they sometimes crushed him between two of them.

Eventually, from chaos, a kind of order emerged, the magnets grouping themselves into little subgroups, all being held in place by invisible lines of force. At the center of the grouping was one particular magnet, the largest of all. It dwarfed Stauer's dream body, as it dwarfed one little magnet held tight. Somehow Stauer knew it was important to free that little one. He swam to it, though how he swam in atmosphere or vacuum he hadn't a clue. In dreams, one never asks.

He pulled and tugged; he set his dream feet against the major magnet and tried pushing off with his arms. Nothing worked. Dimly, Stauer began to realize that the little magnet was not merely held in thrall by the huge one, but that all the other sub groupings contributed their share to fixing it fast in place.

"They have to go," the dream self said, aloud.

Still swimming through the void, Stauer aimed for what looked like the smallest and weakest grouping of magnets. He built up speed as he neared it. Then somehow, as can happen only in a dream, his orientation changed to feet first, even as his speed picked up to an amazing rate.

He struck the magnet with his feet, causing it to spin off, out of control, until it was lost in the distance. Taking a glance at the captive, Stauer saw that it was looser in its orbit about the great one. He began to head for the next smallest group . . .

Wes sat bolt upright. In a whisper, rather than a shout, he said, "I wasn't sleeping, Sergeant."

"Huh? Wha'?"

With a broad smile painted across his face, Stauer gently nudged Phillie. "Honey, I think I've changed my mind about making love tonight. Afterwards, say if I give you a minimum thirty minutes of post coital cuddle time, would you mind making breakfast, no pork for my guest?"

"Cynical bastard," she muttered sleepily. She rolled over onto her back even so.

The first faint traces of light were filtering through the window of a spare bedroom holding a much sleep-deprived Wahab. He could have slept through that easily enough. What he couldn't sleep through was Stauer shaking him like a rat in a terrier's mouth. Wahab opened one baleful eye to see a boxer-shorted, broadly smiling Stauer shouting,

"Get up, you black bastard. Get your lazy ass up. And don't tell me about jet lag. I don't care. My girlfriend's making breakfast and we've got some *planning* to do!"

★CHAPTER FOUR★

I was shipwrecked before I got aboard.
—Seneca, *Epistles*

D-160, At Sea, MV *George Galloway*

In the peculiar loneliness of a storm at sea, the ship plowed the waves. At the bow a white rush of foam lifted, split, and curled to each side. Astern, it left a faint trail of whitish water and cavitation bubbles, the trail soon disappearing under the twin influence of wave and mixing.

Above that trail was a name, in Latin letters. It would never have done to have given the ship any obviously Islamic name. In the paranoid world that was, all such were inherently suspicious. Still, let it not be said that the naval arm of Al Qaeda was completely lacking in a sense of humor. If they couldn't give the chartered ship a holy name, they could at least honor one of their foremost unholy allies in the west.

Of the workings of the ship itself, a mildly seasick Labaan had little clue, even though operating a small boat was certainly in his repertoire. Instead, while the other three remaining with the team alternated turns guarding the prisoner, well chained below inside a shipping container, with long sessions making obeisance to the sea over the side, Labaan searched the news for any indication that Adam's disappearance had been discovered. So far as he'd been able to determine, there'd been not a whisper. There were disappearances all the time, of course, so he'd had to use a fairly narrow set of search parameters. After several hours of trying, however, and scores upon scores of searches, he'd come up with precisely nothing.

So typical of the Yankees, he sighed, meaning New Englanders and New Yorkers, specifically, not Americans, in general, *not to care about or report a crime in their backyard, while so desperate to fix all the ills of the world everywhere else.*

Labaan logged off of one search engine and pulled up a purely spurious e-mail account. This one contained in the draft folder a passage from the Jewish Torah and Christian Bible, Isaiah 11:6. *Ah, good, Asad has made it home safely.*

Another message informed Labaan that the transfer of his men and cargo, scheduled to take place at Port Harcourt, Nigeria, was on time and fully prepared.

Be glad to get the boy off my hands, actually, when the time for that comes, Labaan thought. *Though what he's in for . . . and he seemed like a pretty nice kid, too, the one time we talked, if a little too full of the nonsense his professors have been pouring into his head. Well, until I am relieved of responsibility, I can at least keep him healthy . . . and maybe even knock some of the silliness out.*

★ ★ ★

A dim battery-powered lantern swung overhead, not so much bathing as lightly wiping with light the container in which Adam had awakened. He was certain of three things. He was on a ship; the rocking and swinging of the light told him as much. He was chained—literally chained, by the foot, like a slave—inside some kind of big metal box with corrugated floor, roof, and walls. And he was in very serious trouble.

No, I am certain of four things, he thought. *I am also certain I am seasick.* He reached out for a bucket they'd left for him and emptied the contents of his stomach into it.

Afterwards, he was able to think a little more clearly. *Ransom?* the boy wondered. *My father would pay almost anything in ransom to get me back whole and sound. Not that I'm worth it, or would be if I weren't an only son. Somehow, though, I don't think this is a kidnapping for ransom. For one thing, while I can't be sure, the people who grabbed me struck me as Habar Afaan clan. The one who called himself "Labaan" surely was one.*

When, the boy lamented, *when will they learn that blood is no solution, that the answer is in forgetting ties of blood and seeing our common humanity?*

And what will they want from me? Almost he laughed at himself. *Me? Nothing; I've nothing to give or to take from. They wouldn't be grabbing me for ransom; their clan chief, Gutaale, is even more sticky fingered than my father, keeps even more concubines and still doesn't lack for money.*

No, it's not going to be money they're after. They're

going to use me to exert control over my father, to increase and improve the position of the Habar Afaan over the Marehan. I think that means they'll never let me go. Or never let all of me go anyway. I'm likely enough to lose an ear or a finger as proof they've got me and are willing to do anything to me.

Adam had the thought calmly, but then felt a sudden wave of fear and terror as the thought translated itself to a mental image. He could almost see the knife coming down on a trembling hand—his own—to slice off a finger, or flicking past his eyes to sever an ear from his head. For a moment, but only for a moment, he almost gave in to tears. He killed the tears with a self- and culture-deprecating laugh.

We're as bad as the Arabs. Me and my brother against my cousin. Me, my brother, and my cousin against the stranger. Clan and tribe over all. Steal what you can for your own before another tribe steals it first. Or, as in my case, steal a member of another tribe. You can use him or her like a slave or, better still, use the slave to force his family to do your bidding.

God, why do you hate Africa so?

Then again, thought Labaan, *there's really no reason to mutilate the boy. Surely his father knows that Gutaale is willing to even without being told or shown. I mean, okay, maybe if we have to produce proof beyond a video that we have him, we could send a finger or something. But I really don't think that will be necessary. I'll tell Gutaale as much.*

Then again, I know what the chief is planning. At some

point the head of the Marehan is going to balk. He has to. And then, I suppose, we'll have to send him a piece of his son, or his son a piece at a time, until old Khalid thinks better of it. Well, hopefully that won't be my job.

Labaan logged off of the ship's computer and stood up, yawning and stretching. *I should probably sleep some. Before I do though, I'd best check on our passenger.*

The moving steel bars that held the door in place shifted, lower sliding up and upper down, as a central handle turned. Adam braced himself for something really unpleasant. Unconsciously, he grasped his fingers together as if to shield them.

Instead of a man with a meat cleaver, though, Labaan walked in, unarmed and unaccompanied. Adam sensed there was someone unseen on the other side of the door.

Labaan glanced around the interior of the corrugated metal box, taking in the water jug, the tray of food, the thin—and none too clean at this point—blanket-covered mattress, and the bucket, bedpan, and piss bottle. It was a lot less trouble and risk to move those than to escort the captive several times a day to relieve himself.

"You are well, Adam of the Marehan?" Labaan asked.

Adam nodded, silently. Almost he'd blurted out that they'd never get away with this, that his disappearance would be reported, by Maryam the Ethiopian, if no one else.

But if they can disappear me, they could disappear her, too.

Instead of letting his mouth put his girlfriend in danger, Adam asked, "Where are you taking me?"

"From here to Port Harcourt, Nigeria. From there we'll be going by air to another place. You don't need to know where that is."

"But . . . *why*?"

Labaan remained genial when he answered, "You are young, boy; you are not stupid."

Adam gave off a deep sigh. "Fine, I know why. But what's the point of it? A little temporary advantage from my father? Eventually he's dead and I'm dead and things will reverse. This is a temporary advantage for your people—you are of the Habar Afaan, yes?—and nothing more."

"Everything is temporary advantage in Africa, Adam," Labaan said. "Everything. When things are crumbling around you, all you can hope for is temporary advantage. Shall the sailor, shipwrecked at sea, worry about the distant shore or about his own next stroke? About the forest in the distance or the piece of timber that can keep him afloat for now?"

"If he doesn't at least look for the shore," Adam countered, "he's unlikely to reach it."

The older man sighed then, countering, "And so are we, young Marehan, and so are we."

D-157, Bandar Qassim, Ophir

A fairly large, wooden, motorized dhow thumped lightly but regularly against the edge of the dock in the almost rectangular harbor. Well-armed and apparently disciplined guards patrolled the landward side, the breakwater, and the docks themselves. This late at night, the sounds of ground traffic were minimal, though off in the distance could be heard the sound of a marine engine, fitfully starting, over and over, and then choking off into silence. Waves rolled and they, too, could be heard whenever not drowned out by that apparently defective engine.

Light there was aplenty, for here, if nowhere else nearby, streetlights worked and the local power plant produced electricity to feed them. Even had there been neither, inside the dhow the boat's own batteries fed enough juice to keep the interior lights going, without a continuous need for the engines to run.

Seated, cross-legged, on a cushion on the lower deck, Gutaale's belly rested approximately on his lap. On the opposite side of the cabin sat a Yemeni, near in appearance to the chief of the Habar Afaan, and likewise with a not unimpressive gut. The Yemeni's hand rested lightly upon a closed laptop.

"Half in three days," Gutaale told the Yemeni, Yusuf ibn Muhammad al Hassan, "the other half on delivery." The sun had been up and high when the two had begun their haggling. It was only well after its setting that they'd agreed on a price within a tiny fraction of the initial offer. The fact was, both men enjoyed the haggling for its own sake.

"That's fine," Yusuf agreed. Once a price was set, the Habar Afaan had already proven himself a man of honor as far as payment went. He had, for example, already paid for the lease of the *George Galloway* and payment to its crew. Those payments Yusuf split with his business associates in al Qaeda, who leased and ran the ship he owned.

Yusuf, on the other hand, was a man of fairly narrow honor. Oh, he'd produce the arms. He was quite reliable that way. What he'd told nobody was that he also intended to provide better arms to the rivals of the Clan Habar Afaan. This would, of course, require the Habar Afaan to purchase still better arms from Yusuf. And so on. And if Yusuf and his associates had chartered to Gutaale's people a ship for a little kidnapping? Well, the Marehan needed but to ask, and produce the cash, and Yusuf would lease them as good a ship and crew or better. Same with al Qaeda, really. Though for them, to gain their trust, Yusuf had had to go far out of his way to create a prayer bump to indicate a piety he didn't remotely feel.

"You do understand," the Yemeni said, "I am only getting the things on a ship, a ship that will be poorly guarded, and that ship to the local waters. It is up to your maritime *mujahadin* to actually seize the ship and its cargo."

"Yes, of course," Gutaale agreed, with a confident shrug. "And the trainers will come?"

"About three weeks later," the Yemeni answered. "It will take you that long to get the equipment off-loaded and moved to where it can't be seized back again by the Russians." *Should they try, which, given the fracturing among them, and the degree to which one splinter answers as much to me as anyone, seems unlikely. But let the Habar Afaan think this is a more perilous enterprise than it really is. It helps keep the price up.*

"I will also need . . . " Gutaale stopped speaking as the lights suddenly dimmed.

"Captain!" shouted the Yemeni. "Start the engines. The light is failing."

D-150, Bonny River, Nigeria

The nighttime lights of Port Harcourt, seen through the smoky haze of the town and reflecting off clouds above and in the distance, were nothing much, despite the nearly four million people who lived in or near the place. Less impressive still were the lights of Okrika, a suburb of the main town, and it was closer. No, what attracted the eye were the plumes of natural gas fires flaring to either side as the Galloway made its careful way up the river.

Labaan stood on the bridge with the ship's captain, the bridge crew, and Gheddi. The captain was speaking into a ship's telephone.

"The ambulance will meet us at dockside," the captain said. He hesitated before asking, "I know you are going to the airport, and not Port Harcourt Teaching Hospital. But if I might enquire . . . "

Labaan shook his head no. "Captain, what you don't know can't do you any harm." Turning to Gheddi, Labaan ordered, "Cousin, let us go prepare our charge for transportation."

Adam's clue that they'd entered a port or something, at least, not on the high seas, was that the lamp overhead had mostly stopped swinging. Of the subtle change in the tenor of the ship's engines he was not really aware. Mentally, he began preparing himself for fight and flight.

They'll have to unchain me, he thought. *If we're near a port, or even a coastline, and if I can get free for ten*

seconds, I can leap overboard. I'm a good, well, a decen,
swimmer. I can be ashore and running like hell before they
can catch me.

He thought he sensed footsteps outside. Sure enough,
the steel rods that held the door in place began to slide. A
thin crack appeared, the flickering light that marked it
faint, at best.

Make yourself meek, Adam, the boy told himself. *Lull*
them, if you can. Maybe they'll be slack enough to give you
your chance.

Within moments of the door opening, Adam knew
there would be no chance. Labaan entered, followed by
three more men. Only one of them, the one called
"Gheddi," looked particularly hostile. The others, however,
didn't look bored or slack. Over one shoulder, one of these
carried a stretcher with straps attached.

Labaan had a hypodermic syringe in one hand.
Holding it point up, he squeezed the plunger until a few
drops leaked out. "This is a mix of an hallucinogen, a small
admixture of an opiate, and arachidonic acid. It will not
harm you permanently, though it will relax you even while
making you see things that will not be there. It will also
give you a fever. Will you cooperate or—" Labaan's head
inclined to indicate the others "—will you have to be
restrained?"

Meek, Adam reminded himself. *If it doesn't matter*
here, it might still, later." He held out one arms and began
to roll his sleeve.

"No," said Labaan. "I am sorry. This needs to go in
your buttocks. Drop your trousers please."

★ ★ ★

The moon was up and shining through the smoke of the town as Gheddi and Abdi carried the insensate Adam down the ship's gangplank, one man at each end of the stretcher. The boy moaned incoherently, and thrashed a bit. Straps on the stretcher kept him in place.

At the foot of the gangplank sat an ambulance, white with an orange stripe that narrowed toward the front. The ambulance doors were open, a couple of white clad emergency medical technicians standing beside them. Neither lights nor sirens were active.

Labaan and the captain of the *George Galloway* had been chatting amiably by the brow. The captain would no more say what his next mission was than the African would. He did admit, "I have to pick up some people in Northern Ireland."

The two shook hands farewell. Labaan walked down the gangplank to join his men and his charge.

Once the boy was loaded, and the kidnapping party had joined him in the back of the ambulance, the lights came on and the siren began to whoop.

★CHAPTER FIVE★

The niceties of peacetime are blown away
like cobwebs, and men are allowed to become what,
under their skins, they have never ceased to be.
—Martin van Creveld, *The Culture of War*

D-124, San Antonio, Texas

Phillie had never seen, really couldn't have imagined, the speed with which Stauer's apartment had been converted into a headquarters. She might have called it "organized chaos," except that she sensed the chaos was more apparent than real while the organization, for all that it was hard to trace the lines of it, was both real and natural. The woman was used to chaos; after all, she was an ER nurse. But this kind of chaos was of a totally different quality and quantity than any she'd experienced before.

It had begun with Wes grilling his African friend. Of that grilling, Phillie had caught only snatches over the sound of frying bacon, for her and Wes, and frying bologna, for Wahab. Having to use two separate frying pans had been a little odd.

"You know or can reliably find out where those people are?"

"No problem, Wes."

"It's going to be a minimum ten million for personnel costs, several times that—*many* times that—for facilities, equipment, transportation, and supply."

"No problem, Wes. My chief will transfer to an account I'll set up and give me permission to disburse as needed. There'll have to be an accounting."

"Sure. To be expected. I'll need a bunch of your people—"

"Bad idea, Wes. The reason I know or can find out where those people you want are is that we have low level informers, slaves and outlying septs, in the Habar Afaan. They've got them among us, too. We can maybe use a few really *close* kin. No more than that though."

"Then add fifteen—no, twenty—million to the personnel costs."

"No problem. How much to get started? And can you take me to set up an account my chief can make a transfer to?"

"Phillie will take you," Stauer had answered. "At least we can set up a local account until we can have one of the people I'll invite set up something more discreet." Phillie found it also a little odd that he didn't even ask if she would, but just assumed it.

Because I'm part of the team? she wondered. *Because he's just taking me for granted? That can wait; no sense taking offense until I know it's really been offered.*

While Phillie had taken Wahab downtown to make arrangements, Wes had gone shopping. He'd come home just after she and Wahab returned. He had with him half a dozen high-end laptops, plus a dozen and a half each sleeping bags and air mattresses, a big coffee maker, several cases of Lone Star, a case of mixed hard liquor with mixers, paper plates, plastic utensils . . .

Phillie guessed that Stauer must have been making phone calls on the way because the door knocking had begun before noon and hadn't apparently ended yet. Oddly, every man at the door had asked the same question as soon as it opened: "Free beer?"

As if the chaos weren't enough already, Wahab had taken Wes' car to the airport to pick up a few more people. He wasn't due back for a couple of hours. And *still* the pizza boxes had begun building up in the kitchen.

She heard Stauer shout from the dining room, in which room the table had disappeared under maps, printed off by sections on the color printer and carefully taped together, "Gordo, you got a line on a ship yet?"

From the living room came the shout back, "I've got five possibilities. And two small subs . . . well, three, but one of those is a little big. And a fast patrol boat up in Finland but it would need to be re-armed. But I need a decision on the assembly area. We've got a line on eighty-five plus square kilometers in South Africa, but it's only near, not on, the sea. Natal, don't you know. It's a safari lodge so it does have some buildings—five of 'em suitable for barracks, I think—and the firing of weapons would be unremarkable. Six million bucks. I've also found two parcels in Brazil, deep in the Amazon, no facilities what-soever but along a navigable river leading to the Amazon and then the Atlantic. One of the Brazilian pieces is five million acres—think 'Massachusetts'—for twenty-five million; the other's about one point two million—think 'Rhode Island, plus'—for about half that. The second one's closer to Manaus, which has its good points and its bad. The realtor's being cagey; both are really old royal grants and may have some unusual attributes.

"Whichever parcel we go with," Harry Gordon continued, "we'll probably need something to navigate the river for supply purposes. I'm working on that, too. I've got a handle on something that maybe would do for a forward assembly area, if we need it; anything up to sixty thousand acres, fifty-five acres abutting Nairobi National Park, for four hundred and seventeen K, USD. Also, if you're willing to stay in the U.S., I can get you forty-five thousand underground square feet, also under about fourteen feet of reinforced concrete, on two hundred and ten acres near Denver, and a similar facility in Washington state. And there's a one hundred and seventy-five thousand acre parcel in Guyana for about two bucks an acre."

"Skip Denver! As for the other parcels, gimme a recommendation! And if it's Brazil or Guyana come up with tentage figures! Kosciusko will be here in an hour or so and you can figure out the ship with him!"

Phillie shook her head with wonder at all of it. It was just all so exciting. And Wes seemed to radiate energy and sheer happiness in a way she'd never seen before.

That wasn't the only change that had come over him. In the time they'd been together, he'd always been the perfect, and perfectly accommodating, gentleman. If she'd wanted to eat Mexican, Mexican it had been. If she'd wanted to see a chick flick, then it was off to whichever movie had tears running out in waves under the exit doors and the sound of wet vacuums slurping up the residue of broken, celluloid hearts. She'd never asked, but she was pretty sure that if she had asked to see Klingon Opera—had Klingon Opera existed—he'd have gone along.

She had the sense now that that prior accommodation had been indifference as much as gentlemanliness. Certainly, he didn't show much tendency to accommodation now, for her or for any of the dozen or so men who had, so far, assembled on the apartment. Wandering from ad hoc work station to ad hoc work station, coffee pot in hand, she thought, *Maybe I should thank you for not listening, God. He seems so happy. We'll have to see.*

She walked up to Stauer and took his cup from his unresisting hand. She filled it, and returned it.

"Thanks, Phillie," Stauer said, without looking at her. He seemed engrossed in conversation with someone she vaguely remembered had been introduced as "Ralph." *Mmmm . . . last name . . . Boxer, I think. Yeah, that was it.* Boxer was about Wes' height, not in such good shape, and a couple of years older. She still thought his graying hair was distinguished, sexy even. And the suit? Well, Phillie was also one of those not particularly rare women who could be and usually were turned on by a nice suit. Boxer's had to be Brooks Brothers or something just as good.

"You need to assemble a strike team soonest, Wes," Ralph was saying. "There's a chance, a slim chance but still a chance, that I can find where the boy is being held or moved to. He may be moving at the time and you'll have to strike fast and hard."

Ralph Boxer was, in terms of retired rank, the third

senior man present, though Phillie didn't know that. An Air Force two star, he'd resigned in lieu of submitting even one more report to the White House that was generous with wishful thinking and economical with the truth. Boxer's own moment of truth had come when two pilots were shot down and killed after one of his intelligence summaries had been doctored by the next echelon up because the White House simply didn't want to hear that the enemy in Afghanistan had grown considerably stronger as a result of its own political mismanagement. He'd made it as noisy a resignation as he knew how. The papers had ignored it.

"Problem is," Wes countered, "without some idea of where he'll be it's nearly impossible to plan. If you find him, you might find him someplace where we can't get arms for the team. He could be at sea and we've no way to get a team to a ship."

"Victor can always get us arms, I think," Boxer said. "Anywhere at all."

"Well . . . yeah," Stauer conceded. He grimaced, "But for God's sake, not Victor."

"What's the matter with Victor?" Ralph seemed truly perplexed.

Stauer shook his head. "You never know who Victor's reporting to."

"Sure we do. He's reporting to FSB, the successor in interest to KGB. So? This is not something the Russians are going to object to. And we don't necessarily have to tell Victor what the arms are for. As for arms-free countries, there is not a one Victor can't smuggle into, given a little time. And once they're in hand, the team can carry what it needs by chartered plane or ship . . . or yacht. The rules then are all different."

Stauer still looked skeptical. "Victor, huh?"

Boxer nodded. "I think so. If we had all the time in the world we could use somebody else. There's an Arab in Yemen, I've heard, who's starting to make a name for himself in the trade. But when you need to start a war in a hurry . . . "

"Victor," Stauer finished. He said the name in the tone of a man who's just been told he's got an incurable disease. "Well, I suppose it's not as if he's a complete stranger."

"Indeed not," Ralph said, with a broad smile. "Now if you'll let me get to work until Bridges and Lox get here . . . "

"Bedroom upstairs. The one that's not full of boxes. I hung an S-2 sign on the door. There's a spare computer in it."

"That'll do," Ralph said. Patting a black nylon case, he added, "But I brought my own computer. It has certain . . . mmm . . . features, that yours won't. Now what about that strike team?"

"You know Terry and Biggus Dickus?"

"Terry Welch? Sure. I didn't know Thornton was available."

"Terry's pulling together his old team, part of it anyway, maybe as much as two thirds or three quarters."

"They're all out of service?"

"Got caught up in the same shit I did," Stauer answered.

"Fair enough then. Though two thirds of Terry's team won't be sufficient. You need more men, and some under-water demo guys."

"Biggus Dickus will be working on that."

After Ralph had left, taking his bag in hand, Phillie asked Wes, "Who's Victor?"

"Russian arms dealer," Stauer answered. "No, that's not descriptive enough. Victor Inning is the most unprincipled, unscrupulous arms dealer of any nationality in the world and perhaps in the history of the world. His main virtue is he will supply arms to anybody, no questions asked, and at what—I have to admit—is always a fair price. Ralph and I used him two or three . . . hmmm . . . three times in the past, when we had a mission and needed non-Nato arms delivered in a flash. He keeps his own stocks, his own ships, and his own little air force, too, Air Luck. Though he doesn't maintain the planes for shit, so they only stay up by luck. Still, what he doesn't have on hand he can usually get in a hurry. Speaking of which," Stauer turned his head and shouted, "Ken, have you got the basic OPLAN and Table of Org and Equipment yet?"

"Not yet!" came the return shout from the extra downstairs bedroom.

"Slow bastard! Hurry up!"

"Is it always this much fun?" Phillie asked.

"Oh, hell, no," Stauer answered with a laugh. "Usually it's sheer misery because you spend ninety-five percent— well, eighty, anyway—of your planning time prepping or giving briefings for a succession of military morons and civilian mental midgets . . . "

"We're going to need AMLs, or those with a mix of Ferrets," Ken called from the bedroom.

"Why?"

"Most common combat vehicles in Africa. Just

about everybody over there has them. Would raise no eyebrows."

"I know where to get Ferrets," Gordo chimed in, from the kitchen. "Nine of 'em for sale in the UK for dirt. They'd have to be rearmed. AMLs are tougher. South Africa had and built thousands, but they've replaced them all with Rooikats and Ratels. The ones they've got have all been designated as targets."

From upstairs, Ralph shouted down, "The South African ammunition budget is for beans, these days. If those things have been designated to be turned into targets most of them are probably in near perfect shape at Tempe, near Bloemfontein."

"How does he know all this?" Phillie asked.

Wes sighed and answered, "Ralph used to be Assistant Deputy G-2 for the Air Force— "

"G-2?" Phillie asked.

"Intelligence. Then he was with the JCS—the Joint Chiefs of Staff—for a while. I understand they put him to pasture when he bitched one too many times about shading the intelligence reports going to the President. We used to work together, sometimes."

"A general?"

"Honey, there are *three* generals here. They're the ones who look really old, except for Ralph, and are wearing ties."

"But you were only a colonel." She wasn't all that familiar with the military but she knew a general out-ranked a colonel.

"Tools to the man who can use them," Wes answered.

There was the muffled sound of a toilet being flushed. A few moments later another man, maybe five-nine, graying and thinning hair, minor paunch, emerged from the master bedroom. "I need somebody who can hack into DCSPERS, MPRI, Blackwater, and Triple Canopy." Officially, Blackwater was called "Xe." In fact, everyone outside of corporate headquarters still referred to it as "Blackwater."

"What for?" Ralph asked from upstairs.

"Identify personnel. Cazz says he can produce the core of the Marines. I can cover the mech force cadre. Welch has part of a small team in hand or en route. I still need pilots, fixed wing and rotary, both, plus a UD team, and more special ops types. And medical personnel, cooks, couple of sappers, an admin puke to help me . . . "

"I can do that, or Bridges or Lox can when they get here. You'll have to be patient."

"Patience, my ass; I'm gonna kill something."

"Who's that one," Phillie asked in a whisper.

"That's the adj . . . the adjutant. Seamus Reilly. He's only here because he hopes I'll give him a strike mission. He hates being a personnel guy. Sadly for him, he was very good at it." Wes considered that for a moment, then added, "He was good at a lot of things."

"Will you?"

"Give him a strike mission? Maybe. Well . . . probably. But it depends on who else shows up. That said, Reilly's in the unusual position of being able to pull in about half a mechanized infantry company—maybe a full one, if he really tried—just from people who worked for him over the years. Just you watch, too. He's going to pull enough of them in and then present me with a fait accompli. I can hear him now: 'Well, they're my *boys*, Wes. They wouldn't *follow* anyone else.' Never mind that most of those 'boys' are anywhere from early forties to mid fifties."

"Is it true that they wouldn't follow anyone else?" Phillie asked.

Stauer sighed. "I've known two, maybe three, commanders in the Army that the troops cried over when they left. I've only known one who, after he left command, the troops formed grievance committees and went to demand of the higher commander that their old commander be returned to them. That happened with Reilly, if all reports are to be believed, at least three times." He sighed again. "Yeah, I suppose I'm going to have to give the son of a bitch a strike team."

"Anyway, Reilly's one of six men I've called who can bring the cadre for their own units with them. The others are Terry Welch—he was a Special Forces type—and Bill Cazz, a jarhead, plus Ed Kosciusko, retired Navy, and Mike Cruz, who was a jarhead aviator. Also Richard Thornton who was a SEAL."

"Jarhead?" Phillie asked. She knew what a SEAL was, from the movies.

"A Marine."

"Oh. Reilly said he needed medical personnel. Would an ER RN do?"

"It would help," Stauer conceded. "But before I let you volunteer we'd at least need to have a long talk."

The front door opened. Someone called out, loudly, "Free beer?" In walked Wahab followed by several more men, each clutching a small overnight bag. "Excuse me, Phillie," Stauer said as he turned to the door. "An army marches on its stomach."

He clapped one of the men on the shoulder and said, "Matt, Ralph is expecting you upstairs." To another, a tall, stout black man who looked to be about seventy years of age, he pointed at Phillie and said, "Sergeant Island, that's the lady of the house. If you would see her about messing arrangements?" Stauer's tone of voice contained a lot more respect for Sergeant Island than Phillie had heard him use with anyone, ever. Phillie had a couple of internal reactions to Stauer's words, pleasure at *lady of the house* and annoyance at the assumption she needed help with feeding people.

Then again, I've never cooked for even a dozen men, and more keep coming. Maybe I need to listen to Sergeant Island, or even let him take charge.

"Phillie," Stauer added, "Master Sergeant Island's bible is the 1910 Manual for Army Cooks."

"All the wisdom of the world, in one volume," Island said righteously. "Everything since is either mere commentary or obvious decay. The 1896 manual is, of course, very good, too, but a bit dated."

To a third, a big bruiser of an obvious ex-soldier, he said, "Terry, I'm turning over my lodge to you and your boys. It's one hundred and seventeen acres with a log cabin down in Somerset, about twenty-five miles from here. I've already drawn you up directions. Go upstairs and pick whatever weapons I've got you think might be useful to train with until we have something more concrete for you to work with. At the lodge there are four Class IIIs, all suppressed, one Sterling, one Uzi, one Smith and Wesson Model 76, and one MP-5. There's also a single PVS-7"—night vision goggles— "with enough batteries for . . . well . . . a while. Ammunition for all of them is in the cabinets upstairs." To the last newcomer, Stauer said, "Ed, one of my guys is working on finding us a ship or ships and a sub. He's in the kitchen; answers to 'Gordo.' Go figure it out."

"But I still don't understand what the mission is?" Ed Kosciusko said.

"Ah, that's easy. We're going to invade somebody by sea, land, and air, destroy a small navy at anchor, maybe blow some bridges, smash a minor air force on the ground, and in general have the time of our lives."

★ CHAPTER SIX ★

> We cannot blame colonialism and imperialism
> for this tragedy. We who fought against
> these things now practice them.
> —Joshua Nkomo

D-150, Port Harcourt International Airport, Nigeria

The ambulance doors were open, showing one weakly thrashing body, with sweat simply pouring off of it, a clustering of vomit about mouth and chin, emanating incoherent moans. Even in Port Harcourt, the stench arising from the body was something noticeable.

To either side of the stretcher-borne young man, seated along the walls facing inward, were six other men, all wearing masks and latex gloves. Four of these were Labaan and his cousins. Their bags were piled toward the front of the ambulance. Labaan, seated at the right rear, passed over his and three other passports to a stout customs inspector wearing a green beret and a short sleeved, gray dress jacket with epaulettes and sundry insignia Labaan had not a clue to the significance of. He actually rather doubted the insignia had much significance.

The inspector fanned through the passports quickly. He couldn't, after all, so much as see the faces of those purporting to be their owners. As for the fifth man, the one on the stretcher . . .

"His is in his pocket," Labaan said. "We were afraid . . . "

The inspector's eyes darted to the softly moaning body. He answered, in clear, clipped Nigerian English, with just that trace of upper class British accent, "I understand completely. But you see, I'll have to explain to my supervisor . . . "

Labaan reached into his shirt pocket and withdrew an envelope. "This is a letter of explanation from our captain," he said. The envelope was much fatter than any simple letter needed to be. It was unsealed. The inspector handed back the passports and took the envelope.

The inspector opened the loose flap and ran his thumb along the top of the stack of bills contained therein. *About two thousand Euros. Half for my boss . . . no, a quarter for my boss. After all, he didn't have to take his life in his hands getting close to this diseased creature. Then, too, my job is keeping undesirable things out of the country. This one wants to leave, or would if he were able, and so I am just doing my job in helping him, and them, leave.*

The inspector glanced over the letter. *Good, it says nothing about money.* He then took the three quarters of the stack of bills he had decided were his due, stuffing the roll in his left trouser pocket and leaving the remainder for his boss. *On second thought, no, if I leave five hundred he'll assume there's more.* The inspector took another two hundred, folded that, and slid it into his right breast pocket. That way, when his boss shook him down for the rest he could produce that. His boss might even give him back a hundred.

"Everything seems well enough in order," the inspector said. "And your casevac flight to Cairo is standing by. Damned odd plane for a trip to Cairo, though."

"I'm told it's what was available," Labaan answered.

"Yes, well, not my problem. Enjoy your flight and"—again the inspector's eyes darted to Adam's body— "good health to you."

Unseen under his mask, Labaan frowned. *Poor Africa, to have such servants.*

The Kenya Airways Saab 340 already had its engines running. Not having a rear ramp, it was suboptimal for a medical flight. Nonetheless it had been available to Labaan's chief, Gutaale, at an acceptable price. What did the chief care, after all, about four men having to manhandle a stretcher up a narrow set of boarding steps?

The flight attendant was female, extravagantly so, and dressed in a striking red uniform, complete to scarf. Equal opportunity had not yet hit most African airlines and, given the typical quality of the service, it was generally felt to be a good idea to give the paying cargo something to think about besides the accident rate or the probability that someone in the maintenance crew had taken a bribe to accept inferior replacement parts.

Kenyan Airways was actually much better than the norm is this regard. Nonetheless, its reputation suffered for the sins of the rest, hence the perceived need for pretty staff. Like Labaan, his team, and Adam, the stewardess was the result of millennia of admixturing with the Arabs across the Red Sea, albeit to a lesser degree. Thus the light brown skin, softer than the African norm hair, and somewhat softer features.

If the woman thought it odd that an emergency medical flight had been contracted for nearly a month prior, she said nothing. Indeed, she was far too occupied in trying to back out right through the airplane's walls to think of much of anything. She didn't have a medical mask, and tried—quite futilely—to cover her mouth and nose with one hand. The other was busy scratching at the wall behind her.

Ignoring her, except for a quick and appreciative glance at her chest, Labaan led the others to the rear of the aircraft. "Get him out of the stretcher and into a seat," he ordered. "Don't clean him up yet."

D-149, N'Djamena, Chad

In fact, the inspector's observations about the aircraft chosen for a flight to Cairo were spot on. You just couldn't get there in a Saab 340 without at least three stops, one of which was guaranteed to be a rotten, problematic layover in either western Sudan or southeastern Libya. This would have mattered, too, had the plane actually been going to Cairo. It wasn't.

Labaan glanced out the window of the plane at the rows of military aircraft lining one side of the runway. *French*, he thought. *The one European people which didn't give up its empire here. And, arguably, the controllers of the only "countries" in Africa that haven't decayed to complete ruin since decolonialization.*

In his heart, Labaan knew that wasn't true. Were the "former" French colonies run a bit better than the norm? Yes, some of them, but there were a few decolonized African states that were doing well, for certain values of well. His own wasn't among them and that knowledge perhaps clouded his thinking on the subject. Conversely, the country they were in, quite despite—or perhaps because of—French tutelage, had the distinction of being rated as the most corrupt country in the world, some years, and never better than seventh from the bottom.

Of course "it's all the whites' fault," Labaan thought. *Isn't that what all the black studies people said at the university? Except it isn't. Though conquered once, Ethiopia was never really colonized. It's a mess. "The imperialists mixed up tribes and thus guaranteed conflict." Which would seem to be true except that Rwanda and Burundi have the same tribal mix they had before the Euros showed up. They're the very definition of a mess. And of my own "country," the less said the better.*

I'm barely old enough to remember the euphoria of decolonialization, though I've heard enough about it. I wonder if there's a man or woman in Africa who wouldn't prefer things to go back the way they were under colonialism? What did that expat Canadian cynic say? Ah, yes, I remember: "By comparison with the sonofabitch system, colonialism is progressive and enlightened."

And at least back then we could all get together in peace, love, and harmony in hating the whites. Now we only have each other to hate and fear. And to steal from, of course.

There was a youngish white man, tall, muscular, tanned, blond, and bearded, waiting for the Kenya Airways flight as the hatch opened. The white's sweat-stained shirt was unbuttoned halfway to his navel.

Labaan took one look and thought, *God . . . no! Not one of them, not here?*

"Dude," the white said, as Labaan reached the foot of the debarking steps, "the plane . . . it's bogus . . . it's broken."

God save me from Californians, Labaan thought. *It wasn't enough to have to go to school with the mindless twits. Even here, without a surfable beach for over a thousand miles, they find me to blight my existence and insult their own language.*

"And you are?" Labaan asked.

"Lance, dude."

Of course. Lance. "What's wrong with the plane, Lance?" he asked.

The California expat's real name was Roger. Since, however, he was acutely conscious of his origins, he went by "Lance." Lance threw his arms in the air and answered, "Man, I dunno. I'm still trying to figure it out."

I knew everything was going too well, Labaan thought, calmly. For the first time since beginning his mission he felt comfortable. This was Africa, after all, and things were not supposed to go well. *Besides, God must have his little joke with us.*

"How long to fix it?" Labaan asked.

"No clue, dude. Nobody here can do a fucking thing with it, and I mostly just fly 'em."

"Of course," Labaan sighed. He began rubbing his forehead against the headache that was beginning to build. *There are maybe three hundred kilometers of paved road in this country, he thought, and most of them are not between here and our next stop. Fuck.*

Hmmm . . . we could hire some camels and drivers. And that would take weeks . . . maybe months. That would be too late. The local airline would be a bad option. We can hardly trust our prisoner not to make trouble and if I inject him again nobody would let him on their flight. Rent a van, truck, or bus? I shudder. Stay here until the plane is fixed?

Labaan took another look at Lance. *A rental vehicle it is.*

Labaan sipped a coffee in a small shop overlooking the buses. His compatriots were with him. So was Adam, who had been tranquilized but not given anything else beyond that. Abdi had liberally sprinkled the boy with some imported brandy, enough so that he reeked of it. Labaan watched as the drivers of the various conveyances busied themselves with fixing luggage to the roofs of their vehicles even though there were no paying customers yet.

"What is all that?" he asked his waiter.

The waiter laughed, broad white smile showing in a friendly black face. "The buses don't leave until they're full. So they put the fake luggage on to convince people that they're nearly full so that more people line up to get on their bus. In a strange way, it even works as those who are best at looking like they're ready to leave are most successful in getting people aboard so they *can* leave."

"I see. And yes, I see how that could work."

And I've no time to fuck around with this; I'll just rent the whole bus. The budget will cover that.

"Make sure the driver has the tank filled before you take off," the waiter warned. "Sometimes they'll deliberately run out of gas so they can take up a collection among the passengers."

Labaan thought the driver's demand for rental of the bus to be outrageous.

"You think so, sir?" said the driver. "Come with me."

The driver then led him to the nearest gasoline station. Labaan took one look at the cost of a liter of fuel and said, "I agree. Here to Abéché, at the price you quoted."

★CHAPTER SEVEN★

The villainy you teach me I will execute,
and it shall go hard, but I will better the instruction.
—Shakespeare, *The Merchant of Venice*,
Act III, Scene I

D-123, San Antonio, Texas

It was very late. While some of the crew could be heard arguing quietly, or in the case of Kosciusko and Gordo, not all that quietly, most were asleep. Phillie could hear still others typing on keyboards. She was amazed that any of them were still on their feet. She heard footsteps and looked up as Boxer descended the staircase.

"Well," said Ralph, walking down the stairs, "Victor's going to be a problem."

Stauer, currently poring over a map with Wahab, looked up and asked, "Why's that?"

"He's been caught and is in a Myanmar jail. Lox and Bridges are working on a complete report of the situation."

"So much for Victor," Stauer said. "Now who replaces him?"

"Nobody," Boxer answered. "The only other one who both could have and would have, Israel Efimovich, is in an Italian jail. And that Yemeni I mentioned is too much of an unknown quantity."

"Well that sucks moose cock. Suggestions?" Wes asked.

"Spring one of them. I'd recommend Victor, in part because he's better at his job than Efimovich, in part because his operation is probably much more intact, and in part because a Myanmar jail has to be easier to spring him from than an Italian one. After all, the Italians have been practicing on the Mafia for decades."

Stauer nodded and turned to Phillie. "Hon," he said, "would you call Terry at the lodge and have him come here?"

"But it's so late . . . "

"Trust me, babe, that's not an issue."

"You're actually going to free Victor Inning from jail?" Wahab asked. As an African, he was more than ordinarily sensitive to the various wars fed by the likes of Inning and his competitors.

"You knew we were going to use him, Wahab," Stauer said. "What difference how we get him? I mean, does your chief want his son back or not?"

"Speaking of which," Ralph interjected, "I know how the boy left Boston. I think I do, anyway."

Both Stauer and Wahab were interested in that. "How?" the African asked. "And how do you know?"

"I did a query of queries," Boxer answered. "About six weeks ago someone at sea, on a ship christened the *George*

Galloway, did a number of searches for kidnappings and disappearances reported in Boston. Can't think of any good reason for someone to do that who wasn't concerned expressly about kidnappings in Boston. The *Galloway* also left Boston the morning after the boy disappeared. It was next seen in Port Harcourt, Nigeria. After that, the trail goes cold, unless the boy's still aboard."

"I wonder what the crew could tell us?" Stauer mused.

"I doubt they'd tell us anything," Boxer answered.

Stauer gave a wicked grin. "Yes they would. It's only a matter of making sure they understand their real priorities. Can you track down where the ship is and where it's headed now?"

"Piece o' cake," Boxer answered.

"Phillie," Stauer called out, "tell Terry to bring his tame SEAL, too."

"Use four men to take down one ship with a crew of maybe twenty or twenty-five, when they've got no warning that we're coming?" the SEAL asked. He sneered, "Piece o' cake."

The SEAL, more exactly the *retired* SEAL, Richard "Biggus Dickus" Thornton, had arms the size of Terry Welch's legs. And Terry's legs were not spindly. Even Stauer found the man's sheer bulk and obvious strength almost intimidating.

"But," Biggus added, "We'll have to hit it in or near a port, preferably as it's leaving, so I'll need the ship's schedule some time in advance. Also architectural drawings, arms, a way to get there, NVGs"—night vision goggles— "preferably PVS-21s—"

"I can get you PVS-7s," Gordo interjected, "or something just as good. But 21s just aren't to be had on the open market."

Biggus thought about that before agreeing, and then adding to his shopping list, "I'll need scuba gear for four, a boat, a padded extending ladder, a . . . "

"Just give me your list," Gordo said. "I'll see what I can do."

Bridges looked decidedly skeptical.

Ralph waved a finger. "Chief," he said to the SEAL, "don't be so sure how easy this will be. Bridges has traced back all of the *Galloway's* stops and routes for the last couple of years. I think they're not just a carrier for hire. I suspect they're AQ Navy, either owned or leased."

Al Qaeda Navy, so called, was a collection, some suspected a very large collection, of merchant vessels owned or crewed by that terrorist organization.

"Really," the SEAL's face was lit with a feral smile. "In that case, what was professional has just become personal." He faced Stauer and asked, "Sir, if I find, after boarding, that they are AQN, can I terminate the lot of them?"

Over that Stauer didn't hesitate a moment. He had his own grudges. "Yes. Or anything else you can imagine."

"You know," Gordo said, "if we're going to off the crew we could save a few million by taking over the *Galloway*, rather than buying our own."

"It's tempting," Stauer conceded. "But I think it drives up our chances of being compromised. Better just to scuttle it at sea. If, that is, it really is AQN."

Kosciusko wandered over and said, "Forget using *Galloway*; it's not big enough for our purposes.

"Oh, well," said Gordo. "How will you know if it is AQN?" he asked of Biggus.

"I find a mosque on the ship," the SEAL answered, with a shrug, "that's no big deal in itself. But if I find a crapload of Al Qaeda literature, weapons over and above maybe two rifles and a pistol, anything remotely smelling of explosives or detonators, money much in excess of what a ship normally carries in the safe, a dungeon, complete with chains, code books, how-to-make-a-suicide-vest videos, CDs with Daniel Pearl's or Fabrizio Quatrocchi's head being sawed off . . . "

Gordo held up his hands, palm out. "I get the picture, Chief."

"Slave girls being transported are also not uncommon indicators," Thornton finished.

Bridges, who had been silent for some time, took the opportunity to say, "Most of what you've asked for, Chief, even if Gordo can get it for you, you can't take it with you."

"Why the hell not?" Biggus Dickus asked.

"The Euros are often quite sensitive to things with military potential, even if they're not actual weapons. Night vision is one of those things, for example. And firearms are really touchy. Once you have something on a boat or plane it isn't that much of a problem; it's getting it from one to the other."

"Shit! I've always been used to travelling under orders, with whatever we need on hand. This is . . . different."

"We'll figure out something for you, Chief," Stauer said, then turned his attention to Welch. "Terry, yours is in most ways a tougher mission, even though we know where Victor's being held. How are you going to do it?"

Welch frowned. "We can get his lawyer to set up a hearing at which Victor will have to be present. That gives us a certain time he'll be outside of the jail and a probable or certain route. The problem will be getting him out of country after that."

"I don't want any Burmese police killed," Stauer said.

"Makes it tougher, of course," Terry said. "Not impossible, just tougher. It will also make getting him out of the country tougher. I'm going to need an airplane and a pilot, or, better, a helicopter and pilot, both to bring us in and to bring us out again."

"Mike Cruz isn't due in for another two days," Stauer said. "He's going to be our chief wing wiper."

"Marine chopper pilot with a Ranger Tab?" Welch asked.

"I didn't know you knew him, Terry?"

"I don't, Wes; I just heard about him. He'll do."

Stauer turned to Welch and Thornton in turn, then asked, "How many days until you can give me a plan we can go with?"

"Three days," Welch answered. Thornton weighed that for a minute before nodding agreement. "Sure, three days."

D-121, Corpus Christi, Texas

Seagulls whirled and swooped along the shore. A warm breeze came off the Gulf, carrying with it the not entirely unpleasant smell of the sea, which was to say, the smell of the shore. A number of people, a plurality of them neither white nor black, but brown, cavorted by that shore. A smaller number of people, most of them white and all of them older, watched from a café on land.

Mike Cruz—and it was "Mike," rather than "Miguel"—had arrived a bit early, the night before. Then he, Stauer, and a small cadre had driven the one hundred and fifty odd miles to this coastal city and port to explain the facts of life, of ships anyway, to the landlubbers, Stauer, Boxer, and Gordo. Cruz pointed across the bay to the USS *Lexington* and said, "That's really what you want."

Cruz was a retired Marine, retired and bored. Normally, he ran a farm in middle-of-nowhere, Pennsylvania. Occasionally he did some teaching, or defense work, under contract.

As a younger man, a much younger man, he'd served as a very junior infantryman at the tail end of Vietnam. Following that, and despite the glasses he now wore perched on his nose, he'd gone commissioned, then to Army Ranger School, then switched over to choppers, the heaviest kind. As far as his emotional relationship between Marine infantry and Marine aviation, he sometimes said that he felt like a man "torn between two lovers." He was pretty attached to both.

That wasn't why he'd come though. He'd come because *I was just so damned, bloody bored. I doubt I was alone in that.*

Kosciusko, the mostly bald ex-naval officer, smiled at the stocky retired Marine and said, "I don't know about him, but I sure as hell would like one."

"Delusions of grandeur," Cruz announced.

"Doesn't really matter," Gordo said. "It isn't for sale.

Matter of fact, there's not another aircraft carrier for sale anywhere. Not so long ago it was a different story, the old *Minas Gerais* was even up on eBay. It's been sent to the breakers already."

"Wouldn't matter," Boxer said, "even if it were available. We need stealth, which in our case means complete lack of remarkability."

"Couldn't afford the crew if the thing were invisible. So a cargo ship?" Stauer asked.

"Yes," Kosciusko agreed, "except with a big but. You want the ship able to launch and recover helicopters—which isn't that hard—and fixed wing aircraft, which is really fucking hard. We could maybe build a temporary flight deck, if we had a long enough ship."

"Except that flight deck has to be something that can be quickly assembled and disassembled," Boxer said, "or we lose our stealth. Even I can't hide something that looks like an aircraft carrier continuously from the eye in the sky."

"We can get some genuine short takeoff birds," Cruz added, "which will reduce the need for a flight deck but of those that will take a really short roll before takeoff, the very best that are available are only really available in kit form."

"Which means we'd have to set up a factory and build them."

Stauer nodded, and said, "And I trust you have some recommendations."

"We need that abandoned missile base for a factory," Gordo said, "the one in Washington state. Two point eight million, plus maybe a few hundred thousand and ten days to a couple of weeks or so to make it halfass livable. The planes, of which we need about eight, take two hundred and fifty to five hundred man-hours to turn from kits to aircraft. Call it five hundred. That's four thousand man-hours."

"Why the missile base?" Stauer asked. "I would think any old warehouse—"

"The kits are made in the Czech Republic," Gordo said, then amended, "Well, some are made in Canada but the Czechs have a tradition of closed mouthedness. FAA lets them in on the presumption they'll be put together by a home builder. But *eight* of them? No, we're setting up something more like an industrial operation. Bound to attract attention from the FAA if noticed by someone and reported to them. So we move it out of sight."

"And I need them ready within the month," Cruz said, "and it will be two weeks to set everything up."

"So," Gordo continued, "even if we work the builders twelve hours a day for fifteen days, that's a building crew of, oh, call it twenty-three or twenty-four, with a foreman, every one of which is a security risk."

"But we have a solution," Ralph said, smiling.

"Why does that smile make me worry?" Stauer asked.

"Because you're a natural paranoid," Boxer replied. "In any case, we can solve both the labor problem and the security problem in one fell swoop."

"Oh, really? Tell me how."

Boxer jabbed a finger toward the beach. "Mexicans. *Illegal* Mexicans. They'll never complain to any authorities. And anyone who thinks Mexicans don't have an amazingly strong work ethic—at least until inner city liberals get their sticky paws on them—is an idiot."

Stauer rubbed his jaw, considering. "It has a certain elegance to it, I admit," he said.

"And we can train them as ground crew in the time between finishing assembly and crossing the line of departure for the mission," Cruz said. "We can add armaments aboard ship."

"But what about the runway. These planes . . . ?"

"Czech designed CH 801's," Cruz supplied. "They're basically Fieseler Storches, if you're curious."

"Right. Czech. They'll still need some space to take off."

"Four hundred feet or so, with full loads," Cruz said. "Well, really less because they'll start off well above the sea and moving into the wind . . . but four hundred to be safe."

"So I suggest a container ship," Kosciusko said. "We pile the containers high to get over any masts, or cut the masts to drop them, then lay PSP or AM-2—"

"AM-2 is better," Cruz said.

"No doubt," Gordo agreed, "but I can get an unlimited supply of PSP"—perforated steel planking, or Marsden Matting; it was used to lay airfields essentially overnight—"in the Philippines. World War Two leftovers, and in as good a shape as the day it was delivered to the islands. They use it for fencing down there."

"What about the choppers?" Stauer asked.

Gordo answered, "Russian Hips. Used, I can get as many as you want for under two million a copy."

"And we can pile the containers in such a way as to leave spaces for the Hips to land in," Cruz offered. "Then we cover them with tarps. From the surface, nobody will see shit, and from the air . . . well, camouflage is a wonderful thing. Same deal with the landing craft; we load them in by the sides, build container sized frames to hold them, and cover them with tarps. Or cover them with cut out container sections."

"But who can fly Hips?"

"Besides an infinity of eastern Europeans," Cruz said, blowing on and then buffing fingernails on his shirt, "I can. Exchange program to Kremenchug Flight College, back in the mid-nineties."

"You have a line on recruiting some eastern Euros, then?" Stauer asked.

"Guy who taught me is living not so large in Tver," Cruz said. "Goes by the name of Borsakov, Artur Borsakov. He's pushing seventy, was a colonel, as a matter of fact, in the Soviet-Afghan War . . . *early* in the war. He can round up the other pilots, crew chiefs, and whatever mechanics we need. I figure we can pick up the two choppers Gordo found, enough spare parts, the ground crews, and fly the whole assembly to link up with the ship somewhere around Vladivostok. Or anywhere else, really."

"We need two," Stauer said. "That means that unless we have at least three we will end up with one working."

"I can get a third," Gordo said. "I told you, 'as many as you want.' You want the water float kits installed?" he asked Cruz.

"How much?" Stauer asked, even though the question wasn't directed at him.

"Another seventy-five thousand over and above the five point one million for the Hips. And Mike's going to need funds to buy spares once Borsakov identifies which spares we really need."

Stauer looked the question at Cruz.

"We're gonna fly off of and then to and from a ship; the floats would make sense," Cruz said. "Shit often goes wrong, ya know?"

"All right," Stauer agreed. "And the ship?"

Gordo scowled. "For reasons beyond my ken," he said, "shipping costs are much higher than what I expected them to be. At least for the size we want they are. I recommend leasing one."

Stauer turned to Wahab and asked, "Will your chief go for a lease?"

Wahab liked Stauer immeasurably. He appreciated, too, what the American was trying to do for him, his people, and his leader. But he was a little miffed that all this conversation, all this planning, all this spending of his chief's money, had been discussed almost as if he weren't there. He pushed the feeling and the thought away. *I am not here for pride's sake, but for my people's.*

"What's the cost of purchase?" Wahab asked Gordo.

"For what we want, anywhere from eighteen to sixty million USD."

"And to lease one for . . . what, three months?"

"Much less than the figures I gave you. Maybe a million, two hundred thousand, if we can get a three-month charter. Four or five million if we have to go for a year. I haven't asked for a quote yet but we are talking a small fraction, and we can always sublease any time we haven't used."

Wahab turned his facer to Stauer. "Lease one, Wes. We're already getting over fifty million in known, planned costs, and those are only so far. Sixty million for a ship will send my chief over the edge."

Stauer grimaced. "One advantage to buying, as opposed to leasing, is that you can get the money back on a purchase, but the lease is just lost. Still . . . you're the boss."

"Just his representative," Wahab corrected. *Though I appreciate the honorific.*

"What about the sub and the patrol boat?" Stauer asked.

"We've got a couple of issues there," Gordo said. "The patrol boat's no problem; I've already contracted with the Finnish company that owns it for Biggus Dickus to take delivery next week."

Gordon was no fool. *Stauer said 'you're the boss' because he is the paymaster, and we'd better keep him happy.* To Wahab he said, "The purchase price on the boat was so low I figured I'd better jump on it. Hope that's okay."

"Sure, Mr. Gordon," Wahab agreed. *He only said that because Stauer dropped the hint.*

"It's unarmed, of course," Gordo continued, "but we can fix that later, after Terry springs Victor from durance vile. And Biggus doesn't need an armed boat anyway.

"The sub, however . . . well, I narrowed it down to two that would do, one of which is perfect and not particularly expensive. That one's in Croatia."

"Problem is, Wes, that the Croatian one is still military. Well . . . naval. It's one of those Yugoslav-built commando carriers. Plastic, don't you know. But *because* it's military, buying it would raise questions and attract attention. Neither of which we want."

"Right," Gordo sighed. He reached into his pocket and pulled out a folded piece of paper. Unfolding it, he handed it over to Stauer.

"A minisub painted up in killer whale motif?" Stauer

asked, passing the sheet over to Wahab, who looked and shrugged.

"Mmmm . . . yeah. It *used* to be military, Swedish, but has been sold and resold enough to drop off the screens. Sea Shepherd owned it for a while, hence the paint scheme. Less than half a million bucks and capable of getting a couple of Biggus's boys to the harbor where they can mine the other side's boats."

"Right," Stauer said. "Orca the friendly killer sub it is. Now what about the assembly and training area?" That question was directed to Wahab.

"My chief will pay for the smaller one in Brazil," Wahab said, "but he insists on retaining ownership." He looked embarrassed when he added, "Yes, I know he agreed that the assets purchased would be part of your fee, but this is land and the land's a lot of money. A ruler in Africa never knows when he's going to need five thousand square kilometers of jungle on another continent to hide in."

Stauer kept his face blank, even as he thought, *Go ahead and break your agreement with me, Khalid. Don't be too surprised if I don't keep to all the fine points concerning my agreement with you.*

While Stauer was thinking that, Boxer reminded himself, *Brief Wes that Khalid has probably stolen and stashed away something between two and three billion dollars. Might help his—our—bargaining position.*

"Keeping supplied up there?" Stauer asked Gordo, changing the subject.

"The same landing craft you're planning to use for the assault. Or . . . "

"Or?"

Gordo reached into another pocket and pulled out another sheet of paper. This he also handed to Stauer. "Or we can buy a hovercraft. Frankly, if you really need the landing craft, and you do, we'd wear them out making constant runs up and down the Amazon. Might lose one, too. This"—his finger indicated the sheet of paper—"can deliver a couple of tons every three days. That's enough, if we bring the heavy shit in initially by landing craft, and purify our own water, to supply us in the middle of nowhere, Amazonia."

Stauer thought about that. *No . . . no. A hovercraft operating on the Amazon daily is going to attract attention from the Brazilian authorities . . . and they're borderline paranoid. Besides, I don't know where to get a hovercraft crew we could trust. They're just not that common.*

"No hovercraft," he told Gordo. "Think of something else."

"Oh, well, just a thought," Gordo said. "If no hovercraft then we can use the mix of the landing craft, the Hips, and maybe some fixed wing, since we're buying a couple of Pilatus PC-6s, anyway. And I can charter some Brazilian river craft. The engineers can hack out a strip and I can order some extra PSP from the Philippines. Hell, maybe that will work better." Gordo frowned momentarily. "No, I'd better order the extra PSP from Calumet in the States. More expensive but we'll get it sooner."

★CHAPTER EIGHT★

Development aid is one of the reasons for
Africa's problems. If the West were to cancel
these payments, normal Africans wouldn't even
notice. Only the functionaries would be hard hit.
Which is why they maintain that the world
would stop turning without this development aid.
—James Shikwati, Kenyan economist

D-149, N'Djamena-Abéché "Highway," Chad

"Oh, God," moaned Adam, seated between Abdi and
Gheddi, "what is this?" The boy covered his mouth and
nose with his hands and began to cough and sneeze from
the thick dust that swirled around the bus. His kidneys
were in agony from the pounding they'd taken from the
combination of bad shocks and worse road.

"I believe this is called 'foreign aid,'" Labaan
answered.

The captive looked confused, and from more than the
aftereffects of the drugs he'd been given.

"Foreign aid," Labaan repeated, with a sneer. "You know: When guilty-feeling Euros and Americans shell out money, ostensibly to help the people, but the money all ends up in the hands of sundry corrupt rulers and their relatives?"

"I don't . . . "

"Understand?" Labaan stood up and, using the bus seats to hold himself erect against the bouncing, walked to the rear where Adam sat. Abdi moved over to open a space for Labaan to sit.

"We are travelling on what is supposed to be an all-weather, asphalt highway. Money was budgeted for it, no doubt by a consortium of Europeans and Americans, governmental and nongovernmental, both. No doubt, too, a generous provision for utterly necessary bribes was built in to every bid . . . well, except maybe for the Americans. For that matter, probably no American concerns bid on the project, since their government is death on paying bribes if they catch someone at it. *Such* an unrealistic people."

If ever someone wore a smile that was three-fourths sadness, that someone was Labaan. "Now let me tell you what happened with all the money that was supposed to go for the road. First, some very high ranking people in this country took the twenty or so percent that was factored into the bids for bribery. Then someone important's first cousin showed up, waved some official looking papers, spouted something in the local language that the contractor couldn't understand. Then, in really excellent French, that cousin explained all manner of dire probabilities and suggested he could help. That cousin was then hired as a consultant. He was never seen again, except on payday.

"An uncle then showed up, in company with four

hundred and thirty-seven more or less distant family members, every one of which was hired and perhaps a third of which showed up for work on any given day, except for payday."

The bus's right front tire went into a remarkably deep and sharp pothole, causing the metal of the frame to strike asphalt and Labaan to wince with both the nerve-destroying sound and the blow, transmitted from hole to tire to almost shockless suspension to frame to barely padded and falling apart seat to him.

"A guerilla chieftain," he continued, once the pain had passed, "perhaps of no particular relationship to the ruling family, then arrived, offering to provide security with his band of armed men. He was, at first, turned down. And then several pieces of heavy construction equipment burned one night. The guerillas were quickly hired. They never showed up either, except for their leader, at payday, but no more equipment was burned.

"Then came the tranzis, the Transnational Progressives, average age perhaps twenty-one or twenty-two, and knowing absolutely nothing about road construction. Indeed, most of them wouldn't have even known what it meant to work. Rich boys and girls, trust fund babies, out to feel good about themselves by saving the world. They filled up every hotel room and hired the few competent, and critical, local engineers to do important things like act as chauffeurs and translators."

The bus had now arrived at a washboard section of the road. Labaan kept speaking, but the steady *thump-kareechsprong* of the road and bus made his words warble almost as much as a helicopter pilot's over a radio.

"More cousins came, and they, of course, had to be hired as consultants, as well.

"At about this time, the accountant for the project arrived and explained that it could no longer be done to the standard contracted for. The substrate began to suffer and the thickness of the road to be reduced. The demands for money, for the hiring of spurious workers and spurious services, never ended. With each mile of road, that substrate became less to standard and that surface became thinner."

Labaan shook his head. "And then came the first rain . . . "

At that moment, both front tires went into a large, more or less linear hole, adding the screech of metal as the fender twisted to all the more usual sounds.

"As I said: '*Foreign Aid.*' And it doesn't matter a whit whether it come from NGOs, quangos, governments, or rock stars; it never does a bit of good. Never. Fifty-seven billion United States dollars come to Black Africa every year in aid, official and unofficial, Adam. Fifty billion is deposited to foreign accounts by our rulers."

D-148, nearing Abéché, Chad

"Fucking foreigners!" the bus driver exclaimed. The bus began to slow as the driver applied brakes. Pretty much unconstrained by asphalt at that point, a cloud of dust billowed upward.

"What is it?" Labaan asked. He didn't wait for an answer because when he looked out the large front window he saw half a dozen armed "men" standing in the road.

Labaan wasn't leader of the team merely for his age. "Abdi, Gheddi, get low, take your submachine guns, exit the back door. I don't think they'll see you with all the dust."

Abdi and Gheddi quickly pulled zippers, opening their cylindrical carry-on bags and removing from them submachine guns which already had magazines loaded in the pistol grips. Crouching low, they scooted to the rear door of the bus and twisted the handle to open it. One after the other they oozed out to the ground, hit, and rolled. In the dust raised by the bus they were not noticed. Gheddi took the time to run after the slowing vehicle to shut and partially lock the door behind them.

Like his subordinates, Labaan opened the small carry-on bag at his feet and removed a firearm, in his case a pistol. He looked to the opposite side of the bus and saw that Delmar was doing the same. Both men held their weapons low, where they wouldn't be seen until the last minute. "Delmar, you work from the rear," Labaan added, "I'll work from the front."

"What is it?" Adam echoed Labaan, except that the captive sounded hopeful.

"Guerillas, rebels, bandits . . . hard to say. Driver?"

"I don't know that there is any difference," said the driver without turning his head. He continued to apply the brakes until the bus came to a full stop amidst a self-generated cloud of dust and a concert of squealing brake pads and rushing air.

"And don't think they're here to rescue you, boy,"

Labaan said. "Look at the scruffy bastards. They don't even know of your existence."

The bus door opened. Three "men" boarded, all in civilian clothes. One carried a Kalashnikov. The other two had bolt action rifles of considerable antiquity. The rifles were longer than their bearers, who looked to be twelve or thirteen years old. The Kalashnikov carrier seemed older, perhaps nineteen or twenty. All were dirty, shoeless, and in near rags. And the weapons looked worse than they did. With the bus so close to the three who remained outside, Labaan couldn't see the tops of their heads, though he could see rifle muzzles pointed at the driver. *More children*, he assumed. The three on board joked and laughed among themselves in a language Labaan didn't know.

God, Labaan asked silently, *why do you hate Africa so?*

The elder, and obvious leader, stepped up to the top of the step and, without a word, cuffed the driver across the face. He then grabbed the driver by the back of his shirt and threw him down the steps and onto the dirt and chunks of disassociated asphalt outside.

Men normally helpless against fate, suddenly given the power of the gun. How many places have I seen this?

Labaan tried to put a look of fear on his face. He wasn't sure he was succeeding. *Then again, acting was never my discipline*. It was no matter, though; looking around he saw that Delmar looked afraid and Adam seemed absolutely terrified. Labaan cast his own eyes down, lest eye contact reveal to the gunman that Labaan was not precisely a helpless civilian.

For a moment Adam thought about shouting out who

he was and what his father would pay for his return. *Labaan won't kill me; neither will he let Delmar. They need me alive. But . . . that man and those boys just might, on general principle. They've that look of the hyena about them, rangy, mangy, feral, and hungry.* He shivered.

Labaan trusted Delmar enough not to make that confirming look. He kept his eyes downcast until the eldest of the bandits was no more than six feet away. Then, wordlessly, Labaan raised his pistol and opened fire.

Adam screamed aloud as the first shot was fired. From his vantage point, he saw a spray of blood erupt from the back of the bandit with the newer and more evil looking rifle. The bandit began to fall backwards. Even as he did, two more sanguinary fountains sprayed out of his back.

Delmar stood to his full height at the first shot, his pistol gripped in both hands and rotating downward to target the other two. That these were children mattered not a bit. Adam saw the one nearest the front, the one farthest from him, frozen in shock. The shock ended when a single bullet exploded the boy's head like an overripe melon.

The middle boy dropped his rifle and turned to run, screaming and throwing his hands into the air. Both Labaan and Delmar turned their pistols on the boy's back, firing so close together that Adam couldn't tell whose shots were whose. The boy was flung downward over his erstwhile friend, bleeding and ruined.

Down below, from the rear of the bus where Abdi and Gheddi had taken firing positions, an altogether more violent firing burst out. In less than a second, so it seemed to Adam, the muzzles that had been visible ahead of the bus disappeared. There was a brief pause and then his two submachine gun bearing captors appeared ahead. They aimed downward. With three more bursts of fire, it was over.

Adam, trembling, pushed his head out an open window and threw up.

"And that's foreign aid, too, boy," Labaan said.

Adam was back in his chair, still trembling and gone comparatively pale, as Labaan and Delmar dragged the two boys' bodies out. A few minutes later the driver reboarded the bus and grabbed the feet of the only bandit who had been of age and fully responsible. That gunman, as had the children, left a trail of blood along the tattered rubber matting of the floor.

It seemed like a long time to Adam before everyone reboarded. The four captors sat and began to disassemble and clean their firearms, taking care to reload the magazines as well. The driver took a broom out from somewhere under the bus. He gathered some dirt in his hands and, reentering, began to spread it over the blood stains. With the broom he spread the dirt around, collecting up the blood.

"It attracts flies," the driver explained, unnecessarily. He then swept the dirt forward and down the steps.

When he looked down, Adam saw that indeed flies were beginning to settle on the remnants of the blood. He looked up and out the window, mostly to avert his eyes from the sight. This was worse, as vultures were settling in a mass not so very far away. Once again, Adam stood and stuck his head out a window to vomit.

Gheddi laughed at the captive, earning a sharp rebuke from Labaan.

"I remember you, cousin, the first time in action. Be polite, lest we bring up things better left forgotten."

With a scowl, Gheddi turned back to his firearm.

When he'd finished, and resumed his seat, Adam gasped, "They were just children and you shot them in cold blood. Like animals." He seemed to have forgotten his own earlier comparison to hyenas.

"They *were* animals," Labaan answered. "Feral," he added, unconsciously voicing Adam's own, earlier thought. "Clan- and tribe-less. No one will miss them. And the world is better off without them. I don't know their precise crimes, yet that they had a lengthy list of them I have no doubt."

"I doubt they had kidnapping on those list of crimes," Adam said, raising a grin from Labaan.

"No, probably not kidnapping, unless you count temporarily, for purposes of rape. And what I do for my tribe is not a crime."

★CHAPTER NINE★

Courage is the greatest of all the virtues.
Because if you haven't courage, you may not have
an opportunity to use any of the others.
—Dr. Samuel Johnson

D-120, San Antonio, TX

Warren Zevon's "Lawyers, Guns, and Money" was playing from the computer's speakers as Phillie walked into the office.

"Is what we're doing legal?" Phillie asked of Bridges. "I asked Wes and he said you used to be a lawyer and I should talk to you."

Matt Bridges, late forties, balding, glasses, pushed himself back from the computer where he'd been working on the standard enlistment contract, and setting up dummy corporations for the procurement of everything from land, to ships, to aircraft, to rubber boats. He rotated his chair and began drumming the fingers of his right hand over and around his mouth. He actually knew the answer, already, but this delay gave him a chance to appreciate the sheer good looks of Philomena Potter, something all the crew liked to do when chance offered.

"Have a seat, Phillie," Bridges said, indicating with on hand the chair normally used by Ralph Boxer. When she'd sat down, he continued, "The answer is yes, in part, and no, in part. It's complex.

"The overall operation is legal. We are hired by a foreign entity that has practical sovereignty over a part of the Earth's surface to accomplish a hostage rescue. That's legal. Not even in violation of sundry treaties against the use of mercenaries, since it's more a police function than a military one. To that end, we are buying a ship, aircraft, arms, equipment. That's all legal.

"Moreover, while that entity has practical sovereignty over an area, nobody recognizes anyone as having legal sovereignty over what used to be the overall country. The former state has no diplomatic presence anywhere. It has no national government. No one accepts passports from there. Pirates operate from there and no one local even tries to control them. International law-wise, it's a black hole and anyone can do pretty much anything there.

"*However*"—Bridges's chin went up on the how and down on the ever—"Terry is taking a team day after tomorrow to Myanmar, to spring a legally held prisoner from custody. That's illegal. Biggus Dickus Thornton is going to pick up a patrol boat for sale in Finland, which is legal, but then intercept a merchant vessel at sea, and either interrogate and release the crew or kill them and sink the vessel. That's illegal."

Phillie suddenly had a sinking feeling. She'd been so

caught up the excitement at first, the air of sheer energy as Wes' apartment turned into a headquarters, that she hadn't thought enough about it.

"It was also, for example, legal for us to buy that old missile complex. It will be legal for us to assemble some light aircraft there. *How*ever, it is illegal for us to transport a couple of dozen bright looking Mexican illegal immigrants there to put those kit planes together."

"We are not going to be importing any illegal weapons into the United States. On the other hand, we are going to be importing a very large quantity of extremely illegal weapons into Brazil. We are also, unless Stauer takes my suggestion and goes in by sea, going to smuggle some portion of them into Kenya, illegally. Moreover, while many of the items we are going to purchase will be legally acquired, a fair proportion are likely to have been stolen— misappropriated, anyway—from *somebody's* arsenals."

"Oh, dear," Phillie said aloud. She looked at Bridges. "You're a lawyer. Why are you taking part in this operation that has so many illegalities to it?"

Bridges sighed. "Lots of reasons. Personal loyalty to Wes. Money? That, too." He shrugged. "But mostly because I am just so fucking—if you'll pardon the expression— *bored* with my life. This is the most fun I've had in *years*. Worth being shot over if we get caught in Africa."

Phillie's already very large and very green eyes widened still further. "Ummm . . . did you say '*shot*'?"

"Well, that's become traditional there for people whom they can fit in the category of mercenary, and even though we technically aren't, they're not too keen on the letter of the law."

"Thanks, Mr. Bridges," she said, rising unsteadily. *Shot*?

"Please, call me 'Matt.'"

"Okay, Matt. Thanks. I have some thinking to do."

"One other thing to think about, Phillie," Bridges said. "If it helps any, we're doing some illegal things, but we're doing them in a good cause."

Chewing her lower lip, she nodded and left. Bridges turned back to his computer, tracing the planned route of MV *George Galloway*.

Phillie's excuse had been that she needed to go to her own place to pick up some clothes. In fact, she just needed to be alone to think.

Her apartment was considerably closer to the hospital where she worked than Stauer's was. It was also considerably smaller, and much less neat than her lover's usually was. The bedrolls littering the floors back at Wes', and the piles of pizza boxes and pyramids of beer cans, had rather changed that. Her place was also, and this mattered, considerably quieter than the other.

She wasn't a cat person, and the complex didn't allow dogs of a size that would make her consider a dog to be "real." Thus, she only had to move some clothes to make room to sit. She did, then thought better of it and went to the kitchen sink, under which she kept a bottle of bourbon. She rinsed a glass that looked clean enough anyway, then bent down, opened the cabinet door, took out the bottle and poured herself a stiff one.

A quick stop at the refrigerator garnered some ice cubes. With that, drink in hand, she returned to her living room and sat down, kicking off her sneakers and putting her feet up on the glass-topped coffee table.

"What the hell have you gotten yourself into, girl?" she asked, rhetorically. "What kind of sentences do they give people who do what Wes is planning to do?"

She sipped at the bourbon, laid her head back, and stared at the ceiling.

The problem, Phillie told herself, *is that I am stuck on a sliding scale. Right now, Wes is utterly attractive. Right now, as near as I can tell, I'm in love with him.*

She shifted gears to think about that. *In love with Wes? Let's see, pitter-pattering heart when we near to being together, even if I saw him just that morning? Check. Ache with emptiness when we're not together? Check. Perpetual horniness? Check. Dreams about raising children together? Check. Me pleasing him feels better than him pleasing me? Check. Think about him all the time, even to distraction? Check. Swallow rather than spit? That one's a no brainer. Of course.*

Willing to go to jail *for him? Harder . . . buuut . . . check.*

Willing to go to jail for him over something like this? Let's put that one off for a minute.

Another sip of the bourbon. Another. Another. *Jail? JAIL?* Big long drink; glug-glug-glug.

Phillie got up again. This time she stopped at the refrigerator first, to get ice, before going to the sink. When she returned to the sofa she brought the bottle with her.

She was thinking much more clearly now, she was certain. *Back to sliding scales.* Sip. *In three years the age of the men I'll find attractive is going to be about sixty. Sip. In eight years, when my biological time bomb clicks out, they'll be closer to seventy. Sip. And that's just impossible. I'll never have a baby if I wait that long. And I wanted THREE of them.*

Sip. Sip. Sip. Glug-glug. Pour some more.

Not going to be a mommy if I'm shot, *either. Sip. Sip, sip, sip.*

The warm caramelly taste of the bourbon filled her mouth. *Would prefer it was Wes.* A pleasant glow had spread across her body. *Prefer that was Wes, too. But SHOT?*

Then again, it has *been fun these past few days. Fun like the ER never is. Sip. And isn't a person entitled to at least one real adventure in life? Sip. And to have it surrounded by men like those Wes has collected? They would never let me be shot? Sip. What am I worried about?*

Sip. Well there's still jail . . . the chance of jail. No matter, I already agree that Wes is generally worth jail. Worth jail for this, though? Well . . . this thing he's doing makes him happy. And maybe that's enough.

Phillie heard a key enter the lock of her apartment door. The bolt fell back with a clump. The door opened and in the doorway she saw Stauer. She nodded to herself, half drunkenly, then stood up and walked to meet him. One hand reached out and pulled him inside. She closed the door shut behind them.

"Bridges told me you were—"

"Shut up, Wesss," she slurred, turning the interior lock. She turned and put her hands on his shoulders, pushing him against the door. "Ah'm going with ya on this, so ya better get me fitted for armor. Meanwahls, we haven' ha' any tahm for this since your crew showed up . . . " Phillie's accent tended to revert to rural Texas when she'd had a few. Her hands fumbled at his belt as she began to sink. He thought she was falling and reached to hold her up. She shrugged his hands off and finished sinking to her knees just as the belt came undone.

Phillie took him in hand and gave a few light flicks with her tongue. Then she looked up at him, smiled, and asked, "Did Ah evah tell ya Ah'm in love with ya, ya bad old man?"

Phillie lay asleep and lightly snoring, her head on Stauer's chest and one long leg thrown across his. His right arm cradled her head and wrapped around to cup one breast. With the left hand, he stroked her cheek.

A man is only as old as the woman he feels, Stauer reminded himself. *But I foresee the day coming fast when I'll have to mainline Viagra.*

And why are you here with a woman—hell, she's nearly a girl—half your age, you dirty "bad old man?" She's not just a convenient port in a storm, so to speak. Never has been. Been with her longer, too, two years now, than any woman I can think of.

Okay, so why?

Well, it isn't just the sex, as good as that is. Process of elimination maybe? The fact that women my age or near it rarely look good, while women much younger than Phillie, or even her age, are usually, to be brutally honest, just airheads? Or, even if that's not fair, and it probably isn't, we just don't, even can't, share world views?

Yeah, all right. Maybe that's part of it. Phillie because so many others are just poor fits. But that's not the whole story.

His eyes jerked in Phillie's direction. *I wonder if you'll ever guess I told Bridges to give it to you with both barrels, to see if you'll scare off. Kind of confirms my judgment, generally, that you didn't. Was it a dirty trick? Well . . . yeah. But, on the other hand, you didn't scare off. So we'll be fitting you for armor tonight, and tomorrow morning you report to Terry's people down in Somerset for the quickest basic combat training course in history.*

Not that I intend for a New York minute letting you fight; but you have to become part of the team. Course, if Terry downchecks you then you're not going past Brazil.

D-119, Somerset, Texas

The sun was just peeking over the horizon as Phillie pulled up to the lodge in her car. Terry Welch was there to meet her. She didn't really know what to expect. She knew she was scared, and that a lot of that fear came from ignorance. Yet what she thought she did know about scared her still more.

But I said I'd go through with it. So, God damn it, I'm going through with it.

She looks half terrified, poor thing, thought Terry, as he watched her car pull up to the lodge. He had his doubts, more about himself and his team than the woman. She . . . impressed him. *I've never tried to teach basic training. And I've never trained a woman. Neither have any of the boys. This ought to be . . . interesting.*

Terry had considered and rejected the time honored method of inflicting hell on the new recruit. It wasn't that he or his boys objected in principle; after all, they'd all been through it so many times and so many ways that most of them had lost count. Rather, it was just that to get any good effect from a hell week simply took time, a week or two. And they didn't have it.

Instead . . .

"Fifteen minutes to get into running gear, Miss Potter," Terry said. "The boss said you were probably fit enough. I want to make sure. You can change in the house."

When Phillie finished throwing up, about one hour (plus the six minutes' changing time) and seven miles later, one of Terry's teammates was standing by with an assortment of guns, some of them taken from Stauer's little armory, but rather more than that from the boys' own collections.

"Miss Potter," announced the very broad shouldered and very black Master Sergeant (Ret.) Robert "Buckwheat" Fulton, "there is no time to make you a marksman. Instead, I am going to familiarize you on these weapons, to include assembly and disassembly, cleaning, and use in close quarters battle. It is unlikely you will have to use any of these, or anything like them, except in close in, personal defense. Pay attention . . . "

Phillie's ears were ringing, despite the earplugs Fulton had insisted on, and every nail on her fingers was broken but for one. She was dirty, greasy, and pretty sure she smelled bad. It didn't seem to bother any of the men at the lodge, however. And she was *so* tired.

"This is a GPS, Miss Potter," said former warrant officer Jose "Little Joe" Venegas, standing perhaps five feet five in his boots. Little Joe laid the device on the table in front of her. "You may have something like it in your car. This will be different." He next picked up a map, announcing, "This is a one over fifty thousand scale map of this area." Replacing the map on the table, he picked up a green cylinder with some projections. "And this is a compass . . ."

D-118

They'd finally let Phillie get some sleep, sometime after three in the morning. And awakened her at five-thirty.

"This is a protective mask, Miss Potter . . ."

"All clear . . . GAS!"

"This is a knife, Miss Potter . . ."

"This is body armor, Miss Potter, and these are the ceramic inserts that supplement it. Put it on . . ."

"These are practice hand grenades, Miss Potter . . ."

"Miss Potter," said Sergeant First Class (Ret.) Rob "Rattus" Hampson, a Special Forces Medic, "you are already medical personnel. I won't waste time, but you need to know how to do some things that are the same as done in an ER, but without the ER's facilities, and with a lot more injured folks than there are people to help them . . ."

D-118, San Antonio, Texas

" . . . the Magellan's surveyor is already looking the ship over," Ed Kosciusko explained. "It's fairly new; I don't expect his crew to find any problems."

"You're absolutely certain you can get the landing craft down into the water with the just the one crane?" Stauer asked.

"It's technically a gantry, Wes. And, no, when you have one of anything then there's always the chance of failure. But every other ship Gordo and I came up with that had more than one was suboptimal for launching aircraft. Those things get in the way. This is the only one we found that was available, at a reasonable price to lease, for a reasonable time, that was also long enough to create an airstrip atop the containers."

"Crew?"

"Gonna join me in Hong Kong," Ed replied. "And no, they don't know anything except that I asked them to crew for me."

"Okay. Scares me, though, just one . . . "

The door to Stauer's apartment flew open, showing darkness lit by streetlights beyond. In walked Phillie. She was dirty. Her face had several abrasions. Both knees of her pants were ripped, and the left one hung down several inches. Reilly, standing near the door, made a waving motion under his nose, so apparently she stank, too.

"Fuck you all," she said, loud enough to be heard over the entire place. Without another word, she began walking straight to the master bedroom. The sound of running water began and didn't stop for a long time.

"How'd she do, Terry?" Stauer asked as Welch followed her in by about a minute behind.

Welch smiled broadly. "Not bad for the time we had. Give us a few months and she could find a place on a B Team. She's a good girl."

"Thanks, Terry. You're boys ready to move out to Myanmar?"

"Yeah, all set. I was concerned about evacuation, but Cruz is going to get the best Hips, piloted by him and his Russian pal, sitting on the Thai side of the border until we call. If Inning's lawyer will play along—and I am betting that Victor picked his lawyer based on his utter lack of principle—then it should be okay."

Ralph Boxer took Terry's hand and placed in it a card. "Memorize this and destroy it. It is a valuable contact within Burma."

Stauer was waiting when Phillie finally came out of the shower. She seemed like a sleepwalker. He stood, being a gentleman and all, and said, "I'm told you did pretty well. To the extent it was a test, and it mostly was, you passed."

She shambled over to him, put her arms around his neck, laid her head against his chest, and began to cry. "Oh, Wes, it was *awful*."

★ CHAPTER TEN ★

There is another huge structural problem for UNHCR,
for every agency, and that's the relief budgets.
The emergency budgets are always easier to get than
development. So you can get the emergency money
with hardly any trouble. Development funds are much
more difficult to get. So, the temptation is to keep
everyone in a perpetual emergency situation rather
than to work towards their integration.
—Dr. Barbara Harrell-Bond, OBE

D-147, Abéché, Chad

Abéché wasn't the middle of nowhere, but you could see
the middle of nowhere from there. That is, you could if
the dust had settled enough to see much of anything. That
only happened, though, in July and August when the town
got most of its annual nineteen inches of rain. The rest of
the time? Forget it.

It was the kind of place that in a travel guide discussing
nightlife, things to do, places to see, places to stay, etc.,

there would be zero entries. Even the airport only operated in the day.

For all that, to Labaan the most disappointing part of the town was that somehow—inexplicably, impossibly—Lance was waiting for the party near the airport parking area when they arrived. They found him by the plane they'd last seen in N'Djamena, reclining on a folding lawn chair, with a reflector held under his chin to help get that perfect tan.

"Dude," Lance said, "the day after I saw you I tried to crank it and it just started to work. Maybe a vapor lock in the engine. Dunno. But good to see ya, dude. You ready to head on out?"

Labaan resisted the urge to shoot the idiot American. *But only because we need him for now.*

"Vapor lock? In a *turboprop*?"

"Dude, I dunno; I just fly 'em. You want me to take you to Kosti or not?"

With all the humanitarian aid and human rights workers flooding eastern Chad, nobody much cared about a single Pilatus PC-12 leaving with a human cargo. Lance told the control tower he was leaving. Nobody answered. With a shrug, he gave a little power to the plane's sole, nose-mounted engine and taxied to the runway. There he turned left, heading west. At the western end he did a one eighty, waiting for a flight from Care to clear off.

"Dude," he called to Labaan, "open the hatch and look behind us to see if anyone's trying to land." When Labaan didn't move, Lance added, "Dude, I'm *serious*."

Sighing wearily, Labaan did just that. Having looked

from directly behind to directly overhead, he closed and dogged the hatch and shouted over the engine's roar, "You're cl—"

He couldn't finish before Lance had given the engine full throttle and was racing down the runway, shouting, "Kawabungaaaa!" The plane's deck moved out from under Labaan's feet, tossing him off the bulkhead rearward of the hatch and then to the floor.

I will kill this man, Labaan thought to himself, as he crawled along the deck to his seat. *Not all the lives saved by America around the world are enough to justify his continued existence.*

"Hey, dudes," Lance called out over his shoulder, "Look down below. Refugee camp." He twisted the control yoke and tilted the Pilatus over on its port side to give his passengers a view.

"There are twelve of these," Labaan told Adam, "all spread more or less in an arc east of Abéché. At least, there were twelve. There may be more now. And they keep growing. Someday, I suspect, the entire population of Africa will be in refugee camps where well-meaning Europeans and Americans can feel good about themselves for all the wonderful things they do on our behalf."

"You don't much like the whites, do you?" Adam said.

Labaan shrugged. "Whites in themselves? I've no strong feelings one way or the other. But the ones who come to help us? The twenty-year old dilettantes who come to teach our people how to farm land they've been farming for five thousand years? The ones who then give out so much food that it doesn't pay to farm anymore? The ones who ensure that both sides to our innumerable and interminable civil wars are fed, thus ensuring that the wars will go on forever? I despise those whites.

"Worse, though, are the ones who brought us Marxism, or brought some of our people to their lands to teach them Marxism. Imperialism never did us the harm that that one miserable European pseudo-philosophy has.

"Worst of all, though, are the ones who bring money, lots and lots of money, that feed our kleptocrats and give them both the means and the motivation to retain power. Always for good purposes does that money come," finished Labaan. "Always for evil purposes is it used."

"Imperialism did us plenty of harm," Adam objected, heatedly.

"Did it?" asked Labaan. "Ask anyone in a position to know, anyone old enough, if they'd rather things stay as they are or if they would, if they could, go back to the old days. Not one in a hundred wouldn't rather have the Euros back in charge. Unless we could talk the Americans into taking the job."

Adam went silent, turning his head and eyes to the front of the plane.

Labaan wasn't letting go, though. "Of course there are *some* people who like things as they are, especially the kleptocrats like your father who could never steal as much while the imperialists were in charge. Like my own chief, for that matter. And the people in the former French Empire couldn't go back, since there's nothing to go back to; the French kept their empire in everything but appearances."

★ ★ ★

The sun was well behind the Pilatus now, shining in thin streaks through the port side windows and painting those in bright lines on the seats and walls. Adam asked, "So what is our problem, then?"

Labaan shook his head. "Countries. Countries that mix tribes and clans."

"How so?"

"Because when you're a minority—or even something less than an absolute majority—in countries such as we have, and you're in a position to steal, then you're only stealing from other tribes on behalf of your own. Why, it's immoral not to steal then, before someone else beats you to it and disadvantages your own tribe."

"Well, yes, of course countries are wrong," Adam said. "Someday, when all of Africa, and all of mankind, live under a single roof . . . "

Labaan started to laugh. The laughter grew and grew, filling the plane with sound even over the sound of the motor. "Is that the nonsense you learned in school, boy? I suppose it must be; since they tried to teach me the same things when I was there. Family of Man, is that it?" Again, Labaan broke down in howling laughter. "Join in the Family of Man, boy? Those people running those refugee camps back there? They joined the Family of Man, and they're doing very well by doing little good, too. And the people that supervise them from plush offices in New York, and Paris, and London? They're in the Family of Man, which only means they've no moral connection to anyone but their own blood.

"Family of Man, my ass! You create a Family of Man, and one government, and the whole world will become

Rwanda or the Congo writ large. And you know what, boy? There'll be no escape from it, either."

"Kosti, Sudan coming up," announced Lance, from his pilot's seat.

Labaan gave one last look, a look half full of regret, at Lance as he stepped off the plane. *Yes, perhaps for the betterment of mankind I should have shot him. But he did, at least, refrain from shouting "Kawabunga!" when he dove for the strip. And the landing was, for a dirt field, acceptable. Even so, I predict that Allah shall punish me in the hereafter for my failure to better the lot of mankind in this one case.*

Looking around, Labaan saw exactly what he expected to see, a dusty van with a couple of men in it, waiting for him and his party. The driver's seat was empty.

"*Warya*, Labaan," the driver called out as he stepped around the van, buttoning his fly.

"*Warya*, Bahdoon," Labaan called back, walking forward to shake hands with his brother and slap him on the back. He did those things, then took Bahdoon's shoulder in his hand, gripped it, and shook it. "You, Brother, are the first thing that's gone right since leaving Nigeria."

"You must tell me about it on the way."

"I will, I promise. And Suakin, it is ready?"

"*Haa.* Very ready. We have the archeologist uncle is supporting, the permits from the government here, the arms, the video equipment, beds, food, cooking implements . . . everything you called for in your list."

"And all the men have been strip-searched for private means of communication?"

"That, and their money has been taken away. I purchased thirty women, right here, for cooking, cleaning, and sex. I promised them, as you insisted, that they would be given their freedom in three years."

"It is well, brother. And now, if you will take us to Suakin . . . "

Bahdoon nodded and said, "Surely." Then, spying Adam, he said, "The captive doesn't look like much, does he?"

"I think he has a good heart," Labaan said. "But his brain is contaminated with silly European and American notions."

D-146, Suakin, Sudan

The cut and dressed coral walls were covered by a sheet. This was necessary as, so far as Labaan knew, Suakin, the ancient port on the nearly circular island in the middle of a bay, was the only town in the world, or in the history of the world, to have been made of coral building blocks. If seen, those blocks were a dead giveaway.

In front of the sheet, on a cushion with his arms bound behind him, Adam sat facing a video camera. There were guards beside him, but they were standing with only their legs and the bayoneted, downturned muzzles of their Kalashnikovs showing. Labaan, the interviewer, was off screen entirely. Adam's chin was sunk onto his chest, resting on the one size fits all robe they'd given him to replace the filthy clothes—mere rags now—in which he'd been taken.

"Lift his head," Labaan ordered. "Let his father, Khalid, see who he is."

A Kalashnikov muzzle moved slightly as the guard holding it shifted to put his fingers through Adam's hair. The boy winced as his head was pulled back, showing his face to the camera.

"Tell your father, boy, are you being, and have you been, treated well?" Labaan asked.

Despite the pain it cost him, Adam twisted his head to free it of the grasping fingers. Even so, he had taken the hint and kept his eyes on the camera lens as he answered, "I have been kidnapped, drugged, endangered, chained like an animal, and threatened with torture, mutilation and death. But I am fed and watered, and reasonably healthy, Father."

Later, after the filming was over and the disc on its way, Labaan had taken a much ashamed Adam to the guards' quarters, a rather large coral-walled barrackslike room. Unveiled women, some older, some younger, were scrubbing floors on hands and knees. They got to their feet when they saw Labaan enter.

"You're going to be with us a long time, Adam," Labaan said. "I see no reason to make your captivity any worse than it must be." His arm swept around the room, taking in the women and girls. "Pick one," he said. "Pick one for yourself to care for you and to ease the burden of your sorrows."

"I can't," the boy said. "It's wrong to enslave people, even women . . . even Christian women, as I suspect these are."

"They are," Labaan confirmed. He mused for a minute, then said, "If you can't pick one for yourself, I'll pick one for you." His eyes roamed over the women until they came to rest upon one of the younger ones, an Ethiopian, tall and slender like most of her people. She was quite pretty, Labaan thought, pretty enough to keep the boy's mind occupied. "You, girl, what's your name?"

The girl lowered her eyes and answered, "Makeda, if it pleases you."

"Don't worry about pleasing me," Labaan said. He pointed at Adam and continued, "Please him. He's your new master."

★ CHAPTER ELEVEN ★

Ship me somewheres east of Suez,
where the best is like the worst,
Where there aren't no Ten Commandments
an' a man can raise a thirst;
—Kipling, *Mandalay*

D-116, Yangon International Airport

The last place Terry Welch and his team wanted to be at the airport was the Theravada Buddhist Temple lookalike VIP lounge.

"I thought Burma was socialist, Terry," Rob "Rattus" Hampson said, looking out the bluish windows at the gold trim visible outside. A college boy, one who'd enlisted into special forces straight out of school under the old "X-Ray" program, Rattus made a considerable effort to keep abreast of things in the world. He could have made, indeed, had been making, quite a fine living as a physician's assistant on the outside. But when Terry had called, saying, "Free beer," the old code for "Alert," he'd looked inside himself, discovered that, deep down, he loathed civilian life, and come a runnin'.

"The original socialist dictator here," Terry answered, "was clever in many ways. One way was that instead of suppressing religion he enslaved it to the cause. Mind you, since he made any number of key decisions based on numerology, I'd suggest he was probably sincere about Buddhism, too. Hell, for that matter, adherence to Marxism requires a faith that's almost religious."

Little Joe Venegas looked around, trying very hard to keep from his face the disdain he felt. "Place gives me the creeps, and it seems so fucking obvious."

Venegas, like Hampson, had found gainful employment in the civilian world, after retiring, following the dustup in Afghanistan. In his case, though, it was in IT, since before striking for warrant he'd been a communications sergeant. Like Hampson, he hadn't really cared for civilian life. Perhaps the thing he'd loathed most was the big, blustering bastard who ran his shop. So when Buckwheat Fulton had called, passing on Terry's message, Little Joe had walked into his boss's office and said simply, "I quit." He'd then made reservations for a flight at night, a couple of nights hence, terminated his lease, and ordered his furniture picked up and stored. Then he'd waited for his former boss to leave work, beaten the living bejesus out of him, never saying a word as he did so, and left.

"Never heard of "The Purloined Letter," Little Joe?" asked Rattus.

Joe didn't answer immediately but instead looked around at the various businessmen, jet setters, and do-gooders flying to or from the latest conference at some luxury resort. "Well, we're mostly the right age to fit in, and the suits help, but old as we are, Rattus, not a one of us has a gut to match most of these fuckers. And most of them have cell phones glued to their ears."

"Point," Hampson conceded. Then he pointed with his chin at a well dressed blonde with prominent breasts. "But then again, she has neither a gut nor a phone."

"Point. You figure they're natural?"

Hampson, though a former "delta," or Special Forces medic, shook his head. "Out of my league, training-wise. But probably not. There is no such perfection in nature."

"Terry," Little Joe said, nodding his head in the direction of a short and prosperous looking businessman, approaching with one underling in tow and a newspaper tucked under one of the businessman's arms. He had thin lips, long earlobes, a flat, wide nose, and the somewhat subdued epicanthic fold often found among the Burmese.

"I see our Mr. Nyein, Joe," Terry answered. "Split up, per plan."

Little Joe and Rattus Hampson cut right without another word, except to each other, heading to the lounge's bar. The other members of the team were already waiting, scattered about in ones and twos. Nyein's flunky headed towards the bar to link up with Little Joe and Rattus, and lead them to their hotel. When the other team members saw the flunky shake hands and then leave with Hampson and Venegas, they began to follow in a loose gaggle, Buckwheat taking up the rear. The flunky dialed a number on a cell phone, said nothing, then put the cell phone away.

Terry, meanwhile, took the nearest seat. Mr. Nyein sat down next to him.

Nyein opened his paper and began to read, or to seem to. His cell phone rang. He put down his newspaper, answered the call and began to speak. "Our friend Pugnacio," he said, referring to Boxer, "asked me to lend you a hand."

Terry took out his own cell and pretended to make a call. "And we appreciate this," he answered.

"The problem is, however, that the entire situation is much more complex than Pugnacio led me to believe."

"This doesn't surprise me, somehow," Terry said.

Still seeming to speak into the phone, Nyein said, "I will get up and leave. Wait two minutes and follow me but no further than the pickup ramp. I will swing by to get you in a blue BMW 328. After that . . . "

Nyein made the introductions. "Captain Welch, Major Konstantin, Mr. Naing. Captain Welch, Mr. Naing is Mr. Inning's attorney here. Major Konstantin is a . . . "

"I am a business associate of Victor's, Captain Welch," said the major in almost accent free English.

Terry took one look at Konstantin, heard his spoken English, and said, "You're Spetznaz."

"Not precisely," the Russian corrected. "Once upon a time I was in a somewhat similar group. Now I work for Victor. It pays the bills."

"And you are here to get him out?"

Naing, as typically Burmese looking as Nyein, answered, "Everyone wants Victor freed, Captain Welch. Since Myanmar is an outcast state, the government needs him out there feeding us arms. Major Konstantin has not the connections to keep the business going . . . "

"Victor is very cagey and clever that way," Konstantin said, stone faced.

"You need what?" Nyein asked. "Arms? Transportation somewhere?" The Burmese shrugged. "No matter. While Russia itself doesn't seem to care about Mr. Inning, certain interests within Russia want him back to doing the work he does so very well. And I need to be paid."

"Which you will not be," Konstantin said, "until my principal is free." The Russian turned toward Terry, asking, "What is it you need with Victor?"

"I don't have the full list," Welch answered, though that was only true insofar as he didn't have the full requisition on his person. "In general terms, from him we need arms and ammunition for a small battalion, plus some special equipment, radios, night vision, and some light armored vehicles. Perhaps some few other things in his purview."

"I don't even know where he stockpiles the ammunition," Konstantin said. "I only know that he does and that he's got at least several regiments' worth of arms, to include eight hundred Abakan rifles, stashed away."

"They any good?" Terry asked. "I've never fired one."

"The Abakans? Yes, Captain, they're quite good in terms of accuracy and reliability though the ergonomics are suboptimal. My team has them here along with our version of those nonlethal electronic pistols your people seem to like. As for the Abakans, mechanical training is . . . difficult. And the sharp edges on the metal? Ouch! Not to mention the peep—"

Mr. Naing *ahem*ed. "I hate to interrupt your professional discussion, gentlemen, but we do have a problem to solve."

"Well, my people had a solution," Konstantin said, "until

our helicopter broke down. Fortunately, we were not in the air at the time." The major sighed at the depravity of man. "Time after time I've told Victor, 'You must maintain the aircraft.' But would he listen? No. And we were ready to launch in three days. My men have been spending the last two weeks rehearsing, to include driving in this miserable excuse for a city."

"You have a solution provided you have a helicopter?" Terry asked.

"With Mr. Naing here, along with a certain amount of interested indifference on the part of the government, yes, we do. Why?"

Terry smiled, "Well, as it so happens . . . "

What a sadness, Mr. Naing thought, *that though we were a part of the British Empire, and to a considerable extent inherited the English legal system, we did not, however, opt to keep up British integrity.*

On the other hand, he added, with a mental shrug, *at least we can say we have honest judges who, when bought, stay bought.*

Naing stood and bowed, reaching across the judge's desk to shake hands. The leather satchel he'd brought with him to the judge's office remained on the floor, even when the barrister turned to leave.

The judge could count the money in the satchel later.

D-113, Insein Jail, Yangon, Myanmar

The money had been for nothing more than to get the

judge to agree to a hearing on a particular day. The money being adequate to something not outside of bounds anyway, the judge had agreed. Of course to get to the court, Victor would have to be taken from the jail where he was being held, pending trial.

Located, for the most part, within a sixteen sided, walled complex, perhaps three hundred meters in diameter, the jail was about six hundred meters from the Irrawaddy River. Insein tended toward the primitive, with most waste functions being handled by pot and bucket rather than via plumbing. It stank far, far more than the surrounding rice paddies. Insein—pronounced "insane"—was also notorious for torturing, holding, dumping, and on occasion hanging political prisoners.

There were, however, better and worse conditions. At least one Burmese prodemocracy dissident had had a complex specially built to house her under approximately civilized conditions. Victor Inning, as someone considered by the government to be a past and potentially a future asset, had also been given rather better than normal treatment.

He was unsurprised when Mr. Naing showed up at his cell door, accompanied by two guards. "Court appearance today, Victor," the Burmese lawyer said. "I've moved the judge to hear your habeas petition ahead of schedule."

Inning nodded, stood, and began to walk to his cell door. His eyes searched Naing's face for any clue that rescue might be imminent, but the lawyer's face was set in concrete.

Seeing one of the guards holding up a pair of handcuffs, Victor turned about and placed his hands behind his back.

The guard cuffed the right wrist and then the left. He tightened the cuffs, causing them to make a slight clicking sound, but no more than was required for security's sake. Inning's circulation was, in any case, not impinged upon.

Once outside the cell block, Victor glanced at the permanent gallows standing near the southwest sections of the wall, past the women's quarter. Even though he thought it very unlikely he would end up standing on the structure, the sight still sent a chill up his spine.

Approaching the blue-painted, Chinese-made van, Inning was struck by the word "POLICE," lettered in white across the vehicle's side. *How odd it is,* he thought, *that fifty years after the English pulled out of here, the word for those who enforce law and order is still in the English language.*

The van was actually half van and half truck, having a four seat cab up front and a truck bed behind. One of the guards opened the door for Mr. Naing and Victor, while the other put a hand atop Victor's head to guide him away from hitting it on the door frame.

They're being amazingly polite, Victor thought. *Almost as if they expected me to become a free man, even an important free man, soon.* Again he looked at his attorney's face and again he was met with a cold mask.

Whatever little hope Victor might have had then evaporated when the door closed and he could see that it had no interior latches. A quick glance to the other side of the van confirmed that Mr. Naing was as trapped as he was.

Oh, well, thought Victor, *even if I have to go back it will still be nice to get away from the stink of the prison for a while. I never before knew that some stenches were so bad olfactory fatigue wouldn't set in.*

The van's engine started with a cough. Waving at the guard on the gatehouse at the southern end of the prison, the driver put it in gear and began moving forward. By the time they reached the gate, it was open. The van pulled through and turned right.

Timer's friends called him . . . "Tim." Major Konstantin called him "Sergeant Musin." Timer Musin was a Tatar. Part Tatar, anyway; somewhere in his ancestry were people with eyes not dissimilar to the Burmese. Somewhere in his ancestry were men who had ridden horseback with the Golden Horde.

But me? Nooo. I get to ride this miserable excuse of an upengined moped.

On the plus side, Tim wasn't much taller than the Burmese norm, though his shoulders were considerably wider. His eyes, rather than having the epicanthic fold, were round and green. This didn't matter as his sunglasses covered them. What did matter is that, as a former sniper, Musin had eyesight much better, at 20/8, than the human norm.

Though normally blond, Sergeant Musin's hair had been dyed black the night before. It wasn't the right texture to blend with the locals, though, and so he would cover that, too, with a helmet, before taking off on his—to be charitable—motorcycle.

Musin was perched atop his bike sipping one of the vile local soft drinks when the gate to his north opened. From one hundred meters away, Victor may as well have been sitting at a distance of a mere forty. He was easily recognizable to Tim as being his boss of many years.

Musin pushed a button on his cell phone to dial Konstantin's number, thus initiating an overall conference call among the members of the two co-joined teams. While the call was going through, he put the helmet on his head. By the time he finished that, his earpiece was saying, "Konstantin here, Sergeant Musin."

"I have them, Comrade Major. They've turned off to the west, toward the river. I am following."

★CHAPTER TWELVE★

Those who 'abjure' violence can only do so
because others are committing violence on their behalf.
—George Orwell, Notes on Nationalism

D-113, Insein Road, Yangon

Tim made his last cell phone report as the half van carrying Victor entered the five way intersection where Insein Road joined with and became Pyay Road. With that report, he turned his motorcycle to the left, following University Avenue past the University itself to Inya Lake, a large, tree-fringed watery park within the city, largely surrounded by the mansions of the wealthy. At the intersection of University and Inya Road, he again turned left until the next right turn. This led into the park.

One of the requirements of the mission was that the helicopter that would pick them up needed open space to either land or, at least, come to a very low hover. Open space that was not normally filled with vehicular traffic was generally hard to come by in the center of this city of six million. The lake, at least, was open. It was also shallow enough to wade into for a pickup, should that become necessary.

The helicopters had already taken off from the southern tip of Mae Hong Son Province, Thailand; so much Tim knew. At this point one should be loitering over the river to the east, midway between Yangon and Onhne. Another one, the backup, was about thirty kilometers further out. The third, unknown to Musin, was back in Mae Hong Son with two flight simulators in the back. Both of the active choppers carried auxiliary fuel tanks to give them nearly six hundred miles of one way range. Given that the round trip from Mae Hong Son to Yangon and back was only about forty percent of that, that allowed for a lot of loiter time.

Which is really *good*, though Sergeant Musin, as he parked his motorcycle by one of the public parking spots edging the park that surrounded the lake, *since traffic was especially bad today and we're a fucking hour behind schedule. Also good that the cops weren't in enough of a hurry to take some other route to the courthouse.*

Tim unstraddled the bike, unfixing from the rear seat the small red satchel he carried. This contained a radio for contacting the helicopters, his submachine gun and a half dozen smoke grenades, two red and the rest white. The satchel also held two cartons of cigarettes and a bottle of vodka. These were slightly less important to Tim than his mission baggage.

He walked to the northeast, along a very narrow causeway to where an oval island seemed almost to float on the lake. Four mansions on the mainland and on two other nearby peninsulas framed the oval island. Sergeant

Musin took a quick glance left and right and saw two more red satchels, just like his. *Also good; Kravchenko and Litvinov are on station. And now, if traffic and the police will just cooperate . . .*

D-113, Green Elephant Restaurant, Yangon

Terry Welch and Major Konstantin sipped tea on the sidewalk fronting the restaurant. Both were a little nervous at the hour's delay, Konstantin chain smoking while Welch drummed his fingers on the table.

Slightly to the north, nearly next door, in fact, Rattus and Little Joe made a show of inspecting the wares in Augustine's Antiques. Augustine's wares ran heavily to bronze- and silverware, wooden and stone statuary, furniture both local and colonial, and porcelain. The stuff was sometimes carefully displayed, while some wares were stacked to the ceiling. For all either of the two men knew, it was even as antique as claimed.

On the eastern side of the street, approximately opposite the antique shop, two more of Terry's men sat in a rental car. Another one of Terry's men, known to his friends as "Pigfucker," also sat in a car, motor running. That car was combat parked, which is to say, tail to the curb, in front of the restaurant and ready to launch out into traffic in front of the police van. The remaining men, one of Welch's, Buckwheat Fulton, and two of Konstantin's stood, all also with red satchels at their feet or in their hands, at three of the other four roads feeding in to the five way intersection. The centermost of these had two missions, one along Insein Road and the other at Pyay Road, both north of the intersection. Each man, to include those in the vehicles, had mopeds standing by. Terry, who would carry Victor off, had a full fledged motorcycle. It was only recently that the ruling junta had lifted a city-wide ban on mopeds and motorcycles, which had been in effect since the driver of one had accidentally annoyed one of the generals who ran the country by running into said general's motorcade.

Somehow, thought Welch, *I expect that ban to be back in place within twenty-four hours.*

For what little added security it provided, everyone had been given a makeover by Vladimir Galkin, who was Konstantin's disguise specialist, and widely believed to be homosexual. But, hey, if it didn't bother the Russians who worked with him daily, who were the Americans to object?

It's not really a complex plan, Welch thought, fingers still drumming, *but it sure does have a lot of moving parts. That said, there's only seven of us here, and we each have discreet jobs. One, Pigfucker, to crash the cops. He could do that in his sleep. Three to expand the traffic jam have very simple jobs. And three to secure the pickup zone have almost nothing to do once Sergeant Musin turns off from trailing the police. It really ought to work. We've even got some inherent redundancy.*

Still, if I didn't worry I don't know what the fuck I'd do. Unconsciously, his fingers picked up the William Tell Overture: Taptaptap, taptaptap, taptaptap, tap, tap . . .

All the members of the two teams were on a constant conference call and had been for over an hour. The common tongue was English, since all of Konstantin's men spoke it, while Terry's only had Farsi, Arabic, and Spanish for foreign languages. Besides that, the Burmese police, for the most part, could get by in English, legacy of the long years under the Empire, in case they had occasion to try to explain something away.

Terry had heard Sergeant Musin's report, just as Konstantin had. "Remember, Major," he said, "no local police get hurt. Those were my orders."

"No problem, Terry," the Russian answered. "We don't, my organization doesn't, want any trouble with the Burmese we don't have to have. For one thing, they're potentially very valuable customers."

"All right then. Annnnd . . . " Terry saw the police van moving at no more than ten miles an hour down Pyay Road. Reaching down for his satchel, he ordered, "Pigfucker, get 'em."

Unseen by Terry, Konstantin started his watch in stopwatch mode.

"Pigfucker"—known to more polite company as Darrell Hammell—was a Tennessee ridge runner from the general vicinity of Knoxville. His answer was an altogether too loudly shouted "YeeHAW" and the screeching of tires as he launched his car forward into the right front fender of the police van, stopping himself almost cold and spinning the van almost halfway around. A taxi which had been following the van perhaps a bit too closely almost immediately struck the van on the left rear, further spinning it. Another vehicle behind the taxi struck that, while a fourth, fifth and sixth added to the mayhem. A symphony of car horns arose to assault the ears.

★ ★ ★

And that's my signal, thought *Praporschik* Alexei Baluyev. Baluyev, a Great Russian, very tall and very blond and thus terribly noticeable amidst the much shorter and darker Burmese, stood on the southern side of Hiedan Road, west of the intersection. He bent over to his own little red bag and removed from it a smoke pot. Unscrewing the cap, Baluyev gave it a jerk, yanking the cord that ignited the thing. He rolled it under the auto to his front and, crouching still, padded up to the next car. There he repeated the gesture, even as a cloud of dense smoke was pushed into the lanes of traffic by the wind blowing from the southeast. Amidst the sounds of screeching tires, honking horns, smashing glass, and tortured, twisting metal, Baluyev mounted his moped and began trolling briskly to the east, heading to the rendezvous at the island at the edge of the lake. As he crossed the intersection, he saw to his left that a similar cloud had bisected Insein Road to the north, while another was building along Pyay Road to the northeast.

Ahead of Baluyev, two cars were apparently on flame along University Avenue. To his right, a group of armed men had already surrounded one police van—*the target*, Baluyev correctly surmised—and the traffic cop on duty at the intersection was obviously drawing his sidearm and sizing up the situation even as a wave of pedestrians passed him fleeing the mayhem to the south. Baluyev pulled his cloned version of the American M-18 Taser from his pocket and shot the policeman in the back. The cop collapsed, twitching like a crack addict in sudden, total withdrawal. Baluyev then took the spare cartridge from its holder below the pistol's grip and placed it on the business end of the less-than-lethal weapon. The Taser-clone then went back into his pocket, where Baluyev lightly caressed it before putting the hand back on the handlebars.

Baluyev hurried on, happily whistling "Ochee Chyornya".

Even before the police van came to a rest, Terry's team and Konstantin were racing for it, pulling their weapons from their satchels and firing into the air to frighten away any pedestrians who might come to help the police. Terry and the Russian arrived first, and aimed at the policemen in the front of the van. Both, though stunned by the repetitive car strikes, raised their hands overhead immediately. Little Joe and Rattus arrived a few seconds later. They opened the doors and dragged the slight policemen bodily from the seats, flinging them face-down to the ground. Terry's team had come intending to do the mission, or at least to try to, without doing anyone any lasting bodily harm. Thus, in addition to the tasers provided by the Russians, Rattus and Venegas each had a couple of auto injectors filled with a concoction Hampson had come up with. Once the police were on the ground, and covered by Welch's and Konstantin's weapons, Hampson and Little Joe jumped on their backs, removed auto injectors from pockets, took off the safety caps, and slammed the business ends into uniformed buttocks, sending each of the Burmese cops rapidly into Neverland.

Terry trotted away to get his motorcycle as the two men from the other side of the street, former Sergeants Blackburn—"Blackguard"—and Ryan, ran up. These, too, went to opposite sides of the van, opening the doors and pulling out Mr. Naing and Victor Inning.

"Relax, Victor; it's a rescue!" Konstantin shouted, in Russian.

Mr. Naing was thrown to the ground, a bit more gently than had been the policemen. As Rattus pulled out another auto injector, Naing asked, "Is this going to hurt much?"

"Like the devil," Hampson admitted. "Sorry, Mr. Naing, but it beats prison. And it beats us having to rough you up—worse still, shoot you someplace non-vital—to make it look like you weren't in on this."

"Oh, go ahead and do it, then," the lawyer said with a mix of fear and resignation in his voice.

Rattus nodded once and gave him the shot, in his right thigh. The lawyer squealed once, then went into deep relaxation.

Meanwhile, one of the men from the other side of the street turned Victor around. From his satchel he pulled a set of bolt cutters. "We can get the rest of it later, Mr. Inning," he said. "For now, it's only important that you can hang on to Terry. Trust me, hanging on to Terry when he's driving a bike is a major effort."

With a metallic crack the chain on the cuffs parted just as Terry pulled up on his bike. Little Joe and Blackguard, who had the bolt cutters, physically manhandled Inning onto the bike, placing his arms around Terry. Blackguard then dropped the bolt cutters and pulled out a motorcycle helmet. This was a large size, guaranteed to fit Inning's head . . . which it did with only a minor screech from Victor as the helmet twisted his ear downward. Little Joe slapped Terry upside the helmet. "Go, boss, GO!"

Terry, carrying a still stunned looking Inning, took off

with a roar, cutting across stalled traffic and heading for the oval island.

Konstantin consulted his watch again. *Ninety-seven seconds. You know, we really might just get away with this.* He clapped his hands twice, sending the other five scurrying for their mopeds. He, himself, turned likewise and walked calmly to his own, parked in front of the Green Elephant. Equally calmly, he tied his satchel onto the back of the conveyance, then straddled it, pushing the starter button. The thing sputtered to life as Konstantin sat down. In moments he was entering stalled traffic, between cars mostly abandoned, heading for the other side of Pyay Road and eventual safety. As he moved Konstantin heard police sirens, distant but growing closer.

Of course, our big advantage now is that we are vehicle-borne, while the police are going to have to get on foot to get through the traffic jam we've created.

I hope.

Baluyev saw a Burmese policeman walking west, through the halted traffic, waving his pistol and shouting imprecations in his native tongue. *Oh, oh. We planned for all the known cops but this one was not in the plan. Probably some poor bastard just getting off duty.*

Halting his moped and glancing to his left rear he saw what had to be, from the size, shape and color of the bike, and the fact that there were two big men mounted on it, the American, Welch, and Victor Inning. Apparently the cop saw them as well, as he pointed both himself and his pistol in their general direction, raising his left hand to order a halt.

Baluyev twisted the handlebars to the left and leaned that way as well, laying the moped down on the asphalt. He extricated his left leg and got up to a crouch, even as his right hand pulled out the Taser. Once the cop took up a deliberate firing stance, Baluyev hesitated not a nanosecond, but fired his two leads into the policeman's side. The cop began a twitching descent to the ground.

Trotting over, Baluyev bent down and patted the policeman's cheek. "No offense, officer," he said, in English, with a New York accent. Once upon a time, *Praporschik* Baluyev had been part of a very highly trained team, oriented to doing some very nasty things in the American northeast.

A motorcycle raced by, its wind and smoky exhaust assailing the Russian. He then scooped up the cop's pistol which he saw was an old Browning. This he stuck in his belt before racing back to his moped.

Terry, riding down the now abandoned sidewalk, saw the cop preparing to shoot and was, himself, a couple of nanoseconds from dumping the bike to try to get himself and Inning out of the line of fire. Just before he did he saw the policeman begin to twitch and fall. He recovered the bike to full upright and gunned it past the fallen constable of the peace without a backward glance. He continued east on the University Avenue sidewalk for another five hundred or so meters before cutting left, just inside the smoke screen still bisecting the road. Here Terry had to slow to weave through the stopped autos. He got as far as the westbound lane before he ran into a series of crashed cars so extensive that he thought he might make better time on foot. He stopped the motorcycle and turned around to shout to Victor, "Can you run?"

"Stop this thing and I'll *fly*!" the Russian shouted back.

"Come on then." Terry took a folding stock assault rifle Victor instantly suspected was from his own stocks and tossed it, shouting, "Shoot to intimidate, and only if necessary. Do *not* shoot to wound or kill." Then Welch took his own Taser-clone pistol from his pocket. Leaving his helmet on his head and grasping his satchel in hand, Terry took off at a gallop, Victor trailing close behind. They passed school buildings on the left of the gently curving road, mansions galore—in both senses—on the right. Further to the right, past the irregular line of monuments to conspicuous consumption, a Russian-built helicopter could occasionally be glimpsed between dwellings and through trees, as it came in low over the waters of the lake.

"I see your purple smoke," Artur Borsakov said, his helmet mounted microphone transmitting the message in a warble to the man on the ground below, the one who had announced, "I am popping smoke."

I know I've picked that man up before, somewhere, somewhen, thought Borsakov.

"Affirmative, that's us. Enemy situation is negative at this time, but everyone's not here yet."

Borsakov keyed his mike to internal only and asked Cruz, "What do you think, Mike, land or take a turn around the lake?"

"Land, I think, Artur. After all, the LZ is cold."

"Fair enough." Rekeying the microphone, Borsakov said, "We're coming in."

"Roger," answered Tim from the ground. "Be advised we do not have our principal target here yet."

The months of enforced inactivity, at least of cardio-vascular inactivity, had taken their toll. Inning was flagging, however manfully he tried to keep up. Terry had already had to slow to something he considered a crawl, and still the Russian was falling behind.

They heard an almost comical *toot-toot* behind them and stopped. It was just too silly a sound to be dangerous. Looking to the rear, Welch saw the Russian he knew as Baluyev smiling broadly as he pulled up on his moped.

"Get on, Victor," Baluyev said. Welch immediately began forcibly pushing his charge onto the little vehicle's seat. Once he was there, and his arms placed around Baluyev's mid-section, the former took off again smartly. Terry resumed his foot-gallop.

A number of mopeds belonging to the two teams passed Terry. Though numerous high-pitched horns sounded, nobody offered him a ride until Buckwheat Fulton came to a stop a few feet ahead. Without a word, Terry jumped on the back, facing to the rear, his ass on a metal frame and his satchel clutched in his lap. Fulton gunned the thing, if "gunned" was the right word for an engine that measured roughly 3.1 cubic inches and achieved under four horsepower.

Ahead, they could hear the steady *wop-wop-wop* of their helicopter's rotors, mixed in with the higher pitched whining of its jet engines. In his earpiece, Terry could hear Konstantin ticking off the names of the team members as they arrived and formed a perimeter around the oval island.

Konstantin reported, "Captain Welch, I have everybody here, including Victor, except for you and Sergeant Fulton."

At that moment the moped heeled hard right as Buckwheat turned it toward the island.

"We're about two minutes out," Terry said. He felt for a moment the joy that hangs on the edge of a completed mission, which joy is usually expecting disaster to intervene and cut its life short. "Start loading."

Konstantin pointed at Baluyev. "Get Victor aboard." He had to shout to be heard over the helicopter's roar. Arm around Inning, Baluyev led him up and over the rear ramp, which Borsakov had dropped for faster, smoother loading. (Some models of the Hip have clamshell doors; this was a variant with a ramp able to handle a vehicle up to the size of an SUV.) Others began following by twos as Konstantin called off numbers.

The men were buckling in on the side-mounted troopseats when someone shouted, "Look the fuck out." Everyone turned their head to the helicopter's rear. They saw white teeth and the whites of eyes, both in their way smiling broadly, in a black face. The moped below that face came up the ramp before the driver twisted and dumped it on its side, causing it to slide down the cargo deck, bouncing off this and that and propelling legs upward.

"Take the fuck off!" Welch shouted from the cargo

deck. He was rewarded with the sound of the chopper pulling pitch and lifting off the island. His stomach was pressed to his back. A low tree ahead brushed its branches along the underside just before the Hip twisted in air, assuming a generally easterly heading, on its way back to Thailand.

I love Russian helicopters!

D-112, Headquarters, State Peace and Development Council, Napyidaw, Myanmar

A ceiling fan rotated gently over the desk, not so much fanning the moist air as just redistributing it a bit.

"Well, that went nicely," said the general at the desk to Mr. Nyein. "My compliments."

"All the doing of the Americans and Russians, sir, I assure you," Nyein modestly responded.

The general made a shushing motion with his hands. "Perhaps," he admitted, "but let us not give the foreigners too much credit. Your job was in many ways the most difficult: Getting the arms merchant Inning off our hands in a way that would not hold us up to the world's opprobrium, not annoy him to the point he would no longer do business with us, and with as little harm to our own as possible. And doing it all behind the scenes."

Nyein bowed his head graciously, then asked, "Speaking of which, sir, the policeman . . . ?"

The general seemed momentarily aggrieved. "The one who was shot with an electric gun at the intersection? He died. Congenital heart defect of which no one was aware, least of all himself. Apparently the shock was too much."

"Ah, that's too bad. Still . . ."

"Never mind," said the general. "His wife and children will be well cared for. Moreover, his death validates our innocence. Thus, he died for his country."

★CHAPTER THIRTEEN★

I must go down to the sea again,
to the lonely sea and the sky
—John Masefield, *Sea Fever*

D-112, Hong Kong, PRC

The advent of "communism" to this former British colony had made remarkably little difference to the running of the place. Trade, enormous levels of trade—especially considering the long recession-bordering-on-depression in which the world found itself—still flowed. Ships were built, outfitted, and repaired. Ships sailed to and from the place almost en masse. Indeed, the level of maritime activity was so great that one ship, more or less, being worked on, more or less, or even modified, more or less, invited little notice. More or less.

The ship, for the nonce the MV *Magellan*, rang and hissed with the sounds of workers, busily making the relatively minor mods Kosciusko thought he needed to turn a container ship into an assault transport. Under the guise of strengthening the hull, beams were being welded—and here the ship's sole gantry was proving singularly useful—to provide a resting platform for containers which would leave some open space down below. Additionally, another partial deck of perforated steel, sent up from the Philippines, was being welded very near the bottom of the hull. Space had to be left, and new power leads run, for a containerized, seventy-two-hundred gallon per day desalination plant, being flown in tomorrow from Santa Clara, California.

And there goes about a hundred and twenty k, thought Kosciusko. *But without something like the desalinator, we could never hope to carry so many people for so long. A quarter million liters of bottled water? That would have cost even more and taken up too much space. And that's not even counting predictable losses if we hit any rough seas. Which we will.*

The Chinese were also being paid to add in some extra fuel bunkerage. The ship was capable of almost eighteen knots, fast for a merchie, but maintaining that speed cost in fuel. And, since every day mattered, speed would matter and fuel would be used profligately, as well. Moreover, the day was going to come when the ship would be carrying things no customs agent could be permitted to look at. Since customs agents and ports went hand in hand, any of the latter that could be avoided should be avoided.

There were Chinese at work, as well, on the exterior of the ship, painting it in its new colors as the flagship of the new—courtesy of Matt Bridges—non-governmental, humanitarian aid organization, Mobile Emergency

Relief for Civilians In Fear of UnLawful aggression: MERCIFUL.

Stupid as shit, Kosciusko thought, *though bleeding heart NGO-wise, it's got no monopoly on stupid names. And . . . well, it beats Onward Christian Soldiers, or OCS, which was the first suggestion given. And, thank You, God, 'Titan Uranus' was already taken.*

Then, too, one could read the name as "Merciful Aggression," and that surely fits the mission profile. And I do kind of like that proliferation of clasping hands, doves, olive wreaths, and whatnot.

Rechristening as the *"Merciful"*—though, in fact, no ceremony would take place—would be one of the last things done, the better—if only slightly—to drop off the screens after the ship left Hong Kong.

Three landing craft—LCM-6s—were already en route to Manaus, Brazil. Two of these were coming from Richmond, California, and one from Seattle. They were expected to arrive there via a Panama registered merchie about ten days after the staff and advanced party landed at Gomes Airport, Manaus, to take possession of the huge tract of jungle purchased for an assembly and training area. If sufficient armored cars arrived to begin training with them in Brazil the LCMs would meet them on the Amazon and sneak them in to camp.

And, if not, we're just screwed, thought Kosciusko. *Though there's always highly suspicious fallback position two: buy a couple of turret simulators from the Frogs, if they exist. Not my job, anyway.*

Kosciusko had been something of an odd duck in the

Navy. "Duck," in this case, carried more than one meaning. A former enlisted Marine, Ed had gone to the Naval Academy and elected, at graduation, to enter the Navy rather than the Marine Corps. In the Navy he'd made a specialty of amphibious operations, with a sideline in logistics. This, unfortunately, left him pretty much out of all the more powerful "unions" within his service. He'd never been passed over for promotion. Still, his personnel manager had been direct. "Ed, you've got about two years left in. You better find another job."

Well over fifty now, nearly bald, and with a budding paunch, Ed had been with the merchant service for a while. That had lasted until boredom and the realization that he was a little late for that union, too, sent him into a second, potentially suicide inducing, retirement. He'd been mulching the flower beds surrounding his house when his wife, Elaine, had come out, cordless phone in hand, and said, "Someone named Cruz wants to talk to you, Ed. Said you know each other from the Pakistan thing. By the way, *what* Pakistan thing?" she asked, very suspiciously.

"Need to know, Hon, need to know." *That dickhead, Cruz.*

Cruz had been considerably more cagey about inviting Ed in than his naval personnel manager had been in inviting him out. "Whatcha been up to, Ed? . . . Sounds really dull . . . yeah, I hear ya. Hey, why don't you fly on down to San Antonio. Friend of mine has unlimited cases of free beer . . . Yes, Ed, free beer. You'll understand when you get here . . . he might have some worthwhile piecework for you . . . We'll have to see . . . "

★ ★ ★

Though he'd kept his face a blank, at first Ed had been a little skeptical. Then he'd seen the staff at Stauer's place, heard the money being spent, seen the utter seriousness of the Army and Marine types Stauer had collected. This hadn't completely dispelled his skepticism. Indeed, he'd kept it until Gordo—Harry Gordon—had shown him four container ships he'd found for sale or lease and said, "Pick one and defend your choice to Wes."

With that, they'd had him hooked. *Command the naval portion of an amphibious assault? My so-far-frustrated life's ambition? Be still my heart. Where do I sign? I've only got the one firstborn child. Can I offer you a couple of grandchildren?*

Still, it's going to be a bitch, Ed thought, glancing up at the gantry. *Sure, the thing will move back and forward, but not one inch further back than to reach the middle of a twenty foot container parked in front of the superstructure. That still means that a plane taking off from just forward of that is going to have to pass under the gantry before going airborne. Cruz says he can do it—says any good small plane pilot could do it—and that, in any case, these planes are really short take off.*

But I'm mighty glad I won't be in any of those planes. And, if they really decide to load out the Pilatuses, taking off a PC-6 through that window is going to be hairy, even if they won't have to land again.

Note to self: Talk Stauer out of trying to launch the PC-6s from the ship; be bad on the paint job.

And speaking of landing, those Hips are best put on

the back deck. And there they're going to be tight as shit. And the Chinese still haven't put in the fuel tanks and pump. Yeah, they're working on it. That, and the check's in the mail and I won't come . . .

Kosciusko became aware of a small presence standing behind him and slightly to his right. He turned and saw the tiny boss of the Chinese crew that was doing the modifications. The Chinese spoke English rather well.

"Yes, Mr. Chin?" Ed asked.

The Chinese sighed. "It used to be Captain Chin, you know, skipper."

Ed gave a small sympathetic nod. He'd had enough of the Chinese's background to have guessed it. That, and that the man had been beached a few years before Ed, himself, had.

Chin looked at the deck and said, "You know, skipper, that you are building this thing into a clandestine assault carrier is so obvious to anyone who really looks that I'm surprised you haven't had us paint "USN" in tiny letters all over the thing."

Ed's eyes flew wide. It *wasn't* obvious. He was sure it wasn't.

Chin smiled and said, "Imagine, Captain Kosciusko, that you are a poor country with a rebellious province on, say, an island far out at sea. Imagine further that the greatest power in the world—a great and *hostile* power— had a fleet sitting between you and said rebellious province. How might you consider getting a military force to that island in a way your great adversary would be unlikely to discern? Might you, say, consider using merchant vessels rigged out to transport troops and aircraft? Might you then, say . . . "

Kosciusko understood then. "That's what you used to do in the Chinese Navy," he said, definitively.

"Yesss, skipper," Chin nodded. "For the last dozen years of my service, anyway. And that is why it is so obvious that you are doing the same . . . except that I doubt you intend to take on Taiwan. Now, Captain Kosciusko, I have seen your plans and if I may offer some useful suggestions?"

"What do you want from it?" Ed asked.

"Not much," Chin replied. "Enough money to get a fishing yawl somewhere else than the PRC, and that you take me and a dozen of my crew with you when you go. Us, and our families. Our families are small, what with the one child policy they used to enforce here."

"I don't know about that," Ed answered.

"The alternative . . ." Chin left the thought hanging.

"Let me contact my principal."

"Tell him my *select* crew is all composed of long service regulars with the Peoples' Liberation Army Navy. We *will* be useful."

"One question, *Mr.* Chin," Ed emphasized the "Mr." to remind the Chinese that a ship could have only one captain. "You're a seaman. Why didn't you just grab a ship with your men and leave?"

"And do what? We had no money to set up again somewhere else. Assuming the PLAN wouldn't have simply sunk us at sea. See . . . I probably know just a little too much to let go."

"Fair enough. Why leave?"

Chin sighed, wearily and hopelessly. "Captain, I am a

communist. Do you know what communism means here now? It means that high party cadres are able to shunt tremendous wealth to their children. It means *nothing* else. And I want out. It will be bad enough living under capitalism, I suppose. But it can't be as bad as living under industrial feudalism pretending it's communism."

Chin's face grew wry. "Why, captain, do you suppose I'm not commanding a ship right now? Because all the commands are going to the children of high party cadres, that's why.

"So, no thanks."

"You realize," Ed said, "that there will probably be no more viscerally anti-communist group under the sun than the one you would be working with."

Chin shrugged. "Are they hypocrites about it, Captain?

The corners of Kosciusko's mouth bent down as he shook his head *no*.

"Then I would relish it."

"I'll ask," Kosciusko agreed.

"I can ask for no more," Chin said. "And, since I can see no reason for your principal not to agree to accept a baker's dozen highly trained and competent seamen, I have the following suggestion: You have us welding in two large areas of "hull reinforcement." It's not necessary. Yes, you need a mess and planning deck. But for passageways and such, there's no reason we can't make a normal configuration of containers and simply cut side passages through them. We can also, if you or your principal will pay for lumber, build stairs and ladders to access a second level of containers. I don't think we'll need three levels."

"You think?"

"Yes, Captain. And while we're on the subject, your storage arrangements are suboptimal. There is no reason to have all the food immediately accessible. We can *dump* containers over the side, if necessary, to get at food needed later. And, on that note, you need to add a magnetic attachment to the crane, a rather powerful one. Fortunately, Hangzhou Permanent Magnet Group, Limited, makes them. I can get you a good deal; I have a cousin—the capitalist bastard—who works for them. Moreover, your medical plan doesn't seem to include a decent way to get the wounded down to the facilities. I suggest moving it . . . "

"To where?" Ed asked.

"Superstructure. We don't have time to put in elevators to bring the wounded down to the lower levels."

Kosciusko nodded. "Let me make a phone call."

Although there were a couple of hundred workers involved in refitting the ship, only thirteen of them were clustered, twelve and Chin, at the base of the superstructure, when Kosciusko emerged from making his call. Of those, he didn't know how many spoke English. *Probably none of them as well as Chin does*, he thought.

"You're in," Ed announced, without fanfare. "But you're in until the operation is past and everyone is dispersed. And you won't know what the operation is until we are well at sea and you've all been strip searched for communication devices."

"Our families?" Chin asked.

"Can your wives cook?"

"We have, among the thirteen of us, eleven wives. Two of them are nurses. One, Mrs. Lin, is a doctor, a surgeon. One is a machinist. Another is an accountant. There is a small engine—" Chin stopped momentarily, struggling for the word—"repairer? No, that's not quite right. Repairman? But she's not a man. Anyway, she fixes little engines. Plus a highly skilled welder." He pointed at one of his sailors. "And Liu here's wife is a superb freight crane operator. *My* wife is a naval intelligence analyst. The remaining two can, I suppose, cook."

"Then they're in, too."

Chin passed the news on to his core crew in about three syllables. They didn't cheer, but did smile.

"Pay?" he asked.

"Three quarters of a million *Yuan*, for the lot of you, not counting whatever you make for this job," Ed replied. "Plus the same when the mission is completed. With that, you should be able to put a down payment on a boat."

"It is most fair, Captain," the Chinese agreed, bowing his head slightly. "And, since you have hired us, I promise that we are your men for the duration. And since we are your men, those cradles you're having us build? Three of those are obviously for landing craft, LCM-6s if I'm not mistaken. They're too narrow to be for LCM-8s. But the fourth and fifth?"

"One is for a patrol boat," Kosciusko said. "The other's for a small submarine. Don't worry about the sub; it comes with its own cradle. We just need something to hold that."

"I thought so about the patrol boat. The submarine was within the realm of the possible. But we have a problem, skipper."

"Which is?"

"We need more exact dimensions for both, patrol

boat and minisub cradle, or we risk damaging their hulls if
. . . when . . . we hit bad seas."

"I don't have them yet."

"Then, Captain, we need a lot more lumber and some
hardware and we need to redesign the cradles to allow us
to tighten them down on the things they're supposed to
hold secure. Also some tires we can chop up."

"You have an idea?"

"As it so happens."

*I don't know, thought Kosciusko, whether I ought to
be insulted this guy knows my job—parts of it, anyway—
better than I do, or pleased that he does.*

"And we need some additional structural steel, I-
beams, Captain," Chin added, "W10x22s. Mmmm . . . say
. . . two hundred and forty meters' worth in twelve meter
long sections."

"What for?" Ed asked.

"Helicopter landing pads off of the main deck. And
you need a lot of paint stored. And sprayers, and . . . "

"How are we going to get you and your people out of
here?" Kosciusko asked. "If your departure would be a
security concern . . . "

"I am the only real problem. Well, myself and my wife,
Kai-ying. Most of my people and their families can be
smuggled aboard. For us, we'll have to meet you somewhere
on the water. I . . . we . . . have a small boat. It wouldn't do
to take us out very far to sea, but it would do to link up with
you somewhere past, say, Lamma Island."

"That should work," Kosciusko agreed. "Assuming, of
course."

"Yes, assuming."

★ CHAPTER FOURTEEN ★

Forbid a man to think for himself or to act
for himself and you may add the joy of piracy and
the zest of smuggling to his life.
—Elbert Hubbard

D-112, Mae Hong Song Province, Thailand

Outside the hut in which the former Special Forces and
Spetznaz men rested, Mike Cruz and Artur Borsakov
supervised as their ground crew repainted the helicopters
from World Food Bank colors to new ones, with the words
"Exploratory Mining and Drilling Support, Inc."

Inside, with the snores of his rescuers droning in his
ears, Victor Inning was mildly insulted. *Not a word, not a
blessed word. Here I am, the most notorious arms dealer
at large in the world and the bloody Burmese never
even announced my escape. Oh, maybe they told their
neighbors, on the sly, but as far as a public announcement
goes, nothing. What's the use of smuggling arms to half the
countries in the world, and every continent, when no one*

159

appreciates you for the master of the trade you are? Why, it's almost enough to make me give up the calling.

He snorted softly. *Nah. This is too much fun. Where I'm going to come up with* everything *on the requisition list, however . . . ?*

Inning stopped scribbling in the note book in front of him and asked Welch, "This patrol boat your people are picking up in Helsinki, how big is it?"

"Good size," Welch replied, "eighty feet and change. Why?"

"Well . . . for reasons best kept to myself, I've got a number of equipment and supply sets stashed in various places. They're generally set up to equip a squad, or a platoon, or a company. One of these, for a small platoon, is near Tallinn, Estonia. So they'd have little trouble picking it up with a big enough boat, sailing from Finland. But."

"But?"

"It's a twenty-four man set. Has everything. Arms— suppressed submachine guns, Kalashnikovs, PKs, Dragunovs, and RPGs, in this case—plus ammunition, night vision—yes, *with* batteries—individual equipment, body armor, uniforms. Even combat rations, though they may not be to taste."

Konstantin made a ugly face, which earned him a dirty look from Inning. "Well, Jesus, Victor," the major said, "the meat in the things is fifty percent fat. Okay to make a soup with, maybe, but straight out of the can it's vile," he further explained to Terry. "I'd *strongly* recommend that your people stock up on canned or smoked meat, cheese, and fish in Finland."

"What's so bad about it?" Welch asked.

"Ever have a dog?" Konstantin answered. "Well . . . think of what you fed your dog."

Other than the dirty look, Victor ignored him. "Plus one 60mm mortar and eighty rounds, mixed, HE, HC, and illuminating. Also one 30mm automatic grenade launcher. One heavy machine gun. There's a demolition kit, plus another two hundred kilograms of SEMTEX. It even has scuba—actually rebreathers—since it's near the sea, and two rubber boats, big enough to carry a dozen men each, with small engines. But if I crack it, it's gone to me. It either all goes or none of it does. You people will have to buy the whole set *and* guarantee to move it all out."

"Wherever did you get 60mm mortars?" Welch asked. "The Soviets never made them."

"Portugal via Mozambique," Victor said, further explaining, "They're short range commando types. Eight hundred meters range, max."

"Cost?" Terry asked. "For the set, I mean."

Victor seemed to consider that for a while, possibly subtracting from his initial asking price the value of one rescue from a Burmese hell hole. "One hundred and eighty thousand USD. Trust me; it's a bargain."

"Where do you hide something like that?" Welch asked.

"Baltiyski. The locals call it Paldiski. Or did you mean specifically? That you won't know until the money transfers."

"Don't be silly, Victor," Konstantin said. "They're not going to stiff you over such a measly sum when they need you to get them ever so much more."

Inning considered that. With a shrug, he answered,

"On the grounds of the Orthodox Church. I have the priest on retainer. And, believe me, he needs the money."

"I'm not familiar with the place," Welch said.

Konstantin spoke up. His voice seemed mildly tinged with embarrassment. "It was a Soviet naval base for training nuclear submarine crews. Had its own reactors—two of them—and a mock up of a submarine. Those, and the usual crappy socialist living arrangements. Estonians weren't, for the most part, allowed in. Barbed wire, guard towers. Now that the navy's gone, it's practically a ghost town, some Estonians and a few thousand Russians abandoned by the motherland."

"Sounds lovely."

"Anyway," Victor interjected, "do you want the package, the whole package, or not?"

Welch nodded. He had authority from Stauer to commit a lot more funds than *that*. "How do our people get the goods? Just pull into port, knock on the priest's door, and say, 'Hi, we're from Victor and we want all the weapons you've been hiding?'"

Inning smiled at the sarcasm. "It's a little more complex. There's a code phrase. Once your people give it to the priest, he'll turn over the stuff readily enough. And I can download a map to the church for you to forward."

Welch put a palm across his mouth and drummed his fingers against his left cheek. "All right," he agreed. "The price seems reasonable, even if we don't need all of the equipment. I'll have my boss make the transfer—you *do* have an account you want the money sent to, yes?—later today.

"Now what about the other materiel?"

"All the small arms and smaller items I have or can get. But for the armored cars I'm going to have to go to South Africa. And Israel."

"South Africa I can see," Welch said. "I've been told they had a huge stockpile of the things. But why Israel?"

Inning cocked his head to one side. "There's a company in Tel Aviv that more or less specializes in rebuilding armored cars, especially Panhard AMLs and the South African version, the Eland."

"I don't think we have the time to move the things to Israel, get them built, then move them to Brazil, in time to train crews."

"Good point," Inning agreed. "Israel first then. We'll steal them and then fix them in South Africa before sending them on to Brazil. Or maybe even fix them up at sea on the way."

Victor closed his eyes for a moment, in deep concentration. When he opened them he wrote a series of words, in English, on a piece of paper. He then drew a simplistic map below the word. "This is your code phrase, and how to find the church. I suggest your people go in during the daytime. Night would be more suspicious in a place like that than day. They can move the cache at night. I will notify the priest."

"What if your cache doesn't have what the team needs?" Welch asked.

"Then I can't help you in time," Victor answered. "What's there is what's available within a reasonable time. Still, I think your people will be pleasantly surprised."

At that Konstantin snorted. "Oh, I *imagine*. Except for the food, of course. Once they sniff that swill they'll wonder why we didn't get rid of the reds long before we did."

Which earned him another dirty look from Victor.

D-111, Paldiski, Estonia

It had been about a four hour trip, Helsinki to Paldiski. And that was without really straining the engines for more than was required to test them and the hull. Even at that, the time zone change made it only a three hour time difference.

Biggus Dickus Thornton was singing something about a "three hour tour" as he twisted the patrol boat's tail hard aport to ease it into the completely unguarded small harbor west of the town. They'd considered naming the boat after President Kennedy, what with PT-109 and all, but since that one sank, it was perhaps a bad omen. Calling it the *Mary Jo Kopeckne* had similar issues. But since one person, and a close relative of President Kennedy, to boot, had proven well nigh unsinkable, in any sense, the PT boat now bore upon its stern the name, *The Drunken Bastard*, or *Bastard* for short.

High gray cliffs arose on the right, towering over questionable docks with a few fishermen seated on them. Biggus Dickus cut power and eased in to the docks. One of his team members, a short, dark sort named Michael Antoniewicz, nicknamed by his team mates "Eeyore" because he could carry a house on his back and would sink into the earth before bending under the strain, leapt across the water, rope in hand, to tie the boat off.

There was a gray haired, heavily bearded, cassocked priest there waiting at the dock, as well. The priest walked over and said something in Russian to Antoniewicz. The sailor just shrugged. Despite the Eastern European name, he had not a word of Russian or any other Slavic language.

Pointing at Biggus, Eeyore said, in English, "See him. He has what you need."

The priest held up thumb and forefinger a couple of millimeters apart and said, "I spik leetle Englizh." Then he shrugged, himself, and went to stand by the boat from which Biggus jumped with the grace of a much younger man.

"Father Pavel?" Biggus asked.

The priest nodded as if solemnity was in his very nature.

"Victor sends, 'Saturn-Concert-Bagration.'"

The priest nodded again and said, "You come." He then turned and began to lead the group up the crumbling stairs that led up the cliffs and toward the town.

"Simmons, guard the boat," Biggus ordered the biggest and meanest looking of his crew, barring only himself.

"With *what*?"

"With your dick. And, while we're gone, get us an update on the position and schedule of the *George Galloway*."

At Pakri street the group turned away from the sea. Off in the distance was a white-painted stone church tower. "Lut'eran," Father Pavel said, pointing. Biggus' eyes glanced left and right continuously, not searching for threats, but in wonder at the nearly complete ruin of a naval town. There were apartment buildings, crumbling, not just empty of people but empty of wooden doors and glass windows as well. On the plus side, off to the east, there were at least eight power-generating windmills in sight.

"My name is Ozymandias," the chief whispered, despite the windmills. A few modern artifacts couldn't overcome the wreck of the city. Biggus' eyes glanced at a hand painted sign, in both Cyrillic and Latin letters. "Welcome to Hell," said the bottom half of the sign, in English. "I believe it," Biggus agreed. Below that, someone had added "Gays." Thornton couldn't imagine, *Why the hell should they be worrying about gays, given everything else?*

"You know, Chief," Antoniewicz said, "it's odd. I haven't seen a cop yet."

"What's to steal?" Biggus answered, reasonably.

"My truck if not keep gun," Father Pavel answered.

The stash turned out to be hidden under the crumbling concrete of a ruined building next to Saint George's Orthodox Church. The church itself was one of the very few buildings they'd seen since arrival that was not a complete and utter wreck. The Lutheran church was another. Biggus commented on that to Father Pavel.

"Victor generous," the priest answered. "Finns . . . Swedes more generous to own peeples." He pointed with a finger at a particular section of concrete chunks and said, "You move this. Bring out material. I get truck."

"You heard the man, boys," Biggus said.

Eeyore looked down at the mass. "How the fuck do we move all this shit?"

"The usual way, Michael," the chief answered. "One piece at a time."

By nightfall, the team of former SEALs was standing in a concrete lined excavation that led into the basement of the collapsed building near the church. A large and solid looking metal door barred the way in. Pavel produced a key for the massive lock on the door and opened it. Inside was a single metal shipping container. The priest also had a key for the lock on that.

When the double corrugated doors were opened, Antoniewicz was the first to speak. "Holy shit!" he said.

"I not know vhat inside," Father Pavel said. "Not *vant* know, eit'er. I go. You load truck. I drive to boat once you load. T'en you unload, t'en you go."

The chief answered, "Thanks, Father." Then, turning to Antoniewicz, he said, "Eeyore, you keep inventory. And the rest of us, let's get to work."

D-110, Paldiski, Estonia

The sun was just illuminating the sea to the north and west. The boat was still in the shadows, though distancing itself from the cliffs.

"I still can't believe this shit," Eeyore said, over the *thrum* of the engines. "How the fuck did he *know* exactly what we'd need?"

"He didn't," Biggus said. "There's all kinds of shit we

don't need. And if you think I'm going to trust my life to ex-Soviet scuba gear, you're insane. Your life, maybe. Mine? Never.

"No," the chief continued, "Victor didn't know. He just put in everything that might be useful to a naval op, that he could get and stuff into a twenty foot container. Still, we have what we need. Set course for Londonderry. Three quarters speed."

★CHAPTER FIFTEEN★

"A brave heart and a courteous tongue," said he.
"They shall carry thee far through the jungle, manling."
—Kipling, *The Jungle Book*

D-110, Assembly Area Alpha—Base Camp, Amazonia, Brazil

Monkeys? Check; they could be heard in the distance. Rotting vegetation? Check; it assailed the nostrils. Flowing water? Check; moving in a fine horizontal fashion. Mosquitoes?

"Son of a bitch!" exclaimed Stauer as he slapped one of the little demons into the netherworld, the blood from the bug spurting over Stauer's neck and the collar of the expeditionary dress he, like the rest of the thirty odd men in the party, shared.

"Fortunately, we've all had our shots," said the expedition's doctor, Scott Joseph, a recruit who had taken a long overdue sabbatical in order to go on the operation. The doctor looked for all the world like a cross between Egon, of the Ghostbusters movie, and Noah Levinstein, from American Pie. "That said, there's no shot for malaria. I trust I don't have to explain to anyone that mild diarrhea from the anti-malarial pills is infinitely to be preferred over the twitching awfuls. For that matter, a good portion of the malaria risk down here is Falciparum, which is pretty damned deadly."

"We know," said Stauer. He turned to look over his shoulders. "Sergeant Major Joshua?"

"Sir!"

"This—assuming you don't disagree—is home."

The tall, Virgin Islands black looked around at the jungle floor. The best that could be said of it was that it was high enough not to flood, flat enough for tents, and covered enough by forest growth not to be visible from the air or space without using technical means. He sneered but indicated no more than a general disapproval thereby. "It will do, sir."

Stauer nodded. Between two people who had worked as long together, and knew each other as well, as had he and the sergeant major, a nod was all that was necessary. *Set up the camp,* primus pilus, *as think you best.*

The sergeant major turned on his heels and began taking long strides in the direction of the leased landing craft that had brought the party, along with minimum mission essential equipment, up from Manaus. Stauer smiled with anticipation of the immediate sense of order and discipline that was about to be inflicted on the score or so of troops waiting at the river's edge.

"You sure about the Malarone, Doc?" Stauer asked. Malarone was a multi-drug particularly useful against Falciparum.

Joseph shrugged one shoulder. "Best we can do. Now if you could have found someplace more than nine hundred meters above sea level…"

"Nobody's mapped this area since the 17th century," Stauer said. "We may find such a height, still close enough to the river, in which case we move camp. Remember, though, that with our limited surface transport and needing most of that for construction, 'close enough to the river' is, in fact, pretty damned close. Doubt we'll find anything."

"Fair enough. In the interim, I'll be spraying everything with Malathion."

"Why did you opt for that, rather than good old DDT?" Stauer asked.

Joseph gave off a small snort and began rubbing his hands together. "Brazil has the misfortune to be almost First World. They're just wealthy enough, and just well organized enough, to have almost eradicated malaria. Unfortunately, they weren't quite wealthy enough, or quite well organized enough, to *quite* eradicate it. The local mosquitoes now have a considerable degree of DDT resistance. Besides, the Malathion is almost as good, and almost as cheap. Some would say better and cheaper."

The doctor looked puzzled for a moment. "Say," he asked, "do you think I should go and make sure they set up the camp for proper field hygiene?"

Stauer laughed. "Scott, let me tell you something about the sergeant major. It is mere surmise on my part, to be sure, but I am pretty certain that a hundred generations ago one of Joshua's ancestors wandered in from the desert, after trekking up the Nile, and enlisted in the first Roman legionary recruiting office he came to, rising thereafter quickly to the highest offices to which such a man might aspire. I am also certain, and no one can prove me different, that the knowledge gained by that ancestor was passed down genetically. There is *nothing* you, or I, or anyone, can tell the sergeant major about setting up a camp that he wasn't born knowing."

Joseph rolled his eyes at that.

"Don't believe me, eh?" Stauer raised his voice, "Sergeant Major, how long to dig a six foot deep, twelve foot wide ditch around the camp, and use the spoil to build a wall, after cutting enough timber to palisade that wall?"

The answer came back in about half a second. "To excavate thirty-two hundred cubic meters of dirt and build a wall with the spoil would take, if we had the entire complement here, by shovel, approximately a day and a half, sir. Another day for the logs, though that would delay the engineers building the strip. Do you want a *fossa* and *agger*, sir? I wouldn't recommend it; breed lots of bugs, it would, sir."

"Negative, Sergeant Major. Just curious. By the way, how many shitters and pissers do we need?"

"Thirty-four shitters, sir, twenty-one pissers, assuming the naval contingent never billets here and the air contingent only does so intermittently. Those can be dug out in rather less time and are easier to control for bugs."

"Ahem," Stauer said to the doctor.

"Well, if he's so smart and capable, why wasn't he an officer?" Joseph asked.

Stauer shook his head. "Lots of bright people don't

want to be officers. And of those that are, some are simply happier, for purely emotional and instinctive reasons, at lower levels. Let me give you an example: Reilly."

Joseph had only met the current adjutant and—so Stauer had finally determined—future mech force commander, a couple of days prior. "What about him?"

"He is, without doubt, one of the smartest men I ever met. He is tactically and operationally deft . . . no, deft isn't a strong enough term. He's fucking *great*. He trains troops better than anyone I've ever met, too. Any kind of troops, combat, combat support, or REMF. He *should* have been a four star. You know why he isn't? He doesn't know. At least, I don't think he does."

Joseph shook his head *no*.

"Because emotionally he is only really happy commanding a company, a group that is small enough for everyone to know everyone. He can deal with a battalion, well enough, but he's not really as happy there. See, he needs the fight, close up and personal. Without those things—"

Stauer was interrupted by a German accent, speaking breathlessly. That was the voice of Matthias Nagy, the leader of what would become the engineer section. Nagy was a half Hungarian, half German investment banker with a background in the German Army's Airborne Engineers. He'd been quite happy as a soldier but hadn't liked the direction his army had taken following the fall of Communism. When given a chance to be a real soldier again, he'd taken four months built up leave and jumped on it. His English was approximately as good as his German, with hardly even a noticeable accent.

Sweat poured off Nagy, as if he'd been running through the jungle searching for the area to put in the landing strip, and then run back again to report that he had. Stauer had no doubt he'd done precisely that. Nagy had been one of Reilly's acquisitions and came very highly recommended.

"I found a spot where I can put in a small airstrip, boss," Nagy said. "It will take maybe twelve days, including putting in the PSP. That assumes, of course, that my baby dozer, my grader, and my mini-excavator don't break and that everyone will collaborate in putting in the PSP . . . doctors included."

"Will they? Break, I mean?"

Off in the distance could be heard Joshua's for the nonce harsh voice, shouting, "No, you stupid bastards! The tent pins go straight in, not at an angle away from the tent. Yes, I *know* it's counter-intuitive, but otherwise, when the canvas gets wet and shrinks, the leverage pulls the pins too much, loosens 'em, and causes the tent to collapse. Jesus, do I have to teach you people *everything*?"

Nagy shook his squarish head. "Good man, your sergeant major," he said. "Anyway, sir, the excavator's a brand new Volvo, and the dozer is a brand new John Deere, and the grader's by Caterpillar. Doubt if I could break them if I tried."

"How are you getting them off the boat?" Stauer asked. "The bank's pretty steep and just dirt."

Nagy looked only mildly concerned. "We're going to cut some trees and lay the logs down. Then I'll land the John Deere and use it to get the Volvo ashore, and the two of them to get the Caterpillar out. I've got the cables. Later we'll be building a dock and off-loading ramp."

"And how big does the strip have to be?"

"Cruz said that given the heat and high water vapor content in the air," Nagy said, "I'd better cut out a strip of twenty-four meters by about five hundred. A bit under eleven thousand pieces of PSP, three hundred tons and change. Course, I think he's being overly cautious. The planes are coming in laden, true, but they'll be leaving empty except for crew and fuel. Personally, I think we could get by with a field a half as long and two thirds as wide. Then again, the trees *could* pose a problem with a field that short."

"And how many rubber and other trees are you going to kill to do that?"

"Few hundred, no more," Nagy answered, with an indifferent shrug. Combat engineers *loved* knocking down trees. It was almost as much fun as dropping buildings and bridges. "Well, a few hundred for the field itself. More for some of the other things. And to disguise the shape of the strip."

"All right, then," Stauer agreed, satisfied. "Gordo Gordon has about two weeks to assemble what we need and begin flying it in here."

D-110, Meridien Pegasus Hotel, Georgetown, Guyana

They didn't call Harry Gordon "Gordo" just because it was the first five letters of his last name. In fact, he was fat. He'd always been fat and always had to struggle in the

Army to keep within the strictures of Army Regulation 600-9. This was a shame, everyone agreed, since Gordo was one of the two or three finest logistic minds around. Then again, what could be expected of a regulation dedicated to the elevation of form over substance?

Still, he *was* fat and, as such, had a relatively high body mass to radiating surface. The short version of that was:

"God *damn*, this place is fucking hot! Reilly should be down here; he likes this kind of heat."

"He's got his job up there, boss," answered Gordo's assistant, retired Master Sergeant Warren. "We've got ours down here. And it isn't"—Warren cast his dark eyes around meaningfully at the hotel, the Meridien Pegasus, with its view over the town and the Demerara River—"it isn't as if this is exactly hardship duty."

As if to punctuate the point, a very womanly form in hotel livery swayed up, bearing a tray of drinks. Two of these she set on the table between Warren and Gordo.

Black women weren't usually to Gordo's taste. This one, however, looked to be a mix of black, East Indian, local Indian, and white, and she was to anyone's taste.

"Forget it, boss," Warren said. "Tonight, she's going out with me."

"No problem," Gordo answered. "The first of the Pilatus PC-6s is due in this evening and I want to meet the flight crew at the airport when they arrive. And speaking of arrival—"

"Four hundred and ninety sets, body armor, various sizes, due in, in four days," Warren answered. "And you have no idea what a bitch it was to track that number down from enough different suppliers to not be noticeable and have it sent to Reilly in San Antonio. Twenty-one hundred sets, battle dress, old style, three color desert, due in, in six days. I lucked out with that one, and found a lot of them through DRMO"—Defense Re-utilization and Marketing Office—"at Fort Stewart. Just, and I mean *just*, beat Third Special Forces Group to them. Hats, too. LCE"—Load Carrying Equipment—"I ordered from Israel; that's coming in by air in a week. Reilly's been budgeted fifty thousand bucks for boots for the boys as they show up. Belts, underwear and socks; they're on their own. I did order a couple of rolls of webbing and some generic buckles in case we have to make belts for anyone. The advance party's got enough food for three weeks and their field water purification equipment will do until we can send them the Zenon Mini-ROWPU"—Reverse Osmosis Water Purification Unit—"and, before you ask, that's coming in by air, too, scheduled for ten days from now, with the last of the PC-6s."

Gordo sighed with contentment. Good supply sergeants were such a sheer treasure. "Sergeant Warren, I wish you all the luck in the world with the girl this evening."

"The real bitch is going to be getting enough of the armored cars up the river for the boys to train with," Warren said.

"Not a problem, actually," Gordo said. "The basic chassis will come in kinda openly, minus turrets or arms, as 'all terrain exploration support vehicles.' The turrets we'll fly in.."

"They'll fit a Pilatus Porter?"

Gordo howled with laughter on that one. When he'd recovered sufficiently, he said, "Sure, with both doors open and the main gun sticking out the floor hatch and tied to the fuselage. Nah. No way. But the local 'air force' operates five light cargo aircraft, Short Skyvans. I'm taking the senior pilot of that crew out for drinks and a girl this evening. I imagine he can be bribed to make a couple of extraneous training flights. Of course, that presupposes Victor can come up with enough of the armored cars."

D-109, Menachem Begin Road, Tel Aviv, Israel

Traffic passing down the centrally located major thoroughfare made it all but impossible for anyone not seated at the same table to hear what the Israeli had to say to the Russian. The table was flush against the railing around the outdoor café portion of the establishment.

"You need *what*?" asked the Israeli who went by the name of Dov. Both the men spoke Russian, though both also shared English. While Dov looked essentially western in feature and dress, Victor was done up like a Hassid, curls and all.

"Nine Panhard AML-90s, or the Eland clone," Victor answered, "best possible upgrades. Plus three AML-60s and twenty-four M-3 armored personnel carriers. Of those, I need one in three available for movement by sea *soonest*. And of the M-3s, I need —"

Dov held up one hand. "Stop right there, Victor. The current government is actually trying to stay within the law for arms sales. Knowing you, and I do, there is not the slightest chance you are within *anybody's* law. Moreover, M-3s just aren't possible. We have none in stock that aren't already committed."

"They've never been that common, I suppose," Victor said. "Not like the 90 and 60 versions."

"No, they haven't," Dov said. "But for that matter, it would be perfectly possible to take a 60 or 90 version and remove the main turret. That would leave enough space inside for maybe five or six infantrymen, plus a two man crew. Extending them is also possible, but harder."

"Maybe," Victor said, while wondering, *Will my rescuers be willing to go with those instead of the real thing? They just haven't told me enough.*

"Never mind, in any case, Victor. I can't sell you any. No, not even for a really *big* bribe."

"That's okay," Inning said, his head nodding which made his fake curls swish back and forth. He found that extremely annoying. "I predicted this. I don't want you to *sell* me any. I want you to rebuild the ones I need from some I will get. And I need them rebuilt overseas or aboard a ship. Maybe both. Now does your government have a really big problem with that? You don't need a legitimate end user certificate for mere services rendered and some dual use parts provided, or if you do, you can fudge it. You don't need an end user certificate for giving me the name of the contact there that, I have no doubt, provides you with derelicts in remarkably good shape to rebuild. Because we both know South Africa doesn't use a lot of anti-armor ammunition to train with."

Dov chewed at the inside of his cheek for a while, his head occasionally rocking from side to side. "End user certificate? Mmm…maybe not. Done at sea, you say? Or right in South Africa? Or both. And just how big a bribe are you offering? And how much for the name of my contact?"

"That's all negotiable," Victor said. "It will be large enough. Now tell me what is possible in upgrades."

Dov shrugged. "It's a pretty extensive rebuild: New steering—hydraulic, new disc brake system for all four wheels, new diesel engine—a Toyota, and new wiring. We can put in air conditioning . . . day-night fire control . . . laser range finder . . . armor upgrade for standoff protection from HEAT warheads. Non-explosive reactive is also possible. There's also an option to upgrade the gun to the new high velocity 60mm, basically the same thing we did for the Chilean Shermans. Nice gun, by the way, but we have to modify the turret *hugely*."

A slender, delicate hand with painted but chipped nails grasped one of the unoccupied chairs and pulled it from the table. Into the chair sat an extraordinarily attractive, slender, wave-haired and olive-skinned woman. She was dressed in mechanic's coveralls that completely succeeded in failing to hide her figure.

"Hello, Lana," Dov said, with a frown. "Victor, let me introduce . . ." Dove stopped speaking for a moment when he realized Victor was simply paying him no mind at all.

"They say of many women," Victor said, as if from very far away, "that her hair 'cascades.' I think you are the first one I have ever seen of which the compliment is true. I—"

Victor stopped speaking when he realized than a group of Hassidim had begun to pass, except for one of them who was standing by the railing looking directly at him and chiding him with a waving finger. Victor hunched his head down as if in shame until the finger stopped wagging and the genuine Hassid had walked on with his group.

"Forget it, Victor," Dov advised. "Lana's a dyke."

"Not at all," the woman said, adding, matter of factly, "Tried it; didn't much like it. I've just met very few men I thought worth the trouble and Dov here is bitter that he wasn't one of them. Lana Mendes," she announced, offering her hand.

"You're very beautiful, Lana Mendes," Victor said.

"Don't tell her that," Dov advised. "Tell her she's a great armored vehicle optics mechanic. Tell her she's a first class tank gunner. Tell her she's a fine officer. But never, never, never tell Ms. Mendes she's beautiful."

Lana sighed with exasperation. "As a matter of fact, I used to teach tank gunnery, and now I work as an optics mechanic. And I am a first class reserve officer. But try and prove that in a place like this." She looked around in such a way as to indicate the entire country, not just the local environment. "Dov's right, by the way, you should take the upgrade to 60mm high velocity."

"I don't know about the gun," Victor replied. "I just don't have the authority. I'll check, though. And everything else sounds about right. Now, how mobile and accommodating can you be?"

"We can work *anywhere*," Dov said.

★ CHAPTER SIXTEEN ★

Certainly there is no hunting like the hunting
of man and those who have hunted armed men long
enough and liked it, never really care
for anything else thereafter.
—Ernest Hemingway, *On the Blue Water*

D-108, Londonderry Port, UK

It was already dark when the boat finally entered Lough
Foyle, in the only place where the South, the Republic of
Ireland, was north, and the north, the Six Counties, was
south.

Biggus Dickus appreciated the darkness. *It's just as
well*, he thought. *Even a disarmed and civilian painted
ELCO eighty-one foot patrol torpedo boat is inherently
suspicious. If it hadn't been so fast and so cheap, I'd
probably have turned it down.*

"Biggus Dickus" had booked a berth for the *Bastard*
at one of the marinas dotting the sides of Lough Foyle.

This did not prevent the boat from taking a slow spin around the Lough, through darkened gray-brown waters that were almost without any natural waves.

"There she is," said Eeyore, pointing leftward with his chin. Eeyore laughed softly.

"I see her," agreed Biggus, standing at the wheel of the boat. "And what's so funny?"

"I looked it up. George Galloway is a Brit politician. He's probably an atheist, himself, but he latched onto the Islamics there to launch and support his political career. He even married one of them, a really hot Palestinian girl, though I think she divorced him. He is, in any case, a defensive mouthpiece for Islamic terrorism and an offensive, in both senses, speaker for the gradual subordination of Great Britain to Islam. No wonder they named a boat after him. And naming a boat after him suggests very strongly that that is no innocent ship."

"I always presumed *that*," Biggus said. "Simmons?"

"Here, Chief," answered the former boatswain standing by what once would have been a mount for a .50 caliber machine gun . . . and would soon be again.

"When we berth, you and Morales go ashore. Get a rental and scout out that ship."

"Wilco, Chief."

"And remember to drive on the wrong side of the road."

"Forty-one . . . forty-two . . . forty-three . . . forty-four," Simmons counted aloud as the last group boarded the *Galloway*. "Your count agree with that, Morales?"

The Puerto Rican former SEAL nodded, then added,

"There's no way that ship needs a crew that size. That's twice as many as they need, maybe more."

"Which smells like trouble even if they're perfectly innocent," Simmons agreed. "But where else have you seen young men who looked just like that lot?"

Morales laughed. "Well, besides Afghanistan, Iraq, Somalia, Sudan . . ."

"Exactly. Those aren't sailors and they aren't mostly illegal immigrants. Those are fighters. We need to bring this back to the chief. But first some measurements. I make it as twelve feet from waterline to top of the hull near the bow."

"A little less," Morales corrected. "No more than ten and a half."

"Nah; it's twelve. Look at the containers. In any case, we can two-man-lift a boarder over it. She carries, max, seven hundred TEU."

"Agreed."

Simmons did some mental gymnastics. "I make her as roughly four hundred feet in length and maybe sixty-five in beam."

"About right," Morales said. "She's Antigua registered. Any issues with that?"

Simmons shrugged. "None I can think of. Maybe Oprah Winfrey or Eric Clapton would object to our taking it. But fuck them."

"Not Oprah," Morales said. "I think she's supposed to become Secretary of Cloying Sweetness under the current administration."

"Sweet," said Biggus, though his tone of voice didn't

suggest he found anything too sweet in the news. "I'd thought to get two of us aboard, then wait for the *Galloway* to get out into the sea lanes. Those two could have taken the radio room and bridge, then the rest of us would have intercepted and boarded. With forty-four men aboard, half of them with no likely jobs, the odds of even one man being found are just too good."

"Simple boarding and seizure at sea, then, Chief?" asked Simmons. He looked around the inside of the *Bastard* at the mounds of carefully netted and tied down gear provided by the shipping container in Paldiski. "It isn't like we lack for materiel." Simmons held up a radio-controlled detonator, by way of illustration.

Thornton shook his head. "I don't know there'll be anything simple about it. And it'll be tough to do without them getting the word out. Though you're right about the materiel."

"They'll be leaving soon, Chief," Simmons said. "Otherwise they wouldn't have brought the extra people aboard yet."

"I still don't think we can hide two men aboard with all those extra fuckers roaming the ship out of boredom."

"If not two, Chief, how about one?" suggested Antoniewicz. "I'm a little dude; I can find a place to hide if you can get me aboard."

Biggus shook his head doubtfully. "Bad form to send a lone man off," he said.

Eeyore stood to his full five feet, four inches, held his arms out invitingly, and answered, "Hell, Chief, I'm not even a full lone man. So if we can't send two, let's send three quarters or a half. Bound to confuse 'em."

★ ★ ★

The Russian rubber boat made not a sound as its electric motor forced it through the watery gloom. It passed by *Galloway*'s stern, then drove in under the pier. Once under cover, it weaved between the wooden pilings to the bow. There, it passed under the steel wedge and came around the bow to its port side. The boat came to a stop as it bumped up, still soundless, against the hull. The man at the tiller, Bland, dialed down the power to just enough to keep the rubber tight against the target.

Forward in the rubber boat, Simmons was at the bow, followed by Morales, followed by Antoniewicz. All four men in the boat wore Russian night vision goggles strapped to their heads. These were not the best, perhaps, but they were good enough for this. Without a word all three forward stood low and shuffled to the rubber boat's rounded bow. Antoniewicz leaned forward and put both gloved palms against the hull. Simmons and Morales locked arms and bent low to allow the boarder to get one foot up. They then stood, rocking the rubber boat and almost causing Antoniewicz to lose his balance. He pin-wheeled his arms a bit, moving his center of mass forward to balance again against the hull.

Eeyore felt his heart beating fast and hard as his balaclava covered head peeped over the side of the ship. There was a container marked "Cosco" just in front of him. He could see the letters clearly enough even in the grainy image of his NVGs.

He felt Morales' hand shift to take a position under his right foot. Simmons did so a moment later with the left. Eeyore's upward motion continued until he was nearly waist high to the top of the hull. His hands, gripping that top, moved downward relative to his torso. A push, the swing of a leg, and the boarder was over the top and easing his feet down to the deck below. It was a tight fit between hull and containers. He waited a moment, listening, then leaned over the side to haul up some ordnance the other two passed to him.

And now to find a place to hide and then scout a bit.

He took from his shoulder holster a Makarov pistol, test and familiarization fired on the voyage from Estonia to Northern Ireland. This pistol had some odd features. It had, for example, an infrared laser aiming device, invisible to the naked eye but quite visible to the Russian-issue NVGs. For another thing, there was a shroud around the barrel. Biggus had said the barrel was drilled to allow gas to escape into the shroud, thus lowering a standard bullet's velocity to something less than the speed of sound. From under his right armpit Antoniewicz removed a cylindrical object, the suppresser, and screwed it to the front of the Makarov. The thing would be silent now, except for the working of the slide. And that, over normal ship and port noise, was nothing.

That was one weapon. Across his back Eeyore had strapped another Russian arm, a Kiparis submachine gun. It, too, was silenced and used the same ammunition as the pistol. Thoughtfully, Victor's cache had provided frangible ammunition for both. Less thoughtfully, while the pistol would be very quiet, due to the reduction in velocity below the speed of sound, rounds fired from the submachine gun would be supersonic, consequently rather noisy.

In addition, by his right side was strapped Eeyore's

own handmade knife. Lastly, in various pouches and pockets, the former SEAL carried eight RGO defensive grenades, a radio transmitter and beacon, extra batteries, a piece of thin wire with wooden handles on each end, sundry odds and ends (a small drill and a fiberscope, a fiber optic camera, for example), a couple of pounds of smoked meat and some cans with Cyrillic writing and pictures that suggested *food*.

The boarder looked left. *Nothing*. Then, pistol and eyes reoriented to the right, he sidled along between containers and hull about a dozen feet. There he came to a space between shipping containers of about two and a half feet, or perhaps a bit less. There he doffed his combat harness, submachine gun, and most of the ancillary gear. He kept his pistol as he kept the NVGs.

Just aft of the bow, the container configuration changed, with the outside edges of the above-hull exterior containers resting on double steel pylons, red with rust. It was that kind of a ship. This also left a more or less covered passageway that shielded Antoniewicz from observation from the windowed bridge that spanned the full beam of the ship.

Getting to the stern—really to the superstructure— was tricky. There almost was no telling when someone might round a corner. Antoniewicz solved the problem by ducking in between a row of containers and listening to be certain there were no footsteps or talking. Then he'd come out again, pad quickly to the next row, duck in, and listen some more. Five times he did this before reaching the penultimate gap. At that point there was only one row of containers between himself and the superstructure.

There he waited for perhaps half an hour, accustoming himself to every normal sound the ship might make in this area. Thus, when he heard an other than normal sound, two men, chatting in what sounded like Arabic, their feet ringing on the steel deck, Antoniewicz's heart again began beating fast. He made himself as small as possible in the space, his hand automatically tightening around the pistol. Through his NVGs he caught a brief glimpse of the men as they walked past. They were holding hands. Their other hands were empty.

Doesn't necessarily mean anything, thought the former SEAL. *Not if they're Arabs. Not like it would back in the states.*

Still, I am *stuck here until they go back inside.*

It seemed like hours to Eeyore, waiting in the cramped little space, before the two men walked back to the superstructure. When they did, it was on the other side of the ship. It was only slightly later that the deck was flooded with men, casting off and reeling in lines. Shortly thereafter the engines *thrummed* to life and the ship began moving away from the pier.

The deck stayed pretty active for some time thereafter. Gradually though, as the banks of the lough disappeared and the *Galloway* turned west, the sailors went back to their business. Only then could Antoniewicz come out from his hide and go searching for a place to spend the night and for any signs of Adam. In the latter, he was to be completely disappointed.

The little Russian drill was nearly silent. It went through the thin wall of the first container Antoniewicz elected to try in moments. Through the hole, the former SEAL slid the fiber section of the fiberscope along with another small fiber to provide a minimal light.

The scope had a lot of built in distortion, but not so much that Antoniewicz couldn't see the contents of the shipping container. *Perfect. Boxes.* With his knife he snapped off the inspection seal, opened the container, and removed the first box. This was, like the others, a mid-sized television. He carried the TV to the edge of the bow and dumped it. He watched the progress of the box as the ship moved onward and before it sank, judging, *Eighteen knots. The bitch is faster than we thought.*

He then went back and did the same with another. A third, fourth, and fifth went the same way. The TV sets were heavy. On the other hand, while Eeyore was small; he was not weak.

Crawling into the space thus vacated, Antoniewicz pulled all his gear in behind him and then closed the container's doors. He rearranged the boxes so that, even should someone open the container, they would be presented with a solid set of TV boxes, three by four, while creating for himself a small cubby further into the container.

Then, with the drill, the SEAL made a dozen small air holes on top, plus three or four high along each side.

If it gets too stuffy, I'll make more.

With that, he checked his watch. Running a small wire antenna out of one of the air holes, he sent to the *Bastard,* "I'm aboard and safely hidden. I looked for some sign of the kid, but there's nothing, not a hint. And, you know, a prison has routines. There aren't any here, that I could see. FYI, ship's speed is about eighteen knots. See you at sea." He then drank some water from one of his canteens, wolfed down a bit of smoked meat—*not bad, considering it's not really a Russian specialty*—and went to sleep, one hand wrapped around the silenced Makarov . . .

D-107, MV *George Galloway*

. . . and awakened to the sound of massed firing—full automatic, too—coming from somewhere sternward of his little hide. The sound was muffled by metal walls and cardboard boxes, but was distinct for all that.

"What the fuck!" Antoniewicz exclaimed as he sat bolt upright. His head was saved from a painful impact only by the fact he was so short. "Did the attack start and I slept through it?"

Almost he exited the container to join in. He was fumbling with the inside handle when the firing ceased. He heard something shouted out in Arabic and the firing began again.

They're familiarizing on their weapons . . . or keeping in practice . . . or test firing, he thought. This pretty much ends the possibility that they are comparatively innocent illegal immigrants.

★ CHAPTER SEVENTEEN ★

> If you wrote a novel in South Africa
> which didn't concern the central issues,
> it wouldn't be worth publishing.
> —Alan Paton

D-107, near Tempe Base, Bloemfontein, South Africa

"Tell Dov we've got no M3s for you," the Boer warrant officer, Dani Viljoen, said. The Boer was a large man, broad shouldered, and just beginning to go gray around the temples. Beside him sat a black of the same rank, and similar build, albeit somewhat taller. "Oh, sure, there's one on display down the road but that was just a prototype. And since it's on display we can't steal it without undue notice, and since it's just the one it wouldn't do you much good anyway. And since the thing hasn't run in maybe twenty years it wouldn't be worth the effort."

The black shook his head no. He hadn't said much, generally, but Victor didn't have the impression that this indicated any inferiority between the two. The black, a

Bantu, more specifically a Zulu, Viljoen had introduced as Dumisani, simply seemed the quiet sort.

"What *have* you got?" Inning asked.

The Boer and the Bantu exchanged glances. Victor wasn't sure, not absolutely, but he had the impression that a great deal of information—information to which he didn't have the code—was exchanged in that glance.

"For noddy cars?" Viljoen asked. The cars were nicknamed in South Africa for the British children's television character, a toy named "Noddy" and his toy automobile. "Well . . . a lot of the turrets have been taken off to fit out the Ratels that took over from the noddy cars."

"What's a . . . *noddy* car?"

"Eland," the Boer replied. "AMLs, others call them. Or Panhards. Anyway, the Ratel uses the same turret, so some of the turrets from the noddy cars were put into them, and others have been cannibalized. There's more turrets in 90mm than 60mm, by the way. More left here, I mean."

The black warrant added, "You *can* put infantry in a noddy car, provided the turret's gone. Maybe four men, would you say, Dani?" Dumisani had one of those mellifluous African voices that is an improvement on anyone else's English, sort of Ladysmith Black Mambazo in a prose vein.

"Five in a pinch, I think," the Boer replied, "besides the driver and gunner. Would that do?"

"Can you provide them?" Victor asked. He thought, *Personnel decisions are really* not *in my portfolio for this. But if this is what I can get . . .*

The Bantu shrugged as the Boer laughed. "Enough for an army," Viljoen said. "How many do you need?"

"Nine of the 90mm versions," Victor said. "Three with 60mm turrets. And, since they won't carry as many, call it thirty-six without turrets. Since the ammunition isn't something I normally carry, I need three thousand rounds of 90mm, and about a thousand of 60."

"The 60mm mortar is damned near worthless," the Boer said. "And even three missing would be noticed, since we still use the turrets. I can get you the 90mm versions, nine or twelve or twenty, if you want. I can get turretless bodies, fifty or sixty, I suppose. Okay, *okay*, a *small* army."

"I'll need to consult with my friends," Victor said. "But assuming they can use the turretless ones, how do you get them to us?"

"You got a ship?" Viljoen asked.

"Yes, chartered, my own crew. Some of Dov's people will be aboard to fix the things."

The Boer nodded. "That would work. We can fit three in a forty foot shipping container. We mark them as sent to the tank range as targets. Off the books. Might have to grease the customs man's palm at the port, but nobody here really gives a shit anymore, so we can do that."

"How much?" Inning asked.

Again the Boer and the Bantu exchanged glances. This time they took much longer about it. Victor still couldn't read their faces but there was something . . . he and his wife, Alla, sometimes communicated . . .

"You two are more than friends, aren't you?" the Russian asked.

"Took you long enough to figure it out," Viljoen said.

"But . . . this is South Africa. You're white; your . . . friend's . . . black . . . "

"So?" the Boer shrugged. "He thinks white is sexy. I think black is. And we both despise flaming queens."

Dumisani put up one hand, then ostentatiously bent his wrist before straightening it, all the while sneering profoundly.

Viljoen chuckled, then said, "We were on opposite sides during the Border War, too. Again, so? We're doing this, stealing equipment, I mean, so we can get the hell out of this place and live decently somewhere. Speaking of which—"

"That's part of our price," Dumisani said. "We want out. It would be nice if we could get work we know how to do while we're at it."

"But with money you can go live anywhere," Victor said.

"No," Viljoen corrected. His head nodded towards the Bantu. "He could. But I'm a white South African, and a Boer, which is worse. Nobody wants to take us because nobody wants us to leave South Africa. Open the portals to, say, the United States and ninety-five percent of the whites of this country would disappear overnight."

"Ninety-nine percent," Dumisani corrected. "And then the country would collapse. Which would make progressive minded people all over the world look stupid, clearly a disaster to be avoided. This I did not understand when I was fighting my partner over majority rule. If I had understood, I might have been on his side rather than the ANC's.

"Then again," the Zulu added, shaking his head sadly, "I used to think we blacks could run the country. I think maybe we could have. I think we *should* have. But the last couple of decades have proven only that we *are* running it into the dirt, quite despite could haves and should haves. And I see no solution."

"You still haven't said how much."

Boer and Bantu again exchanged glances. "One hundred thousand Rand, each," Viljoen said, "for a turretless car with a working engine. Two hundred and fifty thousand for one with a 90mm turret with a working gun. No radios included. Plus transportation to the port. I'll have to get you a quote on that. Plus the cost of the containers and port fees and loading fees. Call it ten million Rand, all told. And another four million for the 90mm ammunition. I'm going to have to bribe someone for that."

"Fortunately," Dumisani said, "since liberation everyone can be bribed."

"We weren't," Viljoen said, "as honest as all that even beforehand."

Victor did some quick calculations. *One point five million dollars, give or take. Plus as much for Dov to recondition them. I can charge the Americans maybe four million. That's a fair profit and worth my time. And if the Americans are willing to go for ground mounted mortars, I can provide those from my own stocks.*

"I'll ask if the turretless ones will do," Victor said. "And if a place for you can be found among the group I represent. I suppose, since they're going to be using 'noddy cars,' that people who know how to maintain them would be useful."

"Not just maintain," Dumisani said. "We know how to use them."

Victor was about to comment on that, when his PDA buzzed. It was a text message. He read it, and smiled. *It seems Messrs Nyein and Naing and the government of Myanmar need some arms.*

Assembly Area Alpha—Base Camp, Amazonia, Brazil, D-107

"Ralph," Stauer asked of his chief intelligence officer, Boxer, "just how compromised are we?"

The former Air Force general shook his head. "You're referring to the foreigners? Or just generally?"

"Both?"

"I don't think we are . . . yet. Let me explain."

"Please do."

"Only nineteen of us really know the mission, twenty if you count Wahab. Most of those are here. Reilly and Phillie, back in San Antonio, know. But he wouldn't tell his mother and she's your girl. Harry Gordon and his assistant in Guyana know. They wouldn't tell anyone either. Terry Welch knows. So does Biggus Dickus. Their teams don't know. Cruz knows. So does Kosciusko. They're not going to say a word. Everyone else is pretty much in the dark. Illegal Mexicans are assembling kit planes near Seattle and have not clue one. A bunch of Chinese with Kosciusko just want to escape China."

Boxer chewed at his lower lip for a moment, then said, "In a way, we're not compromised enough."

Stauer's eyes widened, incredulously. "Huh?"

"I haven't told any of my contacts what's up. I need to, or eventually they're going to start asking questions and maybe interfering on general principle. You *know* Victor's reporting to the FSB. But he can only report what he knows, which is that men, arms, and equipment are being assembled for an operation. He or FSB could probably gather, based on the equipment list, that that operation will be in Africa. But since they don't know where, and since Russia has some interests in Africa, or thinks it does, they might want to stop us in case we are going to interfere with those interests. We need to assure them that this is not the case. Brazil doesn't know shit yet, I think. No," he corrected, "I'm sure they don't. But if they get a hint that an armed force of foreigners is being assembled on their soil they will certainly get difficult about it. And a surprise visit by Brazilian Marines would be a 'bad thing,' *marca registrada*."

The last warning, at least, wasn't a surprise. Indeed, the force was taking some pains to ensure the Brazilians stayed in the dark. The management team for the plantation they'd bought on what Khalid thought was his behalf had been reduced in numbers and the remainder segregated far away—thirty-five miles—from the base camp. The camp itself was now, under the sergeant major's tutelage, quite well hidden despite the numbers of tents they'd set up. Supplies and personnel were to come in mostly by air from another country. And the trees were being cut in irregular patterns that tended to disguise the appearance of the field. And the really "dangerous" equipment would be offloaded to landing craft before the ship carrying it even reached Manaus.

"So you think we should bring both the Russians and the United States in on this?" Stauer shook his head. "The idea fills me with dread."

"Yes and no," Boxer said. "I think we should tell them slightly different stories . . . and slightly false ones. I'd like your permission to pass on to the United States Department of State that this is a Russian supported anti-piracy mission. They've had some problems with pirates in the area and so our folks shouldn't balk over that. We tell the Russians more of the truth, that this is a hostage rescue mission. If we have to be more honest about it, we can tell the Russkis just how we intend to rescue the hostage. All things considered, they'll approve. The United States would not."

Stauer considered this, then said, "You can talk to the Russians, since they've already got reason for suspicion. Arrange to take Victor with you. Not a word to State. When do you think you should go?"

"Probably in about five or six weeks," Ralph replied, accepting with good grace that Stauer had only taken his advice in part.

"Fair enough. Now who else is reporting to whom?" Stauer asked.

"None that I know of yet," Boxer replied. "But, once we get people here I'd like your permission to set up a cell under Bridges expressly to monitor any sat-phone traffic."

"Done," Stauer agreed. "And while it's not your bailiwick, what do you think of Victor's proposal to send us a couple of trainers *cum* mechanics with the armored cars?"

"From a training aspect I wouldn't have an opinion,"

Boxer said. "Not my thing. From an intel point of view, more expressly a counter-intel point of view, I don't think it will matter. After all, you're not announcing where we're going until we're all aboard ship and at sea. By then I can *confiscate* all the phones."

"Speaking of communications devices," Stauer asked, "do we have commo up with *The Drunken Bastard*?"

"We do," Ralph answered. "They've got a man aboard the *Galloway*. They'll be striking tonight or tomorrow."

"Think the boy will be aboard?"

"Almost no chance or I wouldn't have recommended we go ahead. But we ought to be able to find out where they dropped him off."

Stauer nodded. "Yeah. Might be worth something." Stauer changed subjects. "What do you think about this proposal to replace the 90mm with that high velocity 60mm?"

"I wouldn't do it now."

"Why?"

"We'll have the anti-tank guided missile Ferrets if there is any armor we have to worry about. And even if there is, there won't be much. We need the larger shell of the 90s to take care of technicals, buildings, fortifications, groups of infantry. Also, I checked. Nobody's ever mounted a gun that powerful in an Eland before and used it operationally. Hate to be the ones to discover that it deranges the turret."

"Point," Stauer agreed.

"And the two South Africans Victor wants to inflict on us won't know anything about the 60."

"Also a point."

D-107, near Tempe Base, Bloemfontein, South Africa

It was evening over South Africa by the time Victor had his answer. With evening, the rats came out. From their table by a window in a small, moderately upscale restaurant the three, Boer, Bantu, and Russian, could watch the rats as they emerged. Streets quiet in the day became quite lively by night.

"You're in," he told Boer and Bantu. "You're even wanted. But it's not a permanent posting. The organization involved is very ad hoc and temporary. It might, and I suspect it does, have unofficial ties to other organizations that may be more permanent.

"The pay is standard for your rank, within the group. In this case it's a bit over three hundred thousand Rand, each, for the entire contract period, which is about three and a half months."

"Shit, man," Viljoen said, "that's a couple of years' pay. What do you say, Dumi?" he asked of his partner. "We can find something, somewhere, if we have two years pay each to live on while we do."

The black seemed disinclined to agree. Two years living expenses was not necessarily enough to start a new life somewhere else. Then, too, "What about our pensions?"

Viljoen snorted in derision. "Love, there aren't going to *be* any pensions paid here soon enough, not in anything that has any value. Maybe if they offered a lifetime of free goat meat and mealie. But why do that when they can 'pay' us in soon to be valueless Rand? And two years pay is over and above what we get for the noddy cars and ammunition."

He turned to Victor. "We won't be *paid* in Rand, will we?"

"No, USD."

At about that time there was a commotion from the street. All three looked out to see a car stopped by another one with a crowd of angry men around the former. The car's doors were locked. No matter, some of the men produced clubs and stones with which they proceeded to smash in the windows.

The man who had been driving the car was dragged out, the broken class of the window slashing his torso and leaving blood trails on the shards. The woman on the other side of the vehicle screamed as rough hands forced their way in and unlatched the door. She too, then, was dragged out. While the male driver was beaten by some of the crowd, others followed the pair dragging the woman off to somewhere. She screamed for a long time, but the police never came.

All of the participants, on both sides, were black.

"I'm in," said the Bantu. "This is no place for a civilized man, of any color."

★CHAPTER EIGHTEEN★

HOMICIDE, n. The slaying of one human
being by another. There are four kinds of homicide:
felonious, excusable, justifiable, and praiseworthy,
but it makes no great difference to the person slain
whether he fell by one kind or another
—the classification is for advantage of the lawyers."
—Ambrose Bierce, *The Devil's Dictionary*

**D-106, MV *George Galloway*,
320 miles south of Reykjavik, Iceland**

In his little, not particularly comfortably fitting,
earpiece Eeyore heard, "We're five miles behind you and
closing at three quarters speed. We'll go to flank once you
report that the radio room and bridge are secure."

"Roger," he sent back. "I'm leaving now. I call; you
come a-running."

"Wilco," answered Biggus Dickus. "Good luck.
Godspeed."

Antoniewicz didn't bother answering that. He

reached down, past the layer of television boxes he'd slept on, and twisted open the rods that held the container's door shut. That made a little noise, a faint screech. Inside the container it sounded terribly loud. Outside, he was pretty sure, the sound would be lost amidst the sea splashing against the bow and the more distant noise of machinery. What he hadn't counted on were the sounds of male passion coming from somewhere very near the container. It sounded like, "*Ana bahebak . . . ana bahebak . . . ana bahebak.*"

With his NVGs on his face, Eeyore eased his head around the half open door and looked in the direction of the sound. *Sure as shit,* and the pun was somewhat intended, there were two of the ships complement—passengers or crew, who knew?—both bearded, with their trousers down around their ankles, one bent over the railing while the other, with both hands grasped tight to the former's hips, belabored his posterior. The one bent over the railing was playing with his own penis.

If they'd just been crew, and unarmed, Antoniewicz might have just passed on. As it was, the Kalashnikovs he saw propped against the inner hull said, *no, too dangerous to let them live.*

The laser aiming device was already on. With a mental shrug Antoniewicz lined it up on the head of the fucker, ignoring, for the moment, the fuckee. With both hands to steady the weapon, he squeezed the trigger until he was rewarded with a moderate felt recoil, the metallic snap of the slide, the *phooot* of contained gas being partially released, and the near disintegration of his target's head.

Oddly enough, even with his brain destroyed, the target's hips kept pumping for a few moments longer, and perhaps even faster. Eeyore had the inane thought, *Gee, I guess sex really is a mindless activity, after all.*

He padded forward quickly, then, just as the fucker's body started to go limp and crumble to the deck, took aim once again, this time at the one bent over the rail. That target's head was not visible, though it might have been to a taller man than Eeyore. No matter, he knew how to get a head up quickly. He shot the fuckee in the kidney. That produced pain so immense, so absolute and ultimate, that the fuckee could only draw air in and twist. As his head raised, the invisible laser lined up on it. The victim never even felt the shot.

Antoniewicz bent down and grasped his second target's legs, lifting and letting the limp body splash to the sea below. He placed his pistol on the deck and grabbed his first victim, hauling the corpse up and pushing the torso over the side. Another bend and heave and that body joined the other in the North Atlantic. The salt spray was not quite enough to overcome the smell of shit-covered dick.

Antoniewicz bent again and picked up his pistol, then gave a little mock salute. Once again, he turned aft toward the superstructure, the bridge, and the radio room. He reported this to the *Bastard*, with the comment, "Two tangos engaged and down. I'm not compromised."

"Roger," came the answer, "we're about three miles out."

As he walked aft, Antoniewicz wondered, *What is it about the wogs, anyway? Is it that when women are held so far down that they're little more than animals, the men have to fuck each other to avoid the sense of engaging in bestiality?*

On the other hand, there's a fair possibility they were just gay. Shit, pun still intended, happens.

The superstructure astern was well lit, well enough, in fact, that it was better for Eeyore to lift his NVGs off of his face and go on ambient light once he was about two thirds of the way back. His eyes were still adjusting from the NVG-induced purple haze as he walked forward. That haze kept him from seeing the expended brass—really thin steel with a faint brass wash on it—until he'd stepped directly onto some and suddenly felt his feet flying out underneath him. He hit, *hard*, knocking his wind out in a way that hadn't happened to him since he was boy.

He lay there on the deck, arms overhead, gasping for air, and silently cursing, *Fucking sloppy wog bastards; never clean up their messes. Dirty motherfuckers . . .*

Antoniewicz became aware of someone tall and skinny, bearing a curve-magazined rifle in one hand, standing over him, outlined in the light from the superstructure. He thought, simply, *I'm fucked*, while—far the worse—feeling, *I fucked up*, and unconsciously stiffened, bracing himself for the bullet he was sure was coming.

Instead the man standing over him said something in Arabic to which Eeyore could only make gasping sounds in reply. Then he bent over, offering his other hand to help the former SEAL to his feet. Antoniewicz took the proffered hand with his own left—never mind the insult that offered, and let the Arab pull him to his feet. He then put his pistol's muzzle under the Arab's chin and pulled the trigger, exploding the head.

A quick lift and push and that body, too, went over the side to splash into the North Atlantic.

"Hold . . . up . . . a . . . minute . . . or five," Antoniewicz gasped into his radio.

"You okay, Eeyore?"

"Long . . . story. I'll . . . be. . . . okay."

It feels a little dirty to shoot someone who was trying to help. Oh, well.

It was a full five minutes before Antoniewicz felt able to continue forward in top form. Since he hadn't heard or seen sign of the *Bastard* he had reason to believe they'd understood and complied with the request for delay. While straining to regain his breath, he listened as best he was able for sounds from the superstructure. There seemed to be something like a party going on at the very bottom of the thing, just where it joined the lowest container deck. At least, the sound seemed like nothing else but a party. And, also, as near as he could tell from sounds, there were twenty-five or so partygoers in attendance.

Mmm . . . too many for the submachine gun. Especially if they've got their weapons to hand. I think five frags—fragmentation grenades—*ought to do for a room the size of the superstructure, especially given the metal walls and the ricochets.*

He flicked his Makarov on safe, then stuffed the silencer into his trousers. Unthinkingly, and perhaps somewhat illogically, he made sure the muzzle would, in the event of an accident, drive the bullet into his leg rather than his testicles. Then he walked to a spot just around the corner from the open hatch from which the party sounds emanated. Eeyore took from one of the pouches he carried two of the Russian hand grenades—RGOs—provided by Victor's cache.

He straightened the pins of each then, holding one in each hand with his thumbs over the spoons, he took the rings in the index fingers of the opposite hands. He pulled his hands apart, taking the rings with them. Walking to stand next to the hatch, Antoniewicz released the spoon held down by his right thumb, hearing the snap of the striker and cap. He began to count—"one thousand . . . two thousand"—as he bent over and bowled the grenade into the room. "Three thousand." He flipped the grenade in his left hand into his right, releasing the spoon in the process. He almost immediately hurled the grenade at the far wall. One of the RGO's nicer features was that it had an impact detonation ability, which was armed about a second after releasing the spoon.

Both grenades went off within less than a quarter second of each other, shaking the walls and setting the partiers to screaming with shock and the agony of jagged wounds. In that enclosed space even the fragments that missed were likely to bounce off the steel walls until they buried themselves in something soft. By the time those went off, he had two more armed. These, too, he donated to the party, even while people screamed from the first salvo. Then he gripped the last one he intended to use, pulled the pin, and sailed it in through the opening.

Eeyore pulled the submachine gun from its position across his back and pushed the muzzle through the open hatchway. He used the steel wall for as much cover as it would provide. Only a few men were standing, and those seemed stunned. For the rest, *Hmmm . . . fewer of them than I expected.* He fired at them, in turn—*brrrp . . . brrrp . . . brrrp . . . brrrp*—until all went down dead or wounded. Most of them seemed as much offended as surprised. Given the nature of the ammunition he was using, it was a fairly safe bet that even the wounded would soon be dead. Frangible was some nasty shit.

"Come quick! Come quick! Come quick!" Eeyore shouted into the radio. "I'm heading to the bridge."

The exterior steps on the port side of the superstructure led halfway up before terminating at a landing. From the landing, a hatchway led inward. Men, about a half dozen of them, were pouring from the doors into the central hallway that ran the breadth of the superstructure. They jabbered excitedly, some of them loading rifles in the process.

Time for another grenade, Antoniewicz thought. He reached into the pouch, then pulled one grenade out, pulled the pin, released the spoon, and counted one second before tossing the thing inward and downward. It exploded before he could quite withdraw his arm. Eeyore gasped with the pain as at least one piece of hot metal penetrating the skin of his forearm, lodging in the muscle below.

"Mother*fucker!*"

He turned into the hatchway and ran down the corridor, firing two to three round bursts into each of the people therein. Their arms tended to flop around as they lost muscle control, even as the frangible bullets broke up inside their bodies. Halfway across was an opening.

Upwards from that ran another set of ladders. Next to the base of those steps was what had to be the radio room.

Eeyore shot the crewman laying on the deck in the radio room once more, to make sure. The crewman was laying face down, feet toward the floor, as if he'd been racing for the radio room when the grenade went off.

The former SEAL changed magazines and fired enough rounds into the three radios as to be *very* certain they were dead. Then, with sounds of something like organization with a heavy admixture of anger growing below and outside, he raced up the central stairway to the bridge.

Antoniewicz reached the top just as one of the crew reached out in an attempt to close and dog the hatch. Eeyore fired at the crewman, a long burst of seven rounds, causing the man's chest to ripple and pulsate under the assault, even as the ammunition broke apart upon entering his chest cavity to expand outward and ruin all the organs inside. Eeyore stepped over the body and found another man inside, this one reaching for a rifle.

Antoniewicz aimed and pulled the trigger again, only to be rewarded with a very disappointing *nothing*. No time to reload, he threw the submachine gun at the crewman, causing the latter to duck behind the bridge's control station. As he was ducking, Eeyore launched himself across the deck, his right hand reaching for his knife. He found it, pulled it, and thrust it generally forward as the crewman re-emerged from his shelter, trying to line up his Kalashnikov.

Antoniewicz couldn't get the knife lined up in time. Instead, he collided with the crewman, knocking both of them to the deck and causing both to lose their grip on their weapons. They rolled over each other for a few turns, with the crewman emerging on top and reaching for Eeyore's throat. The former SEAL batted away that questing grip, and then drove his knee upward into the crewman's groin. The crewman's eyes widened, even as he gasped with the pain.

Putting both hands together to form a flesh and bone hammer, Eeyore batted the crewman on the side of his head, sending him flying off to the side. Eeyore caught a glimpse of his lost knife (he'd completely forgotten about the pistol for the moment) and lunged for it. His hand wrapped around the hilt just as the crewman decided that a little gonad agony was a small price to pay for retaining those gonads. The dripping wound on Antoniewicz's arm flared anew with pain when the crewman grasped his wrist and twisted.

Eeyore formed one hand into a fist and struck the crewman on the ear. Then he twisted his other wrist, pain be damned, and freed the knife. With one hand over his insulted ear and the other outthrust, the crewman begged, "*La, min fadlak, la.*"

"I don't speak Arabic," Antoniewicz said as he feinted first for the crewman's face, then brought the knife down and around and, point first, stuck it into the crewman's stomach. Blood welled out and a scream escaped the crewman's throat. Eeyore ripped downward with the knife, then twisting inside the crewman's body, ripped upward again, effectively eviscerating the man. The scream tapered off into a moan. Then sound, except for that from some terminal thrashing, ceased.

Leaving the knife where it was, Eeyore stood and glanced around quickly. *Now* he remembered the pistol at his waist and drew it, but there was no one else to engage. He bent to pick up his submachine gun and reloaded it from one of the magazines in his vest. Taking a firing position to one side of the control panel, he placed his last grenade in front of him and called to the *Bastard* in a false southern accent, "Y'all come a-runnin', now, y'hear?"

If I could kill the lights the NVGs would give me a considerable advantage. He looked around the bridge for a main light switch or power switch for the entire ship. He found something, a button, and pushed it. The light duly went out on the bridge, except for some faintly glowing red emergency lights. A quick glance out the broad, side to side, windows that faced forward told him that only the running lights were showing on the ship, forward. *Best I can do.*

As Antoniewicz waited, as calmly as one could under the circumstances, for the enemy to make their move, he wondered, *How the fuck did we get ourselves into this?*.

★ CHAPTER NINETEEN ★

Every normal man must be tempted
at times to spit on his hands, hoist the black flag,
and begin to slit throats.
—H. L. Mencken

D-106, 318 miles south of Reykjavik

The *Bastard*, skipping across the waves, showed no running lights whatsoever.

"I hear firing, skipper," announced Simmons at the helm.

"Fuck 'hear,'" said Biggus. "You can see the mother-fucking muzzle flashes." He lifted off his Russian NVGs. "Hell, you can see 'em with bare eyes. Flank speed! Come alongside on the starboard. Morales!?"

"Chief!"

"Stand by on the port side gun."

"Aye, aye."

"Simmons," the chief said, "when we get in the

Galloway's wake slow down to give Morales a reasonable chance to hit something. And us to hook the ladder to board."

"Aye, Chief. You still going in first?"

"Natch."

The sailor sighed. "Aye, Chief."

Eeyore felt something striking the steel deck upon which he lay, followed by muffled screams coming from below.

"Stupid bastards! Don't you realize that your own bullets will ricochet off the steel? And not stop until they hit something soft? Like you?"

There were more bodies now littering the bridge. From his prone position, it was hard to tell how many. But he thought he remembered at least six men going down. Antoniewicz still had one last grenade; he'd used the rest. He figured he'd have to use it, too, for the next rush.

And a bloody good thing you fucks don't have any, or haven't dug them out of storage if you do. Or . . . ah, shit.

In the grainy, greenish glow of his NVGs, Eeyore saw two sparking objects, approximately egg-shaped, he thought, sail up to bounce off the ceiling and then fall to the floor. He opened his mouth wide as he rolled left, back behind the control console. Then they went off in a great burst of light that immediately disappeared to be replaced by thick, dark smoke.

The console saved him from most of the shrapnel, barring what ricocheted off the other metal and found him on the rebound, but not from the concussion, which was bad enough to blow some of the windows out, pummel his eardrums, and to make him feel like he'd had every square inch of his body simultaneously pummeled with an infinity of Louisville Sluggers. To say he was stunned would have been an understatement.

But even stunned men can operate off of long-trained and conditioned autopilot. He rolled out to the right again, felt something dig into his chest, and fired a very badly aimed burst in the general direction of the ladders. He didn't know if he'd hit anything. And he couldn't hear if he had either. He rather doubted it, to the extent he was cognizant enough to doubt.

His hand released the submachine gun's grip and sought under his chest to clear it of the object pressing into him. The hand came to rest upon his last grenade.

"What the fuck? Why not?" he said, and didn't even really hear himself.

Antoniewicz grasped the grenade and rolled back behind the console. He tried sitting up to get his back against the thing but found that what that did to his head just wasn't worth it. Unsteadily he pulled the pin out and rolled back to his semi-exposed position. Quite certain that he wasn't up to throwing the thing, he slid it across the deck with as much force as he could muster. The spoon flipped off as he did.

The grenade slid for point two seconds until hitting a body from which it careened at a low angle. It then hit a dropped Kalashnikov at about the point five second mark. From the rifle it bounced, returning to approximately its previous course. After the passage of point seven seconds it hit the back wall behind the ladders leading to the bridge and bounced forward and down. It hit three steps and a couple of ankles, each about a tenth of a second apart. On the sixth step, which was about as far as the center of the assault party had reached, it had been over one point two seconds since spoon release.

Boom!

Morales began pressing the trigger of the Russian .51 caliber machine gun they'd mounted to the port side at exactly the same time Eeyore's grenade exploded. The grenade flash had the effects of illuminating a row of people ascending the ladders on the port side of the superstructure, and then causing Morales' NVGs to overload, which then left him completely in the dark even as the .51 began spitting out bullets. At the same time, the *Bastard* passed through the ship's wake and rocked violently. This threw off his aim so that, while he fired, he hit absolutely nothing smaller than the ship. And then the *Bastard* was past the point where the corner of the superstructure blocked off any possible target. He heard the shout, "Grenade!" Almost instantly, there was another explosion aboard the *Galloway* and Chief Thornton and two men were hooking a ladder over the *Galloway*'s side and scrambling up.

No sense in sticking with the machine gun anymore. Morales let it go, took off his defunct NVGs, and picked up a night vision scoped Dragunov sniper's rifle. He leaned against the *Bastard*'s port gun tub and, putting his eye to the scope, began to scan. It was a fairly useless activity, even at this short range, as the *Bastard*'s rocking made the chance of a hit a matter of flukes.

★ ★ ★

Biggus Dickus liked the Russki grenades, in principle. *It's quality control at the factory that gives me the willies.* Thus, he didn't even contemplate trying to cook one off. With two of his men, Rogers—known as "Mary-Sue"—holding the bent ladder and Bland—called "Jalapeño," though he had not a trace of Mexican in his background—overwatching with his Russian SMG, the chief pulled the pin, kissed the grenade, released the spoon and tossed the thing onto *Galloway's* rear deck.

The explosion came so soon after Biggus had tossed the grenade that, *Yeah, quality control at the factory left something to be desired. No fucking way I should have held that thing long enough for the impact feature to arm. I could have been holding it, cooking it off and* Kaboom.

Mary-Sue, scrunched low, wasn't fazed by the blast. Besides, he assumed his chief knew what he was doing. As soon as the thing went off, he was on his feet, hooking the ladder over the gunwales, pronounced "gunnels," like "tunnels," which were the hull's uppers.

The chief had been supposed to lead, as a matter of principle. When he delayed for a moment, caught up in the conflicting emotions of very nearly having his arm blown off and relief that this had not happened, Jalapeño charged up, balancing on the balls of his feet. He jumped over the gunwales and onto the deck. He was then caught in a moment of indecision. He'd been supposed to turn left, after Biggus Dickus had turned right. Since Biggus hadn't turned right, his back would be uncovered if he turned left, per the plan. While he was caught in this moment of indecision, one of the ship's company or their terrorist passengers—probably having come rearward to look for more grenades and just having missed being caught in Biggus Dickus' explosion—saw Bland and fired a long burst. Two bullets impacted on the protective plates in his Russian body armor. Twenty-seven went high to very high. One impacted onto Jalapeño's face, killing him instantly and knocking his body against the gunwales, from whence it slid to the deck.

That brought the chief from his reveries. In fact, it brought him to a killing rage. Swearing aloud, Thornton ascended two steps, lined up his laser aiming device on the firer, and fired his own short burst, three rounds, directly into the man's chest.

"Come on, Mary-Sue," the chief shouted as he scrambled up the ladder. The chief did turn right once he'd reached the deck, but there was nothing there to see. He took a step forward to make room for Rogers. Once he felt the SEAL touch down on the deck behind him, and satisfied that there was nothing of danger forward, he ordered, "Take point. Around the superstructure. Go! Go! Go!"

The two SEALs ran toward the bow and cut right, then right again. The terrorists Morales had missed were still lined up on the ladders. As soon as he rounded the superstructure, Mary-Sue opened fire, letting his muzzle climb up the row of enemies. His hose stream of frangible alloy bullets sent first one, then another, then a third and fourth into a Spandau Ballet, their bodies twitching and dancing under the impacts, some of them being hurled right over the railing to crash upon the deck.

It was at that point, caught between two fires, that ship's crew and passengers began dropping their weapons and raising their hands, crying out things in Arabic and Urdu that sounded submissive and plaintive.

The *Bastard* was properly tied off, in tow behind the *Galloway*. All of the enemy bodies had been weighted and dumped over the side. Only Bland's corpse had been salvaged, and his remains, scrunched up like a fetus, were freezing in the big meat locker on the *Bastard*. The prisoners, all nineteen of them, excepting only the ship's captain and first officer, were stripped and secured inside the container that had formerly served as Antoniewicz's hide, the televisions still remaining having been dropped over the side. Eeyore had been left to guard, about all he was good for at the moment, while Morales wired the ship for demolition. Simmons had even managed to tap *Galloway*'s bunkers for fuel to top off his own boat. This was critical as the stop after next, St. John's, in Newfoundland, was quite close to the *Bastard*'s maximum range anyway. That would be important if Narssarssuaq, Greenland, couldn't or wouldn't refuel them.

A search of the containers, such as could be accessed—and most couldn't be—revealed little of obvious consequence to the larger mission. In one they'd found a baker's dozen of teary-eyed, teenaged Romanian girls, living in rags and filth, and grateful to be freed. It had probably been intended to sell the girls somewhere as whores, and quite possibly somewhere in Europe, Canada, or even the United States. It was unlikely that sexual slavery was ever really going to go completely out of fashion, anywhere.

Another had a great deal of explosives, which set

Morales to chortling, as he began carrying the crates to the main deck.

A search of the crew quarters turned up more al Qaeda propaganda than any of them had seen in one place, at one time, in a *long* time. This fit Thornton's rules of engagement for eliminating the entire crew.

They did find one other interesting container, down on the lowest level, that had a chain and a leg iron welded to the container frame. They brought the captain and the executive officer down to it, stood them on chairs taken from the galley, put noosed ropes around their necks and secured the ropes high to a cross piece set up on the top levels of the containers.

"Don't try to bullshit me," Biggus Dickus said, mostly to the wog with more braid on his uniform. "If you're senior merchant fleet people, and you are, you will speak perfectly good English, and you do. I will ask this once of each of you. Who was in here?"

The captain of the boat barely got out, "Fuck you, you inf—" before Thornton had kicked the chair out from underneath him. The noose had been tied very tightly and the captain was a smallish man, and slight of build. The drop was no more than the rope would stretch. Thus the noose barely tightened, at first, not even enough to cut off blood to the brain and certainly not enough to seriously impede the flow of air. It did make talking difficult, what with the forced gagging the captain endured.

"Tsk," Biggus Dickus said, "such bad manners toward your guests."

The captain, naturally enough, panicked as soon as he felt the rope biting into his neck. Mindlessly, like an animal, his feet flailed about for purchase. He set himself to swinging, quite by accident, and three times managed to get his feet against the vertical walls of the containers. This, of course, was not something he could stand on. With each kick the rope tightened by a millimeter or two.

The ship's exec, captivated, watched his captain die slowly. He began to moan with fear and then to pray aloud. As the captain's struggles grew less frenzied, the front of the exec's trousers suddenly grew wet with urine as he lost control of his bladder.

Thornton also watched the captain slowly strangle, but with complete impassivity. He hadn't started out hating "wogs," but after seeing the crisped bodies of his people in Afghanistan, two years prior, he'd learned to. Once or twice he thought he heard the captain trying to speak through his gag reflex.

"Fuck you," he said. "I gave you your chance."

The captain's kicking, twisting, and twitching gradually subsided, though there were occasional interruptions as he somehow found the strength to give another major effort at getting his feet on something. In time, though, only the feet twitched, and the only sounds beyond those of the machinery of the ship and sea were the steady *drip-drip-drip* of piss and liquefied shit sliding off the late captain's toes.

Biggus turned toward the first officer. "As I told the captain, you get one chance. Who—"

"I never knew his name," the *Galloway*'s exec blurted out. He could already feel his bowels loosening, too. "Only saw him twice, *il hamdu l'illah*. Some black we picked up in Boston Harbor. We dropped him off at Port Harcourt, in Nigeria, safe and sound. Yes, yes: Safe and sound."

"Do you know where they were taking him?"

"To the airport; that's all I know. All I know . . . all I know."

"You're sure now?" Thornton asked.

"Yes, yes. Sir, I am sure."

"Good. This is for Petty Officer Bland." Thornton then kicked the chair out from under the exec, and left to check on Morales' progress with the demolition preparation. Before he left the area completely he turned around to where the exec was kicking his life away, as the captain had. "So I lied," the chief said. "So sue me. Doesn't the Koran permit one to lie to an unbeliever? Well, you and I don't share a belief system. Infidel."

Thornton found Morales standing by the gunwales, amidships, connecting one of the radio detonators to a piece of wire. Morales was wearing a wet suit of a very odd design, with the letters CCCP emblazoned.

"You didn't *wear* that shit, did you, Morales?"

"Why not? You said you wouldn't risk your life but ours might be acceptable."

"You know I wasn't serious."

"Yeah, but I needed to use their shit to get down under the hull. I've got five hundred pounds of . . . well, I suppose it must be SEMTEX, or something just like it, based on the color. It was in one of the containers. Anyway, it's down there under the ship. When we set it off it's going to seem like a torpedo hit it, or maybe a drift mine . . . if anyone tries to reconstruct it, that is."

"How'd you get it under the hull?"

Morales pointed to either side. "Two floats connected by a line, with another line in the center of the first one connected to a stanchion at the bow, and a line from each float to the hull. I walked the floats down to where I wanted then, connected the lines, and then sort of keel hauled the stuff under. Course, once I had it roughly in position I had to go down myself—and let me tell you, that center line was mighty useful for that—to prep it all nice and proper." Morales laughed. "This is gonna be *beautiful*, Chief."

Taking occasional time-outs to vomit, Eeyore took the trouble to drill about ninety more air holes in the container into which the prisoners were locked. The men inside the locked container were a tough lot. They didn't panic, not even for a moment, when the door was opened and the strangled, black-faced bodies of the captain and his exec tossed in. They were tough, yet each man there had to wonder, after the door was secured again and the smell of the bodies' loosed bowels assailed their noses, "*Who's next?*"

As it turned out, they all were. They couldn't see it. For that matter, they never really knew what happened to them in any detail, though given more time one of them might have figured it out.

They felt a sudden shock. The rearward portion of their container arose slightly, but only that. Then they heard the blast, and the sounds of tearing metal as the ship's back almost broke. Of course, that was a surprise and, of course, they panicked *then*. The men began clawing at the locked door and at each other. Thus, they never noticed when the previous motion reversed itself and the ship's center sank into the gaseous hole left by the explosion; they were far too busy fighting like rats amongst themselves. And then when the gas cooled and condensed, and the water came rushing in to meet the collapsing hull, they were mostly tossed from their feet as the ship's center raised up high out of the water, completing the sundering into two parts.

The bow section almost immediately began to capsize, spilling that container, along with many another, into the sea. The men who had been on their feet suddenly found themselves tossed to the side and then rolled over as their prison rolled over. Above their own screaming they heard a high pitched whistling sound as water rushed into the air holes drilled by Eeyore a couple of days prior, and supplemented more recently, forcing the air out. At that point, even drowning rats wouldn't have bit and clawed their mates quite so much for a mere few more minutes of breathing time.

"Set course two-seven-two for Narssarssuaq, Greenland," ordered the chief with warm smile. "And, since this isn't the US Navy, break out a bottle of the vodka Victor so thoughtfully put in the cache."

"Hey, Chief?"

"Yes, Mary-Sue?"

"How long to the base?"

"About three weeks."

"We have to stop for fuel, right?"

"Sure."

"Well . . . since we're not dry, can we get something

besides vodka when we do stop? And what about the girls?" These latter were below, wrapped in blankets and badly needing new clothes. Only Antoniewicz's and Morales' uniforms came close to fitting, and they needed those.

"The booze we'll see about. I don't know about the girls, except to go shopping when we get the chance. We can't release them anywhere we're going and can't release them, period, until the operation's over."

"Can we—?"

"Lay a finger on them, Mary-Sue, and I'll cut your balls off."

PART II

★CHAPTER TWENTY★

Old age hath yet his honor and his toil.
— Tennyson, *Ulysses*

D-106, Assembly Area Alpha—Base Camp, Amazonia, Brazil

The sergeant major hadn't put in fossa and agger, of course. He hadn't even set up the camp like a Roman legionary camp. *"No straight lines in nature, sir."* Instead, he'd established a central camp, for most of the headquarters, containing tents for Stauer and staff, plus the rest of the headquarters company, except for the mechanics who would be closer to the river, and a few guest tents for the naval company, should it have to send some people in. The rest of the groups were to be in clusters from there, A Company (Armored) to the northeast and B Company (Marine) to the southwest. The aviation company, such as would billet here, was about a kilometer to the northwest, near where about half of Nagy's engineers were clearing out jungle and rubber trees and putting in the airstrip.

Eventually, once the rest of the detachment of engineers showed up, they'd be putting in a dock and linking the camps with corduroy roads.

They'd need the corduroy roads. Already, under the frequent heavy downpour, the trails linking camps and tents within camps were approaching the state of morass, and that was under very light foot and vehicle traffic, all of that having been generated by the original advanced party of twenty-two, plus the twenty-five later arrivals.

With a light rain that foretold of a soon-coming downpour tapping gently on the canvas roof, Stauer looked out into the jungle from the operations tent. It was already quite dark, and the netting that ran from the edge of the tent's roof to the dark soil below further reduced vision. Add in that the trees kept even most sunlight out and—

"Darker than three feet up a well-digger's ass at midnight."

"Except for the few tents we allow to be fully lit, of course," Boxer said. "Did you expect different, Wes?"

"No. I'm still not certain about letting some tents be lit while others have to stay pitch black."

Boxer shook his head. "The Brazilians know we're here, at least in the abstract and even if they don't know what we are, how many we are, or how many we'll be. If we light everything up they'll get suspicious; a small battalion is way out of line for what we're allegedly doing here. By the same token, though, no lights would also be suspicious."

Stauer shrugged. "I suppose."

"You don't seem very upset that the boy wasn't on the *Galloway*."

Stauer shook his head. "If I'd thought he had been, I wouldn't have launched such an ad hoc 'rescue' mission. We'd have hit with more force and a *lot* more prep. And then our little holiday in paradise"—he sneered at the surrounding jungle—"would have been prematurely terminated. So, no, I'm not sorry. We had to try, as an ethical matter, given the information we had. That it didn't work out is all to the good."

Stauer scowled. "What do you make of those thirteen girls Biggus Dickus found?"

Boxer shook his head. "I'm not sure what to make of it. There were too many for just the crew and the 'passengers' to need. Four girls would have been enough for forty or fifty men. Biggus Dickus says the girls themselves don't seem to know where they were going or why. I suspect they were going to be sold to help fund an operation."

"What's the going rate on a young and pretty female slave these days?" Stauer asked.

"Varies," Boxer shrugged. "A few hundred dollars a head—no pun intended—in some parts of Africa. Maybe seven thousand in Bosnia. More, maybe twelve to twenty thousand, in the European Union or the US. What the fuck are you going to do with them?"

"I dunno," Stauer replied. "Can't let them go. Feel bad holding them against their will, if it is against their will."

"Biggus says they seem happy enough to be free of the *Galloway*. Most of them are only fifteen or sixteen, he thinks." Boxer shook his head with disgust at the innate depravity of Man. "Enlist them, maybe?"

"I can train a decent nurse's assistant in the time we have," Doc Joseph offered. "Maybe even make them full LPNs. Or," he looked pointedly at Master Sergeant Island.

The stout, black mess sergeant shrugged. "Yeah . . . maybe some of them can cook, or be taught to. But, you know, sir, you're already sticking me with some Chinese women. I don't speak Chinese, either version. And I sure as hell don't speak Romanian."

"I speak Italian, four-four Italian, as a matter of fact," Lox offered, with a smug grin. "They're pretty close, closer than Italian and Spanish or Portuguese."

Stauer nodded. "Tomorrow, Lox, try to get a radio link with *The Drunken Bastard*. See what the girls want or are willing to do. Make clear to them that we can't release them for a few months. Tell 'em they'll be paid at . . . shit . . . what rate *should* we pay them?"

"What the market will bear, sir," the sergeant major replied. "Not a penny more than the market will bear."

"All right, Top," Stauer replied, turning from the screen and jungle to the well lit interior of the tent. "But what's the market price for silence?"

To that, the sergeant major had no direct answer. Instead, he asked, "What's the market price for freedom?"

Stauer considered that for a moment, then called for his operations officer. "Waggoner?"

"Here, boss," Ken Waggoner answered, entering the main ops tent from his little side office tent, the two connected by saplings and tarps.

Stauer pointed at a set of three really large chartboards on one wall of the tent. One had a map of the world. Another showed a coastal area of Africa. Between the two was a operational matrix with one hundred and twenty half inch lines running side to side, and a score of lines about four inches apart running top to bottom.

"I see that the *Merciful* has picked up the PSP at Manila, and is supposed to receive the helicopters this evening. Is Welch going to be aboard the choppers?"

Waggoner shook his head. "No. Welch, his team, *and* the Russkis that are part of Victor's business operation are going by air through Port of Spain. Victor says he needs his people in Guyana to help sort and forward what he's going to be sending us there. And I wanted ours here soonest to begin prep for the next stage."

"Any word on the Elands?"

"We haven't updated that part of the board yet, but Victor's charter ship will finish loading them in a few days. They'll be containerized. The Israeli mechanics posing as sailors are already aboard, along with the parts required. Those were loaded in containers, too."

Stauer looked worriedly at the charts. "What's bothering you, boss?" Waggoner asked.

"Just not a lot of slack in the plan, is all."

Waggoner rocked his head from side to side a few times, then admitted, "That's true, but we do have some backup plans if there's a delay in something critical."

"What's your backup if we lose a helicopter while loading or en route?" Stauer asked.

"Bend over and kiss my ass goodbye."

"Good plan," Stauer conceded, sagely. "A better one might be to have Gordo get a line on a replacement."

D-105, 173 miles east of Kota Bharu, Malaysia (South China Sea)

The sea was extremely calm, little more than a glass sheet, with perhaps a few minor imperfections.

Moving at about four knots, just enough to maintain steerage, the ship was one hundred and seven feet in beam, plus a few insignificant inches. The rotor of Cruz's helicopter was just under seventy feet. Subtract from that one hundred and seven feet another sixteen feet for the double stacked containers lining the gunwales of the *Merciful*, plus about four more for the space between the exterior containers and the hull, and it left damned little space to land a helicopter in. They'd move both helicopters and containers once they were well out at sea, but for now Cruz and Kosciusko both wanted the things hidden from casual observation.

Six feet on a side sounds like a lot, Cruz fumed, *until you try to land one of these things in it. Well, at least the bitching ship's long enough . . . that, and the wind's not bad.*

Cruz flew low, his landing gear only a few feet above the water, the better to keep off anyone's radar. To either side of him, in a V formation, the other two Hips, one flown by Borsakov, the other by one of his old comrades, a Cossack by the name of Sirko, likewise flew low. The wash from his main rotor, and theirs, flattened the water below them, pushing it out into little, rimmed and smooth ponds within the sea. Ahead, the *Merciful* had normal running lights glowing, normal except for the infrared chemlights, visible only to someone with a night vision device, lining the side of the hull. That was his near recognition signal. His helicopter, too, showed infrared to the ship's bridge, though his was a design feature, not a hastily tacked on and highly temporary modification.

These waters were among the most disputed bodies of sea in the world, with the People's Republic of China clashing with Indonesia over the area northeast of the Natuna Islands, with the Philippines over the Malampaya and Camago gas fields and Scarborough Shoal, and with Vietnam over the waters west of the Spratly Islands, not to mention disputes, sometimes flaring into violence, between Vietnam, the PRC, Taiwan, Malaysia, and the Philippines over the islands, themselves, plus the Paracel Islands. To mention just a few. And then there were the pirates, who generally avoided the contested areas like the plague, preferring to stalk or lie in wait for ships out in the main sea lanes . . .

The local pirates had proven capable of making entire cargo ships disappear from public view under new names and paint schemes. Yachts were easier.

This yacht, about the size of *The Drunken Bastard*, though narrower in beam, had been simplicity itself to rename and repaint. The pirates had not, however, then sold it. It was too innocent looking, too quiet in operation, above all too *fast* to let go. Instead, once having disposed of the owner, his family, and their crew, the pirates had kept it, the better to advance their own operations.

Tonight the pirates planned a fairly low key operation.

They intended to board the container ship they'd tracked since it left Manila, seize the petty cash in the ship's safe, and leave. They really weren't interested in cargo or holding the crew for ransom; their scouts at the docks who had seen the crew reported that it was, by and large, American. Seizing an American ship in waters where the U.S. Navy frequently operated was dangerous enough; taking the crew hostage was up there with swimming in shark infested waters with chunks of meat tied to one's ankles for sheer risk factor.

Why this should be the one area that the Americans were willing to be forceful over as a matter of course, the pirates didn't know, not being devotees of domestic American politics. It was, in fact, that even a less than entirely successful hostage rescue proved a plus to presidential job approval rating, and the more a plus the more pirates were killed, while the less so as some were saved for trial.

The ship ahead, with the white painted gantry moved almost all the way back to the superstructure, was barely moving. The yacht, on the other hand, was moving and closing the distance between them quickly. At a range of about a kilometer, the pirate skipper lifted a night scope to his right eye. This was a single-intensifier version, once intended for mounting on a light anti-tank weapon.

"That's odd," said the pirate. He pulled the scope away from his eye, closed that eye, and looked again. *Nope, just the running lights.* He put the scope back to his eye. *But there are a dozen other lights that pop up in the scope. And what the hell's that sound?*

The skipper turned the scope toward the sound

and spotted the helicopters, three of them in formation, rotoring in.

"Turn around!" he shouted to the helmsman. "It's a trap!"

Borsakov called Cruz on the radio. "There's a boat out there, maybe eighty or ninety feet long. It's turning around and running like hell. What do you think it is, Mike? Police? Somebody's navy?"

"We saw it," said Kosciusko from the *Merciful's* bridge. "I even readied a party in case it was pirates. Probably not navy or police or they wouldn't be running. Might have been a case of mistaken identity."

"Might have," Cruz agreed. "No matter, *Merciful*, I'll be on station, ready to land in about forty seconds."

"Ground guides are on station and waiting, Mike," Kosciusko replied. "Your spot is marked as Alpha in IR chemlights."

The helicopter passed above the superstructure and gantry, the turbulence caused by them, even at the current low speeds, causing it to shudder and buck. Cruz saw the letter "A" outlined with, he guessed, about twenty-five or thirty chemlights. Still other lights marked the inside edges of the rows of containers lining both sides, rear, and front of the landing area. He didn't bother counting the lights as he was much too busy lining his helicopter up.

Russian helicopters tended to vibrate a bit more than western ones. Thus, Cruz's feet were encased in reverse stirrups to hold them to the pedals. He moved these up and down, slightly, to control the speed of the tail rotor and thus his orientation with respect to the ship. He pushed the cyclic, the control stick, forward, moving his Hip a few meters in that direction, and then pulled it back to stop motion. Satisfied with that, his left hand played with the pitch control, changing the pitch of the main rotor and bringing the bird down several feet.

A quick glance left and right told him that his was going to clear the containers easily enough. He again lowered himself several feet.

At that point, however, Cruz encountered a somewhat more serious surface effect than he was used to. Naturally, helicopter pilots were used to surface effect; they encountered it every time they landed and took off. Normally, however, the air had free means of escape to all sides. In this case, the containers created an open topped box that allowed less air than usual to escape to the sides, hence forced more of the air than usual upward, largely negating the changes in pitch Cruz made.

The helicopter began to shake alarmingly at the violent updraft. *Ugh! Suckage! They never covered this at Kremenchug.* With a nervous sigh, Cruz eased the collective still further, but gently, gently. This had the unlooked for effect of reducing the updraft, causing the chopper to lurch downward. Cruz's heart jumped into his mouth. *Fuck!*

"Artur," he called over the radio, "this is trickier than we planned. The containers have created a sort of up-facing tunnel. You still disperse air forward and back, but there is more of an updraft. Watch out for that and watch your pitch."

"Roger, Mike," came the answer. "I ran into something

like this in a draw in Afghanistan a long time ago. Be really careful to keep level; any lateral variation can potentially spill all the air out one side and send you crashing into the other."

"Roger," Cruz replied, with a calm he absolutely did not feel. *Double fuck. An inch at a time it will have to be.*

Again Cruz nudged the collective and again the Hip dropped until the updraft cancelled out the reduction in effective power. Again . . . again . . . again . . . again . . .

And then the helicopter was sitting on the flight deck, rocking up and down. Mike breathed a sigh of relief and began the shutdown cycle.

★CHAPTER TWENTY-ONE★

"A nation can survive its fools, and even the ambitious.
But it cannot survive treason from within."
—Patricia de Lille,
South African Politician, quoting Cicero,
with regards to a corrupt arms deal

D-103, Durban, South Africa

They came to the port in fifty-three foot shipping containers; the vehicles within driven up on log ramps to reduce the space taken up inside, and with commercial boxes at each end to cover against the chance of a casual inspection. Additional containers had nothing each but three turrets mounting 90mm guns inside. A further two contained ammunition, one with a mix of anti-tank and anti-personnel, the other with a hefty load of TP, or training practice, and a small amount of high explosive. Not a one of the containers was properly and accurately marked.

Victor, Dov, Viljoen, and Dumi were all present for the loading. Only Victor planned on leaving the ship before its departure. The others, billeted in what would nominally have been crew's quarters and in containers, would stay aboard through the rebuild.

"I'm almost surprised you could move so quickly," said Victor.

"Went downtown," Viljoen replied. "Found a bunch of unemployed black fellahs, offered them a thousand Rand apiece for four day's work. Course, it was more complex than that. Had to get them all uniforms and spend a half a day teaching them to at least *look* semi-military. And Dumi and I did all the driving. Paid the same friend of ours in the Ammunition Corps that provided the ammunition to arrange the transportation."

"There's nothing that isn't for sale here," Dumi added.

"Nothing that isn't for sale with *your* people in charge," Viljoen said, smiling.

Dumisani answered seriously, though his eyes said he was joking, "Well . . . I think yours were actually the better thieves, but mine have to work so much harder to catch up."

Victor shook his head. Bad these people might be. Worse than Russia? *Not a chance.* "And your people?" he asked of Dov.

"They're inside the ship and won't come out until we're in international waters. But they're ready and have all the tools and spares needed for the job."

"Can they do it in the twenty-one sailing days to Guyana?"

"Should be able to," the Israeli answered. "Assuming decent—"

Viljoen saw a girl—well, no, not just a girl, this one was clearly a woman—emerging from the hatchway at the base of the superstructure. She walked over to stand next to Dov, though she seemed to be trying not to stand too close to him. She was olive skinned, tall, slender, and extraordinarily pretty; high cheekboned, delicate chinned, with full lips, and with exceptionally large brown eyes. Her long, wavy hair—brown with traces of red—flooded over her shoulders and down her back. Even though he was gay, he still had to notice: beautiful was still beautiful, whatever one's sexual orientation.

"Lana," Dov acknowledged, before making introductions all around. Rather than Israeli, the woman's accent sounded pure Cape English. "Lana's our senior optics . . . person. She's originally from here; Cape Town, wasn't it, Lana?"

"Cape Town, yes," Lana Mendes answered. "Then Israel, then the Army."

"What did you do in the Army, *Boeremeisie?*" Dumisani asked. The term didn't precisely fit Lana; she was neither a Boer nor a farm girl. But the Zulu had meant it well and so she took it. More importantly, Lana had grown up with a Bantu nanny. The Zulu's voice and accent represented something very close to ultimate security and comfort at a level well below the conscious.

"Tank driving and gunnery instructor," she said

"Oh, *really?*" Bantu and Boer asked, at the same time.

D-102, San Antonio, Texas

Both Cazz and Reilly had remained behind since it was their job to recruit, personally, the largest two contingents, the light armored and amphibious infantry companies. Unsurprisingly, they'd each gone immediately for a first sergeant, starting with the best they had known—both of whom had retired as sergeants major—and then working down from there. Rather, Cazz worked down from there. Reilly's first choice had jumped at the chance. Cazz had to strike off two names from his list before settling on the third. Admittedly, this may have been just as well as a former Sergeant Major of the Marine Corps was perhaps a bit too noticeable a personage for what was still, hopefully, a clandestine mission.

Oddly enough, both non-coms were former Marines, since Reilly's choice, Roger George, had spent four years in the Corps, three of them in Southeast Asia, as an infantryman. He'd then gotten out and discovered that civilian life, after the excitement of combat, left much to be desired. The Marines being full at the time, and the Army recruiting system plagued by idiocy on an heroic level, then Corporal George had been enlisted into *the* Army Band, as a piccolo player. That had lasted about four months before he put in for a transfer to First Ranger Battalion at Hunter Army Airfield, in Savannah.

He knew Reilly from approximately the latter's seventh day in the Army, when then Private Reilly had been herded from Fort Polk's replacement detachment to a training company on Fort Polk's South Fort. George had been Reilly's junior drill sergeant through basic combat training.

In any case, Sergeant Major (Retired) and First Sergeant, pro tem, George and Sergeant Major (Retired) and First Sergeant, pro tem, Webster, got along famously. So had they in Vietnam, as a matter of fact, when they'd been members of Second Platoon, B Company, Fifth Marines.

It was truly a small world, and smaller still within the military.

Reilly and Cazz got along. Reilly and Webster got along. Cazz and George got along. But.

"We haven't had any personnel problems or interpersonal issues because nobody's really been collected and shipped onward yet," said Webster. George nodded knowingly on the other side of the table.

"It's gonna be ugly," Cazz added. "With A Company entirely Army—excepting only you"—he inclined his head toward George—"and B Company entirely Marine, I'd expect all kinds of hate and discontent down in the Alpha Alpha. And then when we board ship? Ugh."

"I'm not so sure," Reilly replied. "Especially about aboard ship, where there'll be all kinds of air and naval types for the Army and Marine infantry to get together in peace, love, and harmony, and hate jointly. And then, too, we're all fucking *old*, gentlemen. Too much past that young and full of come and essentially brain dead status of our misguided and misspent youths. The youngest man in B Company will be thirty-seven; the youngest in A Company thirty-nine. That's getting to be a little old for interservice rivalry. In any case, First Sergeants, pro tem, it's going to be your job to squash any of that shit within your companies."

"Easy to say, boss," said George.

"But maybe hard to do," finished Webster. "Once a misguided child too often means always a misguided child, with the emphasis on 'child.'"

"Yeah, well, that's why both of you are going down

with the first major lift, here to Houston, to Port of Spain, to Georgetown, departing tomorrow morning at 10:24."

"You know," said George, "you really ought to keep Webster here to help with transportation. I can handle the Army and Marines well enough until we hit the two hundred man point."

"No," said Cazz and Reilly together. Reilly added, "The critical mass, so to speak, will assemble there. So there you two will be. Cazz and I can handle trans. Shit; with colonels commanding companies and former divisional sergeants major playing first shirts, it's not as if we aren't the most grossly overled military group outside of the Army of Andorra."

"Andorra?" Cazz asked.

Smiling, Reilly replied, "Just reserve officers, no enlisted men or non-coms. They haven't fought anybody in about seven hundred years. Poor babies, too, what with having to carry their own luggage and all." That last was said with a sneer.

"You still can't tell us the mission?" Webster asked.

Cazz took the question, "Not until Stauer says okay, Top. Sorry. I think he'll tell you in Brazil, and give you a chance to opt out if you don't like it."

"That's something, I suppose."

"Oh, and Top," Reilly said, quite certain that George would never back out, "make sure they all know the song, old hands and newbies, alike, before I get there."

George shook his head but half-sang, *"Von Panzergrenadieren, Panzergrenadieren überrannt."*

"Hey, I wanna know that one," Webster said, perking up.

D-102, Georgetown, Guyana

Terry and his boys, and Konstantin and his, looked thoroughly refreshed when they stepped off the plane from Port of Spain. That only added to the intrinsic dislike Harry Gordon had for Special Forces types. He hid it well, generally, but then Terry—*Must resist saying 'Terry and the Pirates,'* thought Gordo—and crew hadn't been around much, first shunted to Stauer's country place and then off to Myanmar. Why the dislike? If asked, Gordon probably couldn't have articulated it. It had to do, perhaps, with a certain 'more military than thou' attitude he'd found in some SF types over the years.

"Had a good time in Trinidad and Tobago, did you guys?" asked Harry Gordon, sarcastically.

"If sleeping well and eating well and drinking well and fucking bloody damned well constitute a good time," Terry admitted, "then I guess you could say, 'yes,' Gordo. And, after all, it's not as if Stauer wanted us here one minute before now. Or that we didn't *deserve* a little I & I"—intercourse and intoxication, the unofficial name for R & R—"after springing Inning from, as you said, 'durance vile'."

Gordo agreed, with somewhat bad grace, and asked, "Who are your new pals? The Russians I heard about?"

Terry nodded and called out, "Konstantin, come meet Harry Gordon; you and he are going to be working together."

"'Working together?'" Gordon asked as the Russian ambled over.

"Part of Victor's contribution to the war effort," Welch explained. "Konstantin and his men are going to help you with transshipment."

"Some of the equipment is coming in mixed, disassembled, hidden, what have you," Konstantin said. "We know how most of it goes together. After all, we've been doing this with Victor for quite some time now. I think you'll find we are useful."

"Can you and your men drive?" Gordo asked. "Can you drive the way they do here, which is to say like maniacs?"

"Ever been to Moscow, Mr. Gordon? Or should I use your former rank?"

"We're all misters or first names here," Gordon replied, shooting Terry a dirty look for his previous use of Konstantin's rank. "Later on, and further south, we can expect to have a more military social hierarchy."

"Works for me," Konstantin answered.

"Good. Anyway, Terry, you and your boys fly out tonight via one of our Pilatus Porters. The people who didn't go to Myanmar are waiting for you at the camp, down south.

"In the interim, there's a safe house between town and the airport. You'll go there and, I guess, that's where the Russians can stay. At least until I work out something better. The safe house is close to Barama Company, with which we've had some useful dealings. Enjoy."

"Useful dealings?" Welch asked.

"They've given us secure computer time and office space, plus access to their truck fleet. We've told some of the bureaucrats hustling them for bribes that death ends all need for money," Gordo said. *You're not the only type of soldiers that know how to make a credible threat of violence.*

D-101, Helmdon, Northampton, United Kingdom

Sergeant Victor Babcock-Moore, black, and Captain Gary Trim, white, both late of Her Majesty's Royal Engineers ("With the rank and pay of a sapper!") took turns ground-guiding and backing the armored cars into their shipping containers, three to a box. The Ferrets were angular little things; at about two meters by two meters by four, they weren't so very much larger than a normal SUV, and rather smaller than some such. Indeed, they were dwarfed by some SUVs, most notably the Chevy Suburban. On the plus side, a Suburban could fit upwards of nine. A Ferret was cozy for two, with their personal gear and the ammunition.

Armored against small arms fire up to 7.62, the scout cars carried a sting of their own in their small, one-man turrets. That is to say, these used to carry a sting. They would again, too, as soon as they were taken to Brazil and modified back. Even then, though, they'd be carrying Russian PKM machine guns rather than the .30 caliber Browning. Exactly how the different guns were to be mounted was still a matter of some conjecture.

Trim and Babcock-Moore had had one task to accomplish before booking a flight for Georgetown, whence to be flown somewhere further on to take up a position as assistant engineer and section sergeant to a small group being assembled for mission or missions unknown. That job had been to inspect and, if found serviceable, buy and ship onward nine Ferret scout cars, Mark II or higher. In this Babcock-Moore had been of rather greater use than had Trim, since the sergeant had actually *been* a Ferret driver early on in his career.

It had been Babcock who'd known to jack up first one side and then the other of each vehicle, turning the forward wheels by hand to ensure the rear wheels on the same sides turned as well. On one occasion Babcock had pronounced, "Blown bevel box, *sir*. They'll have to replace it before we can take delivery." Babcock had said it, as he pronounced everything, in an accent sufficiently superior to Trim's own that had they not been old comrades and friends the former officer might just have been insulted. Instead, given that the sergeant was an immigrant from Jamaica, Trim found it highly amusing. It had been even more amusing when Trim had been a mere subaltern, but the song—"Why can't the English teach their children how to speak?"—had eventually gotten a bit old.

Likewise it had been Babcock who taught Trim how to start the things properly, a complex procedure for what was supposed to be a very simple machine. Babcock, too, had explained that except for hills and such, it was better to start in second gear, that the gear change pedal was not a clutch—"And for God's sake, *sir*, *don't* use it as one."

The engines had all been Rolls-Royce and dating from before the days when nationalization had ruined the British auto industry. They'd all been fine, or better than fine. Of course, they all used gasoline, rather than diesel, and this could be expected to impose certain logistic issues in the future. Still, the engines *were* Rolls and what was a little complexity in providing two kinds of fuel compared to the advantage of utter reliability? (The same could have been said for .30 caliber Browning machine guns, which Victor was sure he could procure. "The Vietnamese have a shitpot lot of them captured in the war there," he'd said. But while changing out the engines would have been a major job for a minor logistic advantage, using .30s would have been no job at all but at a significant logistic disadvantage. Besides, the Vietnamese record for caring for captured arms since the war was not a particularly good one. "No, we'll fit PKMs," Stauer had insisted.)

None of Babcock's checks had incited any anger in the dealer until he'd done a stall check on the first Ferret. This had involved leaving the handbrake on and starting in third gear, then fourth, with the foot brake depressed and the accelerator floored for five seconds.

"What the fock do ye think ye're doin'?" the dealer had asked, belligerently, though he knew *exactly* what Babcock was doing.

"Ensuring my investments are sound," Sergeant Babcock had answered.

"What do you need so many of these things for?" the proprietor asked.

"Movie props," the black man lied, with a perfectly straight face.

In the end, Babcock's checks and insistences had had three effects. One was to drive the cost of the Ferrets up to roughly the six thousand, five hundred pound point, each, on average. The second had been that all nine were reasonably mechanically sound before delivery was accepted. The third was to delay acceptance by about ten days.

Still, "All's well that ends well, and all that rot." The cars were ready now, loaded in containers, even, and would be leaving this evening for Portsmouth, a roughly two hour drive. From there, they'd be loaded on a freighter within the next two or three days, thence to Georgetown.

Trim and Babcock were to fly out as soon as they'd seen the things loaded. Their friends and families knew nothing but that they'd be gone for quite some time.

★CHAPTER TWENTY-TWO★

They are lost like slaves that sweat,
and in the skies of morning hung
The stair-ways of the tallest gods
when tyranny was young.
—Gilbert Keith Chesterton, *Lepanto*

D-100, Suakin, Sudan

Adam could *feel* the armed guards on the other side of the curtain that hung in the coral-framed door. He couldn't see them, generally, nor even hear their bare feet most of the time. They almost never talked when on duty. But the fact of their presence, *that* he could feel even when no other indicator said so.

The room outside of which the guards kept watch was a cubicle of about three meters on a side. Once, when Suakin was still a busy port, it had had plastered walls. The plaster had long since fallen off, except for a few stubborn little traces here and there. It was also an interior cubicle, windowless. What light there was came from bare bulb, run by a generator Adam could hear whining in the distance. Warmth, when needed, came from a light blanket and the slave girl, Makeda. She and he lay under the blanket, on a foam rubber pad with a sheet. A few times a week the girl took the sheet out and washed it by hand, early in the morning.

Adam couldn't be sure how long it had been since his capture. *At least fifty-seven days that I've counted.* But he'd spent enough time sedated or—since arrival here—genuinely ill, that it might easily have been seventy-five or even eighty. Labaan, in any case, refused to tell him, and Makeda didn't know.

"It would just upset you, and for no good end," his captor insisted. "Trust me that you will not be going home any time soon. And if you ever are released, what you return to will not be what you think of as home." *Not after my chief finishes squeezing.* "So try to be happy—as much as you can—in the life you have here, or wherever else you may be brought." The enemy tribesman had seemed to Adam to be almost regretful as he'd said the words.

Adam had to admit that, within certain limits, they'd tried to treat him decently. He credited Labaan for that. Certainly some of the latter's underlings would have been happy enough feeding Adam to the sharks that came in close to the round island's edge on every quadrant. He was well fed, even gaining a little weight back after his descent into some kind of the twitching awfuls a couple of weeks ago. They took him out for exercise twice a day, always being careful to point out a shark's fin, could one be seen. He followed along, in awkward short steps, imagining trying to outswim the fins while manacled.

While the sharks only came to most of the island's edge sometimes, in the east, where the opposite shore was closest, they were always there, their fins clustered thick enough to walk from one to the other. Adam could see land on the other side of the water, a bare thirty meters away. Almost, he felt he could jump such a short span. He knew he couldn't, of course, and with the manacles about his ankles even the less so. The sharks, in any event, were thick at that point of the compass. Perhaps they were fed there by the two guards that likewise seemed always on station there.

The chain they used on his ankles to keep him from running or swimming chafed. *And it would ooze red blood if I were to try to swim through the sharks.*

A doctor checked in on him every few days, the better to ensure his physical well being. The exclusive use they'd given him of Makeda went a long way to seeing to his other needs, physical and otherwise.

Purchased by Labaan's brother, Bahdoon, Makeda was an Ethiopian captured in a slave raid when she was a young child. The girl was about fifteen years old now, as near as she could guess, and virginity was but a distant memory. So, too, distant was the memory of her childhood religion, Christianity. Adam found it both moving and pitiful the way Makeda tried to hang on to barely remembered scraps of her faith. In looks she was much like Maryam, tall and slender, more fine featured than the African norm, and with the high forehead typical of Ethiopians, Eritreans, and some of Adam's own people.

For all her tender years, Makeda was deft in bed in a way Maryam had probably never even dreamed of being.

Whether she took any genuine enjoyment of the act Adam had to doubt. The fine scars across her buttocks suggested she was performing only, like any trained animal. And somehow the passion of her throat never seemed to reach her eyes.

Outside of bed, however, and in the day, she was rather a different person, bright and charming and even funny. Nor was she so timid as to prevent her from laying into the guards fastening Adam's chains about him. "Look at the boy! See the raw red meat you've made of his ankles! How do you think your chief will feel if he gets an infection and *dies*?"

Not that they'd listened to her, at least not until she'd enlisted the doctor's support. After that, while the chains hadn't been loosened much, they'd permitted her to wrap the ankles in soft, clean cloth beforehand. It helped, some. It also increased the amount of free chain by perhaps all of an inch. Adam still had no hope of running or swimming with it on.

And no hope of getting out of this room except with it on. And, since they only give me plastic utensils, no chance of tunneling through these coral blocks.

He'd tried that, of course. His little white plastic spoons had made no impression on the coral whatsoever. Not that the coral blocks, which were basically limestone, were all that hard. They were just harder than cheap plastic spoons and fingernails.

He rolled over and spooned himself to Makeda's warm back, one arm going over her and his hand seeking out a breast to cup. She wriggled backwards against him. *Awake or asleep?* he wondered.

"I'm awake," the girl answered the unasked question. She might not have much cared for the act of bedding, however carefully trained she'd been to do it well. But she much preferred being the property of one to being in the common pool. If Adam wanted her, he could have her.

"You get out on your own, Makeda," Adam whispered. "Do boats ever come to the island?"

"The only one I've seen is the supply boat that comes from the south," she whispered back. "There are fishing boats, but they tie up along the rim of the bay, or sometimes at the causeway that connects the island with the mainland. The ones that tie up on the causeway do so past the guards. Are you planning an escape?" she asked, a tinge of hope creeping into her voice. "Take me with you; free me, and I'll do anything in my power to help."

"I would take you with me," he answered back. "As far as I'm concerned, you *are* free and the men holding you here do so illegally."

"I *am* free, you say," she whispered back. "And if I told you I didn't want you to fuck me anymore?"

Adam shrugged. "Then I wouldn't."

"Really?"

"Yes, really. You are your own person, to choose for yourself. If I've hurt you or angered you so far, I am sorry."

Makeda twisted her head half way around. "And you'll take me with you, if we can escape."

"Yes, of course."

She twisted around inside his enveloping arm. Her own went around him, the left one pushing its way between body and foam mattress. "In that case, pick a hole, any hole."

★ ★ ★

Labaan walked softly, on bare calloused feet, across the smoothly polished blocks that made up the floor. The guards at Adam's door were smiling when they saw him. One lifted a finger to his lips, indicating Labaan should be quiet. The finger then pointed at the portal, through the blanket covering of which emanated sounds of youthful passion. Labaan, likewise, smiled.

Poor children, he thought, *go on and make the best you can of the bad situation fate has dealt you. I was certain*, he congratulated himself, *that I picked the right slavegirl for you, Adam. If you two can find love together, perhaps that will make the fact of your status more tolerable to you both. And don't forget, boy, if you impregnate her and she becomes 'the mother of a child,' that will be a big step up in her status right there. Almost free, in fact. For whatever 'freedom' might mean to a woman in our world.*

Like justice, it doesn't exist except for whatever we can carve out for ourselves and our own.

Makeda was on top, rocking rhythmically as Adam's hands clasped her small breasts almost—but not quite—painfully hard. Without interrupting the motion, she used her own hands to guide the boy's thumbs and fingers to her nipples. "Pinch them," she gasped. "Hard. I like it."

It would be incorrect to say that the girl had never taken any pleasure in sex before. But, if she had, it had always been tempered by the knowledge that she was legally not much more than an animal; that, and the feeling of being worthless dirt that always came afterwards.

This, though? *He said I* was *free!* she thought as she changed her pattern of movement from rocking her hips to spiraling them. *He said I had a* choice! *That must be why this feels as it never has before.*

She reverted from spiraling back to rocking, at the same time lowering her torso down almost to rest on Adam's. He was mindless now, thrusting upwards hard, bouncing her toward the ceiling. His fingers, too, of their own accord, pinched her nipples fiercely enough to cause pain, though even that, mixed with the sensations coming from between her legs, was pleasurable.

She began to moan, then, a mindless animal sound. Her rocking ceased, changing to a reverse thrusting to meet Adam's own. She began to see little specks of light dancing before her eyes. Her moan changed to a long scream, then to a coral-shaking shriek, and finally to a loud, repetitive, "guh . . . guh . . . . guh . . ." which grew softer as she collapsed onto him, shuddering and quaking.

One guard, his rifle placed against the wall, had both hands cupped over his mouth and nose, trying to stifle a laugh. The other, Delmar, was of sterner stuff. He suppressed his own laughter by a sheer act of will. He did say to Labaan, face all smiles, "I grow to like that boy more and more as time passes."

"I know," Labaan agreed. "He's a good boy. Pity he's not one of us."

"Then it would be somebody else's son we'd have taken, since without an heir Khalid couldn't have been chief. And that son or heir would probably be no different from this one. No, Labaan, it's just the world in which we live. We didn't make it. We don't even have to approve of it. We just have to do the best we can in it, for our own."

I hate being owned, Makeda thought, as she lay, still awake, and staring at the ceiling. *It's why I've always faked pleasure, and never let myself feel any of it I could avoid feeling. At least then, inside myself, I had control over myself, I owned that one small part of me.*

So why let myself go this one time? Maybe I'm a foolish girl, but when Adam said he would free me if he could, and that it was my choice if we were to continue to bed . . . well . . . I suppose I believed him. No, I know I believe him. *He's a good boy, a decent boy, a kind boy.*

And he's also my only chance.

★ CHAPTER TWENTY-THREE ★

Like myself, they have mixed the worship of
the God of love and the God of battles.
But unlike myself, they have adequate symbols
of this double devotion. The little cross on the
shoulder is the symbol of their Christian faith.
The uniform itself is the symbol of their devotion
to the God of battles. It is the uniform and not
the cross which impresses me and others.
—Reinhold Niebuhr,
Leaves from the Notebook of a Tamed Cynic

**D-99, Airfield, Assembly Area Alpha—Base Camp,
Amazonia, Brazil**

Recruiting had been done in a rough pyramid, so to
speak, with Stauer calling in a score of his own friends,
for commanders and staff, and these each bringing in
anything from a few to half a dozen to a couple of score,
and these bringing in one or two or three or four each. A
certain number, too, had been recruited by ransacking the

databases of such corporations as Triple Canopy and MPRI, once Lox hacked into those.

Picking the chaplain Stauer had taken on as a personal job. Most chaplains he thought worthless, but there had been a couple . . .

The flight hadn't been that long, really, from Georgetown to an unknown and unnamed strip in Brazil's Amazon, just a few hours of mile after mile of green jungle and brown water.

On the other hand, flying in a tightly cramped aircraft with an unknown pilot, surrounded by nine big, burly and surly bastards that Chaplain (retired) James Wilson just *knew* had to be special operations types, was, at best, awkward and uncomfortable. There just wasn't a lot in common between green beanie and clerical collar, despite both having served in the same Army. They were almost all taller than his modest five feet, eight inches. They were all, even the ones he pegged as senior non-coms, much younger than his fifty-eight years. He had more hair than a couple of them, but his was steel gray while the eldest of theirs was at worst salt and pepper. They all looked like trained killers while he . . . *Well . . . I look like a man of the cloth. Even without the collar I would.*

Point of fact, really, they're a different army, Wilson thought. *We just got paid, mostly, from the same accounts and wore, mostly, the same uniforms and answered, mostly, to the same legal system. Mostly.*

And I suppose they're really not that surly, he thought, *just really, really tired looking and, if smell is anything to go on,* badly *hungover.*

In any case, neither chaplain nor team paid much attention to each other, beyond Welch having introduced himself as they boarded the plane. Of small talk, once aboard, though, there'd been none.

So Wilson spent the flight looking out the small window at the trees passing below. *Not that they're all* that *far below*, he mused. *I wonder why the pilots are . . .*

The thought was interrupted as the plane took a sudden, violent dip downward, causing Wilson's stomach to lurch upward. He barely contained his bile. The special operations types, most of whom had been dozing, awakened with sudden startled cries. Wilson gulped even while thinking, *Nice to know they're human after all.*

Stauer heard the Porter's engine, even muffled through the trees. He caught the briefest glimpse of it. And then the thing was diving for the deck, or—in this case—the freshly laid PSP.

The pilot pulled out, barely in time, Stauer thought. In what seemed mere moments he had touched down on the PSP, bouncing a few times before settling in to a rather nice landing roll. He reversed engines shortly thereafter, slowing quickly to a stop maybe sixty percent of the way down the field.

Nagy was right, Stauer thought. *Cruz was being overly careful. But, then again, this was the* best *pilot Cruz came up with for the Porters. Maybe the others will need a bit more space. And, maybe too, we might have to fly a load or two out of here.*

Harry Gordon, Gordo, had arranged for half a dozen little all-terrain vehicles with dump truck platforms on back to be sent to the camp via the leased civilian riverine landing craft. The things were six-wheeled—though the wheels were covered with rubber treads—and amphibious. Each had a ton and a quarter winch. They drove pretty much like an M-113 armored personnel carrier, having two control sticks to steer and stop. Best of all, they were completely non-suspicious.

Of course, at twenty-six thousand dollars and change, each, they hadn't come cheap.

The ATVs had been there mostly for Nagy's sake, initially, but since he no longer really needed them they'd been parceled out among the other organizations, with two of them reserved to the air operations company. Those two were waiting when the Porter came to a stop. There wouldn't be room for the men, of course. They could walk. *But there's no sense in making them carry all their shit while they do*, Stauer thought. *Not in this heat, anyway*.

As the plane's hatch opened, Stauer adjusted the pull throttle, pressed the starter button, readjusted the throttle and took off to meet his incoming crew, grass and dirt spinning up behind him, until he reached the PSP of the airstrip. The things were a ball to drive, despite the pounding of the junctures where PSP section joined section. The propeller was changing from a blur to a visible set of blades as he stopped the ATV near the hatch.

Terry was first off, tossing an informal-to-the-point-of-ragged salute Stauerward. Stauer frowned until Terry made it more formal. "One or the other, Terry, would be fine," Stauer said. "*Salute or not*, as the spirit moves you. But making a sloppy, half-assed, ridiculous attempt at the thing is just stupid."

Terry nodded and said, "Sorry, boss. Won't happen again."

"All right," Stauer agreed with good grace. "And well done on springing Victor. You and your boys are part of Headquarters"—Stauer pointed down a rutted trail in the direction of the river—"so you billet in main camp. Sergeant Island's been expecting you. You can feed before you rack out. The sergeant major will be by to brief you and your men on camp routine and layout tomorrow morning, 0600. You're on your own 'til then."

Welch nodded wearily, then turned back to the plane from which all of his men had now debarked. "Buckwheat," he passed on to his senior sergeant, "The vehicles can lead off. Mess in the camp, then rack out. Sergeant Major visits us in the morning, 0600."

"Roger, sir," Fulton said. He turned to the rest and ordered, "Column of twos . . . ForWARD . . . March."

"Sergeant Fulton has another mission, too, Terry," Stauer said as the others marched away.

"Recon of the objective?"

"Yes; that and pick up our local attachments. Him and Wahab. Leave in about two weeks. Buckwheat's the only one we've got with both the training and the color to blend in."

"I'm not sure color matters, boss," Terry said. "That place gets overrun with western journalists and other progressive sorts on a regular basis."

"It still matters," Stauer replied.

"Taciturn bunch," Jim Wilson said to Stauer as he watched the backs of Welch's team march away.

"Not so very," Stauer replied. "They just don't know you. Hop in."

Wilson shrugged and tossed his small carry-on into the truck bed in back. Sure, it was still dirty but what's a little dirt among friends. *It's true enough*, he thought, *that I'm a stranger. Even so, I am a man of the cloth. Could they be militant atheists? Never met one in the Army, that I know of, but you never know.* He swung a leg over, grimacing at the *click-click-click* that he felt in one arthritic knee, and climbed over the side of the little tracked amphib, settling down in the cramped passenger seat.

Stauer once again started the ATV, then used the control sticks to head generally around the base camp and its outliers. As he drove, he talked, speaking loudly over the sound of the engine.

"I'm surprised you came," he said to Wilson.

"You called; I came," the chaplain replied. "Even got a portable organ on the plane."

"It's never that simple, Jim. There was an implicit question in there: Why?"

Stauer may never have shown his fangs to Phillie in the time they'd been together. Anyone who had known him before knew also that he wasn't to be balked or stymied. And for God's sake, one should never lie to him.

"I lost my congregation," Wilson admitted. "About six months ago. Little to-do about literal interpretations of the Bible versus more . . . *enlightened* views. Anyway, I got the boot. I was getting desperate when you called, to tell you the truth. Wife and mortgage to support. Two kids in college."

Those were reasons Stauer could accept without

much reflection. He nodded, then pulled both sticks back and locked them, stopping the ATV. Pointing at a collection of olive drab tents under camouflage screens, he said, "That's the main camp. You'll be billeted there. I had sergeant major give you your own tent, about the size of a GP small. Will it do?"

"Sure, Wes. Whatever's available."

"Good enough." Stauer clasped the hand releases and let them go, easing the left stick forward while keeping the right one pulled back. The ATV turned right, then, as he guided it along the dirt path down towards the southern camp, the one that would house B Company (Marine). He pointed this out, too. "Not sure if we should have separate services yet," Stauer said. "Have to see how ex-Army infantry gets along with "former" Marines."

Again Stauer turned the ATV, heading north this time, towards the other outlying camp. "You remember the speech?" he asked.

Wilson sighed. "'Your job, Chaplain,'" he quoted, "'has nothing to do with spreading the word of God. You are not here to comfort the afflicted. Your function is not the saving of souls. You, like me, like the doctors, the lawyers, the everything else, have one true mission: You are here to serve the ends of military effectiveness and efficiency. What you do toward those ends is good. Anything else you can shitcan.' Did I get it right, Wes?"

Stauer laughed aloud. "Pretty good," he admitted, "considering it's been what? Twenty years?"

"Well," Wilson grimaced. "It wasn't like I didn't hear it once a week until I got it through my skull."

"Very true," Stauer whispered. "Very true." More

loudly he said, "I called you, as opposed to someone else, Jim, because out of dozens and scores of chaplains I knew in the Army, you were one of maybe three who could understand that speech, one of a very few I thought was worth a shit.

"Join me in my quarters this evening for a drink, why don't you?" Stauer asked. "Be a good chance for you to get to meet the staff and the chain of command. Some of them you'll already know."

"Like Reilly back in San Antonio?"

"Well, him you already knew, of course. He'll be down later on. What did you think of him?"

"Hasn't changed a bit," Wilson replied, without further comment. Again, Stauer laughed.

"Hey, what's that sound," the chaplain asked.

Stauer listened for a moment, then breathed a sigh of relief. He answered, "With any luck that sound is three LCM-6s that unloaded at Manaus a couple of days ago and are *just* making it up the river to us now."

D-98, San Antonio, Texas

Phillie had never seen the expression "ROFLMAO"— rolling on the floor laughing my ass off—given life in quite the way Seamus Reilly managed. Reilly was, literally, rolling on the floor, occasionally rolling over onto his belly to beat the rug with his fists. And all she'd asked was, "Why can't you be a little kinder, a little more considerate, like Wes is?"

Even Cazz, normally a fairly cold fish, had to smile at

the question. Sure, Stauer had been a different service, but they'd worked together enough to know that neither kindness nor consideration were words that really quite fit. To Reilly, who knew the man very well, the idea was uproarious, even preposterous.

Eventually, after a long and humiliating time of being laughed at by the adjutant pro-tem for the expedition, Phillie sniffed and then walked off in a huff. Once Reilly saw her ass swaying through the door that led to the bedroom, his laughter abruptly cut off. He sat up and brushed himself off, saying, "Kind and considerate," as if they were curses. He did curse, then, as he saw that he'd spilled his drink when the woman's silly comment had hit him. "Kind and considerate."

Cazz shrugged. "She's only seen the dead-inside side of him, bro. She'll see the rest soon enough. And did you have to lay into her quite so hard over chalk seventeen having their shots delayed? She's a girl, you know."

"I noticed," Reilly agreed. "And yes, I did, and yes, I did. That little show was for her benefit, mostly. So when she does see Wes in full fury, or icy exterior, she won't freak over it."

"Man can chew some ass, can't he?" the Marine agreed.

"Sure as shit can when he wants to. Now about chalk seventeen . . . "

"There's a company, Passport Health, that arranges these sorts of things. At least that's the one I know about. I think we can use them, since Phillie ran short *temporarily*."

"Yeah, go ahead and set it up. But she shouldn't have run out. Bad planning. Inexcusable."

"Maybe," Cazz conceded. "Oh, and just FYI, the first sergeants departed Georgetown a few hours ago for base. They should be touching down about now."

D-98, Assembly Area Alpha—Base Camp, Amazonia, Brazil

George and Webster never saw the landing lights on the airfield. They wouldn't have seen them, in any case, because they were all infrared, visible to the pilots in their goggles but not to the casual observer. Even if they'd not been infrared, however, the strip was so narrow that they wouldn't have seen them, anyway, until landing.

"What's this Joshua like, George?" Webster had asked on the flight down.

"Hard ass," George had answered. "Very strong on what he considers the highly limited role of a sergeant major. We never really got along. The man was the senior sergeant major in the old Twenty-fourth Infantry Division and just flat refused to be division sergeant major or even a brigade sergeant major. He thought his effectiveness, any sergeant major's effectiveness, ended once he let himself be pulled above battalion level, or pushed into any kind of battalion than the kind he grew up in. He and Reilly have a mutual admiration society going back better than twenty years.

"Which makes perfect sense," George added, "since Reilly is bughouse nuts. Love the bastard like a brother, mind you, but that doesn't change that he's insane. He was insane as a private and age and experience"—George sighed—"have not mellowed him."

★ ★ ★

"I would not have picked you, George," Sergeant Major Joshua said, in a Caribbean accent gone nasty, as he drove the two first sergeants to their company areas. "That Reilly likes you is the only black mark I hold against what is otherwise one of the finest commanders I've ever known."

"Everyone has some major failings, Sergeant Major," George answered. *I, for example, am having a hard time getting over the fact that while you stopped at being a battalion command sergeant major, I was sergeant major for a brigade and I should probably have your job now.*

★CHAPTER TWENTY-FOUR★

The cruel-tyrant-sergeants . . .
—Kipling, *The 'Eathen*

D-91, International Airport, San Antonio, Texas

By dint of sheer hard work, Cazz, Reilly, and Phillie Potter had gotten the hundreds of men ready and moved from scores of different locations around the United States to Georgetown, Guyana. (And by dint of much harder and hotter work in Georgetown, Harry Gordon and his assistant—with a considerable assist from the aviation company—had gotten them all moved onward to Base Alpha.) Now it was time to close shop and move on. Cazz was heading straight to Brazil, as was Phillie, the latter having a container of inoculations on dry ice in her baggage, for anyone who was missed. Reilly had one more stop to make, to an old Titan missile base not so very far from Spokane, Washington. He'd promised Gordo that he'd see to getting the assembled light aircraft containerized and moved to port. Gordon basically didn't trust aviators to get anything right except the actual assembly and flying. And he, rightly, considered Reilly to be almost as good a loggie as he was, himself.

Reilly wasn't quite so skeptical about the Air Force but, since he did speak Spanish, since all the aircraft assemblers were Mexican, since it was a potential failure point for the mission, he'd agreed to go. Besides, he wanted to get to know some of the pilots who would be provided recon, close air support—sorta, kinda, maybe—and medevac. And those were all up in Spokane, at a long since abandoned, sold, re-sold, and re-re-sold Titan missile base, helping the Mexicans.

They could have flown the CH-801s out of the former airbase, now Grant County International Airport, to the port. Or they could have built them at widely divergent places. But the former—having eight "homebuilt" aircraft with a hell of a lot of Fieseler *Storch* in their ancestry, all leaving from the same place, then landing on the same place, then being partially broken down and packaged to sail on the same ship—might have attracted a little too much of the attention they'd built the things underground to avoid. And building them dispersed would probably have meant quality control problems, to say nothing of the not inconsiderable cost of redundant tools. Of those two factors, only the former had really counted as the cost of the old Titan complex dwarfed the cost of eight sets of tools.

And the other thing, thought Reilly as he sat with Cazz and Phillie waiting for their flight to board, *is that, although Wes never said a word about it, I'd be really surprised if he's going to be willing to let the group we've*

*assembled just disintegrate once this mission's done. No . . .
he's too desperate never to be a civilian again for him to let
that happen lightly. Building the thing in Washington
state, with the title being in Wes' name, gives us an asset
we can use later on.*

*Then, too, he was a lot more intimate with the special
operations community than I ever was. I looked up 'Grant
County International Airport' and the unusual thing is that
nobody flies out of it. Staging area for Special Operations
Command for the Pacific region? It's possible, anyway.*

*I could see that, could see our little group getting a
contract to provide long term support to a staging base.
Might even be kind of fun.*

Unlike most, Reilly hadn't come mostly out of boredom or mostly to find some adventure. Oh, he let on that
he had, because that was what everyone else let on. In
fact, his reasons were much stronger. *God, I was so lonely,
all these years. Nobody I cared about and nobody who
gave a shit about me, either. And if Stauer can keep us
together, I'll never be alone again. Not that I'm ever going
to let anyone see that, of course.*

The loudspeaker nearby boomed, "Continental Flight
One Seventy-eight for Houston-Hobby, now boarding."

Reilly immediately stood, made the most cursory of
nods, and said, "Cazz, Miss Potter, see you at base." With
that he turned and pretty much marched down a dozen or
so waiting areas, before taking his seat to wait for his own
flight to Spokane.

"I'm not sorry to see *him* go off on his own," Phillie
said, once the plane had settled into smooth flight.

"Reilly? A lot of people feel that way," Cazz said. His voice didn't sound as if he was one of them. Phillie said as much.

"He's pretty harsh," Cazz said. "But if it helps any he's at least as hard on himself as he is on everyone else. He's Athenian, so to speak."

Phillie looked confused. "Athenian? I thought he was Irish."

"Oh, he is. And if you don't believe it pour a few drinks into him." Cazz almost giggled, a most unMarine-like thing to do, and added, "He does a pretty good rendition of Rising of the Moon, as a matter of fact. Along with any of about another thousand Irish rebel songs . . . and a fair smattering of American Civil War, Russian, German— heavy on the German, Italian . . ."

"He *sings*?"

"Pretty well, actually, but generally only when he's drunk." *That, or in training, or in action. When he's happy, in other words.*

"Yes, well, 'Athenian,' I believe you said."

"Oh . . . he was born into the world 'to take no rest himself, nor to give any to others.' That's why he's so harsh. He just can't understand for a moment that someone might slack off, take a break, miss something important. Worst workaholic I've ever known."

"If you're telling me he's inhuman, I already knew *that*," Phillie said.

Cazz frowned. "He's human enough." He then laughed. "I'll admit, though, that he's pretty far out on the spectrum of 'human.'"

"Well, I think he's obnoxious."

Cazz looked over at Phillie's face, then couldn't keep from a quick glance at her chest. He looked away and started to laugh.

"What's so funny?"

"Well . . . if you weren't Wes' girl, Reilly would have been very charming—he can *be* very charming, you know, when he has a reason to be—in the hope and not unreasonable expectation of getting you into bed. Since you *are* Wes' girl, hence untouchable, in perpetuity, he treats you like everyone else. Which is to say, like shit."

Phillie looked shocked and a little insulted. "Bu . . . bu . . . but he has a wedding ring on."

Cazz lifted an eyebrow at her. "Such *innocence*. What would *that* have to do with anything?"

Phillie, having a few secrets here and there in her past, didn't comment further.

"Frankly, he never talks about his wife. He might be divorced and bearing a torch, or he might be a widower. Dunno. Never thought it was my business to ask."

D-90, Grant County International Airport (ex—Larson AFB), Moses Lake, Washington

The senior of the CH-801 pilots, John McCaverty, met Reilly outside the main entrance to the old missile complex. This was no surprise; it certainly wouldn't have done to have one of the Mexicans standing guard. All *kinds* of issues with that.

McCaverty put out his hand as Reilly emerged from

the rental car. "Just call me 'Cree,'" he said. "All my friends do."

"Cree, it is," Reilly said, shaking the pilot's hand. They'd never met before. Cree was a bit taller than Reilly, intelligent looking, and fit. They were about of an age, though Cree's hairline had receded a bit more than had Reilly's. "What did you fly in the Air Force?" Reilly asked.

"I didn't fly for the Air Force," Cree answered. "For them, I was a surgeon."

Reilly looked confused for a moment. "Then why—?"

"Never been in action, air or ground. If you don't count dustoffs. Want to be."

Well that *I can understand*, Reilly thought. "Fair enough. Your planes ready to go?"

"Ready, containerized, awaiting the trucks," Cree replied. "But there is a little issue."

"Issue? What issue."

"I want to take seventeen of the Mexicans with me, two per plane plus a chief." Cree looked defensive. He explained, "They're the best workers. Couple of 'em speak fair English, too. Otherwise, we'd never have gotten the things assembled in time. We can't hope to keep these things in the air without these guys."

"Have you asked Stauer or Cruz? Have you explained what the job involves to the Mexicans?" Reilly was being seriously disingenuous here. He'd prepared the manning table and already *knew* the Mexicans, some of them, were supposed to come along. Why this Cree hadn't gotten the word he didn't know. He saw no pressing need to rectify the error. Maybe Cruz was testing this man. *So I'll play ignorant.*

"I dropped a message to Cruz's e-mail, but he hasn't given me an answer," the pilot-surgeon said. "And I don't know Stauer so I don't know what I can get away with. The ones I want to keep think we're going to smuggle drugs and have no problem with that, so I kind of doubt they'll have a problem with what we're *really* going to do. Whatever that is.

"I did have to promise their headman, Luis Acosta, that I'd personally sneak every one of them back into the United States if they had to leave here. He says it's expensive getting into the States."

"Well," said Reilly, "I know Stauer. Stauer knows me. He'd be surprised, maybe dangerously so, if I didn't do *something*, at least, that fell into the category of 'easier to obtain forgiveness' for. Show me the packaged planes and then let me talk to your Mexicans."

"You speak Spanish?"

"Moderately well."

"How will you get them down there?" McCaverty asked. "Assuming you agree, of course."

Reilly thought about that for all of five seconds. "Ordinarily I'd go to one of the services that deal with passenger service on merchant vessels. That won't work in this case, since we want them to go with the planes they built. So . . . I suppose I'll have a chat with the ship's captain. Your Mexicans may be crammed in like rats, but some merchant ships have some open cabins for passage. Or we can simply put everyone in a couple of containers, and ship food with them. The captain most likely wouldn't object to a little under the table cash." He thought some more. "You've got a good relationship with these guys? They'll follow your orders?"

"Yes."

"Then—assuming I can make the arrangements—you will be going with them on the ship while the rest of your pilots fly south to Guyana with me. It will probably suck."

"Fuck," McCaverty scowled.

"Possibly that, too. Your pilots up to this, Cree?"

McCaverty hesitated for a moment. "We've all Army fixed wing and Air Force or Marine light plane pilots, except for me and one other guy. I'm least concerned about him, Smith, because he's our only honest to God carrier pilot. It's going to take some work and some practice getting the rest of us used to landing on a ship."

D-89, Assembly Area Alpha—Base Camp, Amazonia, Brazil

Well, thought Phillie Potter, laying on her back on a narrow cot, lonely and, as near as she could see, forsaken, *I expected to be staring at a tent roof but not all* alone. *Bastard.*

Stauer had met her and Cazz, along with eight other late arrivals, at the airstrip. The tall, skinny black, the one she knew of as Sergeant Major Joshua, had been with him as had another, shorter and stouter black man. The shorter of the two and Cazz had wandered off conversing heatedly on some issue she had not a clue to. Joshua had taken the other eight in hand, marching them off into the jungle gloom. The sergeant major had given Stauer a very odd, almost pitying look over one shoulder as he'd departed.

Stauer had held one hand up to keep her from throwing herself into his arms, pointing at an odd vehicle with the other hand. "Jump in," he'd said.

Wes Stauer wasn't the subtle type, nor the hesitant sort who beats around the bush. "There's no romance between us until the mission is over," he'd said. "Unfair to the troops, if I'm the only one getting his tail wet."

"But what about *me*?" she'd asked. "I've got my needs, too, you know."

"So?" Stauer's voice had really sounded as if he hadn't understood the issue, or even that there was or could have been an issue. "You have a job. Fulfilling that is the only need you have for the next several months."

Bastard, she thought again, moving her hands up behind her head while continuing her upward stare. *Now I understand why you like that asshole, Reilly. You're just the same.*

Phillie's moping was cut short, suddenly and unexpectedly, by a subdued and highly artificial cough coming from the opposite end of the tent. The question, "Nurse Potter?" followed the cough. She sat up and faced the man asking.

"I'm Phillie Potter," she announced to a man she could have sworn she'd seen in a movie. "And you are?"

"Doctor Scott Joseph," the man said. Phillie was sure she'd seen him in a movie, but clearly not as the leading man. "You'll be working for me. Come on, I'll show you around sick bay."

She turned away and lay back down on her narrow cot, resuming her hands-behind-head stare at the canvas above. "Not interested," she said.

"I see," Joseph said, very calmly. Then he shouted out, "SERGEANT COFFEE!"

"Sir?!" answered an eager voice from someone Phillie hadn't seen.

"Nurse Potter seems to be having a morale problem. See to it, would you."

"Sir. . . ."

Phillie never heard the footsteps. All she knew was that one side of her cot suddenly lifted up and she found herself flying through the air before impacting on the muddy ground. And then a mean looking white dude, not so much large as amazingly broad shouldered and solid, was standing above her, hands on his hips and a scowl on his face. "The doctor gave you an order, Nurse Potter. Get on your feet and follow him to the aid station."

Phillie was too frightened even to cry. She never figured out how she managed to get to her feet so quickly. But cry she didn't and stand she did.

"HURRY, Nurse Potter!"

Behind her scurrying posterior, Sergeant Coffee smiled his broadest and happiest smile. *She'll work out*, he thought. *Nice ass, too.*

★CHAPTER TWENTY-FIVE★

They rise in green robes roaring from
the green hells of the sea Where fallen skies and
evil hues and eyeless creatures be;
—Gilbert Keith Chesterton, *Lepanto*

D-88, Gulf of Mexico, Patrol Boat *The Drunken Bastard*

The sun was but a distant memory. Conversely, the rain
and spray were a miserable present reality, coming in
horizontally and driven at better than a hundred miles
an hour sometimes, between boat speed and wind. The
boat was on a water roller coaster, with some of even its
hard-bitten, sea-legged crew vomiting occasionally.
Simmons, who never got seasick, and Eeyore, who was able
somewhat to control it, huddled behind the windscreen,
Simmons' hands gripping the wheel firmly. Biggus Dickus
Thornton, a line running from his waist to a stanchion, was
further aft, looking forward generally, while inspecting the
deck for a minor leak that was making life in the engine
room a misery.

Worse, the liberated slave girls below were doing their best to fill the crew dayroom with vomit, to the extent that Morales and Mary-Sue couldn't keep up with emptying the buckets over the side . . . when they and the girls managed to hurl into the buckets, that is.

The girls all wept and prayed and screamed, in between bouts of vomiting. Though they didn't exactly share a language, but only a language family, Morales didn't have a doubt that they were invoking the aid of the Almighty. That, or perhaps praying for death.

Above, straining to make himself heard over the roar of wind and sea and engine, Antoniewicz said to Simmons, "I fucking told you we should have put in at Havana, you asshole."

"Chief says we push on, we push on," the latter answered calmly, if loudly, likewise to be heard over the roar of the gale. Indeed, he answered amazingly calmly considering the boat was riding through waves almost as tall as it was long. "The last place he wants us or we ought to want to be is Cuba. That's enemy territory, still. Besides, Eeyore, we've made it fine so far. What makes you think it'll get any worse?"

Antoniewicz's face, already a pale green, suddenly assumed a truly ghastly look. "That," he said, pointing astern.

Simmons looked over the stern and saw looming what was absolutely the biggest wave he'd ever seen. His hand automatically reached for the throttle and pushed hard. "Oh, fuck; rogue wave . . . CHIIIEEEFFF!"

Waves at sea, like radio waves and other electro-magnetic waves, operate at a frequency. Moreover, different waves, even in near proximity, will operate at different frequencies from other waves. Occasionally, a series of waves, all normally at different frequencies, will meet. At that point, there can be created an enormous wave, holding within it the mass, and rising to about the height of all the waves operating at the different frequencies that comprise it, together. This is called a "rogue wave," and, once formed, it can swamp a ship, break its back, or roll it over before so much as a "Mayday" can be sent out.

Biggus Dickus Thornton never heard Simmons' call. The waves and the gale were too much for that. He did, however, feel the stern rising rapidly in a way that he hadn't felt the *Bastard* quite move before. He looked astern on his own and saw the suddenly rising mass of foul looking white spray and foam and vertical greenish sea. He didn't have a throttle to push automatically. Instead, he reverted to his childhood, making the sign of the cross—head-abdomen-left shoulder-right—and saying, "For what we are about to receive, O Lord . . ."

And then he felt himself thrown from his feet and sliding to the stern, past where a forty millimeter Bofors had once been mounted, his ass skimming along the wet deck. He never quite finished his prayer. In English. Rather, he compressed it into a long, "Aiaiaiaiaiai!"

Eeyore had a little more warning than Thornton had had. Oh, he still lost his footing and began to slide sternward. But he was able to grip the rope that ran about his waist and stay, approximately, within the confines of the bridge. On the other hand, it hurt like the devil when he smacked his head off of the raised housing, just aft.

"Holyfuckingbastardmotherfuckingcocksuckingsono-fabitchasshole!" This would have upset Mary Poppins deeply, and for more reasons than one.

Still, the stern of the ship continued to rise. Now Antoniewicz slid forward, slamming into Simmons' feet and causing that sailor to fall backwards, losing his grip on throttle and wheel. Rather than try to outdo Mary Poppins' fourteen syllable neologism, Simmons contented himself with a wild, inarticulate "Gaaa!"

Mary-Sue and Morales found themselves against the forward bulkhead, in a tangle of lifejackets and decidedly post-pubescent and nicely female arms and legs and heads and breasts. Had the tangle not taken place in a rising tide of puke, and had the lifejackets not covered all too much of the breast mass, and had the screaming not reached concussive levels of volume and power, they might have enjoyed it. Morales didn't think it was even possible for the volume of the shrieking to go any higher.

But then the *Bastard* began shooting upwards, as near to straight vertical—though subjectively toward the stern—as one might imagine. Morales discovered that, *no, there is no theoretical top limit to the amount of sound that can come from massed female lungs.*

Not being a churlish sort, he elected to join them. "AYAAAHHH!"

Thornton found himself sliding away from the stern and back towards the raised engine housing. By pushing down with one hand, he was able to quarter turn himself so that he impacted sideways, rather than head first. It still hurt, but not as badly as a head blow would have. From somewhere inside the boat, he heard a massed scream.

The combination of boat pointing almost straight down, rising waves, wind and sea, and shooting up like a rocket had totally overridden Biggus Dickus' inner ear. He had no idea whatsoever which way was up, which down. Then, from under the stern, he heard the high pitched whining of triple propellers, spinning out of water. The boat made a last spurt upwards, hung in the air for a long moment, then slammed back down into water. It started to level out, then tilt toward the stern.

This particular rogue wave was composed of four others, in descending order of size and also speed that could have been called, "A," "B," "C," and "D." Having joined at precisely the wrong place and time, from the point of view of the *Bastard*'s crew, these began to separate out again almost as soon as the waves made their final effort to launch the patrol boat into low orbit. A continued on, dropping substantially in height and power, as the rest dropped behind.

The *Bastard* slammed into B-C-D from above. The girls screamed. B then moved ahead, leaving C and D in its wake. The *Bastard*—no water underneath to support the hull—slammed into the remainder. The girls, and Morales, screamed. C then continued on, letting the *Bastard* slip down into the trough formed behind it.

Wave D then slammed into the *Bastard*, hitting at an odd and bad angle. It spun the boat, nearly capsizing it. D smacked Antoniewicz and the chief around like a pimp with a couple of his more recalcitrant and lazy whores. As the boat turned approximately seventy degrees from the vertical, everybody, including the chief and Mary-Sue, screamed.

D-86, 111 Miles North-northeast of *Nombre de Dios*, Panama, MV *Merciful*

Where are they?" Kosciusko fumed. "Where the fuck *are* they?"

Ed had binoculars grasped in both hands, pressed to his eyes, scanning from about ten o'clock to two. His exec, similarly accoutered, did the same from two to six. Chin, as perhaps the most nautically experienced man aboard, likewise searched from six to ten. It was Chin who spotted the boat.

"When did your navy start putting young girls at the helms of small boats?" he asked. Chin concentrated a bit on what he could see of chest of the girl at the wheel. "Well, maybe not all that young."

Kosciusko swung his glasses around to see. "Ugh," he uttered. Not only was there a girl at the wheel, one he'd never seen before, the charthouse itself was about half gone, as were what he'd have expected to see of antennae, the radio mast, the life raft, the lights, the . . .

"What the hell hit them?" Chin and the Exec both shrugged. *Dunno*.

Worse, maybe, than what was missing, the boat that should have danced across the water like a ballerina across the stage limped along, on one engine, at best. And that one seemed to be putting out a lot of smoke. The boat was also riding very low in the water.

They used the gantry to haul *The Drunken Bastard* aboard the *Merciful*, a series of straps passing underneath the boat. Chin's people had gone down to the patrol boat to outfit the straps before returning to the mother ship.

They'd have let the crew come aboard first, for safety's sake, except that not a one of the males had more than three completely functional limbs, except Eeyore, and he was too badly concussed for reliable balance. And none of the girls would leave the men.

The boat lifted out of the water without any sound but that made by the gantry's electric motor. Even the girls were all screamed out. The gantry operator, Mrs. Liu, an itty bitty Chinese woman who smoked *bad* cigars, and was picking up vernacular from the crew at an amazing rate, kept the boat's long axis parallel to the ship's as it rose along the side of the hull. Water poured from its hull. She kept it parallel still as she allowed the water to finish draining, then hoisted it above the gunwales and over the cradle designed and built for it. Once there, she reversed lift, letting the thing settle gently down.

As soon as it touched, Chin's crew were all over it, strapping it down and tightening the screws that moved rubber padded blocks of wood in around the mahogany hull. A ladder was produced from somewhere, and more Chinese boarded up it. After that, one by one the *Bastard*'s crew was helped off, Morales on a stretcher, with several worried looking girls following.

Biggus Dickus Thornton was last off, on his own feet but helped by one of the Chinese as his arm was in a sling. He also had his head inexpertly wrapped. Once on the deck—actually on the roof of one of the containers—of the *Merciful*, Thornton sat down heavily. Kosciusko walked across the container top and squatted down. Chin's people were already erecting the container tops and frame that would hide the boat from casual observation.

"What happened, Chief?" the captain asked.

"Biggest fucking wave you ever saw, sir. Came out of nowhere. I *still* don't know how we survived it. It just came, nearly swamping us, and then—POOF!—it was gone and we were falling. That's all I know. That, and that Simmons and Morales managed to get the girls to pilot the ship to this rendezvous. And the engines are fucked. I *think* we did a complete three-sixty roll, but I'm not sure. We'd have been fucked, too," he added, "except that there was a Spetznaz issue medical kit aboard and one of the girls could read Russian. Most of the medical stores we used up."

"They'll do that, I'm told," Ed answered. "Rogue waves, I mean." *I really don't want to think about the Romanian girls right now.* "Hey look, I have a doctor aboard but she speaks only limited English and has no equipment at all beyond her little doctor's bag. And even that's nineteen-fifties technology. Can you and your men wait until we get to Guyana or, better, to Brazil?"

Thornton's face was gray, ashen. He nodded wearily, and seemed almost confused. "I think so. Nothing wrong with us really but some broken bones and a couple of concussions. We oughta be able to wait a few days . . ."

Cruz and Borsakov, standing behind Kosciusko,

looked at Thornton, at Morales being carried off, and at a very broken and bedraggled looking Simmons and Antoniewicz. They then looked at each other and shook their heads. "We don't think so," Cruz said. He looked at the *Bastard* and added, "This heap shouldn't be in the water again until it's refitted. But Art and I can take one of the Hips and fly these guys to Panama City. There are some good hospitals there, English-speaking, even, and I doubt Stauer will balk about paying for the best care. They can fly to Georgetown later. It's maybe . . . three hours round trip to Panama City and back."

Ed thought about it, weighing the options, the issues, and the problems. *A Russian chopper in Panama has got to be an unusual event. Flying off a ship that isn't supposed to have any is even more likely to raise eyebrows. But we need these guys on their feet by D-30. If they're worse hurt than I hope, they might not be ready. They might never be ready. It's a risk to send them to shore but . . .*

"It's a risk worth taking," Kosciusko said. "Break out a chopper. Land . . . where? Right at the airport?"

"Probably less noticeable than anywhere else," Cruz offered.

"Right. Okay then, land right at the airport. Rent a car. Take them to hospital that way. If it looks like any of them can be released quickly, like within a few hours, wait for them and bring them back. We'll keep it down to ten knots, here."

"Wilco, skipper," Cruz agreed. He was actually senior to Kosciusko, in retired rank, but the latter was skipper of a ship, the former was a Marine, and the captain of a ship is its monarch.

★CHAPTER TWENTY-SIX★

> We become what we do.
> —May-lin Soong Chiang

D-85, Assembly Area Alpha—Base Camp, Amazonia, Brazil

The broad dirt path from A Company's camp, generally to the north, to the airfield passed around the outskirts of Central Camp. Phillie was busy inventorying medicines and equipment lest Sergeant Coffee become more unhappy with her, a fate devoutly to be feared. She stopped what she was doing for a moment when she heard the singing coming through the open portal of one of the aid station tents.

> . . . d Nächte stand nie der Motor,
> Wir stürmten und schlugen
> Und kämpften uns vor,
> Mit den Panzerkameraden treu vereint,
> Immer die Ersten am Feind.

That was odd enough to bring Phillie out of the tent. *German? Sounds like German.* Sure as shit, there was the armored company, in the same battle dress she now wore, marching in four groups, forty files of three and change, the big red-headed guy she knew as George marching by the left flank, all of them singing some bloody awful foreign—*gotta be German*—song. The men in the ranks looked to average somewhere in their early to mid forties, but there were some considerably older ones among them. Sergeant Major Joshua, marching at the head of the column, had to be over sixty, she thought.

Over the singing, George somehow managed to make himself heard. "Column Riiighghght . . . .MARCH!" After another step, the point of the long column turned right, heads erect and arms swinging.

> *Panzergrenadiere,*
> *Vorwärts, zum Siege voran!*
> *Panzergrenadiere,*
> *Vorwärts, wir greifen an!*

Phillie stopped what she was doing and pulled on her camouflage jacket, the same kind as the troops wore though she filled hers out rather differently. *I don't want Sergeant Coffee pissed at me anymore*, she fretted, as she took the time to button the thing. She clamped the broad brimmed hat on her head. Then it was out the tent door, trailing the marching company. She saw a couple of others following. She assumed it was out of curiosity.

She froze when she heard Coffee's voice, "I thought you were doing an inventory, Nurse Potter."

"I was but . . . "

"Never mind. This will be useful education for you, too."

Phillie breathed a mental sigh of relief. "Now come on," Coffee said, "hurry up and we can fall in on the last platoon."

He ran; she followed. She found it hard to keep in step until Coffee said, "Listen to the stressed beats. That's when your left foot hits the ground." Then he joined the singing.

> *. . . Wird jeder Feind gestellt,*
> *Bis die letzte Festung fällt,*
> *Und im Sturm drauf und dran überrannt.*

"How do you know the song?" Phillie asked from the side.

"No talking in ranks," he admonished her. "But I used to be his platoon sergeant for a while."

"Whose platoon sergeant?" she asked, ignoring the admonishment.

"Reilly's, the fucking maniac."

> *Von Panzergrenadieren,*
> *Panzergrenadieren überrannt.*
> *Von Panzergrenadieren,*
> *Panzergrenadieren überrannt!*

Ahead, the dirt path through the jungle opened up to the airstrip's clearing. The volume of the singing, if anything, redoubled. One of the airplanes Phillie had learned was called a "Pilatus Porter" was turning around, midway down the strip. George called out, "Column Leeeffft . . . MARCH!"

Overhead, the Pilatus made a single circling bank of the airstrip, at a range of about a dozen kilometers out. Inside the plane, Reilly barely noticed the turn, and had no real eye for the jungle below. His heart was too full of joy for that.

It's hard when you're a kid, he mused, *and too bright to have any friends. Hard when even the adults treat you like some odd little specimen, neither one thing nor the other. And then you grow some and you find a job you love and, for a change,* real friends, *people you care about and who care about you. And then you find, best of all life's pleasures and joys, a woman that you love and loves you back.*

And then God takes the woman, and fate takes the job, and you're alone, all, all alone. And you stay that way, for years, *alone and miserable.*

And then someone gives you a second chance.

Reilly cast his eyes upward. *God, if this thing works out, please kill me before letting me be lonely again. Please.*

And then the plane was bouncing down the rough runway, and Reilly knew, just knew, that his solitary existence was at an end.

Phillie had to do a double take. The man she remembered as looking vaguely clerklike, suited or in ragged blue jeans, depending, wearing glasses, with a slightly receding hairline and a bit stooped, could not possibly be the same man as the one exiting the aircraft in a single nimble leap to the ground.

But, she thought, *if the words he spoke then—
"Patience, my ass, I'm gonna kill something!"—didn't
quite fit the man who spoke them then, they sure as hell
do now. Why, he looks so young, so rejuvenated, he
wouldn't even look interesting, if he* weren't *an asshole.
Which he is.*

George, who had marched around the column to take
a position in front of it, called out, "Sergeant James, get
the CO's baggage." A tall, skinny sort, Phillie thought he
might have been in his mid forties, rushed over to the
plane, saluted Reilly before throwing his arms around
him, and then let go and reached up to grasp a greenish
flight bag that someone inside threw to him.

Reilly marched, rather than walked, to a position a few
meters in front of George. The latter then saluted and
reported, "Sir, Company A, for armored, regimental
lineage to be determined, all present or accounted for."

Reilly returned the salute sharply, Phillie thought,
even stylishly, and with a subtle confidence that said he
felt entitled to it; that, and that he was pleased as could be
to be able to return it.

"Post!" he ordered. George then faced left and
marched off to one side. Four others, who had been
standing behind, did the same with four more who had
been standing in front. Reilly waited for the movement to
finish, then ordered, "Fall out and fall in on me," while
raising his hands to beckon the flanking platoons inward.

"Gentlemen," he said, once six score and change
faces—some grave, others smiling broadly like himself—
were gathered about, "gentlemen, we're going to have

great fun together."

The best word to describe Reilly's feelings was "home," and the best phrase, "where the heart is."

There was a low and comforting hum of a generator, dug in against excessive noise, sounding from somewhere nearer the river. The tent flaps were raised and tied, letting in a cooling, if damp, breeze. On one wall was a hand-drawn chart that said:

Organizational Manning Chart, Company A

Co—Reilly
XO-FitzMarcach
1st Sgt.—George

1st Plt	2nd Plt	3rd Plt	Mortars	Headquarters
Plt L dr—Green	Plt L dr—Hilfer	Plt L dr—Epolito	Sect L dr—Peters	Conno—Levine
PSG—Abdan	PSG—Moore	PSG—Fletcher	Asst SL—Just	Supply—Dearborne
1st A/C—Conners	1st Sqd—Yee	1st Sqd—Stout	FDC—Olson	Training—Duke
2nd A/C—Con	2nd Sqd—Casky	2nd Sqd—Pilhorn	Gun 1—Velasques	CO's Driver—James
Scout—Snyder	3rd Sqd—Keyes	3rd Sqd—Cubbage	Gun 2—Biby	Medics(Attached)—Coffee
AT—Harvey			FO HQ 2—Mongo	Engineer(A)—TBD
			FO 2—Delluzio	Maint(A)—TBD
			FO 3—White	Translator(A)—TBD

Reilly glanced over the chart, temporarily ignoring his exec. About two fifths of the names were of old comrades, and most of the rest he either knew more distantly or had good reports on.

"Cross out Fletcher and put in Schetrompf, Top," he said, turning away from the chart. "Welch put in a bid to keep Fletcher for his team and, given that Pete became available, I didn't bitch about it."

"Pete opted in?" George asked.

"Yeah, finally. I knew he couldn't stay away. He'll be along in the next few days."

"Scott, you're up," Reilly said to his exec.

"Besides the *song*," Reilly's XO, Scott FitzMarcach, said, shaking his head in pseudo-disapproval at the time spent on that, "we've gotten all the organizational clothing and individual equipment issued. We've got small arms and machine guns and night vision gear issued and the troops familiarized on them. Those Russki burst firers are pretty nice, by the way, but mechanical training took up two whole days and a night. Unlike most Russian weapons, they are not simple, either to use or to care for."

Fitz was standing, briefing from a clipboard. The unoccupied folding chair behind him was part of a semi-circle holding the platoon leaders, all but one of whom were noncommissioned, platoon sergeants, and some section leaders, and the company's small staff, including the first sergeant. The sergeant major, an always-invited guest, stood in back, just listening, as did Sergeant Coffee who would be leading a medical team in support of A Company during the operation. Oddly enough, after George and Joshua, the next oldest man present was Duke, who hadn't joined the Army until the day before he turned thirty-five, and stayed to retirement. He hadn't even needed to, either; Duke was independently wealthy.

"My Russian 120mm mortars are simple enough," said the mortar section sergeant, John R. Peters. He was a big boy, a tobacco dipper and cigar smoker, who'd been out of the Army for almost ten years. Still, some things one never forgets. He didn't forget, now, to refresh his dip, either, fingers pinching out a bit of the worm dirt and packing it between lip and gum. "And we've gotten the gunnery drill down pat." He shrugged. "Gun's a gun, basically. Problem is, I don't have any live ammunition— "

"And we won't have until we get on the ship," Reilly said. "Sorry, but that's the way it is. More or less innocent shit comes up the river from Manaus. War material comes in by air. And those couple of Pilatus Porters we're using just aren't up to carrying enough 120mm ammunition to be useful, even if we could get away with firing it. Not if we're going to eat, anyway."

Peters shrugged broad shoulders. "I know. And that part of it doesn't worry me too much. Like I said, a mortar's a mortar and a shell's a shell. And we've been able to program the TI-84s we've got for the Russki ballistics. But, what does worry me, training-wise, are the forward observers. Their job isn't just muscle memory. And I don't have any shells, or any sub-caliber ammunition, to retrain them on adjusting fire. It's a problem, boss. And Stauer's forbidden me to use smoke grenades, which we do have, to simulate 'rounds' while we have people run around the jungle using GPS to mark impact points. Not that anyone would see the smoke rising above the jungle canopy from ground level, mind you, but that was all I could think of."

"Try this," Reilly advised. "This afternoon, and tomorrow, too, if it takes that long, build a whopping big terrain board. Find a fairly open spot in the jungle for it. Draw up a map—Top, does headquarters have at least one copier?"

"Yessir," George said.

"Fine. Take the map you drew and make some copies for the FOs. Then build a bunker on a hill overlooking, with a restricted vision port, so the FOs can't see anything that isn't to scale; have a trench lead into the bunker so they lose their orientation to the lifesize while crawling up it. Can we get some plastic sheeting to string around the perimeter to hide the trees? Good.

"You can toss grenade simulators to mark rounds. As they get too used to using one observation post, you can be building others. From four different directions, one chunk of ground is four chunks of ground."

"How big you think?" Peters asked. "What scale?"

"How big a space can you find?"

"There's an area maybe two klicks from here," Peters answered, "maybe one hundred and twenty by one hundred and fifty meters. An old Indian slash and burn area. Only a couple of trees inside it and the engineers can take those down for us."

"One to twenty-five scale, then, ought to do."

"Wilco, boss." One thing you could count on with Reilly was that when you hit a brick wall, training problem-wise, he would come up with a workable solution. *Fast*. It was bizarre, really; the man didn't even have to think about things like that; solutions just *came*.

"Physical and medical issues?" Reilly asked, looking directly at his first sergeant.

"Nobody in too bad a shape made it through to this point," George replied. "But we've got maybe a ton, ton and a half of lard to work off before we'll really be ready. Everybody, and that includes the present company, has anything from fifteen to thirty pounds excess baggage."

"God knows, I do," Reilly agreed. Again, he didn't even hesitate to add, "Twice weekly jungle marches, starting tomorrow, full kit and equipment."

Peters looked dubious. "The mortars we got sent are 2S12s, boss. Nice guns but *heavy*. Man, are they heavy.

Maybe four hundred and fifty pounds or so. No way me and my thirteen guys can carry those on a real march. They couldn't when they were twenty, and sure as shit not now."

Reilly looked up at Sergeant Coffee, smiling wickedly. "Can we come up with half a dozen stretchers?" he asked.

"Yes, sir," Coffee replied.

"Good." Reilly looked back at Peters, then around the semi-circle at the rest. "Everyone is going to take a turn helping carry the mortars . . . on stretchers." He looked directly at the gunned armored car platoon sergeant and platoon leader, sitting side by side. "Yes, that includes you."

Neither Green, the platoon leader, nor Abdan, the sergeant, had any problem with that. However, "Maybe we can get away with simulating for the mortars, sir," said Abdan. "But our tankers—okay, *okay*—our gunned armored car crews, absolutely must have some practice with the real thing. Our old M-1s and Bradleys were the definition of sophisticated, gunnery-wise. These things are going to be almost the definition of primitive. And the antitank section will never have fired the Russki antitank guided missiles we're getting. And I gather they're not a whole lot like TOWs or Javelins."

"I know," Reilly agreed. "We're going to handle that a few ways. I checked with Gordo before flying down here. There is a package of South African 90mm training practice ammunition—the same ballistics but no high explosive in the shells, lighter projo, reduced propellant charge—coming, enough for fifty or sixty rounds per gunner. We can use that here without attracting too much notice. Then, once we're aboard ship and out and away from normal sea lanes, we'll toss some sealed containers over the side and shoot the shit out of them with live shell. Same thing with the Russian ATGMs; we'll do practice firing from the ship. Work for you?"

"Works for me," Green agreed. Abdan nodded and said, "Sub-optimal, but it'll do."

"It'll have to," Reilly said. "Speaking of the gun systems, have you figured out how to get the turrets onto the cars once both arrive?"

Abdan replied, "Nagy, the chief engineer, built four tripods out of trees over by the maintenance area, sir. He connected those with logs and added a winch to each. Not a problem getting the turrets on, or pulling a pack when we need to. Note that I said 'when,' not if.'"

"All right, good. And, yeah, 'when.' And now," Reilly said looking directly at George, "talk to me about personnel issues."

"Gun platoon's full up, sir, to include the scout and antitank sections," George answered. "Thirty men. With all the Bradleys and tanks there were plenty of turret experienced folks to choose from and long experience of turret drill, in this case, was key. Levine's signal crew is short one but he says he can manage as long as he doesn't have to lay wire in a hurry. Supply's okay. The infantry platoons are short one man, in the case of second platoon, and two in third. Mortars have a problem." George looked in turn to Peters.

"I need twenty," Peters said, his tongue working at the Copenhagen stuck behind his lip. "Twenty to run the 120s, anyway. In theory, anyway. See, originally when we were going to use the light mortars in the armored cars, I could have made do with two three-man crews, three Forward Observers—who can hump their own radios, and myself and three others for the Fire Direction Center who would also drive two more armored cars loaded with ammo.

"Now I need ten to crew two guns, plus the three in the FDC, plus three FOs, and still four men to haul and sling the much, much heavier ammunition. I've got fourteen, including myself."

"And with the line platoons short," George said, "and the scouts and guns needing everybody they have, and headquarters short one, I've got nobody to plug into mortars."

"How's B Company situated?" Reilly asked.

"I talked to their section chief," Peters replied. "Same problems, only worse. They were also supposed to get 60mm tubes and ended up with three 120s."

"Got a solution?" Reilly asked Peters.

The mortarman shook his head. He put a bottle under his lower lip and spat out some tobacco juice. "Not one I can do anything with. If the company, on the other hand, can give me a little more time to get ready between attacks, we can support. More or less. The range on the guns is good, over seven klicks, so if, say, you drop us off five or six klicks out, and move slowly yourself, we can probably be ready to fire by the time you hit. Usually."

"Have to do," Reilly said. Even so, he thought, *The cooks aren't going to have shit to do once we land. And they're perfectly capable of slinging ammunition. I'll have a talk with Stauer, the sergeant major, and Island about it.*

Standing in the back, Sergeant Major Joshua was thinking, *I wonder how long before Reilly suggests using the cooks to supplement the mortars?*

★CHAPTER TWENTY-SEVEN★

I have never smuggled anything in my life.
Why, then, do I feel an uneasy sense of guilt on
approaching a customs barrier?"
—John Steinbeck

D-84, MV *Merciful*, Georgetown, Guyana

The port didn't even have cranes sufficient for the three
containers holding nine Ferret scout cars. This wasn't a
problem, however, as the ship transporting them did have
an integral crane and the *Merciful* had the gantry to move
them around once they were aboard her. The transfer
took place in the river, west of the port facilities, such as
they were. The Georgetown authorities didn't much care
as long as the deputy chief of customs, a subsidiary to the
Guyana Revenue Authority, got a small donative for his
retirement fund for his subverting of Section 204 of the
Guyanan Customs Act. Since he'd been getting a fair
number of such donatives, of late, from Gordo, his retirement fund had grown handsomely over the last several

weeks. At least in theory. For the nonce, it was all locked up in escrow.

In any case, thought the deputy, standing on bridge of the *Merciful,* watching the containers sway at the ends of their cables as the transfer took place, *what takes place in the river and doesn't set foot on land isn't really my concern. On the other hand, the . . . packages that are due in two days, and twelve,* are *coming ashore. I think I'll need a little more than usual to look the other way for those, if not so much as I demanded for the crates full or arms and ammunition. "Sporting equipment," indeed!*

Though dark, the deputy customs inspector was of indeterminate genetic background. Probably, as were many, he was a mix of English or Irish or Scottish, or all three, with African, Dutch, East Indian, local Indian, and perhaps a spot of Chinese. He wore a uniform almost devoid of insignia but with large sweat stains radiating from under his armpits. He had a badge, and a nametag that read "Drake," an unsurprising name, given the locale.

Trim, Babcock, and Gordo all watched the transfer along with Drake, while Kosciusko sat his captain's chair nearby. The ship's exec, who was in fact a former chief petty officer rather than a commissioned one, supervised more closely.

The Guyanan spoke English, or a near enough dialect of it that the others couldn't talk too freely. Gordo did feel comfortable saying to the Englishmen that they'd be going ashore with his assistant and the inspector, while he conducted some business with the captain of the vessel. Nobody mentioned any further movement for anyone from that point, though both Trim and Babcock understood they would be moving on from Georgetown. They didn't know precisely where they were going, of course, and wouldn't until they were in the air.

The gantry, a container full of Ferrets swinging in the air beneath its extendable arm, whined as the entire mechanism railed towards the stern, then whined some more as the Chinese woman at the controls, that swearing, cigar chewing, Mrs. Liu who had already proved herself deft with the thing, slung the load a bit to port, a bit to starboard, then port again. It whined again, a long drawn out screech, as she lowered the container downward to where a few more men stood just out of the way to correct the container's orientation by hand.

"And that's that," Kosciusko said, leaning his head back against the rest surmounting his chair, as the container holding the last three Ferrets clunked home. "Now we just wait a few days for the next shipment"—Victor's turrets— "to get here."

"You going to allow your men shore leave, Ed?" Gordo asked, once Trim, Babcock, and the Guyanan customs man had departed.

"Is there anything worth doing here?"

Harry Gordon shook his head. "Not really. Booze there is, but you're not running a dry ship. Sex is pretty easy to come by," he added. "And the beaches aren't bad. Usually."

Kosciusko thought upon that for a moment. "Can you arrange to send a dozen or two whores out?"

"I could," Gordo said. "But that's inherently suspicious when you could just go ashore. Plus you've got those nice

Chinese women aboard. Why inflict the whoring on them?"

"Point. All right then; shore leave it is. Speaking of suspicious, that customs agent, is he reliable?"

"Inherently? I wouldn't think so," Gordon answered, "not even remotely. Why should he be? But he *is* loyal to the escrow account we set up and that won't be released until we are long gone and the mission complete."

In fact, Drake was intensely loyal to the escrow account still controlled by Harry Gordon, enough so that—while he might be willing to gouge some, to pad it a bit more—he had no intention whatsoever of screwing up the nice little arrangement he had going. Still, more information could lead to higher donatives. He spoke, mostly to Babcock, in the local Creole that was very similar to the speech of the black sergeant's birth, particularly in its rhythms.

"Yah bais, yah unnastan wah meh ah seh?"

"I understand you, old man," Victor Babcock-Moore answered. "I don't speak it very well anymore, but I understand it."

"Where yah gwhan fum here?"

That was close enough for Trim to catch it. He did, and at the same time caught Vic's eye. Quite unnecessarily, he gave his sergeant the look, *Tell him nothing.*

Vic gave a look back, *How can I tell what I don't know?* To Drake he said, "Oh, we're going to the Pegasus for now, catch up on sleep. Then we're thinking of doing some fishing and maybe a little camping. We'll be leaving in a few days. Maybe as long as a week."

"Where yah learn speak so guh?"

"Public school," Babcock-Moore answered.

"Nuh public school hay teach lahk dah."

"Neither do most of those back home," said Vic resignedly.

Drake nodded. He wasn't stupid and had a suspicion that education was failing around the world even if he wasn't sure quite why. Then again, theoretically better minds with higher class backgrounds and more education than his couldn't agree on why Johnny couldn't read. He looked over the black man and had a sudden, not entirely unpleasant, thought.

"Mah daughter, she speak lahk dah. Mosly. Teach herself. Try kuurect meh ass ever day. Yah bais come dinner tonight?"

The sergeant looked hopefully at his captain. Trim had apparently understood. He signaled agreement with a couple of curt nods. Vic answered, "We'd be pleased to, sir."

"Meh pick yah up de hotel. Faive."

Trim would have been late to the lobby without his sergeant to provide— "Sir, I haven't had cooking like home since I left bloody Jamaica and if you don't move your aristocratic ass"—motivation. It didn't matter much; Drake was half an hour late anyway. This bothered Vic rather more than it did Trim, who didn't expect much from the Third World, to include Her Majesty's former possessions, anyway.

Somewhat surprisingly, at least to Trim, Drake had changed out of his sweat-stained customs uniform and looked really quite presentable in loafers, lightweight slacks, and an embroidered, short-sleeve shirt. He was still driving his government-issue car.

The drive was long and Trim quickly found himself getting used to Drake's patois, enough so that it sounded merely different, about as different as northern Scouse-flavored English, perhaps, or perhaps a bit more so, rather than utterly foreign.

Past the low built city of Georgetown, the car broke into mostly open farmland. Guyana didn't have a lot going for it and many of the people practiced subsistence agriculture.

Still, "What's that?" Babcock-Moore asked, pointing at a gate blocking a road leading into a swamp. The gate had a sign on it: "CGX."

Drake sneered. "Oh, dah de government. Dey sells hunert seventy-five t'ousand acres for four hunert dollars each to an oil company. Never use. Back for sale, Ah t'ink."

Trim did some quick and rough mental calculations, U.S. dollars to pounds, sterling. "That's bloody cheap, Sergeant, even for swamp, roughly two hundred pounds an acre."

"Nah," corrected Drake who, again, wasn't stupid. "Yah don' unnastand. Dat's Guyanan dollars. Maybe four-hunert to de pound."

"Two U.S. dollars an *acre*?" Vic exclaimed. "A *pound*?"

"Bout dat," Drake agreed. "What you expect?" he asked with a shrug. "Like man say: 'Country got no secure border have to sell for what it can.' For us, dat about two U.S. dollar an acre." Drake pointed generally to the west.

"See, Venezuela just over dat border and dem folks, dey got *plans*."

Trim immediately raised an eyebrow. "What the hell are you thinking, sir?" Vic asked.

"Oh, just musing. I wonder if there isn't someone, somewhere, who could provide a secure border."

"Ah."

"Yah dreamin'," said Drake. "Nobody cares enough about us for dat."

Which, Vic reflected, *is probably all too true.*

Babcock-Moore thought Drake's daughter, Elizabeth, was dream enough. She showed her father's mixed heritage, with a touch more African from her mother, long deceased.

Still, thought Trim, *she's pretty enough for any taste. My sergeant could do worse. And,* he mentally added, after spearing a bit of mutton from the stew, *she's not a bad cook. And best of all, when her father pries . . .*

"Father," the girl had said, "these are our guests. Cease, at once."

Which absolutely endeared her to Victor.

D-83, en route to Assembly Area Alpha—Base Camp, Amazonia, Brazil

"Well didn't you at least get the girl's *number*, Sergeant?" Trim asked, over the roar of the Porter's single engine.

The two Brits were the only passengers on this flight. Still, the compartment was crowded. At this point, with the personnel mostly transferred and too much food required to buy it all in Manaus without raising suspicions, Air Gordo was having to fly in a ton and a quarter of comestibles daily. Thus Trim and Babcock found themselves sitting, approximately, upon several sides of beef, a good-sized crate of canned vegetables, and who knew what else.

"She's obviously not that kind of girl, sir," Babcock-Moore replied.

"How do you know if you didn't ask for her number?"

"A gentleman just knows, sir."

Trim looked very intently at his sergeant. "You're actually *taken* with her, aren't you?"

Vic sighed. "She seems very nice," he admitted, and wouldn't say more on the subject.

The two stiffened as they felt the plane shudder slightly and veer left.

"Base camp coming up on the left," the pilot announced over one shoulder.

D-83, Base Camp, Amazonia, Brazil

The drone of an airplane filtered through the thick jungle cover above. Beneath it, one hundred and twenty-nine men, including some of the attachments and minus a couple on duty or sick call, marched on rather less than twice that number of good knees. Reilly, personally, was marching on two bad ones.

I'd forgotten, he mentally groaned, *just how god-damned painful this is. And I never really considered how*

*much worse it would be at my age now. Fuck me to tears.
I thought I had all the character building anyone could
ever need.*

Behind him, in two long lines snaking through the
trees, with leaders spaced out between them, marched
Alpha Company. Sergeant Major Joshua took up the rear,
just behind the stretcher-borne mortars, with First Sergeant
George beside him. On one shoulder the sergeant major
carried a machine gun that he'd borrowed for the occasion
from the armory. He just liked the heft of the thing.

The heavy guns had been rotated among the platoons
several times by now and were now back with the mortar
section. The men lugging them groaned—and not just
mentally—with the effort. Nor were they the only ones
with some cause for complaint.

"Quit bitching, George," Joshua said, *sotto voce*.

"I wasn't bitching, Sergeant Major," George replied. "I
was *observing* that we are all pretty much getting too old
for this shit. My knees are *killing* me. And it's hot."

"Stop quibbling, George. And stop bitching."

"Doesn't that asshole *officer* know it's hot?" complained
one of the larger former tankers, Adkinson by name. He was
tall enough that there'd been some question as to whether
he'd fit inside the turrets of the armored cars. The man
made an effort to look intelligent, though there was some
question about that, too. "And besides, what the hell
purpose is there in us marching? We fight from vehicles.
Typical, dumb as shit officer! If he'd ever been enlisted he'd
have more sense."

Adkinson marched at the tail end of the armored gun

platoon. Just behind him a small infantryman named Schiebel carefully stepped on the tanker's heel, causing him to twist his ankle and fall to the jungle floor.

"Sorry, Adkinson," Schiebel said. He didn't sound very sorry. As he stepped over Adkinson's prostrate form, he added, "And just FYI, the CO was enlisted for four years."

★CHAPTER TWENTY-EIGHT★

Eros mocks Mars.
—Brian Mitchell, *Weak Link*

D-82, Camp Stephenson,
Cheddi Jagan International Airport, Guyana

Gordo poured sweat as from a fountain. It didn't do anything too very good for his disposition, either.

It was sweltering in the hangar housing two of the five
Guyanan Short Skyvans and one large container holding
three partially disassembled armored car turrets on cradles. For various reasons, looming large among them the
fact that Gordo thought the chief pilot, Samuel Perreira,
to be a pure weasel, he had brought along Major
Konstantin and two of his sergeants, Musin and Litvinov,
for a little added muscle. True, the Russians (and Tatar)
were unarmed. They gave the impression of men who
didn't need to be armed to execute murder and mayhem.

Because he was fat, and often looked altogether too
jolly, people sometimes underestimated Harry Gordon's

innate ruthlessness. They likewise tended to overestimate his need to be liked.

"Yes, Major," Gordo said to Perreira, in a very unjolly tone, "we are both 'officers and gentlemen.' Notwithstanding that, you get not a penny from the escrow account until these three items are safely landed at the location I've given you."

"But how do I know—"

"How do you know you'll be paid?" Gordo interrupted. "Because the money is safely in escrow and I can't get it back for myself, even if I try. I can only keep you from getting at it, and that I would have no interest in doing unless you piss me off. Which you will, unless my . . . machinery is loaded on your planes and moved to where I want it before daybreak."

"But . . . "

Gordo turned around, huffily. "Konstantin, get the container back on the flatbed. We're taking it back to the ship."

"I didn't say I wouldn't fly it!" the pilot shouted. "I'm just concerned about payment."

"You will be paid. If being an 'officer and gentlemen' actually matters to you, then you would understand that."

"But you don't understand," the Guyanan said, putting his hands up, placatingly. "Okay, I can accept that I'll be paid, eventually. So can my copilot. But my men"—his hands spread out to take in the waiting ground crew—"are also taking risks and 'officer and gentleman' means less than nothing to them."

Gordo thought about that for a moment. Yes, he did understand the problem. So, "How much to get them—and them alone—working?"

"Seven hundred U.S. dollars," Perreira answered, with just enough hesitation to indicate he'd had to calculate what he thought he could gouge. "A hundred per man and a double share for the chief."

"Travelers' checks work?"

"Yes."

"Then get them to loading. I can handle *that* out of personal cash." Inside, Gordo fumed, *I should have just bought the two Skyvans that were for sale. But then we'd have had to find more pilots . . .*

I wish I could have flown them in Cruz's Russki helicopters, and I could have . . . except that the max ferry range for those requires so much fuel there's almost no redundant cargo capacity. Oh, well.

D-81, MV *Merciful,* off the coast of French Guiana

It was a calm, if hot and humid, day. The engines thrummed below, with a comfortably reliable sound. On the bridge, the air conditioning hummed as well, though it was clearly straining.

"That's Devil's Island—rather those three islands are what we've come to call Devil's Island—passing to starboard," Kosciusko told Cruz, pointing. "It's been closed for decades, though the Euros use it for part of their space program."

"You suppose they'll reopen it just for us if we fail?" Cruz asked.

The question was a joke. Kosciusko considered it seriously anyway, before answering, "No, they'll just shoot us."

Cruz scowled. "Why is it you Navy types so rarely have a sense of humor?"

"Oh, I've got a sense of humor," Ed countered, "except when it's about my getting shot. Besides, I'm a former Marine, so there."

"Speaking of having a sense of humor and getting shot," said Chin as he entered the bridge, "Skipper, have you come down to look at the patrol boat? We've just about got the hull and superstructure fixed, *despite* the four hundred *thousand* screws involved, a good portion of which had to be removed and reseated. But, and it's a big but, we're stuck until we know what kind of armament you're planning on mounting."

Cruz scowled again. Kosciusko waved his hand dismissively. "The Chinese have a pretty good idea of what we're about, Mike. They just don't know where." Turning to Chin, Ed said, "We don't *know* yet what kind of armament we're putting on. Oh, sure, machine guns and such don't matter, fifty caliber, sixty, or even 20mm; those the mounts can take. But the main gun is the question. Our . . . supplier . . . is still working on something suitable."

"It shouldn't be that big a problem, Skipper," Chin said. "It took a 40mm Bofors, once."

Kosciusko sighed. There been a long series of e-mails between himself, Harry Gordon, Stauer, and Victor, none satisfactorily resolved. "If we had a 40mm Bofors that would be fine. We don't and our supplier can't get one. He's offered us the turret, basket, and a frame cut from a BMP-3F. Unfortunately, the 100mm main gun on that has twice the recoil force of the 40mm Bofors that the boat used to mount. Might rip the deck right off. Might split the hull. He can also get us a BMP-2 turret except there's no navalized version and the thing would rust away before our eyes. At the very least the electronics couldn't take the salt air and spray.

"It's a problem. We've also been offered a Nudelman 37mm, which the deck could take . . . if we had a mount. But we don't; it's an aircraft gun. Same story with the 30mm GAST gun—you know, that dual contra-recoiling fucker? No mount and no time to develop and build one. And the tail of an Ilyushin 76 would be a hard fit."

Chin had a sudden vision of a patrol boat sprouting an airplane's tail at the bow and laughed aloud. "Well, we've got to have a decision soon, Skipper. My men and women are about done until we know what kind of gun goes forward. If we delay the repairs much longer then we might not be ready in time."

Kosciusko nodded. "I know. What do you suggest?"

Chin, though a sailor, had been a member of the People's Liberation Army Navy. Thus, he was more up to speed on ground systems than most sailors would have been. "Take the BMP-3F turret. We don't, after all, absolutely *have* to use the main gun. It's still got the 30mm cannon *and* the missiles. And if we have to use the main gun, probably just the once, it would only be in life or death circumstances. In that case, who *cares* about the boat?"

"I think he's right, Ed," Cruz said.

Kosciusko thought about it, thought about the pressing time schedule, and said, "All right. I'll send the requisition to Victor and Gordo, and tell Stauer. He left the decision up to us, anyway, but he might like to know."

"I'll need precise dimensions on that turret," Chin said, just before turning to leave. "With those, I can do the necessary mods even before we get it."

At the ladder leading down, Chin turned around again. "I started on patrol boats, you know, Skipper. I commanded a P-6 before they gave mine away to Tanzania. Love the things."

Kosciusko raised one eyebrow, thinking, *Note to Stauer . . .*

D-80, Maintenance Area—Base Camp, Amazonia, Brazil

"I love it when a plan comes together," Stauer said, watching the turret of an Eland as it was gently lowered down onto the body under the supervision of the two South Africans, Viljoen and Dumisani. Reilly likewise watched, one of the Israelis by his side. The rest of the Israeli crew was still anchored at Manaus, doing last minute touch ups while awaiting the arrival of *Merciful* so they could transfer over the cars that were not to land here. Reilly was speaking to the Israeli, the woman, Lana, softly enough that Stauer couldn't make out what was said. *One thing I'm sure of, though; hot as the woman may be, Reilly wants her for one thing and one thing only, training his troops on the armored cars. Single minded, fanatical bastard!*

Stauer then gave a rueful grin, noticed by no one, as he considered, *And what have you done with Phillie, then, that's so very different?*

No, that was different, he corrected himself. *I pushed*

Phillie aside—temporarily!—*because I couldn't be seen having favorites or having access to a woman when none of the other boys did.* To Reilly, though, that Israeli girl doesn't even exist as a woman as long as she has a "higher and better use," namely prepping his troops to fight. Stauer looked over at Lana again and mentally added, *The man is sick!*

But then, in shape she's a lot like Phillie . . . except Phillie has a better rack. And—Stauer mentally sighed—*I find that I'm missing her. Maybe I need a chat with the Doc . . . a prescription or something.*

Contrary to Stauer's opinion, Reilly was by no means unaware of the feminine charms of the tall, slender Israeli standing next to him. He simply compartmentalized well, even while he made an entry in his personal memory bank: *Israeli girl with high cheekbones and cute, if not large, tits; to lay, as soon as possible* after *the mission.*

Even while he made that little entry in his mind, his mouth was asking, "What will the laser rangefinder do for effective range?"

Lana had taken an instant liking to the man and she knew exactly why. Not that she didn't know, in the way all women know, that he'd just made a mental note: *Israeli girl with high cheekbones and cute, if not large, tits; to lay . . .*

But she was obviously something more to Reilly, that thing she'd been mostly denied when she'd been with the Israeli Army. *He thinks of me first and foremost as a* soldier! *How great is that?*

She chewed at her lower lip a moment before answering, "Depends, sir. It's a low velocity gun any way you look at it, firing a high cross-section, fin-stabilized shell. High crossing winds . . . moving target . . . anything like that and it's a matter of luck and training more than the gun or the fire control."

"Training's going to be a problem," Reilly said. "I don't have and won't get permission to fire major rounds before we move out. And I doubt the TP ammunition we're getting is really exactly the same."

"It isn't," Lana agreed, "but that's not a problem. Our reputation depends on how our products do in combat, when it counts. A lot of armies that have these things they can't afford to fire much. So each car comes with three sub-caliber devices, basically modified expended shell casings filled with concrete, and with a redundant, bore-sighted spotting rifle from the old 105mm recoilless inside. I made sure all twenty-seven of the ones that come with the rebuilds were loaded to come here, to your base camp. Along with about thirty thousand rounds of .50 spotting. We can train to shoot."

I think I'm in love, Reilly thought. *Okay, not really.* "You mean 106, don't you?"

"No," she replied, very definitely. "You called it that, to distinguish it from its failed predecessor, but it was 105mm all the same."

"Really?" *Lust, anyway.*

Alone in her tent, lying on the unmattressed folding cot, wearing sweaty battle dress, Phillie was miserable, *And it's not just because I'm horny. But I never even see Wes, except at a distance. Or in the occasional meeting. Or . . .*

Her moping was interrupted by a knock on the tent

pole. It didn't resound, exactly, but she'd gotten used to the rather different sounds of a lonely jungle camp as compared to the big bright city and houses with doors that reverberated like drums.

"Nurse Potter?" Sergeant Coffee asked. "Are you decent?"

I'm actually pretty damned good, she thought, *not that anyone's tried me lately*. "Here, Sergeant Coffee. I'm dressed."

Coffee stuck his large, squared-off head inside the tent flap. "Message from the commander, Nurse Potter. He needs a medical person at the docks and Dr. Joseph is busy with setting a bone from B Company. Somebody from one of the LCM crews must be hurt."

"Do you know who got hurt?" she asked. "How bad is it?"

"No, ma'am, I don't know"—Coffee had gotten much more polite since dumping Phillie in the mud— "but if myself or one of my apes would have done the trick, I'm sure Colonel Stauer wouldn't have asked for you."

Phillie arose from her cot and, bending, grabbed the medical kit bag underneath.

Coffee grimaced. *Ooo, that's nice*.

"Sergeant Coffee," she said, straightening up, "if you would be so kind would you ask Sergeant Island to hold some lunch for me?"

"Be happy to, ma'am," Coffee replied as he ducked his head out of the tent. "By the way, the colonel's ATV is outside. You can take that."

"Wouldn't know how to drive it, Sergeant Coffee. And the dock's not far."

★ ★ ★

There was no one dockside or on the sole landing craft tied up to it. Phillie supposed the other two were downstream, either at Manaus or bringing another load of supplies in. She swung a long leg over the sheer hull and climbed down, calling out, "Is anyone aboard?" More softly she muttered, "If this is some kind of joke . . . "

A strained sounding Wes' voice called back, "Over here, Phillie." She looked around to the stern, from whence came his voice, and began to walk across the ribbed deck. Where the cargo deck ended there was a steel wall, mostly blank except for one ladder inset into it. She elbowed her bag behind her and climbed up. As her head arose over the wall, she saw another deck, mostly flat, with a upright steel housing and an open hatch in front of that. "Down here," Wes called again. His voice sounded urgent, as if the emergency was dire indeed.

She began to scramble down, first swinging her leg until it connected with another ladder. Halfway down, with her head and torso still above deck level, she felt strong hands on her hips lifting her away from the ladder. Thereafter, she sank into the engine housing so quickly she could barely register a surprised "O."

Her feet touched the metal deck below and Phillie felt herself spun around bodily. One large hand slithered up her back, unhooking her bra with practiced ease, even while another frantically undid the buttons on front of her battle dress jacket. She was about to scream "rape" when a quick sniff told her nose, "Stauer."

The latter hand pushed her T-shirt and bra up and out of the way, even while the other one did something overhead that caused a clang that was shocking inside the close confines of the oil-smelling engine room.

Both hands then struggled with the buttons of her trousers before hooking thumbs in them and her panties and pushing downward. Phillie kicked to try to get the trousers off completely but, as they were bloused into her boots, she failed and remained with her ankles bound together by trousers.

She felt herself picked up again, this time by her bare buttocks. She pulled her legs up and rested them on the forearms that held her. When she was released again, it was to rest her bare skin on the cold, cold block of a very large diesel engine. She squealed at the shock.

"Shhhh," whispered Stauer into her ear as he gently stroked her smooth flanks. "Shhhh. Doctor's orders."

Doc Joseph and Sergeant Coffee watched the boat from the jungle nearest the river. They really couldn't tell if the boat's gentle rocking was from the current, from Phillie boarding, or from her being boarded. It didn't really matter anyway.

Coffee pulled a pack of cigarettes out of one corner and held them out, offering one to the doctor. Joseph declined at first then said, "Ah, what the fuck. Gimme."

He took the cigarette and then puffed it alight in the flame from Coffee's proffered lighter. He coughed a couple of times, then his lungs settled into the smoke.

"You really wrote him a prescription?" Coffee asked, just before lighting his own cancer stick.

"Nope," Joseph said. "I wrote her one, and told him to deliver it."

Coffee snickered. "You don't think it will be a problem with the boys, the colonel having his honey to . . . ummm . . . to hand?"

Joseph shook his head. "No, not if they're reasonably discreet. The troops won't care as long as Stauer doesn't play favorites and doesn't flaunt that he's dipping his wick when the boys can't."

Coffee rocked his smoke-wreathed head from side to side before agreeing, "Yeah . . . probably."

A hundred meters away the landing craft continued its gentle rocking, waves forming from the current as it passed around the stern.

★ CHAPTER TWENTY-NINE ★

*Of all branches of military science, military sketching
and reconnaissance is perhaps the most practical.*
—Lieutenant Colonel A.F. Mockler-Ferryman,
RMC Sandhurst, 1908

D-80, Beach Green Two (tentative),
west of Bandar Qassim, Ophir

Waves washed up on the low tide beach, just west of the
city that was named—so local legends said—for its
founder's camel. All the way out, as far as the eye could
see, there wasn't a rock bigger than two fists held together.
The slope was smooth and gentle. A Marine would have
had an orgasm, just looking at it.

The city to the east had grown tenfold in recent years,
the result of its original tribesmen, scattered all over what
had once been the country, returning to the safety and
security of their own tribe. For all that it now housed
nearly half a million people, it was still a low-built city of
mostly mud brick with wide swaths of tent townships

around it. Animals still walked and grazed in the streets, to the extent there was much of anything to graze from. Mostly, the streets were just mud and garbage and general filth.

At the center of the northern edge of the city, where road and building met sea, was a double port mildly reminiscent of old Carthage in that it had a major harbor area partly enclosed by a jetty, and a small one almost completely enclosed that led off from the major one. To both sides were beaches. Though the sand of the beaches was smooth, generally, just behind them was a series of rough wadis which cut the area of the beaches into segments as little as one hundred feet across. This was common in the area. The wadis presented both difficulties and opportunities. They were difficulties in that they would tend to disorganize and separate any attacker doing a landing and could provide good cover for any defender, opportunities in that if one were to land, and were it not defended, one could take cover quite quickly from casual observation. At least from the ground. Air was another story entirely.

"It's a pity," said Buckwheat Fulton to Wahab, as they walked along the shingle, stopping occasionally to take a digital photo, "that this isn't where we're intending to land the major force. It's the best beach I've seen. Even better than Green One, to the west of here." The camera had an integral GPS, Global Positioning System, to it, so there'd be no doubts about where any given picture related to.

Wahab agreed, saying, "You know more about such things than I do, but even I can see the advantages of the gentle rise of the sands. That said," he pointed with his chin toward the almost rectangular port—it *was* a rectangle but with one corner nipped off—"*they* may have something to say about that."

Since returning home, Wahab had barely had time to see his wife and children. He and Fulton had arrived, briefed Khalid, spent a single night at Wahab's house, and then headed north. Still, one night is better than no nights. *I missed her . . . and ours.*

He turned his attention back to the problem at hand, that, and the relative competence of the black American noncom and the black African officer. *I don't think Buckwheat's any smarter than I am. And I've had schooling, within his own country's armed forces, that is way above anything he should have had. And still he knows more about it than I do. I wonder why that is. Self study? Maybe. We've never been so good, this side of the ocean, at worrying about what is to come or preparing for it. But some of us must have and I still don't know anyone here who understands military operations as well. And there's no bloody racial component to it because this man is black, too.*

He asked Buckwheat about it.

"Osmosis," the American replied, simply. "All my adult life I was surrounded by people who studied these things and did them. You just pick it up, without even being aware that you are picking it up."

"Oh." Then Wahab had a still odder thought. *I could pin general's insignia on this man, put him in charge of our "army," and we would be unbeatable on this continent.*

Fulton looked over toward where Wahab's chin had

pointed. They'd already looked at the recognizable pirate ships, an easy dozen of them, in the smaller, better protected, and almost rectangular harbor. Guards, who seemed unusually alert and well disciplined, walked the docks, the fences, and the jetties of the harbor. As near as Buckwheat and Wahab could tell there were nearly twelve hundred such full time warriors in the town, along with tens of thousands of part timers who might well show up to fight in a pinch. Could Stauer's force take them? Who the hell wanted to pay the price finding out?

In reply, Fulton said, "The boats are toast if we want them to be." He mused for a moment, then added, "Of course, we *do* want them to be." White teeth shone bright in a black face, "And they *will* be. But, depending on how we go about that, it will make many loud noises which would alert people that we're coming. Or here. So we'll take them out but probably only after we're landed else-where and moving. Well after. And we absolutely don't want to tangle with that much tribal infantry. That's why"— he chinned towards the bay—"Biggus Dickus Thornton has the job of sinking the boats and we're not planning on landing a single man near here."

"On which note," Wahab said, "we'd better find another beach."

Buckwheat nodded agreement but said, "Not west of here. Green One is fine for a small team, say, one to take out the stuff on the airfield, not so good for a large. The mountains along the coast could make getting very far off the beach a serious problem. Also it's too long a drive from Objective One."

"South, then," Wahab agreed. "The eastern coast.

North of Bandar Cisman, maybe." The two remounted their automobile. Oddly enough, while everyone back at base in Brazil was making do with ATVs and such, the recon and intelligence party had a Hummer, gift of a charity with more money than brains, which gift had been duly stolen and put on the market, sans engine hood and windshield. Wahab had picked it up for a fair price.

Since purchase, the Hummer had been further modified, this time by the guards Wahab had hired in the town. One of those three stood up in the back of the Hummer, manning a machine gun, while the other two rode the back seat, rifles clutched in their hands. The guards were actually from a sub-clan of the Habar Afaan tribe. Even so, they seemed diligent. Then again, why not? It wasn't as if they knew why Fulton and Wahab were taking pictures, nor even why they'd stopped at certain villages, taking photos of nearly everyone present and providing copies from a color printer that rode the back of the Hummer, taking its juice from the battery.

The beach and the town lay far to the northwest, after a long day's kidney-pounding drive. The sun was sinking in the west behind sand dunes. The Hummer, Wahab driving, had been parked in low ground between three dunes. While one guard, with the machine gun, lay atop the highest of those, scanning the horizon for threats, another pitched a tarp with one edge tied to the Hummer and the other staked to the sand. He used a shovel rather than a mallet, digging holes and burying crossed stakes, with the lead ropes attached, within them. The third guard took care of cooking, a simple meal of azuki beans with a small side of goat. Spiced tea brewed on the fire, next to the pot holding the beans. It gave off the scent of cinnamon and cardamom.

While the guards busied themselves with housekeeping, and Buckwheat fiddled with a small satellite dish mounted on the ground behind the Hummer, Wahab—rifle in hand— watched the guards. Paranoia, in this part of the world, was only good sense unless one was surrounded by close kin.

"What you do?" asked the guard squatting over the fire of Fulton.

"Getting ready to send the pictures we took back to my magazine," Fulton replied. "Anything happens to us, at least they'll have a part of a story."

"Nothing happen," the guard assured Buckwheat. "Here . . . now . . . we have peace. Even stinking, goat-fucking Marehan no bother us anymore."

"Peace is good," Fulton answered, noncommittally. Even so he looked casually at Wahab. Yes, his comrade of the day and hour had heard. No, if he took any offense he didn't show it. Indeed, he was smiling. *Got to love a cool comrade.*

Fulton left the dish for a moment, walking the couple of steps to the computer and checking reception.

"Where you learn do that?" the cook asked.

"Journalism school," Buckwheat lied. *At SWC at Fort Bragg, North Carolina, back when Bronze Bruce was still on the other side of the street.*

"Wish I could learn," the cook said, suggestively.

"Tell you what; when we finish my photo shoot I'll show you. Fair enough?"

"Better than fair," the cook answered. "For that you get extra portion of goat."

D-78, Rako, Ophir

While the United States Army had never been a force in which idiotic personnel management boners were unknown—for example, at a time when it had been critical for Special Forces personnel to be able to blend in with the locals, it had on at least one occasion assigned a black captain to a Special Forces A team oriented to *Norway*, and this at a time when there were virtually no blacks *in* Norway—in Fulton's case it had made the far more sensible decision, deep in the throes of the Cold War, to assign him to a Special Forces Group, the Third, and team oriented towards the fringe where Islamic Africa met Christian, Animist, and Christian-Animist Africa. Thus the continent held few surprises for him. He'd seen it all. As Buckwheat said, more or less frequently, "Thank God my multi-great grandpappy got dragged onto that boat."

He'd said just that, once, after demonstrating the use of a condom to the men of a nominally Christian village. For that particular demonstration, he'd used a stick to simulate the male appendage. The next morning, after he'd arisen, he'd discovered that every married man had used his condom exactly as he'd shown them. Outside of each hut, planted in the ground, was an upright stick and on each stick a properly rolled out condom. He'd thought then, as he thought now, *Thank God my multi-great grandpappy got dragged onto that boat. Tough shit for him, of course, but awful good for me and mine.*

The reason for him thinking so, on this occasion, was

the village into which he and Wahab and their guards had just driven. More precisely, it was the young girl, kicking, crying, begging, and pleading for all she was worth as she was dragged by her feet to where a collection of grim faced women stood, one of them holding a knife, another several rags, and a third a basket that Fulton already knew held acacia thorns. The thorns were a suture substitute.

Who do you blame for this? Fulton asked himself, as he had every time he'd been a near witness to a female circumcision. *The Arabs? Islam? Nope, this predates them. The people doing it? "Nothing is stronger than custom." And how do you change their minds? Answer: you don't; I've tried. Poor little shit.*

Neither Wahab nor the guards so much as blinked when the girl, now concealed inside a hut, began to scream in earnest, heartbreak incarnate. Again, Fulton thought, *Poor little shit.*

Though Wahab didn't blink, he likewise thought, *Poor creature. Thanks to Allah my Alaso wasn't so treated when she was young. Of course, I can't say anything. Even if the mission we are on didn't require "cover," I am already so embarrassed in front of Buckwheat that I want to puke.*

No more than had Wahab or the guards did the chief of the village seem to pay the slightest mind to the girl's voiced agony. The chief wore what amounted to a skirt, below, and in a sort of plaid, no less, with a bright blue shirt and a light, patterned shawl. On his head was perched the snug-fitting, rounded cap, called a "qofe." The chief looked to be truly ancient, from which appearance Buckwheat assumed they were about of an age.

The guards made the introductions while Wahab remained in the background.

"You are an American," the village chief, Zakariye, observed. It was not a question.

"Indeed, yes," Fulton agreed. "Is this a problem?"

"Not at all," said Zakariye. "Indeed, we hope someday to have closer relations with the United States, so says my eldest boy, Gutaale. That, however, is for the future . . . and is in God's hands."

"As are we all," Fulton agreed. While the chief's wives and daughters, modestly wrapped in accordance with their faith but not in the stifling burkas of more fundamentalist regions, served lunch, Wahab busied himself with taking pictures. Eventually, the girl being clitorectomized not so far away ceased her wailing and shrieking.

D-77, Rako-Dhuudo highway, Ophir

Wahab said exactly what Fulton was thinking, "We're so fucked!"

"Why fucked?" asked the guard manning the machine gun.

The reason for the exclamation was the column of dust-covered tanks—at this distance Fulton made them as being either Russian T-55s or the Chinese copy, the Type 59—passing across the road heading north to south. The tanks threw up a thick, linear cloud of dun-colored dust.

"He just worries whenever he sees soldiers he isn't one hundred percent sure are harmless," Fulton lied. "I thought you guys didn't have any tanks,"

"People you call 'pirates' took them from ship," the guard explained. "Maybe . . . a month ago. Radio say we got . . . ummm . . . twenty-four. Me, I think the pirates didn't steal anything and there was a deal"—the guard winked—"under the table between our people and the Russians. But, hey, I'm just hired guard. What I know?"

"I do know," said another guard, "that there are black men training the crews. I never heard of no black Russians."

Fulton suppressed the chuckle that the line deserved, even if the speaker didn't know why it deserved it. *Besides, having to face tanks, even T-55s, in armored cars is* not *a laughing matter. Shit.*

★CHAPTER THIRTY★

The reasons for the current overestimation of
the importance of intelligence in warfare are twofold:
the first is the common confusion of espionage and
counter-espionage with operational intelligence proper;
the second is the intermingling of operational
intelligence with, and contamination by, subversion, the
attempt to win military advantage by covert means.
—John Keegan, *Intelligence in War*

D-75, Assembly Area Alpha—Base Camp, Amazonia, Brazil

"Shit," said Bridges when he saw the pictures Fulton had downloaded via satellite. He then added, "'Dad, get me out of this.'"

"What is it, Matt?" asked Lox.

Wordlessly, Bridges swiveled his laptop around to show his coworker.

"Shit," Lox agreed. He filled his lungs with air and called for Boxer.

Boxer came into the tent breathlessly, followed by Stauer and the operations officer, Ken Waggoner.

"What the fuck was that in aid of?" Boxer asked. Just as Bridges had, Lox answered nonverbally by pointing at the screen.

"Oh, shit," Stauer said, shaking his head slowly. "That I was not expecting. Oh, shit," he repeated, needlessly. "We should have asked the Israelis to mount their high velocity 60mm guns. Too late for that now. Shit."

"Tanks?" Waggoner mumbled. More loudly, he added, "I didn't plan on tanks, boss. Not real ones. Not a bunch of them. Nothing you or this Air Force reprobate told me said we'd have to deal with tanks. Jesus! How the fuck do we deal with tanks in those numbers?"

Boxer, less inclined to lose his head than most, asked, "Where were they spotted?"

"On the road to Objective One," Bridges answered. He took back control of the laptop and scrolled down untill he came to some verbiage. This he read. "Well, just off it, actually. They're based right near there . . . Buckwheat says they're just T-55s or Type 59s . . . probably depot rebuilds . . . maybe night vision equipped . . . but no thermals. No add-on armor, either. Annnddd . . . the crews are barely trained. What he saw was driver training . . . he *thinks*. That, or he says 'they need driver training.' He also says that there are probably two dozen of them."

"Why the *hell* didn't you see them?" Stauer asked of Boxer. "You're tapping all the NRO's shit!"

"I looked. A few weeks ago. They weren't there then." Boxer sounded quite apologetic. "And there was nothing on the news or in the intel channels to suggest otherwise."

Stauer suppressed an urge to unload on the intel type, but, *No, sat recon is limited. And the press is not notably*

*good about honest reporting in this part of the world. He
did the best he could.*

"Chilluns," said Stauer, "this is what we in the trade
call a 'bad thing.' And we need a solution." He considered
for a moment, then added, "Send to Buckwheat that he's
to stay on station." He shrugged, "In country, I mean, not
right there with the tanks. I need to know a lot more about
those T-55s. Everything there is to know, as a matter of
fact." Turning to Waggoner, he said, "And you start working
on a plan to take them out, without compromising the rest
of the operations. If we have to take some risks, elsewhere,
then that's what we'll do."

"Could we get some tanks of our own?" Waggoner asked.

Stauer shook his head. "Maybe, but if so, so what?
They won't be M-1s or anything our armor crews are used
to, so they'd need training and there wouldn't be time to
train. Even if there were time to train, the gantry on the
Merciful isn't up to forty to seventy tons of steel. Even if it
were, the LCMs probably can't carry an M-1 or equivalent.
And even if they could, we couldn't conceal them in a
container. And if that weren't necessary it would still take
too long getting ashore when we'd have to ferry them in
one per boat at a time.

"No, we need to do something else."

D-75, 90mm Range (subcal), Assembly Area Alpha—Base Camp, Amazonia, Brazil

There was a steady *pop-pop-pop*, deeper than from a
normal rifle, or even a normal .50 caliber. This was the

sound of the modified spotting rifles being used for 90mm gunnery training.

When Reilly returned to the range from a short but intense meeting with Boxer and Stauer, all three gun-armed Elands were on line firing. Downrange, in three deep zigzag trenches the engineers had dug, three teams of three soldiers each—the other crews for half the Elands—manhandled silhouettes of generic armored vehicles while the gunners tried to perforate the moving targets.

Lana Mendes was half in, half out of the hatch of one of the armored cars. *I'm not sure which view is better*, Reilly mused. He didn't muse, or view, very long though. Instead he walked up and slapped her hard on the thigh. The stream of mixed English, Afrikaans, and Hebrew (really Arabic, since Israel had had to borrow) curses previously emanating from the vehicle let up momentarily, only to commence again with real fury as she withdrew her top half from the turret. Reilly tried not to notice when her shirt caught on the turret and began to ride high.

As she was fixing her shirt, before she could even begin to lay into him, Reilly cut her off, abruptly, saying, "We've got a serious problem, Lana. Leave Green in charge. Round up Sergeant Abdan. Meet me at my hooch in half an hour."

With that he turned on his heel and walked away. Lana thought, *I like the other view better.*

When Lana and Abdan arrived at Reilly's tent, the other key leadership was already there, seated on Reilly's cot, folding chairs, or the ground. The first sergeant, George, the company exec, FitzMarcach, and the antiarmor section leader, Harvey, shared the cot. The two infantry platoon leaders, Hilfer and Epolito, sat on folding chairs. The mortar section leader, Peters, was already there and seated on the ground, as were Viljoen and Dumisani. Matthias Nagy, who would lead the team of engineers supporting Company A, was likewise in attendance, but standing. Nobody looked particularly happy but Harvey looked especially pale.

The first sergeant and XO spread apart to make a little room on Reilly's cot for Lana.

"As I've said, we have a problem," Reilly began. "The other side has tanks, and near enough to one of the key objectives that we can assume they'll pour out to fight once we show up."

"How many?" Abdan asked. "What model."

"T-55s and—we think—twenty-four of them."

Lana looked instantly horrified. "You can't, I mean you *can't* take on tanks, even T-55s, in Elands and expect to survive the experience. They got no— "

"Yes, you can," Viljoen interrupted. "I've done it twice. In Namibia. I'm not saying it's easy but it can be done."

"And were you outnumbered four to one?" Lana asked heatedly.

"Well, no," Viljoen admitted. "We had the numbers, if only slightly, at the point of contact.

"Boss," Harvey said, turning to Reilly, "My Ferrets are going to carry eight missiles loaded, between them, and another dozen stowed internally or on the back deck. That's twenty missiles, max. Sir, do you know why they call them 'missiles?' Because they miss a lot more often than they hit. From my twenty, ideally, we kill seven or eight tanks. That still leaves sixteen or seventeen facing a half dozen Elands. And that's too much."

"Don't count on me to whittle them down," Peters said, spitting tobacco juice into the can that he seemed always to have in his hand. "If I hit something much smaller than the Earth, with a mortar, it'll be a fluke."

Abdan shook his head. "Sir, the boys are already griping about having to traverse the turrets by hand and have the commander double as a loader. If we had four M-1s, I'd take on your two dozen T-55s with a grin. As is . . . "

"Yeah," Reilly agreed. He disagreed about the numbers, though. "Maintenance being what it is, and tanks being what they are, there's not much chance we'd have to take on all twenty-four. Think more along the lines of twelve to twenty." He turned his head toward Viljoen. "Tell us about taking on T-55s with Elands."

"It's simple, Wes," Reilly explained later in the day. "I can handle maybe half of those tanks if they come after us. And they're close enough that we won't have seized our targets before they do come looking for us. They're also close enough to block our egress back to the sea and the ship. Are those targets all that key?"

"Yes," Stauer answered.

"Okay, then my options are A: Hit the tank compound first, before I do anything else, with everything I have, while the fuckers are asleep, killing everything that moves and taking time to thermite the back deck of each one. Understand, though, that the targets might get away.

"If you don't like that, there's option B: Seize the targets: leave the vehicles behind; everybody goes out by air. I won't comment on what this does to the rest of your plan, even assuming we could do it before the tanks are ramming their barrels up our asses.

"Then there's C: Reconfigure the light aircraft due in, in a few days, to attack the armor base. They'll have to linger there, shooting anything that moves, for several hours. My guess is that while they'd cause some delay, even get a few, they wouldn't stop the tanks.

"Lastly is my personal favorite," Reilly continued. "D: Two to four aircraft—call it 'three'—strike the place, along with the mortars, immediately following which I and the Elands roll in and shoot the shit out of it, while my XO takes the rest of the company to the objective to seize the targets. The aircraft can keep any survivors busy while the company links up and moves to the sea. This has some downsides in terms of the likelihood of meeting serious resistance at the objective, and people escaping through a thinner net. I was counting on those 90mm guns to cow the opposition. Oh, and I'm going to need the cooks to supplement my mortar section. In any case, even D has some . . . issues."

Note to self, Stauer thought, *bet with Sergeant Major, pay off, soonest.*

"How about dropping off your engineers to mine the road?" he asked.

Reilly shook his head. "I've checked the maps. The road's a convenience, nothing more. With luck we get one tank that way and then the rest pull off road into the desert and continue the march. And there are no unfordable streams we could drop the bridges to, nor even any fordable ones we could mine the fords of."

"What if I cancelled Welch's mission and sent his boys to take out the compound?"

Reilly wrinkled his nose, this time. Despite that, he replied, "I've got no beef against special forces, but they're just as likely to alert the opposition as to take them out. Only so much shit can be back-packed, after all. And besides, you *need* them for the mission you've already got them on. The whole thing's kind of a waste, from *our* point of view, if they don't do that."

And if Welch's mission doesn't go off, we can't stay together, and I spend the rest of my miserable life alone.

"Yeah," Stauer admitted. "I'm willing to consider Option D. It's very close to what Boxer and Waggoner came up with, by the way."

"Greats minds and all," Reilly said with a shrug. "That said, I've got another problem."

"Which is?"

"My tankers are maybe on the verge of mutiny over the limitations of the Eland. Sergeant Abdan's playing it down, for now, but it has me worried."

"What are you doing about it?"

"For now, I'm sending the two South Africans around to tell war stories. That should prove especially effective since one of them was Eland crew in their border war, and took out T-55s with them, while the other was on the receiving end, if not exactly in a T-55. I'm also going to have to have a long chat with Mendes about talking up the Eland. That's going to be tough, because she thinks we're suicidal maniacs for even thinking about it. And I don't know how good an actress she is. And while I like Option D better than the others, it's still a shitty plan. If they see us coming, we're fucked."

"That's what I told Waggoner."

The explosion had a metallic quality to it: *Blang*. The 90mm subcaliber device sounded and a target to the left front shuddered with the impact. A small puff of smoke told of the hit.

The sound of the spotting rifles, as muffled by the 90mm barrels, was odd, flatter sounding than what the troops were used to in the .50 caliber Browning. Lana rode the back deck, with her head inside the turret. Twenty-one of the twenty-seven available subcal devices were loaded on this Eland, in the immediately accessible ready racks. The platoon leader, Green, commanded and loaded—a tough job in itself—while his gunner, face pressed to the gunner's sight, frantically spun the traversing and elevating wheels to line up on targets that appeared at random, ahead and to either side. The gunner's face ran with sweat from the effort, despite the air conditioning the Israelis had installed, clouding his eyes and fogging up the sight. The bouncing of the armored car on the rough ground made the gunner's job seem impossible.

"Gunner, HEAT, Tank!" Green called out, dropping back to his seat and grabbing a round which he stuffed up the breech. "Three o'clock."

Lana counted off the seconds as the gunner spun the turret to the right. One . . . two . . . three . . . four . . . five, and assume you're dead, gunner, because at this range they can't miss. She thought it, but said nothing.

Reilly wants me to act like I've got confidence; I'll act like it.

The subcal sounded again. Lana didn't need to see the target; she knew it had been a miss from the way the gunner slammed his head against the sight in frustration.

Green, however, having stuck his head up again, did see the miss. Once again he dropped down to his seat, screaming, "Gunner, HEAT . . . "

Lana shook her head. Inside, she felt rising despair. *Shit; it doesn't even matter. Their heavy antiaircraft machine gun can penetrate at this range.*

"Lana," Reilly said, after she confronted him with her fears and doubts, "don't sweat it so much. The tank commanders are not going to spend much time under fire with their heads above the hatch. That's why I have infantry. There will not *be* a manned machine gun capable of engaging except for the coax guns, and those won't penetrate. And while a slow traverse is fatal at close range, it doesn't matter as much at long range.

"You just get my boys trained to engage and hit the targets. Leave the tactics of the thing to me." *Now if only I could come up with something I had some confidence in, myself.*

"Is that confidence," she asked, "or just overweening pride?"

Reilly laughed. "Maybe a little of both. Well . . . " he hesitated, then sighed. He looked her in the eye and said, "Look, Lana, this is the truth. As near as I can tell, it is, anyway. I'm not a good man. I'm sure not a nice man. I've got the morals of an alley cat . . . except that that's an insult to self-respecting alley cats everywhere.

"But there are two things I can do better than anyone I know . . . anyone I ever heard of that's living. I can train troops better and I can lead them in combat better.

"So if you won't have confidence in your Elands, or my crews, have confidence in me. They're going to be about two to three times more effective than you think is even possible . . . because of the way I'll train them and the way I'll use them in action. Do you think these guys came here and are still trying because they lack confidence in me? And, remember, the core of them know me from way back."

Mendes chewed at her lower lip while searching his face for the truth in his words. *He believes it*, she thought. *He really does. Maybe . . . just maybe. And I do like him. Or worse. So . . .*

"Fine. You're that sure?" She glanced at his face again. Yes, he was that sure. "Then I want to come along. You need a maintenance chief anyway, to ride herd on the Boer and the Bantu. And I, at least, won't look askance at Viljoen and Dumi for doing things that I do myself."

Reilly scratched at the side of his head for a half a minute before answering. "Let me ask Stauer if we can afford another . . . man . . . on the rolls." *And did she just send me a hint? Did I suggest it to her with that "morals of an alley cat" line? Shit.* "And if you can't believe we have a chance, Lana, can't you at least fake it, for the men?"

She smiled then and, lifting her chin, answered, "I *am* a woman. Of *course* I can fake things for men."

God, what a wonderful girl.

★ ★ ★

"I see misery in your future," Viljoen said to Lana, later, over dinner.

Dumisani, sitting next to Lana and opposite his lover, began softly to laugh.

Lana sniffed, "Why is that and why would it be any of your business?"

Viljoen rolled his eyes as if the questions were too preposterous to answer. Dumi, instead, answered for him. "Because, countrywoman, you've got it so bad for our 'fearless leader' that we can practically smell you getting wet every time he gets close. Trust me, Dani and I are both pretty good at discerning such things. It's part and parcel of the whole gay thing."

Lana bridled. Her face grew red. She sputtered, "That's . . . that's . . . that's . . . "—her moral outrage collapsed, suddenly. "Oh, shit, what am I going to do? He hardly knows I exist." Then she remembered a perceived mental note of, *To lay, soonest.* "Well, maybe he does."

"Oh, he knows," Viljoen countered. "We're pretty good at reading body language that way, too. As to what you're going to do, I'd suggest rape if you're impatient, seduction otherwise."

"I'd thought that being treated as an equal, and an equally valuable soldier, meant more than being treated like a woman," Lana said, sadly and wistfully. "It's not a crime to be wrong, is it?"

"No crime, no, Lana," Dumi replied. "And don't listen to my partner. Seduction you can do. Rape would be right out."

To Lana, the tone and tenor of the Zulu's voice, so

much like that of the woman who had cared for her as a child, was inherently authoritative.

"I don't understand why he's never come on to me," she said. "I mean, I'm pretty sure he has me on his list. But never a hint, or at least never one he intended to give."

"He's a pro," Viljoen said. "I mean, I'm pretty sure Dumi and I make his skin crawl, but he suppresses that in the interests of the mission and the organization. Equally, you make certain parts of him vibrate like a tuning fork—no, we can't hear it; that's just a guess—but he pushes that back, too, and for the same reason."

"Seduction, huh?"

"Seduction."

★ CHAPTER THIRTY-ONE ★

No man is free who is a slave to the flesh.
—Seneca, Epistolae ad Lucilium, XCII

D-91, Suakin, Sudan

Things had been worse. For one thing, he'd developed an infection, a few weeks back, from the open sores where he'd once been manacled. They'd stopped shackling Adam's legs together, long enough for the sores to heal, and never quite gotten around to putting the shackles back on. He could walk almost like a free man, now.

Almost as if they were free, Adam and Makeda walked hand in hand in the pre-morning darkness. His guards walked, politely enough, a few steps behind. They were not so far back, however, that they couldn't hear what was said. And Adam had learned already that if he whispered they simply closed the distance.

Across the water, one largish building shone electric lights. Besides that emanating from the portholes of a dhow which had shown up the previous night, those were the only lights to be seen, close in. Adam turned his head over one shoulder and asked the guards what it was.

Before they could answer, Labaan spoke out from the darkness. "It's a prison, boy, and, yes, we considered putting you in it. Be happy we decided differently. The place is a near double for what I imagine Hell is like.

"And here, at least, you have the girl."

Adam nodded, then squeezed Makeda's hand. *Yes, at least here I have the girl.*

"You must think I'm a whore," Makeda whispered, after a bout of particularly fierce and frantic lovemaking. She was definitely growing fond of the boy, and even beginning to trust him a bit.

Adam smiled and shook his head *no*, while thinking, *I think you're very good at your job and there's a part of me that would like to cut the heart out of whoever trained you in it. Because, in a better world, I could take you home and present you to my father as my wife. In the world that is, they'd never accept you as anything more than a slave and concubine.*

Makeda wasn't fooled. "It's all right," she said. "I understand. There's no place for you and me to be together after . . . if we ever get free of this place and these people. Get me free, though; that's all I ask."

"There is such a place," Adam replied, softly. "Far away, across Africa, over the sea. I've lived there. It's real."

"America? Where the streets are paved with gold? I've heard of it."

He shook his head, rustling the pillow. "Yes, there . . . though the streets aren't paved with gold. Still, it's a place

someone can get a fresh start in life, a place where the
only slavers are the . . . frankly, the Arabs and other
Moslems that immigrate there. Oh, and the odd Hindu or
Filipino. And even those the Americans will send to jail if
they catch them. Fine them too for the wages their slaves
should have been paid, with interest.

"Sadly," he added, "I am as much a slave as you, or
maybe more so. You, if free, could go to America. Me? I
have obligations to take over my clan when my father dies
and those I can't . . . shit." He rolled his head on the pillow,
staring at the ceiling, the moonlight filtering in showing a
look of mixed disgust and despair on his face.

"What?" she asked.

"I just realized. I mean *really* just realized. Labaan was
right. Blood, for us, counts for most and I, no matter what
they told me at the university, am just as much a member
of my culture and supporter of my clan as he is. Shit."

"I don't see what the disappearance of the *Galloway*
has to do with us," Labaan said to the Arab seated opposite.
Both men sat on placed on the rugs that covered the
polished coral floor. "Yusuf ibn Muhammad al Hassan,
from Sana'a," the Arab had introduced himself as. He'd
come in on the dhow riding at anchor in the bay. It was he,
so it was said, who had arranged for a ship bearing arms,
among them T-55 tanks, to be in a position to be seized by
the clan's seafaring rovers. The Arab had come in from
Yemen by dhow, the same dhow as brought supplies every
eight to ten days.

"It didn't just disappear," Yusuf said. "It blew up.
That's odd enough, in itself. But the area has been swept

and not a single body or piece of a body has been found. That's really odd."

"So what do you think happened to it?" Labaan asked.

"If I had to make a guess, I'd say either British or American or possibly even Zionist special forces overtook it at sea, boarded it, and captured the crew. Except that I had the ship transporting more than just the crew. There was a major strike force of *mujahadin* aboard, as well, and they would not have gone gently."

"All those forces you mention are highly capable. They probably have some method of incapacitating a ship's crew before they even board."

"Maybe," Yusuf half agreed. "But it is still oddly coincidental that someone went after this particular ship so soon after it transported your people and your prisoner."

"Stranger things have happened," Labaan said, with a shrug. "I would think it much more likely that it was the presence of that same strike team you mentioned that alerted whoever took over the ship."

Yusuf cocked his head to one side, shook it to and fro a few times, and again said, "Maybe. Still, I thought you ought to know. And, per your chief's . . . request, I could hardly call you."

"I appreciate that," Labaan said, "as I appreciate the trouble you took to bring us word. And I will increase security because of it. Even so, we are small change, here. I think whoever went after your ship was after the *mujahadin*, not us."

"You're probably right," Yusuf agreed, with good grace.

D-90, Suakin, Sudan

There were four guards, not counting Labaan, when Adam and Makeda were brought out for their evening walk. Labaan looked apologetic as he announced, "I've received word of some strange happenings. The details don't matter. What does matter is I have to increase security on you. I'm sorry."

Adam looked from guard to guard and answered, "What difference, two or four. There's still no privacy."

"It's more than that," Labaan said. "I won't . . . we can't . . . put the leg irons on you anymore, but . . . " He signaled with a toss of his head at the guards. One of these produced a set of manacles, old things, a little rusty on the surface, and rough, but solid looking for all that.

Adam began to protest. "Like a . . . " He cut himself off. *No sense in reminding Makeda of her official status.*

"I'm sorry," Labaan repeated. "But turning the two of you into one package makes it that much harder for someone to take you away."

And impossible to swim, Adam thought. *Dammit. There goes that plan . . . if I can call it a plan . . . since I still had no good solution to the sharks.*

Makeda took the wrist manacles in stride, or at least seemed to. Who knew what anger and hate burned inside the heart of a slave? Adam, on the other hand, felt a deep, burning sense of humiliation.

"It will only be when you're outside," his captor assured Adam. "And I really am sorry." Labaan, feeling mildly dirty, turned and left. They could hear his footsteps scrunching on the coral gravel for some time after.

The sun setting to the west over the waters of the bay framed Makeda in bright orange as she walked the rubble strewn road circling the island. She had the swaying grace common among the woman of her people, that grace being partly driven by culture and example, and partly by the mere fact that they tended to be so tall and slender. Adam walked at her side, holding her hand. This was the easiest way, since the two were cuffed together at the wrist.

The guards hadn't said, "Now try to swim in that position," as they'd linked the two. At least their mouths had said nothing. Adam thought their faces betrayed the words even so. At least most of them had. One, Adam had thought, looked almost apologetic. He thought, too, that they seemed more alert than they'd been for some time.

"Before you were brought here," Makeda said, "before they put up the fence, we were allowed sometimes to associate with the locals." Her chin indicated the surrounding waters. "They said there used to be yachts that came here . . . often, even. And a ferry from Yemen that came almost every day, instead of the one that comes about once a week or ten days now."

"Not anymore?" he asked.

She shook her head, a motion as graceful as her walk. "Too dangerous now; pirates . . . slavers . . . kidnappers for ransom. They said they used to make a pretty good living from the yachts and the tourists. Some of them hoped they might restart the slave trade that used to run through here . . . but most were skeptical that they could."

"I hope they can't," Adam replied. He exhaled, despairingly. "My father had slaves, too, though we didn't call them that. Still, that's what they were. I never thought about it back then. About where they'd come from, who missed them at home. Some of them, too, had been with our clan for generations. Those were like family."

Her eyes flashed. "Not pieces of meat like me, you mean?"

"I *didn't* mean that. What I meant was that the whole thing is wrong. And it took meeting you for me to realize it."

"And what can you or anyone do about it?" she asked.

He lifted both their hands, the ones that were manacled together, for illustration's sake and said, "Now? There's nothing either of us can do now. Maybe someday."

"It's a nice dream, anyway, isn't it?" she replied.

Their walk had taken them by the dock. The dhow was still there, thumping gently against the dock. The crewmen were busily scurrying about, preparing to leave. Their Arabic cries carried across land and water.

As long as I'm dreaming, Adam thought, looking longingly at the dhow, *what dream gets me in command of that boat, with the crew doing my bidding, to get the hell out of here?*

Bribe the crew? Even assuming I can get aboard, they're none too likely to accept me as someone whose family could pay the price. Force the crew? With what? He looked over at the guards. *They'd kick my ass, if I tried to grab a rifle, even if they wouldn't just shoot me out of hand. Kill the crew? Even if I had the skills and strength for that, which I don't, I couldn't run the boat. And I've got no teacher to pass on the skills, even if . . . hmmm. No, I suppose not . . .*

Dhuudo, Ophir, D-74

Most likely the slave market of Suakin never would reopen, despite the fervent hopes of some of the people who lived nearby. This didn't mean there was no trade in slaves; there was. In fact, the trade had become quite impressive again across the world. By some estimates there were more slaves on Earth, in absolute numbers, than there had ever been before. To a large extent, those estimates depended for their size upon definitions of slavery that were perhaps a bit too expansive for accuracy's sake. Nonetheless, there were perhaps millions, certainly hundreds of thousands, of slaves kept and used, bought and sold, around the globe that would have met Cato the Elder's definition of a slave: A tool that speaks. Most of these were female, and if they could speak it was not for that ability that their owners valued their mouths.

Still, although female slaves had values that males did not, for most buyers and owners, there was still a market in healthy males.

What's mah bid fo' this fahn, healthy, young buck niggah? Buckwheat Fulton mentally sneered as the bidding opened on a boy of perhaps fourteen or fifteen. Manacled, the boy was black, as was Fulton himself, and had features, like the retired master sergeant, more negroid than the locals who tended to resemble very dark Arabs. On the other hand, in contrast to Fulton, the boy looked absolutely terrified.

Bidding was fierce, unintentionally egged on by a group of whites seated on benches near the low stand on which the auctioneer displayed the wares.

"What the hell are they up to?" Buckwheat asked of Wahab, a flick of his chin indicating that he meant the whites.

Wahab shrugged, as if with indifference. *If the genital mutilation of the girl in Rako had been an embarrassment, how much more so this barbarism?*

"Some anti-slavery society or other?" he said with a shrug. "A church group? No telling. They collect money then come here to 'ransom' the slaves, which has the side effect of driving the price up, hence making it more profitable to raid for slaves and increasing the number who are taken. Of course . . . what was that?" he asked, after Fulton muttered something or other.

"I said," Buckwheat replied, "'thank God my multi-great grandpappy got dragged onto that boat.'"

"Oh. Well, anyway, as I was about to say: Of course, given a choice between paying to ransom slaves, thus ensuring more are captured, or using the money to buy arms for the tribes that are the usual victims of the raiders, naturally you western types prefer the least violent and least effective—really, the most counter-productive— approach."

"I suppose they do," Fulton answered. If Wahab understood that Buckwheat had just said that *he* was not among those who preferred nonviolent and ineffective solutions, the African gave no sign. He did, however, think, *And when I pinned general's insignia on you, if I could, I wonder if you might lead us in a war to free the slaves? That would be something. Or to create a country from scraps? It always takes a foreigner to do that, someone not part of or beholden to a clan. When this is all over, you, and I, and Khalid, are going to have a long, long talk.*

With a clap of hands, the auctioneer indicated that bidding was over. He pointed toward the group of whites who had been successful in outbidding the poor locals and shoved the slave lightly in their direction. The whites made a great show of huddling around the boy, in the guise of protection, and a greater one of striking off his manacles. One of their number took pictures for posterity's sake or, more likely, to feature in pamphlets designed to raise money. As the whites led the boy off, another slave, female this time and considerably younger than the boy, was mounted on the auction block.

"Come on," Fulton said, standing up. "If I don't get away from here, I'm going to kill somebody."

★CHAPTER THIRTY-TWO★

It is very reassuring, when confronted by an
approaching enemy tank, to know that across one's
shoulder is the most modern shoulder fired rocket
in existence; or that the man a yard or two
away is diligently tracking the tank through the sight
of a MILAN or TOW missile . . . But there are
times when none of these comforts are within reach,
and one has to do the best one can with what is
available, and that may not be much.
—Ian Hogg, *Tank Killing*

D-73, Assembly Area Alpha—Base Camp, Amazonia, Brazil

FitzMarcach's face said "doom." First Sergeant George
shook his head, doubtfully, as Reilly's finger traced across the
map. "They'll murder us, boss," George said. "There's no
cover, either getting there or once we are there. We'd be—"

At Lana's knock on the tent pole, Reilly, his exec, and
his first shirt both looked up from the map they'd been
studying. The diffuse jungle light was still bright enough,

in comparison to the tent, to strain the eyes. This caused the Israeli woman to appear more of an outline than a person. *Not that it isn't a nice outline*, Reilly thought, then mentally added, *After the mission, asshole. There'll be time, opportunity, and* rightness, *then*.

There were other outlines, much less distinct, behind Mendes. Reilly thought they were the two South Africans, standing behind her. He repressed the distaste he felt about those two, primarily because they were reasonably discreet about their status and were, in fact, pretty damned good armored car mechanics. *Good troops, as a matter of fact. Not their fault, what they are. Then again, not my fault if it makes my skin crawl, either. And if being together helps them push away the solitary nature of life, who am I to criticize?*

"Come on in," he said, flattening the map down on the field table between himself and George. "Have a seat . . . err . . . seats," he amended, when his eyes had adjusted well enough to make out Viljoen and Dumisani in detail. Behind them, he saw, were the German, Nagy. and the two Brits, Trim and Babcock.

Aha, the foreigners' union, Reilly thought. *Well, why not? They're a better mirror than most*.

Mendes went right to the point. "We've been talking it up to your men. But it's not working."

"That's not exactly right, *baas*," Dumisani corrected. "It's working with about two thirds of them, some, anyway. Others are neutral. But there's a smaller number, maybe half a dozen, who are listening to one of them—"

"Adkinson," Viljoen said. "I've seen the type before; chip on his shoulder, big head, tiny brain. Not competent to be in charge of anything big and resentful as hell of someone who is. Nasty toxic bastard. He's even starting to infect your infantry and most of those guys are devoted to you personally. Why the hell did you take him on, anyway? Leave aside that he loathes Dumi and me because we're gay . . . or maybe because we're foreign . . . or maybe both. You never should have hired him."

Reilly glanced quickly and guiltily at George, who said, "His record was clean and even pretty good. And he was available. There wasn't any obvious reason for the boss not to take him on. And, yes, I knew he's been a source—okay, okay, *the* source—of trouble for the last few days."

"Well," Viljoen said, "you would have been better off if he'd been *un*available."

"What's his beef?" Reilly asked.

Viljoen shook his head, not with confusion or doubt but with disgust. "He'll claim he's only concerned about the tanks and the implicit violation of the contract here. It's bullshit; if it hadn't been tanks, it would have been something else. He's just that type."

"Dani is understating the man's abilities," Dumisani said. "He's actually not stupid. He wouldn't be so dangerous if he were. He's fairly clever, in fact, clever enough to hide what he's doing behind care and concern and a sort of bizarre notion of professionalism."

Reilly looked at George. "Why hasn't the sergeants' mess taken care of it?"

The first sergeant chewed at his lip a moment before answering. Rocking his head from side to side, he said, "They're waiting to hear from you. Frankly, they're scared, Boss, scared enough that they're not sure whether to beat Adkinson's ass or join him in a mutiny. You have to talk to them."

Reilly sighed, then brushed fingers through somewhat thinning hair. "Among my many other military failings, Top," he admitted, "is a vast inability to bullshit people. I haven't talked to them about it because I don't have an answer to the problem yet." His finger indicated the map. "None of the options are good. The more I think about them the less good they seem.

"Suppose we hit the tank compound first. Okay, we can probably wreck that tank formation. But the more I think about it, the more certain I am that everyone in that village will scatter to the bush and we'll fail the mission. They're going to hear the shooting, after all; the compound's not *that* far from the village.

"Stauer's already said we can't just take the town and evac everybody by air. He doesn't think we can do it in time even if he gave us the air. Again, the more I think about it, the more I'm inclined to agree.

"I don't think a few light aircraft can do it alone and I don't think I can afford to split our force up either, even if we have air support.

"So I'm stuck. I *wish* to hell that Stauer had ordered the high velocity 60s."

"Oh, sure," Lana said. "Those can penetrate a T-55 right through the front glacis. At pretty fair range, too."

"Mmm . . . yeah." Reilly made it almost a curse. "But we don't have them. What we've got is 90mm soft recoil guns that can—"

"They can kill a T-55," Viljoen said. "I've done it . . . well, with help. But it helps if you can get them from the flanks. I remember the first time we ran into them . . . "

Reilly, Mendes, George, and the rest all stood bent closely over the map. Trim watched, too, but it wasn't really an engineering problem. Babcock-Moore seemed distant and distracted, staring up at the tent ceiling when he wasn't staring at the door flap.

Reilly's right index finger drummed the map at a particular spot. "I'll have to clear it with Stauer," he said. "It's a major change to his plan. *Major.*"

"But you can believe in this?" George asked.

"Yes," Reilly answered.

"Then tell the troops."

"As soon as I talk to Stauer." He thought for a moment, then said, "Formation on the airfield, tomorrow morning. Call it eleven hundred hours. And pass the word to Gordo that I want at least two of his Porters waiting on the airfield at that time. Plus I need him to make a deal with his Guyanan contacts to hold a few people more or less indefinitely.

"Also, Top?"

"Yessir?"

"Identify the dozen or fifteen of the most reliable non-coms and troops we have. Issue them arms and ammunition. Also give me a list of the least reliable people we have."

"Schiebel in charge?" George asked.

"Good choice, yes," Reilly replied.

Trim gave a tight smile and added, "And there I was going to volunteer my sergeant."

Reilly raised an eyebrow and asked, "Why's that?"

D-72, Assembly Area Alpha—Airfield, Amazonia, Brazil

Stauer and Phillie stood off to one side, along with the Sergeant Major. Stauer looked, if anything, jolly, in stark contrast to Joshua's scowl. Phillie was beginning to believe that the sergeant major had been scowling so long it had become his natural facial expression.

On the other side of the field two Pilatus Porters thrummed softly, their engines idling. Behind the Porters Reilly stood, centered on the airstrip's perforated steel surface. Mendes stood beside Reilly, along with the two South Africans, and what looked to be about a dozen armed men, close behind.

Stauer asked of Joshua, "Is he fucking her, do you think?"

Phillie blushed, just slightly. The Sergeant Major's scowl simply deepened. "Nope," he said, shaking his head. "He might have, before she signed on with us. Now? Not a chance."

Stauer nodded and agreed, "Yeah, you're most likely right."

"It's not like she wouldn't say 'yes' in a heartbeat," Phillie said, softly.

"What's that?" Stauer asked.

"Oh . . . it's written all over her face. She wants him *bad*. A woman can tell these things, you know."

"But he wears a wedding ring," Stauer objected.

"You might be surprised how little that can matter," Phillie said. She didn't offer to elaborate.

Before Stauer could enquire—which is to say, pry—further, they heard George's voice through the trees, counting off the simple cadence: "One, two, three, four . . . left, right, left . . . left, right, a-left." Some of the troops began to sing the company song before the first sergeant cut them off with, "Shut the fuck up, goddammit. It's not a singing occasion."

"Is he going to shoot somebody?" Phillie asked. "I mean he's got those armed men . . ." Her voice trailed off. It was pretty horrible even to think about.

"Only if necessary," Joshua answered, completely tonelessly. Phillie looked over at his face and saw that, remarkably, his scowl had disappeared, replaced by something that was almost a smile. She asked about that.

"I love to see a master at work," Joshua answered. The sergeant major went quiet then, watching through narrowed eyes as George gave the commands to maneuver the company into a position centered on Reilly. He was no more capable of failing to evaluate even the simplest military evolution than a politician was capable of keeping his word or speaking the truth when a lie would serve better.

Phillie noticed that the engines of the Porters began to cut out as the company approached the runway. She asked about that.

"He considers it 'poor art' to actually have to raise his voice to a shout," Joshua explained.

"Do you know what the problem is?" Stauer asked Phillie. "I mean the real problem?"

She just shook her head.

"In any company, in any army in the world," he began to

explain, "there are about, oh, anywhere from half a dozen to at most a dozen people who really make things work. I mean the real go getters, the ones you can completely rely on. Those guys, and girls sometimes, make up the real chain of command."

"The difference between a good company and a bad one is often how closely that real chain of command mirrors the legal and official chain of command. If all the real movers and shakers are, say, privates or junior noncoms, it can put a company into a state of unofficial civil war in a heartbeat.

"I've seen a company where the *real* commander, the man everyone turned to for guidance, was a staff sergeant on crutches."

"Yes," Joshua said, "but Sergeant Ortiz *made* that company."

"Oh, I agree, Top. No argument. He was even able to mitigate the damage that red headed bastard, McPherson, did. But he could have just as easily *un*made that company."

Stauer sighed, realizing even as he did that *I find myself doing a lot of that, lately.* "Our problem, and Reilly's problem, is that we don't have half a dozen to a dozen really great guys per company. We've got about three dozen in each company."

"Post!" Reilly ordered. Unusual for the command, not only did George walk around to the back, along with the platoon sergeants, while the officers moved to stand in front, but the armed men behind Reilly also fanned out to both sides, half boxing the company in.

Reilly smiled, looking directly at Adkinson and saying,

"I understand that some of you are a little unhappy over the opposition we'll allegedly be facing . . . "

"But that should be a good thing, shouldn't it?" Phillie asked.

"No, ma'am," Joshua said, shaking his head. "When you've got that many superb people there just isn't enough to keep them all busy doing great things."

"With some folks, it doesn't matter," Stauer continued. "They'll do the job they're assigned, even if it's beneath them, and await opportunities. Some people, however, can't do that. Some, too, are natural troublemakers whom you could get good use from if you had the time to plan how keep them busy, but otherwise, they just create discord."

"But Reilly doesn't have the time," the sergeant major said. "He'd really prefer, deep down, to win people like that over. I imagine it hurts him inside that, in this case, he can't."

Adkinson wasn't sure why Reilly looked directly at him. Sure, he'd been complaining about the prospect of taking on tanks in armored cars, but that was professional, the obligation, as he saw it, of a noncom to keep officers from doing stupid things. He also didn't understand why the planes were standing by, still less the armed guards. In all, he didn't like the look of any of it.

Still, certain of his own rectitude, and acutely conscious that few NCOs and virtually no officers met his standards, he stood calmly enough, listening attentively to the usual officers' bullshit.

"I'm a little disappointed," Reilly said, with a seemingly

friendly nod, "at your lack of faith. But it's only a little, because I wasn't sure myself how we were going to take them out until quite recently. I'm a lot more disappointed that those of you with, shall we say, troubled hearts didn't come to me.

"That was the time I would have explained things. Now? Too late." Reilly jerked his thumb at the waiting Porters. "You want out? Git! I'd rather go in with a dozen men that were willing than ten times that who aren't."

The ranks shuddered, but no one moved. Whatever Adkinson was thinking—Reilly glanced at him again—his thoughts never reached his face. *Hypocrite*. The faces that belonged to the other two names given by George, Slade and Montgomerie, looked worried. *You should have thought of that before joining in with the malcontent*, Reilly thought.

The Israeli—and Lana had taken the effort to look particularly good for the event—and the two gay South Africans walked forward and said, loudly enough for all to hear, "We'll go with you, sir. We'd make a better noddy car crew than any you have, anyway."

Reilly nodded, thoughtfully, just as if he were deeply touched and just as if they hadn't rehearsed that part.

Sergeant Epolito, standing being his platoon, gave the order, "Third Platoon . . . take . . . seats." He then looked at Reilly and announced, "Sir, the Third Herd isn't going anywhere." He then sat himself and folded his arms across his chest.

That part they hadn't rehearsed. *But some things you can just count on*, Reilly thought. *I knew Epolito would never desert me or let anyone else do so.*

Peters, with the mortars, followed. Then Schetrompf, a very Marty Feldmanesque little guy, gave the order, "Seats." Headquarters came right after that, with the "armor" platoon seating themselves at Abdan's command.

Reilly nodded again, this time thoughtfully. "So you want to see it through?" he asked.

"Yessir . . . Yes, sir . . . sir . . . "

"Okay . . . we can go ahead. But there are a few of you I wouldn't trust with the lives of the rest of you." Reilly looked very pointedly at Adkinson again and said, "You all signed contracts giving us right and privilege of arrest, of summary punishment, and dismissal. Corporal Schiebel!"

"Sir," answered one of the armed men standing around the company.

"Please place Adkinson, Slade, and Montgomerie under arrest. They are stripped of their rank within the organization. Their pay is forfeit and will be placed in the unit fund. Bind them, and toss their asses on the first of the Porters. Take two guards to escort them to where they're going."

"Sir!"

"Sergeant Babcock-Moore?"

"Sir!"

"Your officer informs me you have some business in Guyana. Accompany the prisoners, oversee Corporal Schiebel until they're safely deposited, and return in no less than three days."

"But . . . "

"No buts."

"Sir!"

Reilly turned away to hide a slight smile. *So I'm making a little downpayment on loyalty? So what? Cheap at the price.*

★CHAPTER THIRTY-THREE★

Justice renders to everyone his due.
—Cicero
There is no such thing as justice—in or out of court.
—Clarence Darrow

D-72, Camp Stephenson,
Cheddi Jagan International Airport, Guyana

The hangar, while quite large, was crowded. Along one wall lay nine containers, side by side and ends toward the wall. Dark-skinned men, none of them in uniform, removed various sections from eight of the containers, assembling them into small airplanes on the hangar's concrete floor. The metal sliding doors were just open, and no more than required to ventilate the oven. Beyond that could be seen a single Pilatus Porter, its engine apparently still running. From the Porter four men took turns carrying in three squirming, struggling, blanket-wrapped bundles.

Gordo ignored the cursing and grunting as Schiebel and his crew dropped the last of the three tightly wrapped blankets-with-legs-sticking-out to the concrete. One of the bundles didn't squirm much, and the legs twitched only feebly. Sergeant Babcock was sporting a sore shin where one of the prisoners had managed to kick him during the flight. He hadn't kicked the prisoner— Montgomerie, it was—back. Instead, the black Brit had taken it in stride while Schiebel knelt beside the man, gripped his head through the blanket, and hammered it to the Porter's uncarpeted deck until Montgomerie had gone unconscious.

"Be easier," Schiebel said, wiping sweat from his brow, "to have just dumped them over the ocean from way fucking high up. The boss always was too soft hearted."

Harry Gordon ignored that, except to think, *If Reilly or Stauer had thought it necessary, that's just what they'd have had you do, Corporal.*

Both Drake and Perreira, the Guyanese pilot, were there, as well. Perreira had no real further personal business with the group assembled in Brazil, nor with Gordo specifically, since he'd already moved the turrets to Camp Alpha. Still, he had useful contacts and Gordo, while still thinking the man a weasel, had decided that he was probably a mostly honest weasel. Drake did have business still, notably arranging through his police contacts for the three Americans wrapped in blankets to be held incommunicado for some months in a jail far, far to the west. It had cost a little extra to find and employ a small country jail house where not one of the jailers except the sergeant in charge spoke a word of even Guyanese Creole, let alone English. Unless Adkinson, Slade, and Montgomerie could converse in Akawaio they were going to be pretty much out of communication.

"What are they being charged with?" Gordo asked of Drake.

"De bais ah in violayshun de immigrashun," the Guyanan answered, definitively.

Somehow, Vic thought, *it just sounds better with that accent.*

"Works for me," Gordon agreed, not thinking it worthwhile to mention any number of extraordinarily undocumented persons in Guyana at the time, not least among them a number of Mexican aircraft assemblers and mechanics. "After all, they are here, in Guyana, without visas."

"Exactly," Drake said. He said it so well that Gordon took a double take.

"Meh gyal, she teach meh. Speakin' o' dah, you kam dinner, boyo?" he asked of Babcock-Moore.

Before the sergeant could agree or Gordo could comment, McCaverty, better known as "Cree," sauntered up. "We'll be assembled and ready to go by about nineteen hundred, tomorrow night."

"Roger," Gordo replied. "You'll space out at half hour intervals. My sergeant will meet you on the road six miles east of the bridge over the Takutu river. He'll have a pod of fuel and will mark the landing zone with infrared chemlights. You'll refuel there and then continue on to base. You guys have any problem with a rough strip landing, at night?"

"None," Cree assured. "What about my Mexicans?"

Gordo pointed with his chin at the Porter that had brought in the three prisoners. "They start leaving on that, just after you do. Most of them will beat you there. The rest go tomorrow."

"They don't speak a lot of English," Cree advised.

"No matter," Gordon said. "A lot of people at camp speak Spanish. Morales from the SEALs will be going with them, along with Antoniewicz, now that they're out of hospital. They'll be taken care of."

"Fair enough."

D-71, Assembly Area Alpha—Base Camp, Amazonia, Brazil

Phillie was a San Antonio girl, and part Mexican to boot. Of *course* she spoke Spanish. Lox spoke Spanish, too, along with Tagalog, German, French, Italian and a smidgeon of Arabic. Konstantin had sent down Sergeant Musin, who shared Russian with at least one of the Romanian girls, and English which was the organization's lingua franca. Nobody in the camp spoke Romanian. Still, they had reason to believe between all those languages that they'd be able to get their point across enough to teach the girls to serve as back up scut work medical personnel.

Thus, it was with more annoyance than pleasure that Phillie asked, "You all speak English?"

"Some not so good," the senior girl, Elena said. "Some better. Mine"—she put her hand out, palm down, and rocked it— "okay."

"Then why the *hell* didn't you tell the men who rescued you?"

Embarrassed, Elena looked down at the tent's dirt floor. "Not know they rescue," she said. "At first think they just capture to resell. Later on, when know they not like that, ashamed to admit . . . we . . . lie."

Phillie shook her head. She was beginning to discover that the world was a much suckier place than she'd been led to believe. And it didn't seem to be getting any better. She chewed her lip for a while, then said, "Sergeant Lox?"

"Ma'am?"

"I think you've got better things to do. You're dismissed." Phillie was rather pleased that she'd said that approximately like Wes would have. "Please stop by the aid station and ask Sergeant Coffee to come here."

"Yes, ma'am. Do you need Tim?"

"No, I don't think so."

Lox nodded and turned to leave, signaling with a head jerk that Tim was to follow.

Turning back to the girl, Elena, Phillie asked, "What do you understand about our circumstances and yours?"

"You are military group," Elena answered, without hesitation. It got harder then. She struggled, "Private, not belong . . . not . . . ummm . . . owned . . . " She shook her head; no, that wasn't quite right. "Not *controlled* by national government."

"That is correct," Phillie agreed, but added, "Also not protected by any national government. In light of that, what about you and the others?"

Again, Elena didn't hesitate a moment. "We all talk and agree, once we understand . . . back on little boat. We owe you *big*. We help."

"It could be very dangerous."

"We help."

"Then we've got ten weeks to turn you girls into competent medics and medical assistants. Let's go check with supply and see about your uniforms, boots, and other gear. There'll be a lot of it."

"Good," Elena said, looking down at the ratty, way oversized sailors' coveralls she wore. "Got nothing else to wear. Got nothing we own."

Yep, the world is a far suckier place, and not in a nice way, than I've been led to believe.

One of the Romanian girls said something in her own tongue. To Phillie it sounded hauntingly like Spanish . . . but was just enough off as not to be intelligible. Whatever the girl had said, Elena reached over and smacked her head.

"What was that for?" Phillie asked.

"Not all of us unwilling be sold as whores. She wanted know when we get to see men."

Aha. Then before we hit supply, "Sit down, girls. Let's have a little chat about the rules . . . and under what circumstances you can break them." She looked around at the faces, pretty in general, slightly olive for the most part, much like herself, but, "Wait a minute. How old are you?"

"I am . . . sixteen," said Elena, the senior. "We are all sixteen or seventeen except for Adriana, Irina, and Tatiana." On the last name Elena once again struck the girl—apparently Tatiana—she'd slapped before. "They is . . . umm . . . are fifteen."

"Aha," Phillie half smiled. "Very *different* set of rules then. *Very* different. Rule Number One is NO. Rule Number Two is, in case of doubt, refer back to Rule Number One. Rule Number Three, on the other hand, says Rule Number One, NO, is continuously in force. Rule Number Four . . . "

★ ★ ★

Coffee heard Phillie's voice coming from inside the tent set aside for training the foreign girls, " . . . is known as the 'two girl' rule. That means that I better never find one of you alone. You will always be at least in pairs. This includes, most *especially*, going to the latrines, the toilets, in the middle of the night. Rule Number Six . . . "

Coffee smiled—*quick study, our girl*—and then coughed. "Phillie, you sent for me?"

The girl called Tatiana began turning her head very quickly to where the voice had come from. This movement ceased and her eyes returned to straight ahead in a flurry of Romanian and a loud *crack*.

Phillie ignored the slap. She said to the sergeant, "Despite what we thought, these girls all speak English to some extent. I think that means we can get a lot more use out of them than planned. So I suggest that instead of me teaching them how to clean floors and instruments to standard, or to empty bedpans, you ought to be teaching them how to be real medics."

"Makes sense," Coffee agreed. "Let me clear it with Doc Joseph."

"Fine," Phillie said. "In the interim, girls, Rule Six is . . . "

D-70, Assembly Area Alpha, Base Camp, Amazonia, Brazil

"And that makes eight," Waggoner said, as the last of the CH-801s touched down on the strip. "Amazing damned things," he muttered, as the plane came to a stop in what looked to be about twenty-five meters. "Just amazing."

"It's just a somewhat redesigned Storch," Cruz said. He'd come upriver to camp from the *Merciful* on the supply ferry. "Arguably not quite as good as those birds were. Considerably smaller wingspan, though, and that—" he glanced around at the trees towering over the strip "—counts. It'll count aboard ship, too."

Under a tree, not five meters away, Cree, who'd come in first then taken over directing the landings, breathed a sigh of relief as he placed a radio microphone down atop the radio he'd propped up against the tree. The radio, as well as those aboard the CH-801s, was in the clear. There were encrypted radios available, but they'd been either in Brazil or in transit. The planes had had to make do with commercial jobs, all unencrypted. Everybody else on the base already had encrypted radios, Russian-made frequency hoppers; a bit heavy, but effective enough for all that.

In the dark, Cree's Mexican ground crew was already pushing the last of the light planes under the trees. More specifically, they pushed it under a camouflage screen they'd erected under Sergeant Major Joshua's tutelage earlier in the day. Mac was one of the denizens of the camp who spoke rather excellent Spanish, the result of spending many years as an instructor at the jungle school at Fort Sherman in the old Panama Canal Zone; that, and having married a girl from Colon, Panama. Sure, the accent was substantially different, as was much of the slang. Even so, he'd spent enough time around Mexican Spanish speakers to more than get by.

"So what's left?" Joshua asked Waggoner. The latter started; he hadn't even been aware the former was still in the area . . . and Mac had never learned to smile in the dark to let people know he was around.

"Bring in the half dozen or so translators Wahab is rounding up," Waggoner answered. "That's it . . . well, that and finish training here and then load the *Merciful*. Not a bad job, all things considered," he added. "From a standing start to a joint-combined battalion size task force in fifty-six odd days."

"Nope," Mac agreed. "Not bad at all. 'Course, all of our own people are already basically pretty well trained. And even some of the foreigners."

"*That* was a help," Waggoner said. "I wonder if it's ever been done before."

"It has," Joshua replied. "Many times, if not in exactly the same way or for exactly the same reasons."

"Really?" Waggoner asked. "Where? When?"

"Depends on what aspect you mean. The minutemen of 1775 mustered from unmobilized and fairly untrained militia in a matter of literally minutes to hours. The Massachusetts militia then began a siege of the British in Boston within days. The Continental Army assembled in mere weeks. None of them had nearly the level of training most of our people came to us with.

"From Hitler's order to begin planning the invasion of Norway to the first German troops setting foot on the ground was about ten days less time than we've planned on and if the Germans already had a force in existence, the scale of the thing was much greater and the anticipated opposition much more ferocious. Eben Emael and the associated bridges were more on our scale, and if those took a little longer to prepare, from Hitler's order to

Student to the actual assault, the Germans were also doing something rather new and, again, against worse opposition.

"Then there were the *filibusteros*, or the Texian Army under Sam Houston . . . Go back to how quickly the Romans not only trained a fleet to face Carthage, but actually built one from scratch. And let's not forget—"

"I'm talking about creating a mercenary force of roughly battalion size, very quickly, from scratch," Waggoner interrupted. *Sometimes I wonder if the colonel isn't exactly right about the sergeant major, his ancient ancestor, and legions of Rome.*

"Fifth Commando, Congo, 1964."

"Oh."

D-69, Kamarang, Guyana

"Ohhh, my fucking *head*," moaned Montgomerie, seated against a brick wall with his rear end on a filthy floor. He'd been out of it for over a day and was just now coming to his senses. When he wasn't puking from concussion. When Corporal Schiebel decided to knock someone silly, that someone would stay silly for a while. "Where are we?"

"I don't know," said Adkinson, standing and staring out the open, unscreened bars of their common cell. It was dark outside, with just a hint of morning's light in the east. Adkinson's forearms were through the bars, with his hands grasping them. "Guyana, somewhere."

"You don't know?" Slade asked, voice dripping with contempt. Slade sat on the one, narrow, mattressless bunk in the cell. "But you know everything, I thought. You sure fucking acted like it and talked like it."

"Fuck you, Slade," Adkinson said. "You didn't have to listen to me."

"And I wish to hell I never had, asshole. I *needed* that money."

A jailer came in. At least they thought he was probably a jailer. He looked old, if not exactly feeble, and either entirely or at least mostly Amerindian. He wore no shirt and only cut-off trousers, remnants of what might once have been a police uniform. A canvas belt and rusty pistol hung at his ample waist. The jailer set a tray of something down on the floor and then, using a pole, pushed it through a small opening at the base of the cells bars.

"Let us the fuck out!" Adkinson said, turning from the barred window. The jailer answered with some language that didn't seem to have any Indo-European roots whatsoever. Naturally, innately sure that he'd be listened to if he just spoke loudly enough, Adkinson raised his voice. The jailer just shrugged and turned away.

Slade stood up and walked over to the tray, bending and picking it up. He sniffed at it. "Food," he announced. "But I'm not sure what kind."

Adkinson was about to give a smart answer when he felt a sharp prick in his neck. He slapped at it. "Son of a bitch!"

"Ohhh, my *head*," Montgomerie repeated.

"Hey, does it seem to be getting hotter in here?" Slade asked.

★CHAPTER THIRTY-FOUR★

> Once a Chekist always a Chekist;
> Chekists cannot be former or corrupt.
> —General Vladimir Smirnov, FSB

D-69, near Lubyanka Square, Moscow

Russia, at least, had gasoline freely available. The thick and fearsome traffic outside the old headquarters of the Cheka and its progeny said as much. The noise, of horns, of badly tuned engines, and of cursing drivers and pedestrians, was equally fearsome.

"I *like* it," said Yuri Vasilyevich Chebrikov, to Ralph Boxer, in a little café down a side street off the square, not too very far for an old man to walk from his daily travails. As tired as he looked, indeed, the skin around his neck and eyes and along both sides of Chebrikov's face sagged, he still managed to make his daily walk, rain, shine, or—commonly enough—deep slush.

Both Ralph and Victor visibly relaxed, now that Victor's father-in-law, who was also a deputy director for

Russia's Federal Security Service, had given at least this much of a verbal blessing to the project. Victor had given the old man the bare bones of the thing before Boxer arrived.

"There are, however," Yuri continued, "a few conditions to my acquiescence." He turned his eyes, which were much warmer than his profession would suggest, to his son-in-law. "How long have you known the plan?" Yuri asked.

"In this detail, Yuri Vasilyevich, about thirty-six hours," Victor answered. Boxer didn't, of course, volunteer that he had not given over the entire plan.

"You understand," Ralph explained, "that we wanted to bring this to the highest authorities, which Victor, sadly, was not."

"What would you have done had I said 'no'?" Yuri asked.

"Gone ahead anyway," Ralph answered. "It's too far along to stop now."

"And if the United States had said you could not?"

"Gone ahead anyway," Boxer answered confidently, though he was not really as certain that Stauer would have balked his own country.

"Have you asked them?"

"No, nor will we."

Chebrikov smiled. "Then let me suggest to you that if they had said 'no' you would not have gone against them."

"Possibly," Boxer admitted. Changing the subject, he asked, "You said you had conditions?"

"Yes. Two big ones and several smaller ones. The big ones first?"

"Please," Ralph agreed.

Yuri patted Victor's shoulder affectionately. "My son-in-law is to go with you, to have full access to your facilities and everything you do, and free ability to report back to me." Yuri waited to see if the American balked on that issue. If he had objections, they hadn't reached his face yet. Yuri continued, "Secondly, I want your people to add a mission." He turned back to Victor and asked, "Is Konstantin's team still mission capable?"

Victor had a sudden image of mopeds racing through the jammed streets of Yangon. "Yes."

"Very good." He turned back to Boxer. "There is an Arab, a Yemeni, from Sana'a, who was instrumental in the hijacking of one of our ships. He is to be punished, seriously and severely punished. We want you to attach Konstantin and his people to your organization, and get them in a position to destroy this man, this Yusuf ibn Muhammad al Hassan. Information on his location and target status will be forthcoming, assuming you agree."

There Boxer balked. "We can't. We're shoestring as it is. We've no way to get Konstantin to him, and no way to extract him and his men afterwards. And, in any case, why us? You represent the Russian Empire, reborn. Surely, you can get this one Arab."

It was Yuri Vasilyevich's turn to sigh. "We can't get him because he is . . . Ralph, do you mind if I call you Ralph?"

"Not at all, sir." *And why not the honorific? The old bastard's been in the intelligence business since I was a child.*

"Civilization is dying, Ralph. All over the world. Everyone in a position to know knows that much."

Boxer rocked his head back and forth. Yes, he knew civilization was, broadly speaking, on the ropes. He wasn't convinced it was hopeless, yet, but, *yes, on the ropes*.

"States," Yuri continued, "once powerful states, are falling to gangs. Borders cannot be controlled. 'Idealists' fight amongst themselves for control of the drug trade. Piracy is as rife as the reduced sea traffic nowadays can support. Economies are collapsing; even your own Dow Jones Industrial Average is below three thousand, less than a quarter of what it once was. Unemployment, underemployment, and misemployment approaches twenty-five to thirty-five percent in the nations that are doing *well*. Fifty percent in some others. Your own president is a would-be Stalin in Birkenstocks, a doctrinaire—what's that wonderful Yankee term?—ah, yes, a doctrinaire watermelon determined to see you into the industrial stone age.

"National consensus, which some deride as consensus to wage war together, but is also consensus to live together, at least locally, in peace and mutual aid, is dying *everywhere*. And adolescent—or, at least, sophomoric—Kantian pipe dreams will not take its place. Civilization is dying, Ralph," the old Chekist repeated. "Or, at least, it's very, very ill."

"One of the things that happen when that happens is that people start looking out for themselves and their own. We can't take on the Yemeni because he is backed by Saudis and because *we* are fractured and that wog banker has his support, all bought and paid for, right here." Yuri's old, gnarled finger pointed towards the square. "Right over there in the Lubyanka."

The old man's hand shook. Whether it was with the palsy of age or simple human rage, Boxer couldn't tell. Yuri half-whispered, "And no one knows who they can trust anymore."

His voice rose again to a normal volume, "That's why I want the Arab punished, and *severely*, not only to teach a lesson to those who would grab our ships but to cut off from financing the people right here inside Russia who are simply members of foreign criminal gangs."

"We still don't have a way to get Konstantin from where we must be to strike to where he must be to strike," Ralph objected.

"Oh, yes, you do," Yuri said. He turned his attention back to his son-in-law and asked, "Victor, do you still have the capability to move, say, two MI-28 helicopters?"

"They'll fit in the largest shipping containers?" Victor asked.

"Barely, but yes, if you take off everything extraneous, the nose, the tail rotor, the main rotor and its mast, the landing wheels, and the side weapons pylons." Yuri didn't bother to explain how he had that information at his fingertips. In his line of endeavor, such things were a given.

"Then, depending on from and to where, Yuri Vasilyevich, yes."

He asked of Boxer, "Can you fit another two helicopters on your ad hoc assault transport? Can you house and feed four aircrew and nine or ten ground crew, plus Konstantin and his people?"

Boxer hesitated fractionally, pulled up the image of the ship in his mind, along with the three helicopters it carried. "I . . . *think* so. They'd have to speak English to fit."

Yuri smiled. "You're an American. If you think you can; you can. And, yes, they'll speak English. I am going to get Victor two brand new MI-28 helicopters, plus ordnance for them. He is going to get them to your ship. They can carry three passengers each and can take Konstantin's team to where it can do the most good.

"Oh, and as a special favor, and since we have owned a goodly chunk of your State Department since at least the 1930s, I am going to tell one of our people there to ignore anything having to do with you and your operation, and to make sure no one else pays it the slightest attention, either. And you can keep the helicopters when they're done; they'll be far too 'hot' to bring back here. Besides, I owe you for springing my son-in-law from the jail. Consider them to be my thank you note."

"We . . . *appreciate* this, sir," Boxer answered, even while thinking, *I'd like to have the names of your people at State. Not that you would give them up. Hmmm . . . did Stauer know this would happen? If so, how? Note to self: Long chat with Wes, soonest.*

"By the way, sir," Boxer asked, "what was on the ship this Yemeni arranged to be grabbed?"

"Tanks," Yuri replied, his face darkening.

"I will," he added, "be sending Major Konstantin a target folder. May I trust your discretion and good judgment in not *looking* at it?"

D-68, Assembly Area Alpha—Base Camp, Amazonia, Brazil

To the west, farther from the river bank, in one of the

tents that had been set aside as a sort of senior leaders' mess and club, some of the commanders, senior noncoms, and staff were singing one of those vile German war songs they seemed so fond of.

At least, Phillie Potter thought as she left her girls' tent to make her way through the nearly pitch black, *at least they're not in an Irish mood tonight. God, those songs are so* depressing. *I wonder why the hell they seem to cheer the boys up. There are a lot of things about soldiers I will never understand.*

She'd learned to stop for a minute or five, light depending, to let her eyes get accustomed to the darkness before she tried walking. She still did, even though she'd grown used to the path to Stauer's tent by walking it every night.

Finally, just able to make out enough of the tent and vehicle silhouettes to orient by, she started to step off. She'd also learned, the hard way, to give the tents a wide berth as their guy lines were always anchored some distance past the tent wall. Fortunately, the corduroy street Nagy and his engineers had put in helped to keep her on the right path, and without any unexpected holes to break an ankle in. She came to an ATV she recognized not by any distinguishing feature of its own but by where and how it was parked. Even if that hadn't been there, she could hear from a different tent than the one she sought the sergeant major, plus George and Webster, talking in normal voices. She turned there, off of the corduroy and onto some familiar sandbags, then slipped through the double canvas barrier, through the netting, and into the light.

"Wes," Phillie said, head facing toward the tent's dirt floor, "we need to have a long chat."

"Shoot," he replied, looking up from some paperwork he'd been about.

"It's . . . it's . . . I don't know where to begin."

He thought she looked seriously nervous, very unPhillielike, as a matter of fact. "Sit," he said, pointing toward the cot. "Think. Relax. Talk when you're ready."

"I thought I *was* ready. But . . . " Phillie sighed. "Nothing to it but to do it, which is to say, *not* to do it."

Now Stauer was very confused. "To do what?"

"It. You know, the wild thing? Make the beast with two backs? Make love? Fuck. I mean we can't. Not anymore. Ummm . . . fuck, that is."

He smiled; this was very unPhillielike. "Okay. Just out of curiosity, why?"

"It's the *girls*," Phillie almost moaned. "Those Romanian ex-slave girls. I laid down the law to them: 'You will not get laid. Period.' How can I do it when I told them they can't?"

Stauer smiled at the irony. "You seemed pretty put out yourself when I first told you no."

Her head rocked. "Yeah. I know. But that wasn't so much the sex; I was mostly hurt because I thought you didn't love me anymore. And . . . "

Yes?"

"Well. I've been learning a lot here, even if I don't understand it all. And . . . one of those things I've learned is that I have to command myself before I've got the right to command anyone else."

Stauer's smile changed from ironic to something

approaching idyllic. "Did I ever tell you what a great girl you are, Phillie?" he asked.

She sniffed slightly. This whole conversation was hard. "Not in those words exactly. Well, not outside of bed, anyway."

"Well, you are. And for a lot more reasons than what you can do in bed." The smile disappeared, to be replaced by a very, very serious expression, like someone in deep concentration or—as she would insist later—someone attempting to shit a brick. "Moreover, since I'm not getting any younger, what say that when this is over we get mar—"

He couldn't finish the sentence because Phillie was on her feet, racing the short distance across the tent, throwing herself onto him and, in the process, knocking them both to the mud. After that she was too busy covering his face with kisses for him to get a word in edgewise, except when she said, "Yes!"

"-ried?" he finally managed.

"Yesyesyesyesyesyesyes!" She pulled back from showering him with kisses long enough to ask, "Umm . . . you want a quickie before I become a nun? A blow job, anyway?"

He laughed and reached up to stroke her hair, saying, "Oh, hon, you have no idea how much. But . . . courage of your convictions, Phillie. It can wait."

She laid her head down on his chest and whispered, "Thank you, Wes. That was the right answer."

In the next tent over, Sergeant Major Joshua stuck out one hand, palm up, saying, "Pay up, gentlemen." With fairly bad grace, Webster and George pulled out their wallets, peeling off, each, fifty United States dollars.

"How the fuck do you do that, Joshua?" Webster asked.

"Got to know people in our business, First Sergeant. Got to pay attention. Got to have had Sergeant Coffee come tell you a story about a young woman being assimilated into the military, what she said to some young girls, and what such a woman is likely to do."

"Bastard," said George, sotto voce, as he counted out two twenties and a ten. "How about a bet on something else?"

★CHAPTER THIRTY-FIVE★

*Africa is a cruel country; it takes your heart
and grinds it into powdered stone—and no one minds.*
—Elspeth Huxley

D-61, Bajuni, Federation of Sharia Courts

Buckwheat thought the city was almost amazingly green compared to the bulk of the area.

"We get an annual monsoon here," Wahab had explained, while driving their Hummer through. "Mind you, that's always followed by an annual drought so the green doesn't last. Then again," the native African sighed, "nothing very good on this continent lasts very long. Still, we used to grow a lot of grain in this valley and could again.

"At least for a while, we could."

"Until the next round of civil war?" Buckwheat asked.

"Until the next round of civil war," Wahab agreed, swinging the steering wheel over to pull through a gate in a wall fronting the street. That turned out to be a mere shortcut. He kept on going through a courtyard then popped out on another street, on which he took a right. As if to punctuate Wahab's admission, a volley of gunfire burst out from what had to be a stadium, ahead and on the right. The gunfire was followed by screams and then a small mob of people exiting one of the stadium gates.

"Stop," Fulton said, holding his left hand up, palm forward. Once the vehicle had halted, he stepped down from the Hummer and walked to the stadium gate, now clear. A young man, perhaps eighteen years old, sat beside the gate, with his back against the stadium wall. His head rested on arms folded across his bent knees and his body shook with sobbing.

Buckwheat looked inside, through the gate, carefully.

In the middle of an athletic field, barely visible for the fifty-odd young men surrounding her, was a girl in a red dress, buried to her waist and with blood pouring from her head and face. All of the young men were armed, rifles slung across backs and fist sized rocks in hand. Perhaps a thousand people filled the nearest seats in the stands, watching the punishment.

The girl wasn't screaming, though she rocked back and forth as silent tears rolled down her cheeks. The tears left clear furrows in the blood. She could have been anywhere between twenty and thirteen years of age, though Buckwheat guessed it was most likely closer to the latter. As he watched, one of the surrounding young men threw a small rock, striking the girl on the front of her neck and forcing her back. She began to gasp, as if trying to suck air in through a windpipe that had suddenly swollen. The men taunted her, imitating her strained gasping.

Wahab walked up, bearing a rifle in one hand. "What is happening? Who is that girl?" he asked the weeping young man sitting by the gate.

"My sister," the boy forced out. "She was raped and they found her guilty of adultery. My . . . sister." He broke down in sobbing once again.

"What was that?" Fulton asked. When Wahab explained, he shook his head and said, as he often did, "Thank God my multi-great grandpappy got dragged onto that boat."

"Give me your rifle," he demanded of Wahab, holding his hand out.

Wahab shook his head, tightened his grip on the weapon, and said, "No. There is nothing you can do for that girl. It is the law. It is a rotten law, but it is still the law. And those men slowly killing her will still kill her, and also you, if you interfere. I would be . . . sorry to lose you, Buckwheat."

Tightened grip or not, Fulton reached out with snake-like speed, snatching the rifle from Wahab's hands. As he settled into a kneeling supported firing position, his left side resting on the left edge of the gate, Buckwheat said, "They're too intent on pulverizing that girl to even notice me until I open fire. You've got two minutes. I suggest you go get some more ammunition for this and the other rifle. I intend to see just how far your chief's protection will extend to those who intend to rescue his son."

A sort of low moan, punctuated by occasional rifle shots, permeated the air above the stadium floor. The moaning came from the survivors of what had been fifty-three young men, formerly engaged in stoning a girl. The bulk of the men had been shot in the back, some when firing first began and others as they fled that fire. With each shot the volume of moaning grew less.

Bang. Robert Buckwheat Fulton walked gingerly across the grassy field, his rifle generally pointed toward the ground. *Bang.* Every few steps, he would stop and fire another round—*bang*—into the head of someone who appeared to him to be still breathing. In all, he did that eleven times—*bang*—before he reached the spot where an older brother dug with bloody hands to free a younger sister from the pit into which she had been half buried. Wahab followed, his rifle up towards the now empty stands.

"How?" he asked, repeatedly. "There were fifty of them! *More* than fifty! How?"

"President's Hundred," Fulton said, in explanation, as he took aim at the head of another breather just past the girl. The retired sergeant's voice was pure ice. *Bang.* "Camp Perry, Ohio. Motherfuckers never had a chance." *Bang.* He looked down at someone who was not only breathing but conscious. "How do you like it when someone else has a gun and can shoot, asshole?" *Bang.*

"Oh," Wahab said. He looked over at the girl and said, "We can go now, Robert."

Bang. "Has the kid got his sister free?"

"No point. I mean, yes, but . . . she's dead."

Fulton bit his lip. "I see." *Bang.*

"Come on, Robert, we must go meet the chief and our attachments to your force."

"Sure. Be just a few more minutes . . . Hey, want a little cat's meat, motherfucker?" *Bang.*

D-53, Bandar Qassim, Ophir

"I hear there was a disturbance down in Bajuni," the old sept chief, Taban, said to Gutaale at the evening *majlis* in the latter's palace courtyard. "No one seems to have any details, but apparently a frightful number of young men were put to death by Khalid's decree."

"It's all falling apart down there," Gutaale said confidently. "Even faster than I predicted. Soon we'll be able to take it all."

Taban shook his head doubtfully. Even so, he had to admit that seizing the other chief's only son and heir had been masterful. *Or at least, I can't point to any one thing that hasn't worked out as Gutaale predicted. The lands we have demanded have been evacuated and turned over. Unrest is apparently rife in the enemy capital. Khalid's position is said to be crumbling. Still, it doesn't feel right. And I can't explain why.*

D-44, Suakin, Sudan

The sun wasn't quite up yet, nor had the *muezzin* begun the call for prayers. Under a bare lightbulb, in his own quarters, Labaan dipped his *canjeero*, a thin, pancake-like bread similar to Ethiopian *injera*, into a side dish of beef, cut small and boiled in *ghee*. Ordinarily, breakfast, or *quaraac*, was his favorite meal. This one . . . wasn't. *Neither, come to think of it, did I enjoy yesterday's, or the day before's, or any lately. Nor lunch nor supper either.*

His fingers dipped the rolled bread, dipped, dipped, then simply opened up and dropped it into the bowl. Standing, Labaan walked toward the part of the building wherein his captive and his gifted slave girl were kept. The guard on the door nodded, respectfully, which nod Labaan returned. The bare coral walls weren't really something one wanted to rap one's knuckles against. Instead, Labaan made a little coughing sound to announce himself.

"Are you and the girl decent, Adam?" Labaan asked.

In answer, there was a rustling of cloth, as if someone were hurriedly dressing, then the hung fabric covering the door was pulled partway aside. Adam, wearing a clean white robe, slid out sideways through the narrow opening, closing the door covering behind him. It was dark in the room, Labaan could see.

"Makeda is sleeping," Adam said. "I don't want to wake her."

"You'll spoil the girl, young Marehan," Labaan said chidingly. "But never mind. Even a slave can sleep in sometimes. I assume you haven't had anything to eat yet." The older man inclined his head, saying, "Come on."

The guard wasn't there for the girl; he was there for Adam. As the captive followed Labaan along the coral floor, the guard stepped in behind, his rifle at high port. After all, the boy wasn't chained.

At his own quarters, Labaan motioned for Adam and the guard both to have seats on the floor. The guard laid his rifle down on the side opposite the boy. There was no reason to throw temptation his way.

Once they were seated, Labaan retrieved his dropped piece of canjeero and popped it into his mouth. With his other hand he indicated the tray holding the bread and the bowl of beef. Adam hesitated until the guard reached over, ripped off a piece of the bread, rolled it and dipped it, scooping up some of the beef.

They ate in silence for some time until Labaan said, "I have been thinking about the . . . security arrangements, Adam, and I had a thought."

Adam raised one eyebrow, inquisitively, but said nothing.

"There is a thing the Europeans have, maybe the Americans, too; I'm not sure. It's called 'parole.'"

"Which is?" Adam asked.

"Your 'parole' is, among other things, your word of honor that you won't try to escape. I've watched you for some time now. You're a good boy, a good man, really. If you gave me your word you won't try to escape then I can dispense with the damned, bloody shackles. Give you more privacy." *Feel like less of a heel, though you don't need to know that.*

"It would mean more, this 'parole' of which you speak, if I had the faintest idea how I might escape," Adam said. "I don't, not that I haven't thought about it."

"I'm sure you have," Labaan agreed. "Be unworthy of you not to at least try to think of a way. Allah knows, I've spent enough time, both before and after your capture, thinking about how to prevent it." The older man's hand swept around, indicating, so Adam thought, not merely the building in which he was held but the entire abandoned city. "So will you give me your parole? You word as a man of honor that you will not try to escape?"

"It wouldn't matter," Adam replied. "With or without my word, I can't leave here. I can't leave the girl. You knew that would happen when you gave her to me, I'm sure. But for what it's worth, fine, you have my 'parole.' Such as it is."

Labaan nodded, more relieved than happy. "I'll give the orders not to shackle you anymore," he said. "And I'll pull the guards back out of earshot from your door. Who knows; maybe without us listening you'll get that girl with child. Then I'll have a better hold on you even than she is."

"Do you have children, Labaan?" Adam asked. The guard scowled; Adam had no idea why.

For a time Labaan was silent. Then he said, sadly and perhaps a bit distantly, "I had. Two girls. And a wife, of course."

"Had?"

"Dead. Killed."

Adam suddenly felt sick. Sure, Labaan was his kidnapper. But even in that he was only doing his duty as he saw it. In every particular, otherwise, he'd been as kind as he could be.

"I'm so sorry," Adam replied. "Was it my . . . " He let the question trail off.

Labaan shook his head. "Your people? No. No, I don't know who killed them. It was during the troubles that attended the breakup of what used to be a country. But I am sure of two things. One is that the Marehan had nothing to do with it; my family was nowhere near any place your people inhabit."

"And the other?" Adam asked.

Again Labaan went silent for some time. "And the

other," he finally answered, sighing, "and the other is that whoever did it, they were not of my people. Which is how I learned that one can only have faith in one's own blood."

★CHAPTER THIRTY-SIX★

Oral delivery aims at persuasion and
making the listener believe they are converted.
Few persons are capable of being convinced;
the majority allow themselves to be persuaded.
—Johann Wolfgang von Goethe

D-42, Assembly Area Alpha—Base Camp, Amazonia, Brazil

The twice-weekly marches had gradually been worked up from six miles at a fairly slow place and minimal equipment (barring the heavy mortars, which were always brought along for pain's sake) to twelve at a near killing pace. It was hard on the old men's knees, in itself, but their weight was dropping and that helped a bit. Maybe more importantly, they'd gotten used to regular pain again, pain in the back, pain in the knees, pain in the feet, and pain in all the muscles in between.

From the "street" outside of his darkened tent, Reilly heard the first sergeant giving the orders, "Foot inspection in thirty minutes. Platoon sergeants take charge of your platoons." This was followed by Platoon Sergeant, ex-Sergeant Major Schetrompf shouting, "You pussies don't need thirty minutes. Besides, the sun—such as it is—will be down by then. Squad leaders, you have ten to get 'em ready. Snap and pop, assholes, snap and pop." Epolito added, "The same goes for you, Third Herd."

Reilly made his way to his cot and sat down at the foot of it, wearily and heavily. "Oh, *God*," he moaned, softly, "my feet hurt."

Lana came in, dropped her rucksack down, plopped her shapely posterior on the ground, and leaned her back against the tent's center pole. She was wearing a green T-shirt that stuck to her body in all the best places. "You know," she said, "there's a lot to be said for just being a girl . . . pampered . . . soft . . . protected . . . spoiled. Maybe this whole feminist thing is a bad mistake."

Reilly knew she wasn't serious, or not entirely serious. "You heard Top. Get your boots off."

"I can't," she replied. "It hurts too much even to think about."

That much he did believe. He flipped the shoulder straps off of his rucksack and lay back, then rolled off the cot to the tent's dirt floor. On all fours he crawled toward her until he'd reached her feet.

"You don't have . . . "

"Shut up," Reilly said, as he began unlacing her boots. He undid the laces on both before pulling off first the left one, then the right. Thickly cushioned but now wet boot socks followed. These, smelly things that they were, he stuffed into the boots. There was just barely enough light to see by, filtering through the tent's roof, walls, and door.

At least there was now that his eyes were accustomed to it.

He examined her feet with a critical eye. "Tsk," he said, on seeing the prominent blisters. "You don't march much in *Tzahal*"—the Israeli Army—"do you?"

"Not so much," she admitted. "Not since the fifties when we went almost completely mechanized. Oh, sure, there's some in initial training and then rarely after that." She thought about that last statement and amended it, "Really rarely."

"It shows. How long have they been like this?"

"Couple of weeks."

"And you didn't see the medics?" His voice was full of reproach, even as his mind thought, *Good girl. Tough girl. You make me proud of you.*

"I'm not a whiner." *And besides, I didn't want to disappoint you.*

"I guess not," he agreed. "Wait here while I go get Sergeant Coffee."

He started to rise but her hand shot up and pulled him back to the ground, considerably nearer to her than he'd been. "Wait," she said. "It can wait."

"For what?"

"For this." She used both hands to grab him on either side of his head and pulled his lips to hers. He resisted, at first, but she had powers—God-given ones—far beyond his merely mortal ability to resist. One hand, his left, intertwined itself in the great auburn waterfall of her hair while the right, operating entirely on genetic autopilot, sought its way under her T-shirt, behind to her back, and then to the clasp that held her bra. A pinch of the clasp, a twitch of the finger and thumb, and it was loose, her breasts free. That hand then moved to cup the left breast softly but firmly.

She broke the kiss and moved her mouth to his ear. "Would you prefer to fuck me or to make love to me?" she sighed, breathless. "You can have it any way you want, any place you want it."

The spell she had him in wasn't broken, but it had been weakened by the breaking of the kiss. He backed off slightly and answered. "I'd prefer it when this is over."

She stiffened. "Damn! It's your wife, isn't it? I don't care if you're married. I want you *now*!"

He smiled, more than a trifle sadly. Untangling his hand from her hair and holding it up, he wagged his fingers and asked, "You mean this? I'm not married; I'm a widower. I wear it in memory." *And because it made me feel a little less alone. I think it did, anyway. Though maybe sometimes it reminded me of how alone I was.*

"But the men . . . ?"

He shrugged. "They don't know, except for a couple of them. No reason to tell them."

"Bu . . . oh, never mind. You don't want to make love until the mission is over?"

"Bad policy, I think."

Her hand went to his trousers, grasping him through the fabric. She looked around. Yes, it was fully dark by now. "We'll compromise," she said.

"Huh?"

"Just relax," she answered, pushing him back. She twisted her body and began to bend her head, even while her fingers worked at the belt and buttons of his trousers.

She was perhaps less expert in this than he had been with her bra clasp. Still, enthusiasm counts for much. Her hand felt around softly. "Ah, good," she said, in a husky voice. "I'm not orthodox but for some things I prefer kosher." As she bent her head over him, she added, "This isn't sex; that's what everyone says. But at least it's intimate, and emotionally satisfying, if not physically. And don't worry; I'll be the best little trooper you ever saw after this; no favoritism for me. But you will fuck me immediately after the mission is complete. *Immediately*!"

After that he wasn't in any mental position to argue the point, his brain being much deprived of blood and oxygen.

Oxygen deprived or not, Reilly wasn't nearly finished before he pulled Lana off and said, "Ah, screw it. Let's fuck."

"What the fuck do you want, George?" Joshua asked irritably.

Framed in the door of the sergeant major's, the light illuminating his features beatifically, George smiled, stuck out one hand, palm up, and answered, just softly enough not to be heard outside the tent, "I want my pound of flesh. He did her. Hah!"

"He fucked her?"

George hesitated. His hand dropped slightly. "Well . . . not exactly. She blew him though. I heard it. Most of it. I came back to collect before he actually finished."

"Thought so. You're an eavesdropping piece of shit, George. Besides, it doesn't count; ask the former President of the United States. For that matter, ask any fifteen year old; not that there's much difference between the two. He's got to fuck her—and before the mission—if you want your money back, First Sergeant; that was the deal."

George turned on his heel and stormed off without another voiced word, thinking, *Bastard*.

D-38, Assembly Area Alpha—Base Camp, Amazonia, Brazil

The Eland moved cautiously up the trail, its turret moving left-right, left-right, under Dani Viljoen's deft spinning of the wheel. Beside him sat Lana, her eyes scanning for threats—targets, in other words—and one hand resting on the ready rack of training rounds. Up front, Dumisani drove. He'd come to driving late in life, a byproduct of South Africa's former policy of oppression and suppression of its black population. He'd never quite gotten the hang of civilized driving. For a combat vehicle, this was no detriment but quite the opposite; Dumi could and would do things with a vehicle that had no place in civilized driving but were entirely appropriate in combat.

All three wore helmets on their heads, with boom microphones and cushioned speakers surrounding their ears. With these they communicated through the intercom system when the roar of the engine didn't permit normal conversation.

"Our girl here seems pretty happy, wouldn't you say, Dumi?" Viljoen asked. His manipulation of the traversing crank was automatic, leaving his brain and mouth free to tease the woman.

"Leave her alone, Dani," the driver said, with just a trace of menace.

"Not a chance," Viljoen responded. "How many times has it been now, Lana? Seems like every day since the last foot march you've disappeared for an hour or two."

"Fuck off, Boer," the Israeli woman replied. Then, "Gunner, HEAT, Tank!"

"Identified," Viljoen said. "Target."

"Fire."

The muzzle flashed. The .50 caliber subcal wasn't nearly enough to rock the armored car. They still felt the blast on their skin. Downrange, a plywood target shuddered. Lana was already slinging another round into the breech as Viljoen announced hit.

"Repeat. Fire."

"On the way . . . hit."

"Driver, move out."

"So how many times has it been, Lana?" Viljoen asked again.

"Has what been?" she asked.

He pulled his face away from his gunner's sight and said, "Don't be silly."

She shrugged. "Do multiples count? If so . . . ummm . . . eight . . . . no, nine. But you can't tell anybody."

"Wouldn't dream of it. I would, however, suggest that you make sure to wipe your chin before you leave his tent. And take off your shirt beforehand, too, because semen on mostly green camouflage cloth is pretty noticeable."

"I didn't!" she exclaimed.

"Actually, Lana," Dumi said from down at the driver's station, "you did. At least twice."

"Oh, God, did anybody else notice?"

Dumi answered, "Just Schiebel and Sergeant James, I think. Don't worry; they won't mention it. But *eventually* . . . "

"It would be simpler if he'd just screw me all the time," she said. "No muss, no fuss. But he's so worried about being caught . . . " Then, "Driver halt. Back up. Back up!"

"Gunner, HEAT, tank!"

A very confused and conflicted Reilly watched the half of the armored car platoon for which he had vehicles maneuver through the bare floored jungle. He realized he had eyes only for Lana's Eland and so forced those eyes away. When, after a moment, they went back of their own accord he physically turned away and began the walk back to camp, head toward the ground.

Not far from the armored vehicle training area began the ranges. At the first of these, the Marine company worked their PUS-7 simulators for the their Victor-supplied RPG-7s. Cazz, standing behind the firing line, waved. Reilly returned the wave, politely, then looked down again, continuing on.

Past the antitank range, he came to a square, marked-off open area where one of Sergeant Peters' mortarmen ran from spot to spot, a radio on his back, dropping simulators to mark rounds called in by forward observers.

Nothing I can do there that Peters can't do as well or better, he thought, then continued his trek.

He stopped to let a Ferret pass him by, the scout car dragging behind it an empty container on log rollers. Some of Nagy's engineers took turns moving the rollers to the front of the container as they were rolled forward. The engineers dripped sweat in the equatorial heat.

And that's where we're going to hide the vehicles, the military ones, anyway, when we leave. Who knows; maybe we can recover them some day. And, if not, they'll make some interesting matters of conjecture for some future archeologists.

On the other side of the container Reilly saw Stauer, deep in conversation with Chaplain Wilson.

Guilt, Reilly thought. *What I've got is a bad case of conscience. I mean, when you fail to meet even the very low standards you set for yourself . . .*

On the other hand, between having a company again and having a worthwhile woman again my life is pretty much complete again. And so, of course, I feel guilty over that, too.

He walked over and said, first to Wilson, "I wish you were a Catholic. Since you're not," he turned to face Stauer, "Boss, can I have a private word with you?"

From off in the distance came an irregular pop . . . pop . . . pop from the Dragunov range. From a droning plane above the airfield small dots could be seen falling. Parachutes opened up over the dots, slowing their descent. From last night's command and staff meeting, Reilly knew that a couple of the translators were being trained to jump.

"No," Stauer said, shaking his head firmly. "No, you can't be relieved and turn command over to your exec. He's a good guy but he's not you and I need you. And, no, especially are you not relieved after you lobbied so hard for the position. No, I can't get another crewman to replace Mendes since a) I don't have one and b) it's unlikely anyone else will be willing to serve with the two gays. We're just not that enlightened a group; sad but true. And I can't begin to tell you how *disappointed* I am in you. *You*, of all people, should have known better than to get romantically involved with a subordinate."

And am I the world's greatest hypocrite or what?

Head hanging, Reilly admitted, "I know. It . . . she was on my not-to-do list until much later but . . . well, things sort of got out of control. And now . . . now I don't know what to do. I can't stand the thought of putting her at risk."

Stauer scowled and growled, "Then I strongly suggest you do everything in your power to minimize that risk, company commander. Because we're still going in. She's still going to be commanding an Eland. And you still have a mission.

"On which subject, are you ready to start burying equipment, striking tents, and moving your people to the *Merciful*?"

"Yes, sir."

Stauer nodded, then asked, "You want a suggestion?"

Reilly just nodded, guiltily.

"When we pack out of here, move her in with you, all open and above board. There'll be less damage that way than if you keep sneaking it."

"I'll think about it, sir."

★CHAPTER THIRTY-SEVEN★

If the highest aim of a captain were to preserve
his ship, he would keep it in port forever.
—St. Thomas Aquinas

D-32, MV *Merciful*, Manaus, Brazil

The ship was anchored at the stern, with the bow, guided by the current, pointing downstream, toward the Atlantic. Behind it, the lights of the city shone, their rays bouncing off of the thick clouds overhead and illuminating river and ship, and the jungle framing both. Coming, as it did, from everywhere, the ambient light fairly obliterated any chance at deep shadows.

Not so much fortunately as by plan, the *Merciful* was anchored toward the north bank of the river with no ships or boats between it and the bank. Still, when the landing craft put-putted in, passed the ship, then turned to face upstream, perhaps someone on that bank might have seen it maneuver to a position alongside the merchant vessel. Perhaps that person might have seen the lowered boarding ramp or the long line of men, lugging rucksacks and other impedimenta, depart the craft up the ramp before disappearing through an open hatch in the ship's side.

"But," as Kosciusko observed, "anyone looking at this boat at three-thirty in the fucking morning needs to get a life. Besides, the authorities are a lot more interested in people who come in illegally than in people departing for just about any reason."

"This is so, Captain," Chin agreed.

"By the way, we have a new assignment for you and your men," Kosciusko said.

"The *Bastard*?" Chin asked, his face carefully blank. *Be still, O my heart.*

"The *Bastard.*"

D-30, MV *Merciful,* five miles past Santarem, Brazil

The ship didn't rock much, here in the waters of the Amazon, except on a turn, sometimes, or when another ship passed it going in the other direction. Down low in the hold, in Stauer's quarters, a twenty-foot container, lit by a bare bulb hanging from the ceiling, with a narrow folding cot, a small field desk and a pair of folding metal chairs, even the wake of passing ships was barely to be noticed.

He lay on his cot, staring upward, seething inside.

God, we've gotten away with so much, so far. I can hardly believe our luck will hold. But it has to.

Tomorrow, once we're past Brazil's territorial waters, I have to brief the men . . . oh, and the women, too . . . on the mission. They might balk. Be a laugh, which is to say a crying shame, if after all this they decide they don't want any part of it. Will they? I don't know. I'd have told them more from the beginning, if I could have been sure none of them would go running to the authorities. What if they want to run to the authorities now?

Simple, we lock anyone who balks in the containers they don't know about, the ones Chin set up . . . the ones with the bars. We can hold as many as fifty that way.

And no hard feelings. Anybody who doesn't want to stay in needs the excuse of being held against their will. What's the most they could be charged with then? Illegal possession of personal firearms in Brazil? No one's going to extradite for that. Well, I don't think anyone will.

Least of my problems, anyway. What if the planes break down? What if the helicopters do? We've run the landing craft kind of hard these last couple of months. What if they break down? What if they break down when we've got half the force ashore?

Fuck, fuck, FUCK.

Konstantin and the Russians? How do I know I can trust them? Boxer thinks they're solid, that the old man in the Lubyanka wants that Yemeni punished and no more. Oh . . . I suppose I can trust Boxer's judgment on such things. And we will have Victor Inning, the old man's son in law, as a hostage. That counts for something.

Once ashore? Fuck. There are so many things that can go wrong ashore I don't even want to think about it. Reilly fails? . . . Well . . . no. Reilly won't fail. Neither will Cazz. Unless, of course, the armored force near Rako doesn't fall for the bait. What then? Shit.

*Then I tell Reilly, "Move to contact and destroy them."
He'll get butchered, of course. But I wouldn't bet on his
not winning anyway. Though he won't be going after the
town with what he'll have left.*

Stauer had a sudden image of a headline in the *New
York Times*. "Mercenaries Massacred." *And wouldn't the
bastards be popping champagne corks over it, too.*

And what am I going to say to the men? What if . . .

D-29, MV *Merciful*, 107 miles northeast of Forteleza, Brazil

The open area that was normally used for a mess hall was
packed. Only those absolutely essential to running the
ship weren't present, and those Kosciusko had briefed
separately. The men had listened quietly, as Stauer went
through the operations plan. From their faces, he didn't
detect any real problem with that side of things. Then
he'd turned it over to Bridges for his part of the show.

"And those are the legalities of the thing," Bridges
finished, after briefing the company on just that.
"Colonel?"

Stauer stood up and walked back to the podium as the
lawyer vacated it. "All right," the colonel said, "now you
know. And now you've got a decision to make, each of you.
It's too late for us to just let you go if you want out. You
know too much, as they say.

"So here's the deal. Anyone who wants out, who isn't
willing to face the legal consequences *or* the combat can
opt out now. We've got some reinforced containers, with
running water and latrines, cots and all that shit. You'll go

there and you'll *stay* there. You'll still be paid the base monthly rate until the operation is over, but you won't get the combat rate.

"Make your decision, now."

"Told you they'd stick, sir," Joshua gloated, as Stauer forked over a hundred dollars. "Gotta know people in our business. At this point, on the one hand, a lot of 'em want their combat pay. On the other, a lot of 'em feel that they were already as guilty as sin and actually going through with the thing won't add six months to anybody's sentence. That's not the big thing, though."

"No?" Stauer asked.

Joshua shook his head. "No, sir. Most of the men didn't really give either a second thought. They'd signed on for action, action was promised, and they, by God, intend to have what they signed on for."

As the sergeant major put the money away, he felt a tap on his shoulder. George was standing there with his hand out. "I believe you owe me fifty bucks, Sergeant Major," he said.

"Why's that, George?" Joshua asked.

"Because she's moved into his quarters," the first sergeant said. "That's a tight fit unless he manages to occupy some of her very personal space, don't you know."

D-28, MV *Merciful,* at sea

The sea lanes were still pretty crowded here, far too much

so to break out weapons to test fire, or rehearse the more complex dance of reconfiguring to launch aircraft and land grunts. Indeed, it was extremely important, for the nonce, to look and act as innocent as humanly possible.

This didn't mean there was nothing to do. Below, among the hidden decks and compartments, groups of men clustered around sand tables holding models of men and boats, terrain features, buildings, towns, harbors . . . even a few fake trees made from lichen for those few places that trees were important. Stauer moved from table to table, listening, watching, occasionally offering bits of advice and less frequently giving directives.

Some of the terrain boards and models were incomplete and always would be. Welch's team—himself, Grau and Semmerlin, snipers who would bear large caliber, silenced, subsonic sniper rifles, Graft, a machine gunner, Issaq Abay and Haayo Abdidi, Marehan tribe translators who had made it through jump and weapons training in Brazil, Pigfucker Hammel, Ryan, Little Joe Venegas, Buttle, Dalton, and Mary-Sue Rogers, detached from the SEALs—neither had nor could have had more than the slightest idea of the interior layout of the building that was their objective.

Stauer watched Terry's team take turns moving the toy soldiers representing themselves across the features of a small scale palace built to a large scale model. Abay and Abdidi seemed fully integrated to the thing, even dropping out and taking on others' jobs as the rehearsal went into variables like people being hit.

"You've got a problem," Stauer said, after calling Welch aside.

"What's that, sir?"

"Anyone can take over for anyone else on your team, correct?"

"Yes, sir; everyone knows everyone else's job and weapons."

"No they don't," Stauer corrected. "Your two translators are a potential point failure source. Yes, you have two to allow for a backup. But your plan has them both exposed to full risk, even after one of them gets hit. That, you can't permit."

Terry thought about that for a second, then another fifty-nine or so. "So if I lose one, I've got to immediately wrap the other in thick bulletproof gauze before continuing."

"I think so," Stauer said, "since there isn't and never was a chance of making your entire team conversant in the local language."

"Right. We'll change the plan then."

"Stout lad," Stauer said. "Be proud of you if you had figured it out for yourself."

Across the deck, Konstantin's boys did much the same as Welch's. They had a related problem in that they really hadn't more than the most general written notes on the internal layout of the much larger palace that was their objective. No more than Welch's could Konstantin's team—himself, Baluyev, Litvinov, Galkin, Musin, and Kravchenko—know the rooms, corridors, and entrances of their target, in Yemen. The Russians had one advantage in this; they had a spy who was expected to guide them once they were on target.

Though the Russian team hadn't changed since long before Myanmar, there'd been a number of minor personnel changes over the months, and more in the last couple of months and weeks. Terry had had to detach Buckwheat to accompany Wahab on strategic recon. A three man supplementary team had been built to send to those two. This consisted of Rattus and Fletcher, reinforced by Sergeant Babcock-Moore on the not impossible chance that some demolitions could be required for their mission. Terry, understrength even for Myanmar and freeing Victor Inning, had picked up two translators, plus a number of others to create one full strength team, droppable, depending on the equipment carried, in four to six of the light airplanes.

The five men remaining to Biggus Dickus Thornton's team were two too many to fit in *Namu*, the Killer Sub. That's how Mary-Sue had ended up with the "Army." Biggus Dickus himself, redundant and not remotely happy about it, filled his time with drilling the shit out of Simmons, who would drive *Namu*, and Morales and Eeyore, who were going to get to risk their lives to some Russian rebreathers.

The mechanized and amphibious infantry companies, under Reilly and Cazz, had stayed fairly solid, as had the air and naval components. They were both too big, however, to get everyone around a sand table all at the same time. Thus, they rehearsed only with platoon leaders and sergeant, and section leaders and their assistants. Those people had scheduled time when they'd be able to bring up their subordinates and go through the entire thing, at least on a small scale.

D-18, St. Helena, South Atlantic

With GPS and radio, it was the easiest thing imaginable for two ships to meet in an otherwise unoccupied stretch of ocean. It was not, however, all that easy for two ships to transfer cargo in an open stretch of ocean. This depended on all kinds of powerful and unpredictable factors. Oh, certainly, warships of most of the major naval powers could conduct UNREP, UNderway REPlenishment, in some fairly heavy seas. They were built for it, had crews trained for it, had a lot of experience in it, and were, broadly speaking, equipped for such transfers.

The *Merciful* was not a naval vessel; it was a merchant ship. Moreover, while some modifications, even some substantial modifications, had been made, they'd not been made with the intent of transferring cargo on the high seas. Neither had there been any substantial changes to the ship Victor used to bring the two MI-28s donated by his father-in-law, nor the flight and ground crews.

In all, then, the operation was pretty damned early nineteenth century. This is to say, the two ships needed a sheltering bay, both to operate the gantry and to run the small boats that would bring over Victor, the flight crews, and the ground crews.

"Which is, you know, oddly appropriate," Reilly said to Lana, as they watched the transfer while sharing a drink on the deck forward of the superstructure. George, Fitz, and the platoon and section leaders were there, too. Some, like Reilly and Lana, had their backs to the superstructure.

Others, like the first sergeant and exec, formed a circle farther out. A couple of bottles of scotch were passed around the circle. Reilly considered war to be largely a social activity, thus social events, too, had their place in preparing for it.

"Why's that?" she asked. She sat straight, head resting against white painted steel. She was near but not next to him. Really, she ached to slide over and lay her head on his shoulder. With all the others present, though, that just wouldn't do. And it wasn't that anybody didn't know, at this point, that they were sleeping together. It was that the others could comfort themselves with the illusion that it was just recreational sex, and that Reilly wouldn't care for her any more than he did for them, and wouldn't disadvantage them on her behalf. That required that they still be businesslike in public, with no obvious affection between them.

You've never heard of this place?"

"Don't think so, no. Should I have?"

Reilly smiled. "Maybe." He lifted his right index finger and twirled it around at the surrounding cliffs. "This bay is called 'Prosperous Bay.' I'm pretty sure nobody knows why. God knows, I don't."

"And so?"

He stuck the previously twirling finger in one ear, scratching more for effect than to relieve an itch. "Well, if you were foolish enough to climb those cliffs—and, yes, by the way, it's been done—and walk west-southwest for about, oh, maybe four kilometers as the crow flies, you will come to a house. Its name is Longwood."

The expression on Lana's face changed. She had heard

that name before . . . but wasn't sure exactly where or what it meant.

Reilly wasn't about to give her any easy hints yet. "Maybe two and half kilometers past that, edging more southwest than west-southwest, is a grave. There's no one in the grave, but there used to be. Some Corsican guy . . . you probably never heard of him . . . "

"Napoleon?" Lana asked, wonder in her voice. "Of *course*! Napoleon! Oh, we have to visit," she said. "We have to. Please? Pretty please?"

"Wish we could, Lana, but we can't. No time. See, they've almost finished swinging over the last container."

She looked at the gantry. Mrs. Liu, the Chinese adept on all things crane and gantry related, was easing the third of three containers over the *Merciful*'s side; a small crew waited on the deck to help guide it into position.

"Maybe on the return trip," George suggested. "Assuming, of course . . . " *Assuming there even is a return trip.*

"Maybe, Top," Reilly said. "I'll bring it up to Stauer. 'Assuming, of course.'"

D-15, MV *Merciful*, 397 miles west of Luederitz, Namibia

Overhead and at a considerable distance, two unmanned aerial vehicles, which needed virtually nothing special to land on or take off from, circled at a distance of twenty-five to thirty miles, ensuring there were no ships that close to the *Merciful*.

Among the other items brought from Base Alpha had

been several tons of dirt in sandbags and a fair number of logs. The logs were laid out in two layers, crosswise, on top of five pairs of containers, thoroughly lashed and chained together. Above the logs were sandbags, layered five deep. Atop the sandbags were erected five Russian 120mm mortars, all set at very high elevation and aimed, generally, over the starboard side. The mortars themselves were along the port side. Aiming stakes, painted green but with a red and white strip bared once some tape put on during the painting had been peeled off, were laid out to the left front of each mortar, at twenty-five-meter intervals. Getting the stakes stuck in had been a major pain in the ass, involving the use of both more sandbags and considerable finesse.

Next to the mortars were three high-explosive shells each, plus a couple each of illuminating and smoke. Around each were five crewmen, three crews of Marines and two of soldiers. A joint fire direction center sat behind them.

The mortars and FDC took up a good chunk of the main deck, which would become the flight deck. Behind that, the forward observers stood on the bridge, connected to the mortar FDC by land lines and field phones.

Between the superstructure and the mortars, Mrs. Liu busied herself with dropping half a dozen sealed containers over the side. The containers would sink on their own, eventually. The mortars hoped to hurry the process.

"Buuut," Peters said to his jarhead opposite number, "the odds of our hitting anything, even by direct lay, from a corkscrewing ship, are, at best, shitty."

"Yeah," agreed the Marine, Sergeant Benevides, a stubby, stocky Ecuadorian immigrant to the United States. "But it'll be fun."

As soon as Mrs. Liu dumped the last of the target containers over the side, Kosciusko ordered a long, wide, and slow one hundred and eighty degree turn. As soon as he was about two miles opposite the line of bobbing containers, he ordered the ship to come to a full stop in place and then turned to the senior of the forward observers, saying, "You may fire when ready."

Flukes, much like shit, sometimes just happen. After missing by as much as five hundred meters, the eleventh round managed to actually hit one of the container targets. Better, it passed through the side above the water, through the side below the water, and then detonated a very short distance into the water. The container was blown skyward, spinning end over end before reaching apogee and beginning to plummet back to the sea.

"You couldn't do that again if your life depended on it," Peters said.

"Nope," the Marine agreed. "And, in light of that, I think we ought to retire the guns on a positive note."

"I concur," said Peters. "Out of ACTION!"

Kosciusko shook his head, watching the sundered container fly up and then splash down. *Some people have all the luck.*

The chief observer announced, "Skipper, they're striking the guns."

"Works for me," Kosciusko agreed. He jabbed the intercom and announced, "Reilly, get your Eland and antitank crews on deck to test fire. I'll have Mrs. Liu bring up the containers holding them and the ordnance."

D-13, MV *Merciful*, 211 miles south of Cape Town, South Africa

Mrs. Liu plopped a container on a section of deck covered with PSP. Immediately, the container was opened on both sides, and a small crew of men entered it, scrunched over, and began pushing out sections of the matting to other teams that waited to either side. She then moved the gantry to pick up and move another.

A siren blared, then the loudspeakers carried Kosciusko's voice. "Cease work. Cease work. The time has run and we are not done. All decking teams, break down the flight deck. Gantry, replace the containers in their hide positions as they are filled.

"We're going to work on this all fucking night and tomorrow night, too, people, until you can assemble the flight deck to standard and on time. Section leaders and company commanders, report when we are stowed and ready to begin again.

"That is all."

D-8, MV *Merciful*, 355 miles east of Dar es Salaam, Tanzania

Lana was squeezed in with Reilly on a single width, folding Army field cot. She awakened, startled by the horrific sound coming from the other side of the closed doors.

Reilly listened, too, for a moment, then began to laugh. "The Boers or the Brits, do you figure?"

"Huh?" She really hadn't a clue what he was talking about.

He shook his head and said, "That sound you heard outside our little nest was a bugle." The call it was playing was *Dismount*."

"Fucking Viljoen."

"That's Dumisani's job," he said.

★★★
PART III
★★★

★CHAPTER THIRTY-EIGHT★

Regard your soldiers as your children,
and they will follow you into the deepest valleys;
look on them as your own beloved sons,
and they will stand by you even unto death.
—Sun Tzu

D-2, MV *Merciful,* fifty miles southeast of Aden, Yemen

It wasn't a moonless night. Indeed, it would be a nearly full moon when that body arose. This, however, was not going to happen until just before one in the morning, local. Thus, barring the minimal lights permitted on deck and the red lights of the bridge, it was darker than the proverbial three feet up a well digger's ass at midnight.

"Yep; darker than three feet up a well digger's ass at midnight," pronounced Stauer with satisfaction. "A UAV we sent out about an hour ago says your landing area is clear. You and your boys ready, Konstantin?"

The Russian breathed deeply then released a sigh. "As ready as we're going to be," he answered. "Assuming we

427

can cut off the target from communication and take it down before any of Yemen's roughly two hundred and eighty modern jet fighters and bombers come to take us out."

"I wouldn't worry about it too much," Boxer said. "If one in ten of the things are working I'd be surprised. And if the Yemenis knew *which* ones in ten, I'd be amazed. And if there are pilots on standby for that thirty or so . . . and if they're fueled and armed . . . and if they don't need permission from echelons above God to launch."

"No," Boxer summed up. "As long as you go in low, make it a ground rather than an aerial attack, and evac quickly you should be fine. Even if you have to call the choppers in for some close support to cover your egress, it should be fine. These people just suck."

"It's that word 'should' that bothers me," Konstantin said.

"You don't have to do it," Stauer said.

Again Konstantin sighed, this time with a fatalism that could only be Russian. "No. The old chief wants that man out of the picture. And I owe favors and have obligations from way back. We'll do the mission."

Somehow, I was sure you would, Boxer thought. After all, he'd met the old man, Victor's father-in-law, and had sensed the kind of abilities that engendered long-term loyalty, to say nothing of everlasting fear.

"It is confirmed by your people that the target is at home," Boxer said. "How they know this I wouldn't speculate."

"If the old man says the Arab's home; he's home," Konstantin said. "Though I, too, wouldn't care to speculate on how." *Because I know the old man has someone in the house . . . errr . . . palace. Code Name: Lada. Or maybe his . . . or more likely her . . . real name. And that's all I know . . . well, and that I'm supposed to get that person out when we go. Wonder why he didn't give us a picture with the target folder.*

And I shudder, because some of what the old man wants me to do . . . I just don't think I can.

With the ship's gantry whining to the sides and overhead, Konstantin left the superstructure by the hatch most level with the container-supported flight deck. He passed between eight inward-facing, small, short takeoff and landing—STOL—aircraft. These were idle with their pilots standing by or sitting inside or on the deck as the mood took them. Two LCMs were exposed, as were the empty space for another and the cradle that had once held the patrol boat, *The Drunken Bastard*. Those craft were already moving to the south, toward a rendezvous on the coast.

Konstantin passed beside three very small off road motorcycles—dirt bikes—strapped under the helicopter's pylons. These were attached to the wing, rather than to one of the two hardpoints on this side. On the other side, he knew, was a weapons container with the arms and equipment his half of the team would need for the mission. There were extra fuel pods on each side to extend the range. The other helicopter, holding *Praporschik* Baluyev, plus Kravchenko and Litvinov, carried the same load. Strapped to their bellies, each helicopter carried a brace each of desert camouflage screens and poles. There were also two weapons pods between the pair, one for unguided rockets and one for guided missiles. They didn't expect to actually need the weapons, not with the chin guns armed and ready. But one never knew.

Looking toward the ship's bow, before entering his helicopter, the Russian noted that the forward mast had been dropped. The helicopters wouldn't need the clearance, he knew, but the light airplanes would.

Inside, Timer Musin sat next to the presumed homosexual, Galkin, in two of the seats in the cramped compartment behind the engines of the MI-28. He reached a hand out to help Konstantin through the tiny door that opened just under the jet engine's exhaust. Though the engine was idling, hot jet-fuel-stinky fumes entered the compartment. Had it not been for Konstantin's bulk filling the door space, they'd have been a lot worse. Musin handed Konstantin a pair of headphones as he settled himself into the altogether too narrow seat, closing and locking the little door behind him. He put the headphones on, adjusted the boom mike and announced, "Ready."

The pilot didn't acknowledge. Instead, the engines began to whine with almost painful force. Then the first MI-28 leapt upward, surged forward, and twisted in air. Once it was clear of the ship, it dove for the surface of the sea, and then began the relatively short flight to the general area of the objective.

D-2, Beach Green One, west of Bandar Qassim, Ophir

The night was still darker than a slave dealer's soul. There were no automobiles on the coastal highway that ran parallel to the beach to illuminate things. Rather, there were no running automobiles. There was one, a Hummer stolen from a nongovernmental organization and purchased from the thieves, just off the highway, parked, idle, and dark.

There was also an artificial light hanging on a ten foot pole, but that light was infrared and most unlikely to be seen by anyone not looking for it and equipped to find it. Under that light, Buckwheat Fulton's world phone sat on his lap, as dark for the moment as the coast itself. He, in turn, sat on his ass, on a lonely beach not far from a lonely city, facing across the Gulf of Aden toward the Arabian Peninsula. Somewhere, not too far to the north, a landing craft bearing three men and two Land Rovers, along with enough arms, ammunition, and other more-than-suspicious equipment to earn several life sentences nearly anywhere, churned its way to the coast.

Beside Fulton, likewise in the sand, sat Wahab. The two had sat in silence for a long time, ever since arrival, really.

"I sometimes miss the communists, don't you know, Robert," said the African, breaking the silence. "Life was simpler then."

"You mean the graft was better," Fulton half-joked in answer. He lifted a set of night vision goggles to his eyes and scanned the sea for a sign of the LCM or the patrol boat he suspected would escort it.

"That, too, of course," Wahab agreed. "Being paid by the Russians to sabotage you, by the United States to sabotage them, and by the French to ensure that the sun never set on the French Empire . . . " Wahab sighed. "Those were good days. Even the Italians occasionally kicked in."

"That's not even counting the stipend your chief got from the Catholic Church for watching out for its interests," Fulton replied.

"Well, of *course* not," Wahab said, shaking his head. "Nor even what the Saudis funneled us. He always gave those stipends back anyway, in one form or another. Taking from God and actually *keeping* the money . . . that would have been wrong. For that matter, I can't even say with a straight face that we ever really screwed the Russians for you, or your side for the Russians."

Fulton shook his head, unseen by his companion. He'd spent quite a bit of time by now with Wahab, and liked the African a great deal. Even so, *Thank God my multi-great granddaddy got dragged onto that boat.*

Wahab went silent again. He, too, searched the sea for a sign of the landing craft. Without Fulton's goggles, he had scant chance of seeing it. On the other hand, without the goggles much more of his attention could be focused on his hearing, better than the American's, in any case, for not having grown up in the industrialized west.

"There," Wahab announced, pointing in a particular direction out to sea. "Not sure how far off, but there's a powerful engine—no . . . two of them . . . straining and they're much closer than a merchant ship is likely to come to the shore."

Fulton redirected his attention, returning the NVGs to his face. At first he saw nothing but the green-tinged surf. He kept looking until first one, then a pair of lights bobbed up above the waters. He picked up his world phone and pressed a button. There was a brief delay as the call was processed.

"Buckwheat, Rattus. I see a light."

Fulton wrapped one hand around the pole and began rocking it to and fro.

"Correction, I see a rocking light."

"That's me," Fulton said. "The beach is clear."

"Coming in."

The LCM's engines still strained, holding it and its lowered ramp snug against the shore and against the pull of the receding tide. Over the ramp came a Land Rover to thump and splash into the surf, before churning its way up to the beach. A second Land Rover followed.

Yeah, okay, thought Fulton. *Maybe they are just about the most reliable vehicles in the world and maybe three quarters of all of those ever built are still running. But the military calculation remains: If you need X at the objective you must start with at least X plus one. Since we really only need one besides the Hummer, we must start with two or Murphy's finger shall lance out and touch us with bad juju. That, or the Buddha will ensure bad karma . . . or God will just fuck us over. Same things, really. And I still remember that limey Marine's ass on fire when his Land Rover decided to spontaneously combust in Kurdistan, back in 1991.*

The vehicles pulled up and out of the water, their wheels bouncing as their frames spouted salt water downward. From the second one Rattus emerged. "Everything's packed and ready, Buckwheat. Including sterile uniforms. Not that those will help us in the slightest."

"Who's the team?" Fulton asked.

"Besides you, Wahab, and myself," Rattus answered, "we've got Fletcher to snipe and a Brit engineer named Babcock-Moore; 'Vic,' he goes by, to help spot. Or blow shit up if required; we've got a demo kit for that, too. He's driving the other Land Rover. Seems pretty competent, if a little formal."

Buckwheat Fulton shrugged. "We can deal with formality . . . even if it *is* a little uncomfortable." He turned to Wahab and said, "Take the Hummer to the safe house in Elayo. We'll follow and hole up."

D-2, MV *Merciful*, Gulf of Aden

"Reduce speed to four knots," Kosciusko ordered.

"Aye, sir," the helmsman replied, reaching out to pull back the throttles on the panel before him. The vibrations felt through the deck immediately lessened and every man aboard was leaned forward.

It was a dangerous move, really, given that the area had been known for piracy for quite some time, and given that the *Merciful*'s escort, *The Drunken Bastard*, Chin commanding, was still far behind, escorting the LCM that had landed Rattus and party on the beach to join Buckwheat and Wahab. Dangerous though it may have been, slowing was necessary to recover the LCM, to regain protection from the *Bastard*, and—for the moment, most importantly—to launch the minisub.

Biggus Dickus Thornton's crew were up next. And

Biggus was not amused by it. He couldn't go. They'd tried, but there was simply no way that three ex-SEALs, plus all the diving gear and explosives, could fit inside the tiny sub if one of the three was the size of Thornton. Even if he would have fit, though, along with the required equipment, the boat's minimal life support could only handle three smaller men. Biggus Dickus used enough oxygen for any two others. Instead, Eeyore Antoniewicz and Morales, both on the short side, plus Simmons, who was big but not as big as Thornton, were going. Biggus had to stay on the ship.

He wasn't happy about it. He'd considered pressing to put just two men aboard the sub. That was, after all, her normal crew. But he couldn't do the explosives job himself quickly enough; it was a two man job . . . and somebody had to stay with the sub or it was going to be a long swim to Aden. His only consolation, such as it was, was that at least he would be spared the humiliation of riding an ex-Sea Shepherd, Orca-painted minisub.

I shouldn't worry, Biggus thought. *This is the least time sensitive of the missions. All they have to do is ensure every potentially armed boat in the harbor is mined before sunrise. Piece of cake, really.*

The mines the group were to use were called limpets. These were very special limpets, however, manufactured in fairly small lots for Soviet naval special forces, during the Cold War, then obtained by Victor and reconditioned. Each weighed about nine pounds. They were generally hemispheric in shape, and measured three and a half inches, at their thickest, by about nine in diameter. To that thickness could be added a small, round projection from which sprouted two pull pins and a small fold-out propeller. Moreover, around their edges were three eye-bolt type screws for affixing them to wooden or fiberglass hulls. Internally they mounted four rather strong magnets.

The pull-pins armed, in one case, internal antihandling devices. These did not necessarily prevent the mines from being removed from the side of a ship or boat to which they had been attached. They did tend to ensure that the diver removing them would have very little time for self-congratulation. The other pin allowed the propellers to spin once removed, and started a preset clock ticking. The propellers, once freed by removal of the second pin, would turn as the target boats moved through the sea, fully arming the mines after about a mile of movement, and self-detonating them after about twelve miles. In theory. Victor had warned them that twelve miles could be fifty or more, or two or less, depending on both quality control at the original factory and quality control among the people he'd hired to recondition the mines.

Those settings could be varied prior to employment. In this case, twelve miles was Boxer's best guess as to just how far the typical pirate *couldn't* swim. "The world has little interest in living pirates," Boxer had said, a point with which Stauer had utterly agreed.

Namu, for so the minisub had been nicknamed, carried thirty-six limpets, four pods of nine each. The pods were a bit over nine inches in diameter, three and a half feet long, and had holes in them to permit water to displace air. In all, like the limpets, they were mildly negatively buoyant to permit easier underwater control.

Thirty-six was rather more than the number of

potentially significant boats expected in Bandar Qassim harbor. Then again, the most important factor in calculating explosive use was "Factor P, for plenty."

Unlike *The Drunken Bastard* and the landing craft, the minisub *Namu* could not be boarded—not safely, practically, quickly, and efficiently, in any case, not with the requisite equipment—after being hauled over the side. Instead, the crew would load it aboard ship, then be raised and lowered to the water as a unit.

It was already hooked up to the gantry by its attached lifting rings. This had been started as soon as the *Bastard* and the LCM had been lowered over the side, then completed as the Russian helicopters had taken off. The slack was already out of the lifting cables.

Biggus climbed up on the cradle holding the *Namu* and looked down on a very scrunched up, tropical wet-suited Eeyore. He could make out Morales's black-clad back just forward of that and the backs of Simmons' legs stretching out to either side along the inner hull. Simmons drove the boat from a padded horizontal bench, on his belly, looking through a clear, round viewport. A metal frame ran from the sub forward of the view port to protect it from accidental impact. Rebreathers—Russian IDA71s, courtesy of Victor—were laid up beside the sub's driver. The limpet mine pods were likewise, but forward of the rebreathers. All the men, including Simmons, were outfitted for a dive, though there was no room for a rebreather for Simmons. There were two Russian built APS underwater assault rifles in there somewhere. These were of very limited utility in air.

"Don't fuck it up, Eeyore," Biggus Dickus said, looking down into the boat's tiny conning tower.

Antoniewicz strained his neck to look up. He shrugged, "What's to fuck up, Chief? Simmons gets us to within a quarter mile of the harbor and surfaces. Morales and I unass, put on the equipment, get the pods, swim in, and mine the boats. Then we swim back to the sub and head toward the *Merciful*. Piece of cake."

"Nothing's a piece of cake, Eeyore." Biggus shook a cautionary finger. "Murphy has his eye on you. His pulsating prong of perversity is greased and waiting for your ass to be exposed. His dangling dong of destiny vibrates in anticipation. The reaming rod of randomness . . . "

Antoniewicz held up a hand. "I read that story, too, Chief. I'm not a future Israeli on a distant planet. This will not be that hard. Trust me."

Thornton sneered, then relented. "I'm just pissed I can't go."

"We know, Chief," Eeyore sympathized.

Biggus nodded his head, then backed off from the sub. He raised one hand, palm up. Overhead, the controller of the gantry saw and pulled back on a stick. The Chinese woman wearing the night vision goggles had had a lot of practice, both in port at Manaus and on the way here. With a whine, the sub began to rise, the cables lightly vibrating under the load. A different whine began as the gantry's arm was rotated outward.

Once the sub was clear of the deck, Thornton scrambled to the gunwale and watched it descend to the water. When it touched and sank a bit, the cables grew slack. The sub began to pull sternward, building up a small wake.

Simmons matched speed and the cables grew slack. From overhead, the Chinese woman released them at the points where they'd held the sub.

"I'm just pissed I can't go," Thornton repeated, in a whisper, as the sub turned away and began its lonely journey to the harbor. He began to turn away, then suddenly turned back to catch a last glimpse of the *Namu*, whispering again, "Good luck, boys."

Good luck, boys, Stauer thought, as he watched the *Namu* eased over the side. His anxiety level was high, though no one could tell it from his face. Indeed, it had gone up, rather than down, with each separate launching. And it would go up still more until the last man was recovered, back on the ship, and heading away.

It was part of the price of command and one of the reasons so comparatively few people could be commanders.

Nothing more I can do about it at this point, Stauer thought, not so much dismissing the *Namu* and her crew as compartmentalizing them into the part of his mind labeled, "Beyond your control."

Stauer looked down at a number of aircraft, idling on the flight deck. *Besides, I've got more immediate problems.*

D-2, MV *Merciful*, Indian Ocean, rounding the Horn of Africa

The moon was just beginning to peek over the ocean to the east. The gantry was rolled all the way back, as far as it would go, towards the ship's superstructure. PSP— perforated steel planking—was laid out between rows of containers lining either side and virtually the full length of the ship forward of the gantry. The forward mast was long dropped.

On the PSP the eight light, single engine, short takeoff and landing aircraft belonging to the group idled. Two of these weren't, strictly speaking, needed for the current lift. They were there, however, assembled and crewed, to serve as backups should one of the six designated airplanes for this part of the mission fail.

Always nice to have a backup, Terry Welch thought, looking at the two extras sitting directly under the gantry. At the same time, unconsciously, he patted the reserve parachute strapped across his stomach. It occurred to Welch that any comfort he derived from having a reserve chute was possibly false comfort; he and his men were going to jump so low that a reserve chute might activate, if at all, only after they had been driven several feet into the ground.

Vibrations ran through the PSP. Whether that was from the airplanes or from the engines straining below to bring the ship up to full speed for the launch, neither Terry nor any of the men clustered around him could tell.

"It's really overkill," said McCaverty, the lead pilot for the mission, glancing down and around at the PSP.

Terry hadn't heard over the massed roar of the engines. "What was that?" he asked.

McCaverty pointed down at the planking, then ran his finger forward toward the bow to where the steel disappeared in the darkness.

"We don't need this much," he shouted into Welch's ear. "At the ship's speed, and with the light loading, we could launch in half this space. Or less."

"Does it hurt any to have the extra safety factor?" Terry shouted back.

"Well . . . no," McCaverty admitted with a shrug. "But it isn't needed."

"I'll take it anyway." Again, Welch's hand unconsciously stroked the reserve.

Again, McCaverty shrugged.

A member of the ship's crew began trooping the portside line of aircraft. "Launch point in thirty minutes," he announced quietly as he passed each group or individual. He said the same to Welch and McCaverty as he got to the forwardmost CH-801. Then the crewman turned to walk the line of planes on the starboard side.

"Load up?" McCaverty suggested.

"Yeah," Terry agreed. Even though it was thirty minutes to launch, his heart began to beat a little faster.

"Need a hand getting to the plane?" the chief pilot asked.

"Getting to it, no," Terry said, beginning the awkward, overladen shuffle to the door. "Getting *into* it? Yes."

The team consisted of twelve men, two per aircraft. Yes, in theory the planes could have lifted three each, plus the pilot. In practice, though, it was just too cramped with three men, fully equipped for both parachuting and combat, to exit the things easily. And where ease of exit meant speed of exit, and speed was rather important, two would have to do.

McCaverty checked that both Welch and his other passenger, Little Joe Venegas, were strapped in for the takeoff. Ordinarily, this would have been the job of a crew chief. Since, however, the table of organization, such as it was, was quite skimpy in some areas, he had to do it himself. Oh, sure, the Mexicans could have done it, but they were busy getting ready the rocket and machine gun pods that would be the next load for most of the aircraft.

McCaverty's was only the third bird to actually start its engine. He was first in order of liftoff, even so. He looked to the side and saw two conical lights come on. One of the ship's crew—though the light allowed past the opaque cones was faint, the pilot thought it might be the same one who'd passed the word to begin loading—signaled by holding them straight overhead and parallel to each other: *Assuming control.* In reply, McCaverty gave a little gas to the engine: *You got it.*

Apparently satisfied with that, the ground guide began walking toward a spot on the center line of the flight deck. The pilot duly followed, then stopped—except for aiming the plane toward the bow—when the guide crossed the lights over his head. The lights moved off to the side with McCaverty's eyes following.

"All my life . . . " McCaverty whispered, as his eyes followed the lights, "all my life I've wanted this . . . just this . . . this feeling of impending . . . crisis . . . this sense of plunging into danger."

One of the batons twirled, then pointed toward the bow. With a half-maniacal cackle of unadulterated glee, McCaverty pushed the throttle forward. The plane vibrated, lurched, and then began to move down the ad hoc air strip. Long before it reached the end of the strip the pilot felt the thing begin to lift, the force pressing him down into his seat.

As the plane left the *Merciful* behind, McCaverty could be heard singing—well . . . *trying* to sing— "Mothers, don't let your babies grow up to be cowboys . . . "

★ CHAPTER THIRTY-NINE ★

Why join the Navy if you can be a pirate?
—Steve Jobs

D-1, Yemen

"Short final," the taciturn pilot said over the intercom.

After the buffeting from flying with the landing wheels barely above—indeed, sometimes skimming—the waves, then barely above the sand dunes, though it didn't skim those, it was a welcome relief to Konstantin when the helicopter went into a low hover. The pitch of the engine changed, as well.

Though he'd never before flown into anywhere in an MI-28, Konstantin was certain that the change in pitch meant a landing. The sudden shudder and bounce as the landing wheels touched down told him his guess was correct.

"*Devaye, devaye, muzhiks*," the pilot said, which translated roughly as, "Un-ass my helicopter, peasants."

Konstantin flipped the small door open and dived out.

He hit and rolled, groaning, "I am getting too old for this shit," before scurrying to take up a position around the helicopter. He couldn't see the other bird, but heard it not far away.

"*Still* darker than three feet up a well-digger's ass," he said, with satisfaction, looking around at the sand dunes that seemed to enclose him on all sides. He flipped onto his back and brought his NVGs down to his face, scanning quickly but thoroughly.

Already, the helicopter was powering down. In the grainy green image he saw the other bird. He saw, too, that the other three men were likewise lying down around it. Closer in he caught glimpses of the two, Musin and Galkin, who had flown with him.

And now we wait for the choppers to power down completely, put up the camouflage nets, break out the motorcycles, change clothes, rest until nightfall, and then . . . we're off.

D-1, MV *Merciful,* paralleling the eastern coast of Ophir

Down in the hull, several layers of containers down, forward of the internal open assembly area, Boxer watched over a UAVs pilot's shoulder as another greenish image, this one on a monitor screen, changed with the movement of the UAV.

"Fuel?" Boxer asked.

"Maybe half an hour," the pilot replied, after checking his somewhat ephemeral instruments. "Not enough to get the thing back."

"All right," Boxer nodded. For a moment he considered the very high amusement quotient in sending the thing to Saudi Arabia where it could be found, after crashing, complete with Israeli markings, on Saudi sands. It would be a hoot, and bound to muddy the waters, but . . . better not.

Feeling mildly guilty, he said, "Well, we do have a limited number of spares. Spend the fuel circling around Konstantin's position until you have only enough to get to the sea. Then head to sea and ditch it. *If you see anything that might be of interest to the Russians, let me know.*"

"Roger."

Boxer shifted his attention to a different pilot and monitor, this one aimed at the port of Bandar Qassim and the airport to its west.

"Sir," said the pilot, "two boats have left the rectangular harbor. I mark them as targets three and seventeen, both presumed pirates. They've split up, one heading west toward the Red Sea and the other heading generally toward . . . well, toward *us.* Maybe an hour and a half behind us, at our current speed and heading. That's assuming they haven't changed course. And about that I just don't know; I can't cover two things with one UAV."

Eyes on his screen and controls, the pilot didn't notice Boxer close his eyes and envision the current positions of the LCM, *The Drunken Bastard*, and *Namu*. The latter, in any case, would be fifty or sixty feet underwater and thus in no obvious danger from a primitive surface ship manned by pirates. The LCM, however, could be in danger if *Bastard* left her to her own devices.

"No," Boxer said. "You keep watch over Bandar Qassim." *But I'd better go see the ship's captain and Stauer.*

"At what time," Boxer called out as he left the control station, "what precise time, did the boat that's tailing us leave port?"

It's a danger, Stauer thought, *but not a disaster.* This, too, was a part of command; to know the difference.

The bridge was still lit only in red. Kosciusko, Stauer, and Boxer surrounded a chart spread on a table. It was, perhaps, a bit primitive, but it worked well enough. On it were several wooden models for the known or presumed positions of six seagoing vessels. For two of those, the pirates, erasers had been pressed into service, one blue-green, the other pinkish. Under the light, they were merely slightly different shades of red, as, indeed, were the faces of the men.

Kosciusko wasn't saying much of anything, just peering closely at the chart and, to all appearances, doing calculations in his head.

"Anything we use has the chance of giving the game away," Stauer said. "If we launch either a CH-801 or a helicopter with rocket and machine gun pods, someone on shore will see the firing or the tracers. Might anyway. If we wait until they're climbing up our ass and engage from here it's the same problem only worse. How sure are you that they're heading for us?"

"I'm not sure," Boxer admitted. "We've only got so many UAVs and so many pilots. But pickings have to have gotten scant for the pirates since the merchant ships have started avoiding this stretch of coast. I figure they noticed us—ground observer, maybe—as we rounded the Horn, and launched then, intending to overtake and take us. They probably haven't clue one about what we are."

"Can we just avoid them?" Stauer asked.

"Do we want to?"

At Stauer's raised eyebrow, Boxer continued, "Even leaving aside the general good to mankind in taking them out, if we don't take them out they just might be in the landing area at precisely the wrong time. And if we lose them by heading to sea, that won't change the risk that they might be hanging around the beach when we start to land."

"I can see the problem," Stauer agreed, then asked, "Did you warn Chin and the *Bastard* about the other boat?"

"Just before I called you up here," Boxer relied. "He says, 'No sweat. Piece of cake.'"

"That's comforting." Stauer said it in a way that indicated it was not at all comforting. "How's he plan on taking them down without giving away what he is?"

"I asked him that. He said that he and the LCM were heading out to sea where there'd be less chance of anyone spotting their fires. He can go further out to sea without risking delay with another operation, though it would surely slow down the landing if we lose a third of our capability."

Stauer shook his head, doubtfully. "The LCM's slow. What if the pirate closes before he can get far enough out?"

Boxer smiled broadly. "He said, 'chop-chop.' He also said—"

Apparently satisfied with his mental calculations, Kosciusko suddenly stood bolt upright, cutting off whatever Boxer had been about to say. "You know, Wes," Kosciusko said to Stauer, "we could kill two birds with one stone here. If we're clever."

"Oh?"

D-1, thirty-six miles northeast of Nugaal, Ophir, and about three hundred feet over ground

The land below wasn't just sere; it was also rough. That meant that the six CH-801s moving across it in a loose staggered trail formation were also moving up and down . . . and up . . . and down and . . .

Terry Welch wanted to puke. *Desperately* wanted to, as a matter of fact. He held it in, no matter how hard the self-willed vomit hammered at his tonsils, because one hurl and it was a safe bet that everyone aboard the aircraft would do likewise.

On the plus side, at least the nausea keeps me from worrying.

And there was a great deal to worry about. He could worry about the planes—especially the lead bird, his own—not finding the right drop zone. Sure, sure, the Global Positioning System—GPS—should ensure that this did not happen. And, sure, McCaverty had shown considerable ability to find the right spot during practice jumps back in Brazil. "But that was yesterday . . ."

Then, too, there was the worry about the self-packed chutes opening properly, and, given the altitude at which they intended to jump, *quickly*. The reserve on his belly may have been a comfort, but it was a small one, if so, because there mightn't be any time to deploy it if the main failed.

Landing? Jesus, landing? Dark, rocky, and anything but flat. And laden like pack mules.

Then there was the hump over the mountains, preparing a hide and hiding out all day, then a night move to the objective, and finally, the assault.

And let's not even get into the timing of the extraction. Or making sure we can get off the airfield at Nugaal, or . . .

"Twwwooo minutes!" McCaverty announced.

Or much of anything else.

D-1, Safe House, Elayo, Ophir

There was no electricity here; thus the only light came from the fire on which they'd cooked their meal and a couple of candles burning on a table. Wahab paced back and forth, nervously, causing the candles to flicker and the slight shadows they cast to shift in random and annoying ways.

"Never done this before, have you?" Fulton asked. A large caliber bullpup rifle—a Russian VSSk—with a long tubular extension, the silencer, sat across his lap.

The African stopped his pacing, clasped both hands behind him, and admitted, "No, nothing like this." Wahab had fought before, of course, as a regular, back when he'd had a country with a regular armed force, and then as an irregular, leading his fellow clansmen against other clans, made of those who had once been his countrymen. That, however, had been different in kind.

"Some people say it's the waiting that's worst," Rattus said, with an evil smile. "Me, I've always thought the worst part was when the bullets were smacking around your head; that, and the incoming artillery. Oh, and the IEDs . . . Jesus! I remember one time—"

Rattus's beginning monologue was stopped by a dirty look from Buckwheat Fulton.

"Relax, Wahab," Fulton said. "Our job is pretty easy. No, it's not without its risks, but overall it's pretty easy. We take the vehicles to a place about two miles out from the airport's military side. Then we split up, go in on foot to a point about half a kilometer from that. Then we shoot the engines until every helicopter or other military plane there is unable to fly or someone notices us doing it. If we can kill that someone, we keep doing it.

"Odds are fair, though, that nobody will notice even if they're awake. The rifles are subsonic and suppressed. The only thing anyone's going to hear is the strike, and that's an unusual enough sound that they're unlikely to know what it is. Or where it's coming from."

"Now get some sleep," Fulton finished. "Big day tomorrow."

D-1 Minisub *Namu*, mouth of Bandar Qassim harbor.

Enroute, they'd surfaced and popped the hatch half a dozen times to get their location with a hand-held GPS. In no case had they stayed up more than as long as it took to pop the hatch and get a reading. But the last previous check they'd made had had them within five kilometers of the target and a small fraction of that of where they should have been on their predetermined course.

The sub was tiny, as such things go, and, though quiet on its own, not particularly well insulated from outside noise. Thus, when the small orca-painted conning tower, or sail, broke the surface, Eeyore could hear the water rushing off and around the boat, even as he saw the line of the surface recede in his port.

"Dead slow, Simmons," he ordered.

"Aye, slow," the boat's driver echoed.

The tower had a clear vision port wrapped around the forward half of it, just where tower met deck. Ordinarily, with a two-man crew, Antoniewicz would have had the port just in front of him. As was, with Morales taking up space, he had to scrunch.

The opening to the harbor was there, about a half a mile off and almost dead ahead. The little difference from dead ahead was not, in Antoniewicz's judgment, worth resubmerging for. *It will do*. Most of the city behind it was darkened, without the ambient glow one normally associated with built up areas of that size. *My compliments to the chauffeur.*

They weren't submariners, really. The formal commands and sequence of events weren't a big deal. In fact, the former SEALs thought it was all a bit silly.

Instead, with a mixture of relief—after all, Simmons could have misnavigated—and satisfaction, Eeyore said, "It's almost dead ahead. Good job. Bring us up past deck level. Morales, you ready?"

"To get out of this fucking can? You couldn't imagine how ready, Eeyore. My fucking back is *killing* me."

"Bitch, bitch, bitch," Antoniewicz said as he stood up and stretched his own back. He didn't take long over the stretch, though. As they'd rehearsed it dozens of times on the *Merciful's* deck, he scrambled out the hatch, keeping low, to the deck ahead of the tower. There he sat down and spun on his butt until he was facing aft again, away from the port. By that time Morales was standing in the hatch well, ready to begin passing over the munitions and equipment.

First out was a pod of limpet mines, with an attached strap. Eeyore took the mine pod and hung it, over the side and half in the water, by hooking the strap over a small stanchion. Another mine pod followed, then the third and fourth.

After that came masks with underwater night vision attachments. These were more or less normal, if wide view, masks, with a single, waterproof image intensifier that could be rotated to either eye. Then followed fins, Phoebus Bio-fins, which did not come cheap. The real advantage to those were that they were so efficient that the user used up much less oxygen, thereby increasing dive time.

The fins were followed by snorkels, fairly light weight-belts with waterproof GPS clipped on, harnesses, rapidly inflatable vests, and rebreathers. Last came two of the underwater useable assault rifles, the Russian APSs.

Simmons stayed inside, still lying prone, with his face to the other clear vision port, to help keep the boat balanced and on an even keel.

While Antoniewicz was donning his equipment, trying to keep the latter from going over the side, Morales turned and slithered out the hatch, to the aft deck, and into the water. From there he swam with easy, effortless strokes to the forward deck and bellied up on it, before swiveling as Eeyore had, to face aft.

In a rehearsed sequence, Antoniewicz lifted the equipment overhead and slightly back to where Morales could grab it and don it. Well after the last piece was gone, after a wait that seemed interminable, but was certainly no more than eight minutes, Morales tapped Eeyore on the shoulder and announced, "Ready."

"Go," said Eeyore, as he eased himself into the water to port and Morales did the same to starboard. Unsurprisingly, the water was quite warm.

Simmons, lying below, felt the boat surge once the weight of the two divers was lifted from it. He swiveled a bezel on his—of *course*—Rolex, then eased himself back and back some more until he was able to squat under the tower. From there he stood and took a look over the bow at the sea. Already there was no sign of his comrades, which was better than the alternative. Turning around, Simmons took hold of the hatch and, ducking back into *Namu*, closed and dogged it behind him. He then carefully squatted before resuming his pilot's position.

Moments later, a very odd looking, orca-painted minisub slipped beneath the waves to wait for the prearranged time to rise again.

D-1, MV *Merciful*

"Chin says the boat that was heading toward him and the

landing craft never showed. And he can't hear a trace of it on sonar either. Course, the *Bastard's* sonar is not, shall we say, of the best. Still . . . " Boxer looked mildly puzzled for only a moment before announcing, "We intercepted some radio traffic. The other one told him they had a firm fix on us. I think that they're going to try to get together to double team us."

"'Think?' Is that a guess?" Stauer asked.

"An educated guess. Still, yes, I could be wrong."

Stauer turned his attention to the ship's skipper. "Recommendations, Ed?"

"Start to take 'em out now, one at a time."

"That will cost time," Boxer observed. "One, we had time for, within the schedule. I don't know about two, though."

"Yeah," Kosciusko agreed, "It'll cost us time. But having one of them show up when we've got seven or eight armored vehicles and a hundred men in the LCMs could cost us the landing and the mission. Then, too, some of what we lose we'll pick up by shaving off the time Chin and the LCM will need to get to us."

Stauer was nothing if not decisive. "Fuck it; do it. If we have to burn out the engines racing to the landing site then . . . well . . . that's our employer's problem."

"Not even his, really," Boxer said. "We could always scuttle the ship and let the insurance company worry about it."

Stauer thought about that for maybe two seconds before agreeing, "True. What do we owe those assholes, after all?"

"Bring her about," Kosciusko ordered. A stream of

orders followed. "Spotters forward. Mrs. Liu"—the chief gantry operator— "to the gantry control. Deck crew hook up an empty container, a forty footer if one's available. Set speed for eighteen knots and I'll buy a case of beer for the engine crew if they can squeeze out twenty." The constant slight vibration one could feel through the deck suddenly became less slight as the engines below strained to put on maximum speed.

★CHAPTER FORTY★

Corsairs against corsairs;
there is nothing to win but empty casks.
—Italian Proverb

D-1, Yacht *One Born Every Minute*, off the coast of Ophir

The pirates had kept the yacht's original name because it just seemed to fit so well, once it had been explained to them.

Times have been better, mused the captain of the yacht and leader of its seventeen man crew. Not that the yacht itself needed seventeen men to run it, of course, but somebody had to man the machine guns, do the boarding, secure the captives, and inventory the haul.

The captain, Nadif, as with almost all of his crew and most of his people, was tall, slender, and fairly light skinned, with features a mix of Arab and African. Gray at the temples, he was just beginning to sprout gray, single, curly hairs all over his head. He thought he was probably about forty-five, but couldn't be quite sure. As a young man, he'd been a fisherman, and a good one. It was that, that knowledge of the sea, that had brought him to the pirates who were, by and large, landlubbers or, in any case, young men with very little knowledge of seamanship.

Rather, the knowledge of the sea had made him an asset to the local pirate group, made them seek him out. He'd have had nothing to do with them, ordinarily. But as a fisherman, years before, he'd found he just couldn't compete with the western, Chinese, and Japanese commercial fishers who had taken so much of the local stock that it had become hardly worth the expenditure of gas for the few fish he could catch. Necessity is a harsh mistress, and with a family to support, pirates flashing altogether too much money, that money driving up prices . . . *Well, what was I supposed to do?*

Victims of our own success, though, Nadif mused. *Oh, for a while we were raking it in. And the whites' and squint-eyes' navies were by and large helpless. Yes, they had their successes, as did we. But they never really understood, or would admit to understanding, how to stop us. Until, in the face of their failure, the fat merchant ships simply started avoiding us, avoiding our coastline, at least, unless the cost of fuel was greater than the likely ransom they'd have to pay.*

I suppose we were "overfishing," too. Nadif patted the console of his little command. *Of course we still manage to take the occasional idiot yachtsman.*

Fortunately, we never became political, or not too political. I can just imagine what kind of reaction we'd have caused if those Arab lunatics on the other side of the Red Sea and Gulf of Aden had had their way. Sure, chop

*off somebody's head for the televisions? Then watch the
westerners get serious.*

Thank Allah we managed to avoid that.

Beneath the deck the engine shuddered and coughed
before catching its timing again. A fine fisherman Nadif
may have been. He was not, however, a marine engine
mechanic. *And Allah? If You could see fit to make the
motor run for just a couple more days? Just a couple? Yes,
yes, I know: The camel limps from its split lip. But what
can one do?*

*Oh, and thank You for sending that fat prize our way.
We appreciate it.*

D-1, four miles northeast of Nugaal, Ophir, and about eight hundred feet over ground

On McCaverty's command, the flight had shifted formation
from a staggered trail to a broad V. This took very little
time. It had also increased its height over ground, which
hadn't taken much more.

The image in his NVGs was so grainy that Welch
almost missed the final landmark before jumping, a thin
dirt airstrip with perhaps four thousand feet of useable
runway. The team had considered simply airlanding at
that runway.

Which probably would have worked, he thought, *for a
part of one night. Since we had to go in a day early, we
couldn't leave the planes parked there in the intervening
day. Sooo . . .*

We jump.

The seat next to the pilot was missing, in order to allow two jumpers to get to the door in turn. In the open space crouched Little Joe. Terry's butt was still half inside, but he had his legs out of the plane with his feet resting on the strut that supported the wing.

"Go!" McCaverty shouted over the roar of the engine and the rush of the wind.

Everybody with normal human emotions had a different point at which the reality of impending danger tended to set their heart to racing and their stomach to fluttering. For underwater demolitions people, that might be when they actually entered the water. For regular infantry it might be when they crossed the line of departure, or LD. For paratroopers, it was often at some point in the jump sequence: "Hook up!" for example. Terry had jumped a *lot*. His heart didn't start *really* pounding until he got the command to "Go."

Ignoring that pounding, and the fluttering in his stomach, Terry stood and swung his rear end so that he faced forward, wind against his face. Then he scrunched down and . . .

It wasn't a jump so much as a letting go. The plane was moving slowly, which had advantages and disadvantages. Chief among the disadvantages was that the forward speed of a plane, in effect, helped the parachute to deploy. Chief among the advantages was that at the current speed, the tail of the plane wouldn't take his head off before he cleared it.

That, and one got a relatively soft opening of the chute.

Falling face toward the ground, Terry felt a slight tug at his back. As he typically did, he counted off aloud: One thousand . . . two thousand . . . three . . . "

When he got to "four thousand" and still hadn't felt the opening shock, his right hand began automatically questing for the ripcord. He forced it to stop.

And then there was an opening shock. *Not bad. Not bad at all*. Terry's hands went to grasp the risers. His stomach settled and his heart rate dropped.

D-1, Yemen

"Not bad; not bad at all," Konstantin whispered as he finished his circuit of the sand-colored camouflage nets he, his men, and the four air crew had put up over the helicopters. The image in his goggles, at this range, was good enough to tell that the nets were properly staked down, that their edges blended smoothly into the dunes, changing the shape of the dunes but not their essential quality.

He walked forward now, coming in the same way he'd left. Behind him he trailed a short length of netting to distort and disguise his footprints. At the end of the net he went to his belly and slithered forward. Sergeant Musin lifted the net for him, making his entrance easier.

"Everyone here?" Konstantin asked of Baluyev.

"All present, Comrade Major," the *praporschik* answered. The warrant officer now wore a long flowing dishdasha and had an Arab headdress, a keffiyeh, in one hand. "The bikes, arms, and clothing from the other helicopter are here, tested—except for the motorcycles—and functioning."

"Radio check with the ship?" Konstantin asked.

"Yes, Comrade Major," Baluyev answered. "And with

the old man, back in the Lubyanka. That last was via the helicopter's radio."

Konstantin nodded, satisfied. He pointed and said, "Galkin, set up shop inside this helicopter. Check everyone's makeup. Then, everyone sleep, except for the guard. One in six on alert. Pilots just sleep. We've got a big day tomorrow."

D-1, MV *Merciful*

While Kosciusko and the bridge crew were restricted to small, hand-held or face-worn night vision devices, the two observers on either side of the bow had much more powerful, tripod-mounted scopes. Thus, it was no surprise when the speaker on the bridge sang out with "Captain, this is Wilcox on the starboard side. I've got 'em at about one o'clock. Two and a half to three klicks away. Looks like a fishing yacht, maybe fifty or sixty feet, hard to say. About twenty in beam or a bit less. Armed men—I *think*—at the bow. She's making good speed."

"Drop speed to eight knots," Kosciusko ordered. "Bearing: zero-two-zero."

"Aye, sir . . . Aye, sir." The engines' throbbing reduced as every man aboard was slightly but forcibly leaned toward the bow and to port.

Stauer shot the captain a questioning look.

"He's—whoever he is—not going to know we're the same boat he's been after. Too dark to pick out colors and we're almost head on to him. I don't want them to have a clue about how fast we can go if we want to," Kosciusko explained. "Not until it's too late, anyway."

"Fair enough."

"Wish we had a couple of barrels of fish guts and blood," the captain said.

"Why's that?" Stauer asked.

"Chum the water."

"Huh?" Kosciusko didn't normally give Stauer the impression of bloodthirstiness.

Kosciusko shrugged. "I'm a sailor. I don't like pirates."

D-1, Yacht *One Born Every Minute*, off the coast of Ophir

Life's so unfair, Nadif thought. *Ordinarily, we're lucky to get a good haul once in two months. But tonight, we've got two ships and only my little command to take them. And the other boat reported engine trouble and that they were heading back to port. No help there. Damn. Decisions, decisions.*

"No matter," he said. "Better a bird in the hand than ten in a tree."

"What's that?" Nadif's helmsman asked.

"What? Oh. We'll take this beneficence and forget about the other. Steer for the target." Nadif listened to the engines for a few seconds, then shook his head with mild disgust. "They're too noisy," he tsked. "Drop speed to one third. After all, it's not like they're not heading our way anyway."

D-1, MV *Merciful*

"Mrs. Liu?" Kosciusko queried over the intercom.

"Here, Skippah," came a lilting voice back.

"You understand the mission?"

"Sho' t'ing, Skippah. You say which side. I swing containah ovah. I wait. You tly ram mothafuckahs. You say drop. I drop."

"By George, I think she's got it," said Boxer. "I also think she's been listening too closely to the deck crew's invective."

"She's loaded every container and piece of heavy equipment we have aboard," the captain answered. "Flawlessly. She's always had it." He heaved a sigh, "And, yes, she picked up the slang pretty quickly. I think she thinks 'mothafuckahs' is a term of endearment . . . "

Kosciusko picked up a small radio from a charging station not far from the ship's wheel, and then turned toward the hatchway.

"Where are you going?" Stauer asked.

"Tight timing," the captain explained. "Hard to control from here. I'll let the helm know when."

The bow of the target loomed above the small pirate craft. The target was maybe seventy-five meters off, making way slowly.

"Speed to one quarter," Nadif ordered, very quietly. "Gently now, gently. They don't know we're here and I don't want them to until we're swarming over them. Grapple, ladder and tie off men forward . . . quiet, damn you!"

Even this close, the pirate was hard to see until Kosciusko pulled on his NVGs. If there'd been much distance between the two vessels, depth perception would have been an issue. As was, with the *Merciful* well elevated over the pirate, gauging distance was relatively easy.

The pirate was veering to come alongside his ship to starboard. *Possibly*, thought Kosciusko, *to pin us and prevent escape. Possibly, too, as an instinctive move to avoid being silhouetted by any light on the shore. Old habits die hard, I suppose.*

He glanced down and said, softly, "But you're going to die harder."

In his goggles the captain saw two men, one to either extreme side of the pirate craft, spinning what he suspected were grappling hooks.

"Mrs. Liu?" he whispered.

"Stan'ing by, Skippah."

"Starboard side. Amidships."

"Logah."

The gantry began to whine as the Chinese woman moved it slightly forward while pivoting the crane to the right. The wheel bearing the cable, too, squeaked as the steel passed over it.

Nadif gave the order, "All stop . . . astern, half power." At the slow speed of the merchie he thought to match its speed to allow his men to grapple and board. Once he was grappled, of course, the target would provide a perfect match for course and speed, at least it would once the *One Born Every Minute* was swung around and tied off with a heavier line.

"What's that sound?" Nadif asked of no one in particular. It seemed to come more or less from above and drew his eyes upward. There, he thought he could see, or almost see, a head looking down at him.

"No clue, boss," the helmsman answered. "Maybe routine . . . oh, shit!"

At his helmsman's cry, Nadif looked down again. The target was turning. Worse, the wash was suddenly spurting rather higher than it had been, even as the port side seemed to boil.

Without another word, effectively on autopilot, Nadif's hand reached over and pushed the throttle fully forward. The engines, not that well maintained at the best of times, began to give whatever they had to give.

First, however, they had to overcome the rearward inertia. For a long moment, therefore, the yacht hardly moved at all.

"Hard right rudder! Full starboard bow thruster!" Kosciusko ordered into his hand-held radio. The captain kept his enhanced vision on his intended victim. He could see, or perhaps only sense, that the pirate below was straining to avoid being rammed.

"But you're not going to make it, you bastards."

By inches and by feet, the *Merciful*'s bow closed on the pirate.

Nadif knew, within a few moments, that he was not going to be able to avoid the merchant ship's bow completely, not with this boat and these engines.

"So let's limit the damage."

Limiting the damage, in this case, consisted of keeping the merchie from harming the engines or propellers, or crushing in the gunwales or hull. Shoving the helmsman off to one side, Nadif took the wheel himself and twisted it hard to port, to spread out the coming blow. It was almost enough. The impact, when it came, was still on the starboard quarter. He and all his men were thrown from their feet as the yacht was struck and then partially lifted up on the bulbous bow. Several screams from the port side told that a number of men had been pitched overboard. They were cut off as the merchie forced the yacht over them, driving them under, probably with serious injuries.

Nadif struggled to his feet and returned to the wheel, though he kept his eyes locked on the hull scraping by his own vessel. He noticed that the merchant vessel's water line was well above the surface, indicating a very light load. *Well, maybe we won't have lost much of a haul.* As a good seaman, even though one who had never been in quite these circumstances before, he intuitively analyzed the forces in play.

I'm pinned against that hull by its swing. But its swing is greatest and strongest here. If I can force my way back, I've got a fair chance of breaking free and away, especially since their rudder's swinging their stern a lot more than their bow. I don't know what I'll do about the men overboard.

He snarled up at the ship looming over his own. *Damned idiots! Do they think they own the sea? Don't they realize there are other boats on the water?*

Cursing that he'd missed—*Well, not quite missed, and it was only a best hope, anyway*—Kosciusko raced to a point just forward of the gantry's base, then stuck his goggled face over the gunwale once again. To his right, a container swung slightly from port to starboard and back again. It reached, on the middle of its swings, just overboard. Doors on both ends swung freely.

"Stand by, Mrs. Liu," he repeated into his radio.

"Still stan'ing by, Skippah."

"Then . . . Mrs . . . Liu . . . on my command . . . DROP, DROP, DROP!"

The yacht was taking on water, yes, but *nothing the pumps shouldn't be able to handle, at least for while.* Nadif hadn't been able to break away from the merchie. He had his rudder hard to port but as the *One Born Every Minute* attempted even a minute turn, the swing of the merchant ship cancelled it, pinning it to the line of the merchie's hull as that hull continued to scrape by. That said, as he neared the stern Nadif could feel the force exerted against his boat lessening.

Nadif was pretty sure his own hull was at least slightly sprung. *Not too bad for the pumps, though, or that thing might have driven right over us. If worse comes to worst I can set the crew, what's left of them, to bailing by hand. Should be able to make it to shore, at least, if not to port.*

Most important to—

Thought incomplete, Nadif glanced up and said, "Fuck!"

The container hadn't quite passed the halfway point of its outward swing when Mrs. Liu released the gantry's burden. One corner struck the gunwale and set the thing to a slow spin. In practice, this meant that it hit the boat below almost edge on, crushing several men under its nearly four tons of weight and smashing one side of the boat to below the waterline. One of the freely swinging doors was almost vertical when it struck. This chopped sloppily through a young pirate on all fours, amidships and through the middle of his body. Blood gushed out across the pirate's deck in both directions. The boy barely had time to register what had happened to him before a corner of the container cruched his skull like a soft boiled egg.

The container strike also listed the boat to port. Pressure from the *Merciful*'s dance forced water in at a rate no practical pumps for a boat that size could have dealt with. The water added to the list until resistance from the water below, coupled with pressure from the *Merciful* above, plus the container-induced list, capsized the smaller vessel.

Kosciusko smiled at the screaming below. He *really* didn't like pirates. Looking down, he said, "See? I tolll' ya." Into his radio he gave the order, "Resume course. Full speed."

"Any survivors?" Stauer asked, once Kosciusko had returned to the bridge.

"Doubt it," the sailor answered, smiling. Turning to the helm he said, "Keep a watch out for the other reported boat. Have the forward lookouts relieved and the new ones do the same."

Unseen by anyone, blood from the sundered young pirate, as well as from various cuts, abrasions, compound fractures, and split skulls, seeped into the water around the ruin of the yacht.

When the container hit, it had thrown Nadif and the helmsman from the yacht's bridge into the water. The pirate skipper had gone under, at first, then surfaced to witness as the helmsman, screaming in panic, was forced under the wreck and lost. Nadif, an experienced seaman, was made of better stuff. Paddling frantically, he swam away from the ship. For a while, he seemed to be losing. But then, he had a chance, he knew, when he saw the merchant ship steer to its port.

If I can hang on until some wreckage surfaces too, I can make it. It's a long swim to shore but not an impossible one.

And then he felt a sharp tug from below.

★CHAPTER FORTY-ONE★

The medics jumped and screamed with glee,
Rolled up their sleeves and smiled.
—Anonymous, *Blood on the Risers*

D-1, three miles north-northeast of Nugaal, Ophir

"You all right, Little Joe?" Welch asked of the swaying Tex-Mex with the pack on his back and a chute rolled up and carried in his arms. Terry's pack was on his back, chute over his shoulder. He carried a stubby and conventional looking Russian-made "Kashtan" submachine gun in his hands, a suppressor extending far past the barrel of the piece.

Venegas didn't answer right away, as if he hadn't quite understood the question. When he did answer, his voice sounded much weaker than normal. "Hit my head on a rock, Terry. Helmet's only good for so much."

"Can you make it to the drop-off point?" Welch asked.

"Not a lot of choice."

"No," Terry agreed, then lifted his goggles and consulted his watch. *And not a lot of time until moonrise, so . . .* "Let's get moving." He replaced the goggles and glanced again at Little Joe. "Give me the chute," he ordered. Looking around, his gaze came to rest on one of the other team members, Darrell Hammell, the Tennessee ridge runner generally known as "Pigfucker."

"Pigfucker, take Little Joe's rifle and helmet," Welch said.

"Roger, sir," Pigfucker replied.

"And Ryan, get his ruck."

"Roger."

"And . . . let's move. Little Joe, stick by me."

"Roger."

The short, thin column snaked and weaved its way up the rocky hillside. Slowly. Very slowly. They moved slowly enough, in fact, that Terry began to worry about getting to their hide for the day and camouflaging everything before sunrise. He turned his torso and head to look at Venegas, following close behind. *No, he's not up to bearing his own load yet. Shit.*

D-1, Bandar Qassim

The newly—indeed *just*—rising moon cast long shadows across the water. It didn't provide much light yet, though in places it made the waves sparkle.

The port wasn't really a natural harbor so much as a slight indentation into the land. It had been improved by man, however, by the addition of four jetties, though three of those actually formed one long, dog-legged jetty jutting into the sea first to the northwest and then directly west.

Antoniewicz and Morales had stopped and surfaced once, before reaching the mouth of the major harbor, to get their bearings. Now, swimming near the mixed mud and sand bottom, they entered the outer port very near the long jetty, then turned east. Since no rivers drained into the sea at the port, or for that matter anywhere nearby, the waters were quite clear. There wasn't even very much garbage floating at the surface, since in a place as poor as this one, the definition of what constituted garbage was quite constrained.

Which is a pity, thought Eeyore, *because with more garbage floating around we could put our heads up to get bearings if we needed to. Well . . . nothing for it. Needs must . . .*

As dark as it still was below the surface, they continued east by compass, as well as by the *feel* of the water, and the small currents, and the sound. The monoculars on their masks weren't a lot of use yet since they needed at least *some* light.

The sound of a freighter, tied up to the dock, with waves and currents shifting it about, was distinctive, a combination of *whoosh*, groaning metal, and the occasional resounding thump.

Target one, Antoniewicz announced to himself. *Though it's probably harmless, part of our job is to* punish *the other side.* He swam upward slightly, his fins propelling him and his hands reaching forward to prevent an unfortunate head-first bump on the hull. Morales followed closely.

Eeyore's right hand touched on the barnacle-encrusted

hull. Both arms flared out as he twisted his fins down to bring him to a complete stop. Morales bumped him from behind, then continued on to target two, a smaller ship farther in.

Antoniewicz's legs sank slowly until he was approximately vertical next to the hull. Once he'd achieved that posture, those legs began automatically to pump slowly to maintain his position. His hand went to his side to draw his knife. With this he scraped away enough of the barnacle mass encrusting the surface to be sure of a good attachment. After he felt around the area he'd cleared, and was satisfied, he reached around and pulled a pod containing limpets to where he could open it and get at its contents. This he did, then he removed from the pod a single mine.

The ship's hull, in planning, had been presumed to be metal, based on the size. This proved to be the case. As Eeyore's hands moved the limpet near the hull, the mine's own magnets pulled it inward. He placed both hands around it and attempted to move it. When it remained stuck fast to the hull, he pulled out first one pin, then the other. The thing was mined now, and woe betide anyone who tried to remove it. Just as unfortunate would be the ship itself once it had moved some distance from the harbor.

And even if the ship doesn't *move*, the diver thought, *in about forty-eight hours we're getting the earth-shattering—okay, the* hull-shattering—*kaboom anyway*.

Satisfied with that, Antoniewicz swam off. Sensing the presence of at least a faint moonlight filtering through from the surface, he pulled the monocular over his right eye and turned it on. *Ah, yes, that's* much *better*. At the next target Morales was just beginning to scrape the hull when Eeyore nudged him. The former stopped what he was doing momentarily and gave a thumbs up. Eeyore saw that Morales, too, had activated his monocular. He continued on his way.

These three biggies in the outer harbor, he thought, *then we link up at the mouth of the inner harbor—north side—and it gets interesting.*

D-1, three and a half miles north-northeast of Nugaal, Ophir

Terry glanced at his watch, did some mental calculations, looked around at the terrain he'd memorized, and called a halt. The team went into a cigar-shaped three hundred and sixty degree perimeter, each man taking a knee. The rear man, Grau, and the point, Semmerlin, each bearing one of the suppressed, subsonic sniper rifles, moved to the center, by Welch, and did likewise. Both used their rifles as crutches to help ease themselves down under the backbreaking load. Little Joe tried to take a knee, but ended up on all fours. He was vomiting onto the ground as Terry spoke in a whisper.

"We're not going to make the planned hide before the moon has this place lit up like Christmas," Welch said. He pointed to the left and said, "There's a wadi—sort of a wadi, satellite imagery showed it has some vegetation—over that way, about a hundred, maybe a hundred and fifty, meters, I think. We'll go there and hole up. Priorities of work remain the same. Questions?"

"No, sir . . . None, boss."

"All right. Back to your places and move out."

The spot selected was actually just past the juncture of a smaller wadi with the major wadi. There were three reasons for this. One was that the confluence, and the resultant greater quantity of underground water, had made the spot rather more lush . . . for certain highly constrained values of "lush." Second was that it seemed to Welch to be less likely to be visited by a passing goatherd, since the major wadi had enough vegetation to feed a good sized herd while the minor held out the chance of losing a goat in it. Lastly was against the possibility of a flash flood, always a danger in the desert where rains, while infrequent, typically came unannounced. They could fill up a wadi very quickly and, the next thing the occupants knew, they were drowning or being carried off, or, more usually, both.

While Grau and Semmerlin kept guard, the remainder of the team—including, somewhat inexpertly, the two translators—excavated one side of the wadi, saving the light colored soil off in a separate pile. Once they had a place big enough to hide the chutes and harnesses, they carried their own in, placed them—really packed them— as tightly as possible and went to retrieve those belonging to the others. After that, the darker subsoil was shoveled over, to be followed by the lighter, dryer topsoil. Then they clustered into three groups, one with Grau, one with Semmerlin, and, between the other two groupings, Little Joe plus the two translators with Welch. Over themselves they erected lightweight sand and brown camouflage nets on very low collapsible poles. This was at least as much for protection from the sun—limited though that protection would be—as to hide from casual view.

And then all but the three on watch went to sleep.

D-1, Bandar Qassim

Morales was sitting on his ass, arms folded, cross-legged, atop an underwater concrete block when Antoniewicz reached him after mining the third small freighter in the outer harbor. He moved his right flipper as if tap-tap-tapping with impatience. If the mouthpiece made it impossible to smile, still Eeyore was pretty sure his teammate was smiling inside.

This shit's fun.

With hand signals, Eeyore reconfirmed what had already been planned and agreed to: Morales would sweep the northern and eastern sides of the inner harbor, mining any boat as large as twenty feet in length, while Eeyore followed the north-south jetty before moving to the southern edge of the port, to do the same. Eeyore had the shorter swim but, since the inner side of that north-south jetty was tightly clustered with hulls, about the same "workload." In fact, if the ship and boat positions hadn't changed substantially since the last satellite update, by the time Morales worked his way through the northern, eastern, and southern sides, Antoniewicz would only be about half done with the western. Morales would then start with the southernmost cluster of boats on that western side.

Reaching down to his right wrist, Eeyore twisted the dial on his wrist compass to a bearing of one hundred and fifty degrees. This was conservative, as it would bring him to a little dogleg jutting eastward from the southern jetty. He'd then follow that around to the targets.

Dragging his underwater assault rifle and sixteen limpet mines, Antoniewicz kicked off on his set bearing. With the fins he wore, and the shape he was in, he'd crossed the roughly sixty meters in about twenty-five seconds, despite the load he was dragging. In his monocular he saw the indistinct outline of what was probably a very bored guard.

And I'm so glad we're using rebreathers rather than tanks, Eeyore thought. *Even if they are Russian and even if the slightest mistake that might let water get at the potassium superoxide would make for a really big and hot bang.*

Antoniewicz turned left and, keeping no closer to the jetty than he had to, swam the long, one hundred and eighty degree turn that brought him to a small vessel that reports indicated was a certain pirate.

The boat was about thirty-five feet long, based on photo interpretation, and likely wooden hulled. It was most unlikely to be metal hulled, in any case. The hull, when his hands inspected it, proved to be nearly barnacle free. Again, Eeyore pulled a mine from the pod and placed it against the hull. There was no magnetic pull. Moving his fins slowly to hold himself, and thus the mine, fast, he placed the flat side against the hull. Then, while he continued to hold with his left hand, the fingers of the right sought the flange on the friendly side of the screw. *No such thing as friendly, when we're dealing with explosives underwater.* This he began to twist until he felt it bite into the hull. He gave it a few more twists, then adjusted his grip and took hold of the screw on the opposite side.

D Day, MV *Merciful*, sixty-two miles west-southwest of Soqotra

They had the LCM re-embarked. Chin's command, *The Drunken Bastard*, waited close by the hull, waiting for its turn. The *Bastard* could have made the trip south on its own, of course, and beaten the *Merciful* there handily. On the other hand, war vessels—and it was one, if a small one—were inherently suspicious. There was also another reason to keep a boat in the water. Thus it would be loaded and carried aboard, in its cradle. That, however, had to wait until . . .

Dropping people off in pitch blackness using a GPS is one thing, McCaverty thought. *Landing my very own mortal body on something moving, on the other hand, is a very different proposition.*

Fortunately, we've got a bit of moon to work with now.

The ship was moving forward at about four knots, just about enough to maintain steerage and a bit more. It moved with the wind, to give the returning planes the maximum possible benefit and lift, since they were doing a bow-on landing. Somewhat unfortunately, the superstructure provided altogether too much shielding from the wind. The benefit would be there, early on, but could be expected to drop rapidly and substantially past a certain point.

"Which means," McCaverty said to himself, "that you would be well advised to actually have landed before that point . . . easier said than done, perhaps."

It had been a long flight and a tiring one. Though physically demanding, the little planes were a dream to fly, up to a point. That point had been reached about an hour and a half ago. Right now, McCaverty and all his pilots were bone weary. Worse, he'd taken a fuel report status from each of them and they'd reported less than twenty minutes' worth of fuel left, in the worst case, and no more than thirty-five minutes in the best, which was McCaverty's own. It would have been a bit better except that the ship, for reasons McCaverty hoped to hear someday, had moved about forty miles from the originally planned rendezvous. This had burned up fuel as the flight took a slightly longer course than had been planned on.

The radio crackled to life. It wasn't Kosciusko's voice, but another's, saying, somewhat cryptically, "Send in your first passenger now."

It took a moment for the pilot to recognize the voice of his boss, the former Marine Aviator, Cruz.

"Roger," McCaverty answered. "Break, break: Number Four; you're up."

"Ro . . . Roger," came the answer back, with better than half a gulp in it.

"Relax, Four. You've done this before."

"Roger that. I didn't like it then and I like it less now . . . making my approach."

Racetracking over the ship, counterclockwise, McCaverty banked his own plane to the left to watch the approach and landing. He wasn't close enough to make out the individual wands held by the deck crewman in charge of directing the pilots. He could see the lights frantically wave and then Number Four pull right and up, aborting the landing.

"What was wrong with that one?" McCaverty asked of the bridge.

"Partly our fault," came the answer, "partly his. Guy's speed was a little off and the deck was coming up. He would have hit it wrong; probably crumpled the landing gear."

"Roger . . . break: Four, get on the racetrack. You'll go in next after two. Two; you're up."

McCaverty unkeyed his microphone, looked at his own fuel gauge and said, "Fuck."

Looking again out his left window, he saw Two land fairly effortlessly. Sure, it bounced for a bit and for a moment it looked like it would veer over the side. But Two's pilot regained control and righted the thing within a hundred and fifty feet of first touching down. Within a couple of minutes, the engine was dead and a portion of the deck crew was pushing the plane back, then lifting the tail to turn it forward again.

McCaverty asked, "Four, are you ready?"

"Roger. If the swabbies can get their timing right."

"Both of you need to have your timing right."

He held his breath, this time, as Number Four came in. He didn't begin to breathe again until he saw it safely landed and being pushed out of the way.

"Number Five, your turn," McCaverty said.

The answer was clear and confident. "Roger."

"Do it. Pay attention to—"

"Six, this is One. I'm practically dry. I've got to get in *fast*."

"You're after Five, One."

Again, McCaverty held his breath as Five came in. His landing was, if anything, smoother than Two's.

"One, Six. Go; but be careful."

Number One didn't answer. McCaverty watched the approach, watched the flight deck crewman trying to wave One off, then watched as the pilot ignored the signal and came in anyway.

Smith, flying Number One, was a hotshot. He knew it; everyone back in the Navy had known it. At least, everyone had known it until he made one little mistake. *One little fucking mistake and they beached me, the bastards*.

But in his own view, he was still a hotshot. Thus, it was confusing when he came in to a flight deck, and none of the signals he was used to as a carrier pilot were present in quite the same way. A landing on a real carrier had what amounted to a lot of automation to help the pilots. This kind of landing was more touchy feely, almost like the carriers of the Second World War.

And it was damned strange. And disconcerting. And *Goddamit, I'm nearly out of fuel. And . . .*

The rising bow caught the landing gear and snapped it off like three spindly twigs. The plane almost flipped over and *did* nose dive into the deck. McCaverty couldn't see it, not even with the NVGs, but his mind's eye provided the detail of the propeller blades shattering into thousands of splinters. For some distance, Number One skidded on its nose, tail in the air. Then the tail came down to the deck. This failed to stop the skid which continued all the way to where Number Five was resting. McCaverty saw people, presumably Five's pilot and the deck crew that had manhandled it as far as they had, scattering to either side, like kitchen roaches when the light came on, as One slammed into its predecessor.

While that deck crew was scattering, a different crew was racing out with large but portable fire extinguishers. If there was any fire, and McCaverty had reason to believe there was, these killed it.

I hope Smith didn't kill himself, McCaverty thought, *because that privilege is owed to me.*

"Up!" Coffee shouted into the female medical barracks containers. He sounded positively happy. "Up, you refugees from . . . " he was about to say "bordellos" then realized that was a little too close to the unpleasant truth. "Up, I said."

In seconds, the area in front of the female medical barracks was a seething sea of half-covered female flesh, not all of it young. Instead of the sound of the surf, however, there was a confused and confusing medley of mixed English, Romanian, and Mandarin.

Phillie led the pack. "How bad is it?" she asked, breathlessly. "Have you notified Doc Joseph?"

"He's already standing by in OR," Coffee answered. His voice went from happy to somber and serious. "Two of them are pretty bad."

"I understand." Then Phillie said something that endeared her to Coffee completely. "Follow ME, girls!"

★ ★ ★

McCaverty's engine sputtered out just as Number Three made a safe landing. It had taken precious minutes to get one of the small earth movers they'd once used in Brazil out on deck to push the wreckage of One and Five safely out of the way. Those minutes had been a few too many.

"I can't land," McCaverty informed the bridge. "I . . . " He checked his position relative to the ship, made some assumptions about his glide path, then continued, "I can splash in about two hundred meters to port. Please have the *Bastard* pick me up."

"Roger. *Bastard* standing by."

★ CHAPTER FORTY-TWO ★

Every carrier landing is graded . . .
—U.S. Navy SOP

D-Day, MV *Merciful*, seventy-seven miles southwest of Soqotra

Drumming his fingers impatiently on plywood, McCaverty sat cross-legged over the chart house. Around him, a puddle formed from the water released by his dripping clothes. The puddle was actually more of a wet spot, as the curvature of the plywood allowed and encouraged excess to run off to the sides. His face, normally cheerful, was grim.

"I'm going to kill that stupid son of a bitch," he muttered for roughly the hundredth time since being picked up.

Powerless, and with full flaps down as he'd neared the water, McCaverty had slowed to just under forty miles an hour. A well timed pull of his stick had lifted the plane's nose up, so that he touched down with the tail. That sudden increase of resistance in the tail had slowed the plane rapidly, though less rapidly than a nose dive would have.

Instead, the tail-touch had caused the tail to nearly rip off and the fuselage to slam down almost vertically. At that, the plane had so nearly stopped that only McCaverty's safety harness had kept him from being thrown into his instrument panel.

While the harness might have saved him from any number of cuts and contusions, or worse, it had had the unfortunate effect of holding him fast inside the plane as the latter had rapidly filled with water—most of it surging through the new gaps by the tail—and gone under. If he'd panicked for an instant, he'd probably never have gotten out. As it was, the plane had been ten or fifteen feet underwater—he really couldn't be sure—before he'd managed to extricate himself and swim to the surface, there to be met by a smiling Chinese with a small life ring from which a line ran to the idling patrol boat.

They'd picked him up, gotten him—wet and shaking, with residual fear, not with cold—aboard, and then eased in toward the ship. He held in his hand, the one where the fingers weren't drumming, a good sized glass of lukewarm whiskey placed there by the patrol boat's captain, Chin.

Bastard inched up to the net that had been hung over the side. Looking up at the gantry's whine, he saw a fairly large platform composed of welded I-beams being lowered onto two projections from the hull. The platform, he knew, would be covered with PSP to provide a landing spot for one of the compliment's five—two of them now in Yemen—helicopters. A similar structure was to be erected on the starboard side, assuming that hadn't been done yet.

Probably hasn't been done yet; I don't see where they've had time.

Chin turned the wheel over to one of his crew and stepped up to where McCaverty sat. "You've a choice, pilot," the Chinese said. "You can wait for us to rig the patrol boat and get hoisted aboard that way, or you can scramble up the rope net."

"I have someone I need to kill," McCaverty answered. "And justice won't wait." He tossed off the remnants of his drink and walked unsteadily to the net.

The hand that helped him over the gunwale belonged to the commander of the aviation company, Mike Cruz.

Cruz waited until McCaverty had his feet on deck before saying, "We now have either one extra pilot or two of them. We don't need you to fly. On the other hand, we've got five men hurt, two of them badly. So, junior birdman, your flying days for us are over; you're a doctor again. No, it isn't because you did anything wrong. Ya done good . . . under the circumstances. Now get your ass to surgery and give Doc Joseph and the Chinese woman a hand."

As McCaverty started to leave he turned his head over his shoulder. "How much damage did it do to the flight deck?" he asked.

"Essentially none," Cruz answered. "Amazing stuff, PSP."

McCaverty, scrubbed and suited now, glanced over the two filled operating tables. There was an unconscious patient on each. On one, an itty-bitty woman, the Chinese doctor, was patiently moving intestines from around what looked to be a large wooden splinter from a propeller. The splinter jutted almost straight up from the body, a nurse holding it in position. As the Chinese doctor moved the guts, she piled them on a table next to the patient. One of the surgical team—based on size, McCaverty guessed it was another Chinese—sprayed a solution over the growing pile of gut.

It reeked.

"You McCaverty?" asked the surgeon at the other table. Blood sprayed through one of his hands while the other, holding a hemostat, sought out the vessel from which the blood spurted.

"That's me," he answered.

"I'm Joseph, Scott Joseph. This guy's a mess. I'll be lucky to save his legs. Really lucky. But that may not matter because his skull's caved in. I cut a goodly chunk of it away to relieve the pressure. But he's got bone fragments stuck in his brain that are way beyond my skill set to remove. I understand you're neuro."

"Yeah." Automatically, McCaverty looked at his hands. *Steady as a rock, which they weren't when they picked me up. Must be the whiskey Chin fed me. Ordinarily, really crappy idea to operate after drinking anything. In this case . . . might be the only possible idea.*

"Well, don't just stand there with your teeth in your mouth. Get to work."

"Yes, sir." McCaverty looked at the patient and said, "We've got to save this one."

"Any reason in particular, beyond the Hippocratic Oath?" Joseph asked.

"Yeah. I need him to get better so I can kill him."

Joseph laughed. "Sheeettt."

D-Day, MV *Merciful*, thirty-two miles east of Ofone, Ophir

"*Mierde*," said Luis Acosta, the headman of the Mexican ground crews, as he looked over the wreckage of the two aircraft under the gantry and pushed off to the port side. "Shit."

Acosta was a bit over thirty years old, short, stout, brown, and with stiff black hair that jutted almost straight up from his hairline before rolling its way back over his head. The other sixteen Mexicans clustered around him, ten on one side, six on the other. All from the same area— Guadalajara—and many of them related; they tended to look much alike. Only one was substantially taller and he was also much lighter.

Manuel, Acosta's number two, and the tall, light skinned one, shook his head and said, "Man . . . Luis . . . no fucking way. I mean no fucking way. Shit. How much time did you say we have?"

"Twenty hours," Acosta replied. "That's when we need to have made one good plane out of these two wrecks."

Manuel looked again at the wreckage. "Man, I can't even tell where one plane ends and the other begins. Shit." Manuel sighed and asked, "What did you say they'd pay us if we can make one out of these two?"

"The bonus? Seven thousand pesos. Each."

"Ohhh. Well, fuck; that's different. What the hell we waiting for? Let's start sorting and inventorying parts, man. Seven thousand pesos and I'll *carve* us any parts we need."

Manuel glared to his right and left at the others. "What

are you *maricones* waiting for? Didn't you hear the man? Seven thousand fucking pesos if we get one of these things running. For a day's work? Move it, you *chingada* assholes!"

D-Day, Bandar Qassim, Ophir

All in a night's work. They'd done it; the thirty-six most dangerous or economically significant ships and boats in the inner and outer harbor were mined. Now, out past the harbor mouth, Antoniewicz and Morales treaded water while waiting for Simmons to raise the submarine.

"Where the fuck is he?" Morales asked aloud. He took his GPS from his belt and raised it above water, pressing the query button as he did so. "We are *exactly* where we're supposed to be. *Exactly*."

"Relax, Morales," Eeyore said. He glanced at his own watch. "Simmons has four minutes before he's due to rise." His face acquired a puzzled look. "Did you hear something?" he asked.

"Something like an out of tune lawnmower? Now that you mention it, yes." Arms being busy, Morales pointed with his chin. "It's coming from over there."

They'd both rotated their night vision monoculars away from their eyes and turned them off once they'd passed the mouth of the outer harbor. Eeyore now rotated his monocular back into position and turned it on.

"Oh, fuck," he said.

The second pirate ship limped; there was no better word.

Oh, sure, cursed the captain, *we went out in high style. looking for the best prize we'd heard of lately. Quite a show, the bow cutting the waves and the men waving their rifles and RPGs like they meant business. And then the fucking infidel engine decided to go asthmatic on us. Even a stinking fat merchantman can outpace the miserable seven or eight knots we can do.*

The captain looked behind him and down and spit at the engine. That wasn't satisfying enough. He turned the wheel over to another and walked to the housing, delivering it a solid kick. *Bastard.*

"Captain," the helm called out, "we've got something coming up out of the water."

Simmons had timed it pretty well, he thought, raising the small sail within two minutes of when he'd been supposed to. Setting the engine to idle, he backed off to all fours then pedaled back to where he could sit and then nearly stand. He took a quick glance out of the sail's forward, wrap-around view port—which was also the direction any threat was most likely to come from—and saw nothing to worry him. Then he reached overhead and turned the wheel to open the hatch. It opened with only minimal sound and with little salt water dripping in. With the hatch out of the way he was able to stand up fully to scan for his two mates. As soon as he stood, he heard the asthmatic coughing of a marine engine in truly sorry shape, coming from close behind him. He barely had time to register the sound and turn when something close by struck the sub, right on the tower.

Nothing cracked, *Namu* was small and slight enough

to give readily in the water. But the angle of the strike pushed it over, rotating the sub about its long axis. The boat—Simmons realized it was a boat—began to ride up on the sub, forcing the turn to continue. And then water began pouring into the open hatch.

"What the hell was that?" the pirate skipper asked.

"I don't know," the helm answered, "but we hit it and it went under."

The captain considered this for a few moments, before ordering, "Engines, all stop. And some of you ferret-faced weasels break out a half dozen or so grenades. Maybe we can force whatever is down there up again."

"By the way, did you see it?" he asked.

The helmsman shrugged. "Yeah, maybe, kinda, sorta."

"What did it look like?"

"Well . . . I didn't see much, but I thought it looked a little like a killer whale. You know, like those ones in the movies."

Struggling against the push of the in-rushing water, Simmons managed to get one hand on the hatch's wheel. He pulled for all he was worth, the water resisting even his prodigious strength. He managed to close the hatch, and to dog it, too, but not before the minisub was more than half full of water and sinking. The lights stayed on, which was some comfort. Life support, however, choked and died. Simmons doubted he'd be able to get the thing off the bottom once it settled down.

With water above his thighs, and the sub slowly sinking, he said, "I'm so fucked."

★ ★ ★

"Come on," Morales insisted, "we've got to go get Simmons out."

Eeyore put a restraining hand on his teammate and answered, "Yes, but not yet."

"Why?"

The answer came in the form of a small flash on the boat, followed within a few seconds by a wallop that came through the water and that felt highly analogous to being kicked in the testicles.

After half an hour, and the expenditure of a dozen grenades, the captain decided that if there were anything down there, it wasn't coming up for anything he could do. Shaking his head again, and spitting once more at the engine, he said, "It was probably nothing. You said it looked a bit like a killer whale?"

Again, the helmsman shrugged. "Yeah. They're rare around here, I know, but they're here. Seemed kind of small, too."

"Hmmm. Small, you say. Well . . . let's get to harbor and get this fucking engine in the queue to be fixed before its mother shows up."

"Oh, man, that *hurt*," Morales moaned.

He and Antoniewicz had swum off as fast as possible once the first explosion had gone off. At the range they'd stopped at, the eleven explosions that had followed had still been unpleasant, but not at quite the kicked-in-the-balls level of pain the first one had been.

"Yeah," Eeyore agreed. "Hey, look, they're moving off.

Let's give them a few minutes and we'll see what we can do, if anything, about Simmons and the sub."

Namu hadn't been all that impressed by the explosions, even though they could be felt. Simmons, on the other hand, had been.

If whoever it was hit me had taken off, I'd have hyper-ventilated, cracked the hatch, let the sub fill, and then swum out. But I can't swim in an area being depth charged. Shit.

Already the air was noticeably stale.

This is not *how I intended to die*, Simmons thought. *Not at all. Shit.*

"This is about where Simmons surfaced," Eeyore said. "He's not going to stop short of the bottom, so head straight down and then north, then east. I'll do the same and head south then west."

"What do we do if we find him?" Morales asked.

"Assuming he's alive but that the sub is fucked, one of us can share a tank until we get him to the surface."

"Yeah."

"Okay, then. Monoculars on. We'll come up every twenty minutes to coordinate."

"Roger," Morales agreed, then headed for the bottom. Antoniewicz followed.

It took three more dives and as many different search patterns before Eeyore's monocular caught the faint glow emanating from the viewport of the *Namu*. He swam over to investigate. *Namu* was lying upright. He could see by the dim glow that the lights inside were still on. Through the viewport he saw Simmons slumped against one side of the tower. He thought, but couldn't be sure, that the sub driver was still breathing.

A series on knocks on the viewport failed to rouse the man. Antoniewicz thought, *Well, he's in for a sudden, unexpected shower.*

Eeyore swam upward a bit, then put his legs to either side of the tower to brace himself. For a few moments he hyperventilated to ensure he'd have enough oxygen when his put his mouthpiece into Simmons's mouth. Satisfied with that, he put his hands in different positions on the smaller, exterior wheel for the sub's hatch, being careful to take positions that wouldn't break his wrists when the hatch shot open, as he expected it to. He twisted, or tried to. Nothing. Again, he sucked air, then put everything he had into twisting the wheel.

Come on, you son of a bitch.

He was rewarded with the sudden springing open of the hatch, followed by a massive air bubble that shot to the surface. He waited a couple of seconds for the bubble to clear, then lunged to a point above the now open hatch. Simmons' head was there, clear of the hatch. He wasn't moving.

Eeyore reached down and grabbed his teammate by the nearest things he could get a grip on, the ears. Again he pulled, this time putting his back into it. Simmons' torso cleared the hatch. Now Antoniewicz could reposition to get a one-armed grip under the arms. With that grip secured, he used his other hand to remove his own mouthpiece and force it into Simmons' mouth. He squeezed once, and then again, to get Simmons' lungs to pump air. Then, legs kicking for all he was worth, Eeyore shot the two of them upward. It wasn't really deep enough to have to worry about the bends.

Simmons was still out of it once they reached the surface. Antoniewicz took some comfort that he was still breathing. He held the unconscious man's head above water while waiting for Morales to show up to spell him.

"Thank God," were Morales's first words once his head broke the surface. "Now what?"

"Remember those few fishing boats that were floating away from the dock in the outer harbor?" Eeyore asked.

"Yeah. So?"

"Well, we're going to take him there. Then we're going to steal a boat."

"You mean a rowboat? I don't think that will work."

"No," Eeyore shook his head. "We're going to rest a bit then steal a power boat."

"But they're all mined, bubba," Morales objected.

"Nope," Antoniewicz countered. "One of them *isn't*."

★CHAPTER FORTY-THREE★

Myself, I don't take any chances.
I talk to Mohammad, to Buddha, to Mr. Jesus H.Christ,
or any other religious honchos I can come up with.
—R. Lee Ermey speaking, *The Siege of Firebase Gloria*

**D-Day, MV *Merciful*, forty miles
north of Bandar Cisman, Ophir**

Phillie showered mechanically, on autopilot, washing away the speckled gore from her assistance in the operating room. She didn't want to think about the emergency surgery, the spraying arterial blood, the desperate and frantic work of the surgeons as they tried, desperately but vainly, to save the life of the injured pilot. She just wanted to be clean, to eliminate any traces of the death, and then go to her cot and cry herself to sleep.

Stauer was waiting for her as she robotted her towel-wrapped way from the showers. His arms were folded and he was leaning against a bulkhead.

"Sorry it took so long to find you," Stauer said. "I had

to go over some hymns with the chaplain. That ran over-
time. Then after someone from medical found me and
told me, I stopped by the girls' medical barracks container.
It was hard to get a word in edgewise, what with all the
Romanian weeping. Eventually one of your girls told me
I'd find you here."

She stopped in surprise as soon as she saw and heard
him. He seemed so calm and, frankly, unconcerned that
she felt a momentary flash of anger. "It doesn't bother you
that one of your people was killed?" she snapped.

Stauer shook his head. "Not especially. It's part of the
business. If you're going to be in this business, and have any
business being in this business, then you have to accept that
death is the cost of doing business." He smiled, slightly,
adding, "You also have to accept that sometimes people will
say really fucking redundant things like that, too."

"I don't know that I have any business in this business,"
she retorted.

Stauer shrugged, but asked, "Didn't you ever lose
anybody in ER?"

"Sure," Phillie answered. "All the time. But I never had
any connection to any of them. They weren't coworkers,
friends . . . well, neither was the dead pilot; I didn't really
know him. But he was . . . "

She stopped for a moment, confused.

Again, Stauer smiled. "If someone becomes important
to you merely because he's a member of the organization
you're a part of, Phillie, then you do have a place in this
business. About the dead . . . well, you try to minimize the
risk and the numbers. But you have to accept that it's
going to happen.

"Frankly, I'm a lot more concerned about not having contact with our team of trained pinnipeds."

She gave him a very confused look. "Pinnipeds?"

"SEALs. The people on the minisub. They should have been done and contacted us by now. Not a word."

"Come on," he said, with a twist of his head. "I'll buy you a drink before the memorial service."

"Memorial service?"

"Sure," he replied. "Just because we accept death as part of the cost of doing business doesn't mean we like it, or that we don't owe something to the dead."

The ship had an open area, roughly thirty meters by forty-five, so far down into the ship it was almost out of the ship. The deck was PSP, held up by the containers underneath it. Sternward and forward, it was framed by containers with single width gaps leading to the super-structure, to the rear, and other containers of various function toward the bow. Several of these containers served as galleys for the unit. Still others were part of the command apparatus. The area itself served in turn as mess and briefing-*cum*-planning room.

This far down, the natural roll of the ship was so muted as to be almost imperceptible to anyone who had spent any time higher up. Indeed, the sailors who had been aboard for three months or more with nary a break swayed themselves in time with what motion there was, but their swaying seemed exaggerated, as if some internal mechanism had adjusted itself to a greater motion, and couldn't adjust back in time.

Chaplain Wilson had set up a temporary chapel in the

area, the maps and sand tables, as well as the dining tables, all being carried off to the sides. He stood now toward the bow, in battle dress adorned with a clerical collar.

Stauer was the first in, followed by Phillie and the staff. Along the starboard side flowed in the mechanized company, behind their leader, Reilly. The Marines, Cazz leading, filed in on the port. Behind Phillie more men, the naval, aviation, and headquarters companies filtered in, staying as much together as possible. Ahead of them, on a sheet hanging down, were projected the words of an old and famous hymn.

Wilson glanced at his organist, seated before the small field organ the chaplain had brought with him to Brazil. The organist—Phillie thought he was from the Marine company—nodded and began to play. She recognized the tune. Even if she hadn't, the words sung by—yes, she looked around and checked—every man and woman present that she could see, ringing off of hull and bulkhead and shipping container would have told her the title:

> "Praise to the Lord, the Almighty,
>   the King of Creation!
> Oh, my soul praise Him for he is
>   thy health and salvation!"

Phillie thought she detected at least one voice singing in Spanish and looked behind her. Sure enough, there were several of the Mexicans, covered in grease and looking inexpressibly tired. Yet from their lips she could make out the words:

> "O, despertad arpa y salterio! Entonad
> "Himnos de honor y victoria!"

On a hunch, Phillie continued searching out the people behind her. There, not far from the Mexicans, surrounded by his engineer section, Matthias Nagy, the German, sang:

> "Lobe den Herren, der alles so herrlich regieret,
> Der dich auf flügeln des Adelers sicher geühret!"

On the chance, she glanced to Reilly, who was singing in English. Sure as crap, next to him was his Israeli girl. Phillie couldn't tell at all what words the Jew was singing, but assumed it was the same song (in fact, it wasn't, though the armored car commander *was* singing the psalm that had inspired the hymn).

This is too weird. At least the half dozen Moslems . . . hmmm? She looked. No, they weren't singing. On the other hand, each of them had his eyes closed, arms folded across chests, and was rocking head and body side to side in time with the music.

Phillie looked front and finally stumbled through the singing. She was of a younger generation and her church was more likely to indulge in modern things, or older ones set to modern music, than in the more traditional hymns. After a couple more verses she saw that the chaplain had raised his arms heavenward.

"Let the 'Amen,' sound from his people again!"

Still singing, Phillie looked at Stauer and saw something

she'd never have imagined as possible. Tears were coursing down her lover's face.

"Gladly forever adore Him!"

Chaplain Wilson dropped his hands. The organ gave its subtle signal and the singing stopped.

"Brothers and Sisters in the Lord . . . "

McCaverty had asked to do the eulogy himself. Since it seemed important, Stauer had let him go ahead. When he was finished, Stauer took his place and began to speak.

"Boys," he said, while thinking, *It's really bizarre to be calling a collection of mostly forty and fifty-year olds "boys."* "Boys, so far, with one significant exception, so good. The team to take out what passes for an Ophiri Air Force is in position. Welch's team is in position. The Russians are in position. Just after nightfall, we'll be in position to begin launching.

"The exception, though, is Biggus Dickus' crew, under Antoniewicz, we sent by *Namu*, the killer minisub, to mine the boats at Bandar Qassim. They may be fine, and their radio down. They may have completed their mission and just not be able to tell us. Unfortunately, we can't take the risk that they might have sunk before they ever got on station. Or been compromised. Or had engine trouble. Or any of a hundred other possibilities.

"How does this change things? Good question; glad you asked. We've got to ensure that the boats at Bandar Qassim don't come after us. So we're going to take one light airplane off the strike we planned for Bandar Cisman, and one from the medevac duty, arm the ex-medevac and send those two north to shoot up the boats at Bandar Qassim."

Stauer gave a truly wicked smile. "Yes, as a matter of fact, that does mean you should try fifty percent harder not to get your ass shot, since it'll be fifty percent harder to get you back here."

"And now, gentlemen . . . " Stauer glanced at the organist.

> "Mine eyes have seen the
> glory of the coming of the Lord
> He is trampling out the vintage . . . "

"What was that about, Wes?" Phillie asked as the conclave filed back to their duties.

"What was what about?"

"That whole thing with the hymn. There were foreigners singing: Jews, Huns . . . there were even neopagans, two of them to my certain knowledge, singing an old Christian hymn. And you? I've never seen you cry over anything. But you cried over that."

Stauer tried to brush off her question by saying, "It was just the beauty of the moment." She wasn't buying it. He continued, "Well, it *was* . . . but it was more than that, too. Those couple of neopagans weren't singing to God, New Testament or Old; they were singing to the rest of us. And the rest of us . . . this is the last time all of us are going to be together in this life."

Phillie shook her head. Stauer couldn't tell if that was lack of understanding or full understanding overborne by denial. He guessed the latter.

His shoulder heaved with a weary sigh. "In a few hours, hon, we begin landing. By this time two days from now, not everyone who's here with us will be on Earth at all. This was our last time in this life for us all to be together. That's what made the moment so beautiful and sad. That's why Jew and Pagan sang Christian hymn, why Russian and German sang together. We were singing, each of us, to each other, saying, 'Comrades, we're together.'"

As if to punctuate, one of the former Marines began singing a new song:

"Michael row the boat ashore."

To which even the mechanized infantry replied, en masse. In that small space, low ceilinged and surrounded by metal, their voices caused the containers, the flooring, and even the hull to vibrate: "HALLELUJAH!"

★CHAPTER FORTY-FOUR★

They that go down to the sea in ships,
that do business in great waters.
—107th Psalm, King James Version

D Day, MV *Merciful,* North of Bandar Cisman, Ophir

A hot wind, carrying its share of dust, blew from the stern to the bow. On the port side, four of the six Elands the LCMs could carry were loaded, while Mrs. Liu gently lowered a fifth down. Infantry and crew either crawled down nets or, in the case of the middle LCM, used the same loading ramp they'd come aboard on. Starboard, the former Marines, much as their grandfathers and great-grandfathers had before them, climbed down stout netting to boats rising and falling with the waters. They had it both better and worse than their progenitors, however. It was better in that there was precisely no reason to expect a hostile reception right at the shore. It was worse in that the boats that were to carry them to land were simple inflated rubber craft, with small, quiet engines. It was also somewhat better in that Chin's people had built from scratch a number of floating platforms that bumped and ground against the hull but that also provided something of a safety backup should a man lose his grip on the netting and fall. The floats had the additional advantage of allowing an easier boarding of small boats that were not normally terribly easy to board.

Chin's patrol boat, *The Drunken Bastard*, sat with its engines more or less quietly idling between the ship and the shore.

While some of the amphibians loaded the boats, and others climbed down the netting, the remainder stood in lines topside for their turn to debark. A few of them coughed, from time to time, whether from diesel fumes, or from the dust, or from a combination of those.

Behind those, near to the ship's superstructure, waited the light STOL aircraft. There were six of these, as the Mexicans had managed to patch one together from the scraps of two. Those same Mexicans now saw to arming four of those with a mix of unguided rockets and machine guns. The other two would fly almost unarmed, and solely to retrieve any wounded from the impending action. These weren't marked for medevac, but at least they weren't plainly armed to the teeth. (Though they did carry a side mounted machine gun, just in case.) The medevac birds had floats that were also wheeled, to allow landing on water or on the flight deck.

Behind the aircraft, though forward of where the helicopters waited, Stauer watched the proceedings from the glassed-in bridge. Being there, remaining on the ship, was a tough call. Yet it was the critical node, the locus of the most critical events, and the site with the greatest probability of cascading failure.

So here I'm stuck, he fumed. *Doing my job . . . worrying.*

Down in the Tactical Operations Center, just off the central meeting, planning, and dining area, Biggus Dickus, worried sick about his missing team, would have sympathized. Under the circumstances, however, he didn't have a lot of sympathy for someone as stuck on the ship and away from the action as he was . . . *especially* when he had three men missing.

And still worse, Biggus Dickus Thornton fumed, *I'm totally unnecessary here. Hmmm . . . I wonder.*

D-Day, Bandar Qassim, Ophir

While he hadn't seemed to suffer any permanent damage as a result of oxygen deprivation, Simmons was certainly the worse for wear, weak and still disoriented. He tended to fade in and out quite a lot, too. This hadn't been helped any by spending a long day in a small boat in a harbor altogether too close to the equator . . . without potable water.

He lay in the boat now, conscious if not a lot more than that, while Antoniewicz and Morales paddled the little craft toward the outer jetty where the pirate vessel of the night before had docked. They didn't know why it had docked where it had—perhaps the captain had simply taken the first available berth for fear of engine failure if he'd gone another yard. Or maybe it was the boat's normal docking station. Insects swarmed a light that hung well above the boat, illuminating it, a portion of the jetty and the surrounding water.

"Or maybe they were lazy," said Eeyore to himself, his voice barely above a whisper. "Or wanted to get out to sea again quickly. Or it's just dumb luck."

"What's that?" Morales asked. He shook his head a little to clear it, wondering if the long, unprotected day in the sun had affected his mind.

"I was wondering if it was just dumb luck that the boat we want is where we can get at it without having to risk the inner harbor."

"Dunno," Morales said. "You bitching about it?"

"Not really. We deserve some luck, after all."

"Maybe the harbor was just too full," Morales offered. "It's not like there was a lot of space between hulls when we were mining them."

"Yeah," Eeyore half agreed, "that could be it, too."

"You still want to go with the direct approach?" Morales asked.

"I think that after a night of swimming and a day in the sun without water we're not really up to anything too clever. So shut up and paddle. And aim toward the harbor mouth; we'll let the incoming tide bring us in to the boat *quietly*."

The oars were put up and both Eeyore and Morales had their APS underwater assault rifles gripped in their hands. These were sub-optimal outside of the water, but could be expected to work for at least a few shots, if it came to that.

Ahead, the pirate boat was quiet enough. The semi-frantic activity of earlier in the day, as someone apparently worked on the engines, was over for the night. There were some men who could be heard speaking and joking near the bow. Their jocular voices carried well across the water.

The slow tide carrying them to the boat also passed them by the long concrete jetty that protected the outer harbor. It was unguarded or, if it were guarded, the guard was looking outward to sea.

Guards in evidence along the jetty or not, Antoniewicz worried. *If it was the engines, and the sound it made before hitting the Namu suggests they had their problems, I sure as fuck hope they got whatever was wrong with them fixed.*

The small boat in which they'd hidden for the day thumped gently against the stern of the pirate craft. There was a name painted there, but Eeyore couldn't read it. The thump was gentle, and made little noise. Morales grabbed the stern of the pirate boat while Antoniewicz scrambled aboard, his firearm held in one hand.

Whether it was the gentle thump or some faint sound he'd made in climbing over the gunwale, somebody on the boat noticed. Or maybe he just needed to relieve himself over the stern. Eeyore didn't know and didn't much care. Someone was coming and that someone had to die. He took an automatic kneeling firing position at the starboard corner of the boat.

Poor bastard did just want to take a piss, Eeyore thought, as the dark, skinny man standing next to the boat's cockpit proceeded to do just that, his urine splashing noisily in the outer harbor's water. He'd have lived a few minutes longer, and maybe longer still, if he hadn't then turned as if to walk to the stern.

It wasn't that big a boat. Antoniewicz couldn't wait. He lightly stroked his weapon's crude trigger, twice. There was a slight recoil, but no sound. Even though the APS had no suppressor, the cartridges themselves were piston driven, the explosion of the charge never leaving the cartridge casing and thus never causing harm to a diver underwater who fired one or, in this case, two.

He wasn't even a pirate, actually, but just one of the few people in the port capable of maintaining a marine engine. He needed to take a piss, and then decided to get something more or less cool from the boat's ice chest, below. Not that he didn't make his living from piracy, he did, at least in part and indirectly. Still, the mechanic could say with a reasonably straight face that he was an honest man, who'd never harmed another human being in his life.

He didn't understand, therefore, why he suddenly felt a shock in his upper chest, just below his neck, nor the pain that followed it. It hurt so badly he didn't cry out. His hand went automatically to the source of the pain. He didn't understand why his chest was wet with the thick fluid, nor why his fingers touched on a small—no more than a quarter of an inch thick—metal dart that seemed to be growing from his chest. No more did he understand the iron-coppery stink of blood that assailed his nostrils.

He might have figured it out, eventually, but the second shot went into his brain, right through his left eye. After that, he wasn't in a condition to figure out anything.

"Get Simmons in the boat and then get it started,"

Antoniewicz ordered, softly, head turned over his left shoulder. "I'll take care of the rest of them."

Gingerly, Eeyore stepped over the still quivering body sprawled on the deck.

The men on the foredeck were simply chatting, laughing sometimes, as Antoniewicz crouched by the side of the cockpit and drew bead on them. He was about to fire when he heard the engine start to life with a shuddering cough. All the men looked up and toward the stern in surprise. Then they noticed him. They didn't go for weapons. Indeed, there weren't any to hand so far as Eeyore could see. Instead, they raised their hands.

Fuck; I can't just kill 'em now. Not after they surrendered.

Eeyore motioned with a jerk of his head and another with the muzzle of his APS for the men to get into the water. No arguments; they stood and jumped. Once they were in the water and no danger, Antoniewicz walked, bent at the waist, placed his APS on the deck, and then picked up and rolled the body of the man he'd killed over the side.

"Eeyore, cast us off," called Morales.

D-Day, MV *Merciful*, North of Bandar Cisman, Ophir

Soundlessly, barring only the slight soft whine of their electric motors, the rubber boats carrying the Marine company pulled away from the temporary floating docks along the ship's hull. The Marines sat on the gunwales of the inflatables, with their rifles and machine guns in their hands and their personal equipment D-ringed to lines that ran down each boat's center, bow to stern. Cazz's boat took the lead, moving forward initially before veering to port and the shore. The other boats followed in trail before cutting right or left to make a deep V.

The electric motors had been selected for silence more than speed. The boats didn't move especially fast, no more than four and a half knots or so. This would see them to shore in an hour.

While the Marines cast off and headed to shore, the Mexican ground crews for the remaining fixed wing aircraft continued the laborious process of fitting their planes, four of them, anyway, with the machine guns and rockets they would carry on their missions.

McCaverty, after the briefest of naps, watched Luis' boys work. As he watched, he fumed, *I didn't sign up for this to be a doctor. And it's not right that they're making me. I signed up to fly and to fight.*

I wonder if that bastard Stauer planned this all along.

"I'd accuse you of planning this," Stauer said to Phillie, as she stood next to Biggus Dickus, "except . . . I can't quite imagine how. Let me make sure I understand." He pointed a finger at Phillie. "You want to get closer to the action?" The finger shifted to Thornton. "And you . . . *you*? Trained pinniped par excellence? You want to go on the standby medevac flight heading north?"

"Why not, sir?" Thornton asked. "I started life as a corpsman. You don't have enough doctors to put them on the medevac birds. I'm a better medic than anyone else here, except"—Thornton's head shifted Phillie-ward—"maybe Miss Potter. Might be a matter of life and death for somebody."

Thornton smiled benignly at Phillie. She'd been a much easier sell, when he'd approached her, than he'd expected.

Stauer glared at his lover. "Did you clear this with Doc Joseph?"

Phillie nodded. "He said with McCaverty in OR, and the Chinese women having proven pretty competent, and the Romanian girls to help, that he's more likely to save people if they don't get back to the ship exsanguinated, in shock, and probably infected."

Stauer was not fooled. Pointing at Biggus Dickus, he said, "*Him,* I understand. He's got people out there lost and he's worried sick over them. But you? I thought I had a sensible girl."

"Didn't you tell me once, Wes," she asked softly, "that a rational army would run away?"

He glared at her. *Not fair to bring up old discussion points, sweetie.*

"I knew what you meant," she continued, "which is almost certainly not what Voltaire intended; that it took something beyond pure reason and rational selfishness to make an armed force work.

"I'm not asking you for this for the excitement," she said, "though I won't deny that the self-satisfaction from doing *everything* I can to help is in there somewhere. But the fact is, I'm either a part of this or I'm not. If I'm not, I don't belong here at all. If I am, then I need to be where I'll do the most good, for everybody."

Stauer turned away from the two, walking to the pot of invariably vile coffee always brewing on the bridge. He filled a Styrofoam cup with the nasty stuff, then sipped it, thinking, It might be the right thing to do. *It might be the only right thing to do. But, dammit, she's my girl.*

Which gives me zero excuse.

"Fine, then. Do it," Stauer said, with something less than good grace.

★CHAPTER FORTY-FIVE★

The Marines have landed,
and the situation is well in hand.
—Richard Harding Davis

D-Day, Beach Red, north of Bandar Cisman, Ophir

The dust became a little more noticeable the closer they came to shore. Behind him, Cazz could feel his radio-telephone operator, or RTO, *hmph-hmphing*, trying to suppress a cough.

The beach was a grainy-green image of sloping sand and light surf in Cazz's night vision goggles. Twenty meters out from it the man on the motor cut power and rotated it out of the water. Thereafter, the rubber boat drifted in under its own inertia. With each meter closer to the beach, Cazz could feel the tension rising in the boat.

I guess it's all pretty academic until you actually get near the beach, he thought.

The boat scraped along the sand and gravel below it, then shuddered to a stop. The company commander was out of the boat and churning through surf to shore in an instant. His RTO followed a few steps behind. The other members likewise slid over the sides and raced forward, except for one, the one who had been manning the motor, who more deliberately picked up a metal stake attached to the bow by a rope. This one walked until the slack was taken up, then dragged the boat farther up until its bow was out of the water. Then he drove the stake into the sand.

About fifty meters up the gently sloping beach, Cazz took one knee. His RTO dropped likewise behind him. Seconds later, the rest of the first boatload ran past him, continuing on maybe another three hundred meters.

Yeah, maybe they're all old codgers like me, Cazz thought, chest swelling with pride, *but we had a lot of time in Brazil to work the kinks out. And, still, "once a Marine, always a Marine."*

Inland, the old men then began to spread out to form what would become a perimeter. These men went prone as soon as they'd reached their immediate objective. Their rucksacks were still behind them, in the rubber boat. They'd send a party of two back to retrieve those after the perimeter was set up and secured.

Cazz looked around behind him to where the rest of the rubber flotilla was coming to shore. As boats touched in, more short lines of men streamed, forming themselves on the first group to go to ground. Almost directly behind him the mortar crews struggled to get their guns and a few rounds each across the surf, two men stumbling and falling once as the uneven ground, the pulse of the water, and the massive baseplate they were trying to hump proved too much.

They'll be a while.

More mortar ammunition, twenty-two rounds of 120mm per gun, would come in by helicopter, later.

D-Day, MV *Merciful*, four miles off the coast

There were three landing craft, each capable of carrying two of the armored vehicles, or three of the Ferret scout cars, or one AML and two Ferrets, to shore at a time. There simply wasn't room for more than that, though the boats wouldn't sink under considerably more weight. The round trip took about fifty minutes. Loading took twenty-five minutes to half an hour, and that only because Mrs. Liu was good at her job. It would be at least five hours from when the first LCM left to when the mechanized company was fully ashore.

Just as Cazz had been the first man to hit the beach, so Reilly, as a matter of principle, was going in the first load of heavy equipment. Lana was already loaded on her boat, number three. Standing with one leg over the gunwale, his foot locked in the net, Reilly passed on last minute instructions to his exec, FitzMarcach.

After five minutes of that, Fitz held up his hands, palms out, and said, *"Enough,* sir. I *know* what has to be done and how to do it."

For half a moment Reilly felt anger building. Then he realized, *Yeah, what the fuck am I doing? He knows what to do.*

"Sorry, Fitz. Maybe I was just remembering back when you were a lieutenant."

"I could do this back then, too. Just relax, boss. Go have fun. Top and I will follow in the last boat to unscrew whatever you fucked up ashore."

"Right. See you ashore."

With that, Reilly twisted to bring his belly to the gunwale, and his other leg to the net. He then carefully climbed down to where the LCM Number One waited. Once he felt his feet touch the cleated deck, he turned to the rear and walked between armored car and hull to stand under the raised cockpit. James, carrying a radio, followed, as he'd followed his chief down the net.

Looking upward, one thumb raised, Reilly said, "Take us in."

Back in LCM Number Three, Lana Mendes felt the sudden surge of the engines as the boat eased away from the hull.

Oh, my God, she thought, *I'm really doing this. It's not a dream. I'm going to go and get to* fight *in an armored vehicle, and nobody's stopped me just because my plumbing's wrong.*

For this, *Reilly, you old bastard, I will even learn your fucking Nazi song*. She smiled then, unseen by anyone, even Viljoen and Dumisani, thinking, *And you can't even* imagine *the other things I'll do for you, for letting me do this*.

D-Day, Beach Red, Ophir

The ramp splashed down, raising spurts of surf and sand

around its edges. Instantly, one of the armored cars' engines revved. The car itself spun wheels on wet, cleated steel for a moment, before the wheels caught traction and it surged forward. Up it went, up the sloping front, before thudding across the space between ramp and hull. It went straight for a moment, then nosed down slightly as it took the ramp into the water. Whitish spray surged around the wheels. Then it was off and moving to the shore.

By the time the next vehicle from LCM One moved off its ramp, Number Two had ramped down, while Number Three was perhaps fifty or sixty meters out from the shoreline.

James following, Reilly walked off, down the ramp, and into the surf. There he was met by Cazz.

"Quiet as soft shit," the former Marine said. "There's nothing out there but us, for at least five hundred meters in every direction. I think this is going to work."

"It's not like we didn't pick the loneliest, most desolate strip of nothing for fifty miles," Reilly answered.

"I know. But this just feels too easy."

Reilly thought about that for a few seconds, then answered, "I think it'll get a lot harder, pretty soon."

"With a little luck."

D-Day, MV *Merciful*

With the Marines gone, likewise the landing craft, a good chunk of the mechanized infantry, and all the special operations types but one, the ship was unusually placid and quiet. Kosciusko didn't have a lot to do; the ship's

Dynamic Positioning System—a computerized method of keeping a ship in the same spot—did its job rather well. Cruz was at the stern with the helicopters. The CH-801s, the six of them left, were mostly ready, though Luis' Mexicans busied themselves with them even so. And why not? Four of the Mexicans were going to ride them as door gunners.

Down in the hold the staff kept track of things nicely. All Stauer had to do was stand on the bridge at the moment, and watch . . .

Watch . . . not much of anything, really. Mrs. Liu's doing a fine . . . oh, shit.

Forward, on the starboard side, a sudden bright glow that should not have been there grew from among the containers.

While the LCMs were away, Mrs. Liu busied herself and her gantry with repositioning containers so that other containers, holding armored vehicles, would have their doors freed so the vehicles could move into the open for loading. She had most of them available to be opened by now. Indeed, all but a few of the vehicles were lined up in position for the gantry to lift and shift them over the side. And most of those few, notably barring a somewhat smoky Ferret the mechanics were working on inside one of the containers, were moving into position for loading.

FitzMarcach lay atop the container with his head over the edge, looking in- and downward at a scout car from the engine of which smoke seeped. The mechanics had the engine cover off and were muttering darkly as they rattled about with wrench and spanner. The driver sat at his station, inside, while the commander of the vehicle stood in the turret hatch, offering helpful and completely unwanted advice to the mechanics. Fitz glared at the thing, as if trying to get it to move by sheer will.

The Ferret seemed notably unintimidated by the XO's glaring. Quite the opposite. Indeed . . .

Suddenly, one of the mechanics said, "Oh, shit," dropped his wrench and went scrambling for the far door to the container. Meanwhile, the other mechanic, followed by the vehicle commander, very nearly flew out the open front door as a large burst of flame erupted from the engine compartment. The flame reached the inside top of the container and spread out in a bright mushroom. Fitz didn't get his head out of the way before the flames singed his eyebrows and made his hairline recede even more than it already had naturally.

And then the flames reached the driver, who began to scream. The mechanic who had headed away from the already open door soon joined him as he discovered that that door couldn't be opened.

There was a fire extinguisher with the Ferret. Neither the mechanics nor the crew had time to use it. Thus, the first people on the scene with any serious firefighting capability were the flight deck crew. They raced over, the first two men jumping from the flight deck level a bit over eight feet down to the level of the armored car containers. These received the heavier and larger than normal fire extinguishers normally found on the flight deck as they were passed down. Then deck crew dragged the extinguishers to the open door from which flames poured and began to spray foam inward.

They could still hear screaming.

At least the screaming's stopped, Fitz thought as he directed the firefighters forward into the container. The thing reeked of gasoline, smoke, burned plastic, and, far worst of all, burned hair and flesh. His own face felt warm where the initial flash had hit it, singeing away a good deal of his hair.

Mrs. Liu had gotten the gantry positioned to lift the container off and drop it over the side.

"Can you handle the flames, Fitz?" Stauer asked.

Fitz nodded and said, "Yessir."

"Because if you can't, we've got to dump it."

Fitz felt heat that didn't come from his reddened skin. "And *dump* our people, *Reilly's* people, over the side without a proper burial? No fucking way . . . sir."

"All right," Stauer agreed. "Get in there and get our people . . . our people's bodies, out. Then over it goes."

At the rate they were squelching the fire, Fitz thought and said, "Give us five minutes, no more. Then we can hook the container up and dump it."

"Fair enough," Stauer agreed.

They found the driver half out of the vision port in front of the Ferret. Apparently he'd gotten stuck there and burned from the rear forward.

"Awful way to go," one of the firefighters said aloud as he and another twisted the charred thing to and fro to wriggle as much as they could of it out of the Ferret. Part of one hip and a leg stayed behind. The Ferret itself was too hot to enter to retrieve those pieces.

The mechanic—what was left of him—was easier to recover. He was scrunched up on the container's floor in a fetal position with nothing much holding him in place except his fingers. Those were wrapped around an up-down metal rod that held the door closed.

"Just . . . break the fingers off," Fitz said. He sighed, "No time to be careful. And we've got the important part."

"Roger," the navy types trying to extricate the body answered. With a gulp, one of them took hold of the mechanic's charred hand and broke the fingers off. They came away surprisingly easily, though they made a sound like crisp bacon being crumbled. It was that, more than anything, that made the sailor vomit.

While the bodies were being carried off on stretchers, FitzMarcach looked up to where two of his own people were hooking the container up to the gantry. One of them looked down at Fitz, questioningly.

He nodded and shouted up, "Signal Mrs. Liu to dump it."

Back on the bridge Stauer watched the gantry lift and swing over the side the container with the burned-out Ferret and small bits of his people inside.

Jesus, he thought, *three dead already, two hurt that I know of, and three we've lost contact with, and we haven't even started the shooting part yet. Shit.*

And my boys, dead like that. He pushed the thought away violently. *Mourn later; there's a job to do now.*

★CHAPTER FORTY-SIX★

Let your plans be dark and impenetrable as night;
when you move, fall like a thunderbolt.
—Sun Tzu, *The Art of War*

D-Day, Safe House, Elayo, Ophir

The text signal from the ship had been simple. "Auth. Cd. RBF. Do it, 02:15 hours, plus or minus 15."

Though some hundreds of miles farther north, the same wind that blew dust from the stern of the *Merciful* and made rubber boat-borne RTOs want to cough raised clouds of dust around the safe house and the town, on the outskirts of which it sat.

Buckwheat closed a wooden shutter, then looped a piece of string around two handles. "Let's go."

Fletcher, Rattus Hampson, Vic Babcock-Moore, and Wahab all sighed. Most did so with a trace of fear. In Fletcher's case it was pure anticipation.

Wordlessly, the five filed out of the safe house and boarded their vehicles in the dusty yard just behind. They left one of the Land Rovers behind. The vehicles started without problem. The team drove nine miles east from Elayo, past the utterly insignificant fishing village of Siyaada, before they killed their lights. They then passed the last major wadi before the airport. At the wadi, they turned south into the intensely, even incredibly rough patch of hills cut by wadis that ran perpendicular the coast.

By compass and GPS they moved another four and a half miles eastward through that, the bouncing of the vehicles causing pain to kidneys and, in Rattus's case, a bit tongue. They came at last to a steep sided bit of ground, small and most unlikely to be investigated. There they pulled the vehicles in tight against the sides and dismounted.

Leaving Wahab behind to guard the transportation, the other four, moving in single file, began the two thousand meter trek to the northeast. They left their gear, most of it, behind, carrying only their weapons and ammunition, dun-colored gillie suits, night vision devices, a GPS, personal communicators, and in Buckwheat's pocket, a satellite phone.

The way led steeply up, past a thin dirt road. They crossed this by simply getting in line on the near side, listening for a few moments, then rushing across as one. On the far side they flopped down again, listening for several minutes after.

Hearts were pounding, and not just from the minor exertions of walking and rushing.

"Okay," whispered Fulton, "now to the ridge."

The closer they came to that feature, the lower they walked, until finally, perhaps a hundred meters shy of it, they went to hands and knees and began to high crawl.

From there, they crawled all the way to it, to a point from which they could see the airfield below.

There they waited while Buckwheat flicked on his night vision scope, took a firing position, and slowly swept the scope's field of view across the airfield. He counted silently as he did, then again, just as silently, as he swept it back.

"I count six Hips," he said, "plus eight fixed wing, four of those jets."

"No change then," Fletcher said. Despite the plain and simple words, his voice held the passionate tone of a man about to make love to a woman he has long desired. "And I agree with your count."

"Good. Let's go."

On bellies now, the men crawled forward another two hundred meters to some rocks. There they stopped while Buckwheat used his world phone to send a brief, pre-set text message. The answer came back immediately, a text message that simply said, "Roger."

"You take this position," Fulton whispered to Fletcher. "Vic, let's go."

Those two then crawled, Buckwheat leading, to a different set of rocks perhaps one hundred meters east of the set they'd just left and about as much closer to their targets. There, once again Fulton used his scope to view targets.

"Fletcher, Buckwheat," Fulton whispered over his personal radio. "From left to right . . . engage."

D-Day, five miles north-northeast of Nugaal, Ophir

The airstrip was about six thousand feet in length, running

east-northeast to west-southwest, paralleling the road that lay to the southeast about half a mile distant. There was a single, white, propeller-driven aircraft at one end of the strip, guarded by two armed men who seemed reasonably alert. Between the main road and the airstrip stood a large house—more of a palace, really. That palace was the objective. It belonged to the chief of Ophir and leader of the Habar Afaan clan, Gutaale.

The palace was surrounded by a wall, at three to four feet in height, more decoration and demarcation than defense. Built into the wall were two buildings. One of these was presumed to be servants' quarters, the other a barracks large enough to hold at least fifty men. In front of the palace were a couple of sedans, one commercial truck of about five tons capacity, and a few rattletrap hoopties.

The chief wasn't expected to be home, since this was only one of several palaces he maintained. According to Wahab's sources, and Buckwheat's confirmation, Gutaale's accountant, however, *was*.

From his prone position, overlooking the airfield, Welch scanned with night vision goggles. He could see the entire area well, or at least as well as could expected through image intensification.

"Grau, Semmerlin," Terry whispered, pointing at the two airplane guards. "There are two men there. They're not in range. So far as I can tell they're not night vision equipped. You two get in range—there's a decent firing position to our left—and take them out."

"Roger," Semmerlin answered, softly. "Come on, Grau."

Both men, like the rest of the team minus the already black translators, wore "Black-is-Beautiful," a creamy camouflage makeup that resembled nothing so much as boot polish.

Terry waited long minutes watching the two guards intently. Suddenly, one of them was thrown backwards, arms and weapons flying. A moment later the other one bent double violently before he, too, fell backwards. With the size and weight of the bullets the Russian arms fired, there was little likelihood of either of the victims living, or giving any trouble if they did.

And I never heard the shots, Welch thought. *I love* all *Russian equipment*.

The two snipers returned fairly quickly, taking their positions behind Welch.

"Gentlemen, well done," Terry said. "Now let's go."

D-Day, two hundred meters south of Bandar Qassim Airport, Ophir

Thwupt . . . Thwupt. Buckwheat's .51 caliber rifle gave off barely a whisper. Not only was the bullet subsonic, the bullpup semi-auto rifle mounted a silencer about the size of four Foster's Lager cans, stacked one atop the other. It wasn't the most accurate rifle in the world, perhaps, but it was accurate enough for this.

Downrange, through his spotting scope, Vic saw chunks fly off the fuselage just above where the engine was mounted. Despite the low muzzle velocity of nine hundred and fifty feet per second, the nearly three-ounce, solid bronze projectile was more than capable of ripping the guts out of a jet engine.

"I mark that as a kill," he told Fulton.

"Roger," the marksman said, adjusting his aim slightly left to the next helicopter in line. *Thwupt.*

"Kill."

"Roger." *Thwupt.*

"Miss," Vic said. "Change mags."

Buckwheat raised his firing shoulder up, keeping as much of a stock weld as possible, then reached over and dropped the empty magazine. Vic pulled that out of the way while Fulton pushed a fresh one into the well.

Thwupt.

"Miss."

"Dammit." *Thwupt.*

"Don't take it to heart; Russki quality control at the munitions factory is poor . . . Kill." Vic hesitated a moment, then said, "Uh, oh."

"Huh?" Fulton asked.

"I think you . . . "

He didn't quite finish the sentence before Fulton's last target started to burn. The fire began with a small flame. The flame became a jet as it heated the fuel behind it to a high pressure gas. From there, it quickly grew, locally, then began to spread as burning fuel spurted onto the ground.

Fulton keyed his small radio. "Fletch; Buckwheat. Screw subtlety. Service the targets *fast*."

From across the airfield, more than half a mile away, came a chorus of shouts as some scores of armed men began pouring out of a makeshift barracks. From farther away came a sound that, while strange to American ears, was almost certainly the siren of a fire vehicle.

D-Day, one mile north of Buro, Ophir

The engine coughed and shuddered once again before settling back, for the nonce at least, to a steady if anemic *thrum.*

This bucket won't make better than eight knots, Eeyore fumed, standing at the wheel he'd taken over from Morales once they were out of the harbor. *We'll never make rendezvous at this rate.*

The town passing to starboard shone a few lights. By the chart and the GPS Antoniewicz made it as being Buro, a nothing-too-much fishing village. It was not on the list of places the contingency plan would have had them hole up at to await a later pickup if everything went to shit.

Which it certainly has, for us, anyway.

Even without the lights of the town, they might have seen it, so far and so bright had the moon arisen.

"Hey, Eeyore," Morales asked, "do you remember that movie, *The Princess Bride?*" He was standing beside Antoniewicz, facing aft with his diving mask on his face and his monocular turned down.

"Sure," Antoniewicz answered.

"You remember that scene where Inigo Montoya asks, 'Are you sure nobody's following us?'"

Antoniewicz thought for a moment, remembering back to childhood, before answering, "Yeah, I remember it."

"Good, 'cause I was just about to ask the same question."

Antoniewicz didn't have his mask handy. He glanced backwards even so to see if the pursuer could be seen in the moonlight.

"Shit," he said.

D-Day, five and a half miles north-northeast of Nugaal, Ophir

Terry Welch wasn't the subtle type. *Thwuptupt*. Two silenced, low velocity shots and the two guards at the gate to the palace grounds were thrown back to the low surrounding wall, bonelessly crumpling to the ground.

Grau and Semmerlin took up the rear as two files passed them, racing for the gate. One of the files, the one on the right, was smaller than the other, consisting of a two-man machine gun team, Graft gunning, one of the translators, Issaq Abay, carrying ammo plus an RPG, and Semmerlin. Issaq had said he could use an RPG and there was no reason to disbelieve him. At the gate, the machine gun team took up a firing position partially protected by the low wall and the mud brick pillar of the gate. Semmerlin cut right. Crouching low to take what cover the wall offered, he ran to the corner, then took up a position to cover any rear entrance to the barracks that might be there.

The rest, eight men with Welch in the lead—Little Joe Venegas having been left behind to guard the packs—charged forward. The rear two of those, Buttle and Grau, cut left to take up security at that corner of the palace. There was presumed to be a roving guard, somewhere on the grounds.

The brace of guards at the door proper to the building weren't as alert as they might have been. This cost them as Welch snapped his silenced submachine gun to his shoulder and fired two quick bursts that spun first one, and then the other, to the floor, spurting blood from violated bodies. As much blood as the men shed, Terry knew as he bounded over the corpses that it was nothing as compared to the damage done inside by the subsonic, but frangible, ammunition he'd used on them.

Terry wasn't subtle, but he wasn't precisely "Hulk smash" material either. He didn't throw his body against the large wooded double doors that fronted the palace. Instead, like a gentleman, he tried the knob. It was open.

He took in the first floor of the palace with a glance. Long wide corridor, rooms to either side, and a broad staircase that led upstairs.

He made a two-fingered gesture at Pigfucker and Mary-Sue. *Here. Guard.* Then he led the remaining three, including the last of the translators, up the flight of stairs to the second floor. Then he unscrewed the suppressor from the muzzle of his submachine gun and pointed it at the ceiling.

"Standby to translate," he told the interpreter. "Prep stun grenades," he said to his two Americans.

Then Welch smiled and said, "Shock is good," just as he pulled the trigger.

★CHAPTER FORTY-SEVEN★

But I've a rendezvous with death
At midnight in some flaming town
—Alan Seeger, *I have a Rendezvous with Death*

D Day, Beach Red, Ophir

Reilly was standing there, impatiently, when Fitz reported.

"The mechanic and the Ferret commander were pretty shaken up, boss," Fitz said. "I figured we ought to leave them behind. Top concurred."

The XO was standing in the surf next to the ramp, with waves washing around his ankles. Behind him a vehicle squealed over the wet steel and into the water. Spray from the armored car's wheels sprinkled his back.

"And we haven't a clue what caused the thing to catch fire," Fitz added. "And, since we dumped it over the side, we never will. Buuut . . . those things were pretty old. We've been lucky so far. They stood up through Brazil, after all."

"Mmmm . . . yeah," Reilly answered. *Mourn later.* "'Luck.' Nothing for it now. You made the right call. Mount up. Move out in five mikes."

★ ★ ★

They moved mostly in a column, with the three remaining Ferrets of the scout section forming a wedge at the point, three hundred meters ahead of the main column. Behind the Ferrets, out of range of any RPGs they might encounter, came the first section of Elands, then Reilly's command vehicle, then the second section, then Second Platoon, the antitank section, also in Ferrets, Third Platoon, the mortars, and lastly the ash and trash of headquarters.

In all, it made a column almost a kilometer long, raising clouds of dust as it roared out from the perimeter set up and held by the Marines.

"Start pulling the boys into a tighter perimeter," Cazz told his first sergeant as the last of the armored cars rolled through.

"Roger, Skipper," Webster said, then turned off to oversee the consolidation.

"Good luck, Reilly, ya doggie Irish bastard, ya," Cazz said at the dust cloud behind the advancing armor.

And now I feel my age, Reilly thought, as his turretless Eland bounced over the rough ground, beating his kidneys like a good son of the Prophet would beat a sharp-tongued wife.

He stood in the space that would have held a turret, with Schiebel on the pintle-mounted machine gun ahead of him and James driving. James was a damned fine driver but, *Jesus, this is rough ground and old technology.*

Two vehicles ahead of him, the commander of a

gunned, turreted Eland turned and flashed him a smile that would have been brilliant in the day. From the posture and shape he knew it was Lana Mendes. He'd have known anyway, since the order of march was by his command.

Almost, *almost*, he'd told Green to switch the order of march from First Section leading to Second Section. He hadn't because it would have been such obvious favoritism that he couldn't have stomached it. Nor, he suspected, could Lana have.

But I can hardly stomach that a girl I care for is preceding me into combat, either, even if only by fifty meters. Fuck, fuck, FUCK! The old rule is good: "Nobody else's wife, nobody's girlfriend, and none of the hired help." Fuck.

Lana was young and very healthy. The bouncing of the Eland caused her kidneys no serious discomfort. If it had, she might not have noticed anyway. The woman's heart sang at riding into battle on an iron steed, emulating the heroes of her childhood: Dayan, Sharon, and Israel Tal.

Turning her face back to the front, she placed her hands on either side of the vehicle commander's cupola. Night vision goggles on, she scanned to the front and to the left. Although it was premature, she ordered, "Viljoen, gun to ten o'clock."

"You see something, Lana?" the Boer asked, although his hand was already spinning the traversing wheel.

"No, just being careful. You should have done it without being told."

Viljoen bit back a snarly reply. Even so, he thought, *No, you should have told me. A vehicle in order of march*

*takes its cue from the one ahead of it, sweetie, or from
SOP. Since we don't have an SOP, and the one ahead of us
is aiming straight front, there was no cue. Ah, well. It's a
little thing after all.*

Reilly was about to pitch a bitch at the First Platoon
leader when he saw the gun of the second vehicle, Lana's,
swing left. Number Three automatically began to traverse
to the other side.

He turned full about and saw the gun and turret of the
next Eland in line, Sergeant Abdan's, moving to the left.
Satisfied, he set his own head and eyes to the front, out to
where the scouts led the way.

While it's possible *to do bounding overwatch with
three vehicles*, Snyder, the scout section leader, thought, *it
just isn't* practical.

Bounding overwatch, a military term meaning, in
essence, one section moving while another watches over
it, ready to fire in support, would have been clearly
preferable when heading into the unknown. This, quite
despite the fact that there was an unmanned aerial vehicle
overhead and forward, scouting in advance of the scouts.
The problem with doing it with three vehicles, and after
the accident on the boat that was all Snyder had, was that
one could either have uneven teams, with lessened security
and lessened confidence for the shorter of the two, or one
could have one vehicle continuously switching from one
overwatch to the other. This last could be done, but it was
somewhat slow and somewhat prone to screw-ups.

Instead, Snyder kept his three Ferrets in a broad

wedge, one—his own—in the center and following an approximately straight path to the objective, the others about three hundred meters to either side—RPG range—to spring any ambush the locals might throw together at the last minute.

Best we can do, I suppose. Well, that, and navigate the company to the objective. "And for that," Snyder said, aloud, "we've got GPS." *Damn, but we've all been spoiled absolutely* rotten *by GPS.*

D-Day, MV *Merciful*

Stauer didn't say anything for a few moments, taking in the screens visible past the UAV pilot's shoulder. One showed a map, and the location of the UAV. Another showed the ground in an image-intensified camera carried on the nose of the aircraft.

"Anything on the ground?" Stauer asked of the pilot.

The pilot shrugged. "Couple of runaway goats. Other small animals."

"How about at the tank lager?"

"Looked at it twenty minutes ago. Nothing unusual."

Boxer and Waggoner walked in and stood behind Stauer.

"We've got no unusual cell phone calls coming from anywhere, yet," Boxer said. "But we do have unusual activity at Bandar Qassim. People loading boats, that sort of thing. And at least one boat that was at its moorings isn't anymore.

"By the way, it looks like Buckwheat and company did

a killer job on the airport to the west of the port, too. Wrecks and flames everywhere."

"Source?" Stauer asked.

"I tapped into NSA."

Stauer shook his head. There was something just so fundamentally *wrong* about a private citizen, even if a retired two star, accessing the most secret means of intelligence gathering available to the United States of America.

Seeing the headshake, Boxer defended himself, "Hey, it's not like I'm giving the information to *enemies* of the United States, is it?"

"I think," Ken Waggoner interrupted, "that we need to launch on Bandar Qassim now, boss. We've got to assume the sub went down somewhere, and probably before completing its mission. If we launch now, the planes will hit just after daybreak."

Stauer felt a twinge at the phrase, "the sub went down." *Mourn later*. He thought a moment before agreeing, "Yeah, do it. But since there's at least one boat missing from the port, have the planes skirt the coast and take out anything sailing our way between here and there."

Waggoner considered that, found it wise, and answered, "Roger. Send the medevac flight, too?"

"Yeah. Have it loiter out of small arms range, though."

D-Day, six hundred meters south of Bandar Qassim Airport, Ophir

•

Maybe this wasn't so fucking smart after all, thought

Buckwheat. He was panting too hard to say it aloud even if he'd been of a mind to. His lungs bellowed, sucking air. *Lord Jesus, it purely* sucks *to get old.*

Bullets cracked and ricochets sang around the team as they withdrew at a dead run. The group shooting at Buckwheat and his people seemed to lack night vision; nothing else really explained that their fire was dispersed along the entire ridge. But they could see well enough that it hadn't come from the sea to the north, and the pattern of wrecked and burning aircraft suggested strongly that it hadn't come from east or west, either.

And, thought Fulton, looking behind him at the advancing figures silhouetted by the burning planes and helicopters, *God, there are a* lot *of them.*

He stopped, knelt, and in rapid succession emptied a magazine at the pursuers. *President's Hundred, mother-fuckers,* he thought, seeing that he'd hit four for five, and the pursuit then slowed radically. *I wouldn't have missed the once except for being out of breath.*

While Fulton fired, Vic passed him by and the scoundrel was hardly breathing hard. As Fulton turned his attention back to the south, and began running again, he heard Babcock-Moore cry out and stumble, then fall to the ground.

Buckwheat changed his direction toward his spotter. In five or six steps he'd reached him and knelt down.

"Hit?" Fulton asked.

"Left leg . . . pretty bad," Vic gasped.

"Right."

Without another word Fulton slung his rifle across his back, bent forward at the waist, and pulled the wounded man to a sitting position. Babcock-Moore gasped as Fulton stood, pulling him to his feet.

Letting inertia hold the black Brit in place, Fulton bent, pulled, and the next thing Vic knew—which is to say, what he knew when the pain subsided enough for him to see again—he was slung across the American's shoulder, the other man's rifle barrel digging into his chest, and bouncing up and down—and *my*, didn't that hurt, too—as the pair of them ran on Buckwheat's legs for the topographical crest and cover.

I am so *too old for this shit*, Fulton thought, then said, "Fat . . . fucking . . . limey."

"I'm . . . not . . . fat," Babcock-Moore gasped. "I'm . . . just . . . big."

D-Day, Rako-Dhuudo-Bandar Cisman highway, Ophir

The road in front of Snyder's Ferret was broad and had been, at some time in the past, more or less paved. He reported having reached it to Reilly, who answered, "Roger, follow the plan."

"Wilco," the scout section leader answered. "Break, break . . . Three, this is one. Cross the road directly in front of you, cut out to three hundred mikes past it, then scout generally west for four klicks, keeping parallel to the road. At four, find a good hide."

"Roger," came the answer.

Snyder continued, "Four, one. *Don't* cross the road. Back off three hundred and scout west five klicks, paralleling the road. Hide when you get there."

"Roger."

Snyder then used his intercom to tell his driver, "Back off fifty, then cut right. We'll follow the road for three kilometers, then find our *own* hide away from it."

The wheels of Lana's Eland thumped and bumped over the broken asphalt of the road, approximately where it had been crossed by Scout One a few minutes earlier. Looking to the turret's right rear—it was still trained left—toward the presumed location of the scout, she found she couldn't see the other vehicle but could make out a plume of dust driven upwards by its passage.

She turned to face forward again. "Whoa, Dumi," she said into her intercom, at seeing a deep and sudden drop into a wadi that she wasn't sure the driver had seen.

"I've got it, Lana, no sweat," the Zulu said. Even so, he let off of the gas and put his foot on the brake.

Lana leaned back sharply as the armored car rolled into the wadi. Its tail swung a few degrees to the left, not entirely out of control but not entirely in it, either. The rolling slide down gave her a distinctly unpleasant feeling, not dissimilar to being in a freefall elevator.

Except the ground here is so much more real, she thought. She had a sudden, horrifying vision of the gun digging into the wadi floor and the Eland doing a pole vault over it.

She began to order, "Viljoen, nine . . . " before she saw that the gunner was already swinging the muzzle farther to the left.

The rear wheels spun for a moment, kicking up rocks. Feeling the back of the thing going out of control,

Dumisani took his foot off the brake and reapplied the gas. The spinning wheels threw more gravel and sand to the rear as the Eland plunged down.

Lana felt herself being thrown side to side in the commander's hatch. For a moment she thought the thing would flip. Heart in her mouth, she almost screamed for the driver to simply stop. Self-discipline stopped her from that. Barely.

At the bottom of the long slide, the angle of the ground under the front wheels changed, causing that end to bounce upwards. Again, *barely*, Lana managed to stay in her position. This was repeated when the rear wheels struck.

Then, to the Israeli woman's vast relief, Dumi was able to apply the brakes for a moment before cutting right and moving out again on the wadi floor. He had to move quickly, too, because the next Eland in line was already cresting the lip of the wadi.

Adonai, Lana thought, *if that was so terrifying, what am I going to do when the bullets start flying?*

By sections and platoons the company spread out in its ambush configuration, reporting in to Reilly as each position was reached.

First to report were Peters and the mortar section, about four kilometers back. That one was simple: "Guns up."

Next was the scout section, its three Ferrets strung out to the west at roughly one thousand meter intervals, two north of the road and one, the farthest out, south of it. These hunkered down in hide positions, plentiful among the deeply cut wadis, while the commanders got out, slung radios on their backs, and crawled to where they could see the road but still not be seen.

The two sections of turreted Elands didn't go as far as the scouts had. Instead, they followed the deep main wadis several hundred meters then began looking for side cuts. These were plentiful and steep, if not nearly as steep as the major wadis' sides were. Into these side cuts the vehicles pulled until the gunners reported that they could see the road. At that point the drivers went into reverse and backed up until there was a fair certainty that the bulk of the vehicles would be hidden. To make sure that was so, each commander and driver then dismounted and put a camouflage screen in front of their Eland. Lastly, they bent and tied the whip antennae down.

The infantry platoons took advantage of the lay of the ground, as well. It was a predictable peculiarity of a wadi system that feeders into the main wadi would be at an angle to it, corresponding to the lay of the ground. Into these feeders the turretless infantry carriers pulled. The dismounted men then trooped along the sides of the feeder, confirming they had a good line of sight to the road. They began setting up directional antipersonnel mines, even as the squad RPG gunners laid out rounds on the ground for easy access and reload.

The AT section, under Harvey, took up a position farther east, well behind the infantry lines.

Once everyone had reported, "In position," or some variant on that, Reilly and James dismounted and walked up the road through the entire kill zone. *Yeah, it's a risk*, Reilly thought, *but still better than having an enemy tank* not *in somebody's field of fire.* The troops adjusted their firing positions from there, reported what they had, field of fire-wise, to their leaders, and then hunkered down again behind cover. Once Reilly had confirmation that the entire KZ was covered by fire, he called the *Merciful* and said, "Let loose the jarheads of war."

★CHAPTER FORTY-EIGHT★

Cruelty has a Human Heart
And Jealousy a Human Face
Terror, the Human Form Divine
And Secrecy, the Human Dress
The Human Dress, is forged Iron
The Human Form, a fiery Forge.
The Human Face, a Furnace seal'd
The Human Heart, its hungry Gorge.
—William Blake, *A Divine Image*

D-Day, five and a half miles north-northeast of Nugaal, Ophir

Plaster from the bullet-shattered ceiling was still raining down as men, some armed, others not, began stumbling into the hallway. Some rubbed sleep from their eyes. Most were, at best, half dressed. The two Americans with Terry on the second floor fired at all armed men as they appeared. Sure, maybe the accountant who was the prime target had come out with a rifle but if Stauer didn't like it, he could do the thing himself.

Once those flurries of fire were done with, Terry thundered through his interpreter: "THE ACCOUNTANT WILL SURRENDER HIMSELF NOW OR EVERYONE IN THIS COMPLEX DOWN TO THE LAST BABY SUCKING THE LAST TIT WILL BE PUT TO DEATH!"

"Say it again," Terry ordered the translator. "Only this time put a little insane hysteria into it."

"THE ACCOUNTANT WILL SURRENDER HIM-SELF NOW . . . "

Even as those words thundered, an altogether different kind of thunder, this one accompanied by a sort of lightning, began in the grounds outside and on the lower floor.

Graft, the machine gunner on the gate, snugged his *Pecheneg*'s stock a little closer to his shoulder as soon as he heard firing commence inside the palace. His scope was trained on the sole door from the barracks into the grassy compound.

The *Pecheneg* was yet another among the remarkable series of innovations and improvements attributable to the Russian, formerly Soviet, arms industry. The thing was, at core, a PKM machine gun, modified with a heavier, radially ribbed barrel, with a sleeve around the barrel through which cooling air was drawn. The barrel itself was nonchangeable in the field. This didn't matter so very much as the cooling arrangements allowed the gun to fire up to six hundred rounds in one continuous burst without overheating. No other single barreled, air-cooled machine gun, meant to be fired from the ground, could boast this, though the First World War's Lewis Gun might have come close.

Graft proceeded to put that nearly to the test. As the ready squad from the barracks piled out of the door in a confusion of arms and legs and rifles, he trained on the foremost, depressed the trigger, and walked his six hundred and fifty rounds a minute across the squad, then back again. Some of his targets fell immediately. Others did a version of the ballistic ballet, there on the grass. A few screamed and someone began to cry.

Some of those felled tried to crawl away, but Graft was having none of that. Lifting his shoulder slightly to depress the muzzle, he fired three more bursts at the crawling men, stopping each in his own blood trail. In his scope Graft saw sprays of blood and chunks of flesh fly up from the shattered bodies.

"God, I *missed* this," Graft said, just as grenades began going off in the first floor rooms of the small palace, driving glass shards out onto the courtyard. "Good hunting and no limit."

Semmerlin snickered as he heard Graft's machine gun chattering behind him. *Be my turn soon.*

He didn't have long to wait. Whoever was inside the barracks had probably seen the gunner's handiwork and decided that the courtyard was no place for Mrs. Dheere's little boy, Achmed.

Achmed, or whatever his name really was, slipped out the back with a few friends. Semmerlin let them run perhaps one hundred, one hundred and twenty meters, and opened fire, engaging the rearmost man first and working his way forward. Achmed, if that's who was in the lead, heard and felt nothing until the three-ounce bronze bullet passed through his chest, wrecking heart and lungs and pitching him, already dead, to the ground.

"Graft," Issaq Abay asked, "you want me to use RPG now?"

"No, Issaq," the gunner answered, without taking his eyes from the scope. "They're pinned in there. No sense in giving them a reason to want to come out yet."

"Okay, I do what you say. Still . . . want to use RPG *now*."

"Just wait. You'll get your chance."

"Give me a chance," came the shout in English from one of the rooms farther down the hall. A set of underwear on the end of a curtain rod was shoved out the door. "I am the accountant. Please don't shoot anymore."

"Cease fire except in defense," Terry told the subteam with him on the second floor. Immediately, all but the translator, Abdidi, dropped to one knee, keeping their weapons aimed toward the back of the building. Explosions and bursts of fire continued on the floor below.

"Come out," Terry ordered.

The rod with its makeshift white flag dropped incrementally, then sagged to the floor as a man in a clean robe, wearing glasses, emerged. He took one look at the assault team and dropped the rod, frightened even more than he had been during the shooting.

Welch beckoned for the man who claimed to be the accountant to come forward. Hesitantly, he did.

From his breast pocket Terry withdrew a plastic bag. From the bag he took a single accounts sheet. He handed it to the man who claimed to be the accountant and asked, "What's wrong with this?"

The accountant, if accountant he was, shook his head in disbelief. "You came here in the middle of the night? Killed so many people? Just to have me check your books?"

Terry placed the still warm muzzle of his submachine gun to the man's chin and asked again, "What's wrong with it?"

After a gulp, the man looked over the sheet, saw that the number at the bottom was exactly nine off, and said, "Transpositional error. It'll take me a minute to . . . "

"Never mind; you're the accountant." Terry lowered the muzzle.

"Yes," the accountant agreed. Nodding his head vigorously, he said, "Yes, yes, I am."

"You know all of Gutaale's accounts? His codes?"

"Yessss."

"Very good. Pigfucker, take charge of Mr . . . "

"Dayid. Jama Dayid," the accountant supplied.

"Take charge of Mr. Dayid and get him downstairs to Blackguard. Then to the parking lot. Hotwire a couple of suitable vehicles and flatten the tires on the rest."

Another first floor explosion, followed by a burst of fire, punctuated Welch's command.

"Clear down here, Terry," Ryan called up. "But we've got a dozen civilians."

"Abdidi, tell the rest of the people up here to come out with their hands up and empty! Tell 'em we're going to burn the house but if they cooperate we'll let them out before the fire."

★ ★ ★

Once downstairs, Welch saw two armed men lying on the floor at the back of the house. *That would be the roving guard, I suspect*. He went to the front door and called out, "Grau, you engage anyone?"

"Not since we took down the gate guards," the sniper answered.

"All right. I'm pretty sure the roving guard's here and very dead. Roust the people in the servants' quarters out and bring them inside here."

"Roger."

"The rest of you, except for Blackguard, who will watch the prisoners, take up firing positions on the barracks side window. Abdidi, call out to the barracks that they are to surrender, same routine as the other."

"Yes, sir."

The first response of the guards remaining in the barracks was to fire on all the palace windows. Abdidi, unfortunately, was a little too exposed. One bullet—and even random bullets can hit, sometimes—took the top of his head off. A substantial piece of his skull was still flying through the air, from there to bounce off the far wall, as his body hit the floor.

"Kill 'em all," Welch ordered.

"RPG now?" Issaq asked.

"RPG now," Graft agreed.

The translator set the launcher on his shoulder and stood up enough to raise it just above the top of the wall. He shouted something in his own language that Graft took to mean, "Backblast area clear!" Then he let fly at the barracks, blowing a hole in the wall and sending a stream of hot gasses inside.

After two more shots with the RPG, the remnants of the guard force attempted to stream out both doors. Both Semmerlin and Graft had a field day—*way* overlimit. Some tried to surrender but Welch had ordered no prisoners and neither the sniper nor the gunner were much inclined to disagree.

Issaq fired a fourth shot, and then a fifth and final. Somewhere between the two, the building caught fire.

A woman, tall and slender, walked up to Terry. She was veiled, but removed the veil when she reached him. Her cheekbones were high, her complexion quite smooth, and her eyes were absolutely *huge*. He thought she looked a bit like a model whose name he couldn't quite recall. *Married to some ambiguously sexual singer . . . what was that woman's name? Anyway, this one looks pretty good by the light of a burning barracks.*

"You . . . American?" she asked, in very badly accented and hesitant English.

"Yes, we're Americans," Terry answered.

The woman gestured with a sweeping hand and said, still hesitatingly, "I . . . Ayanna. We . . . slaves. Christians. Some . . . Moslem . . . too. You take . . . with. Please . . . take with."

"'As he died to make men holy,'" Blackguard Blackburn quoted.

Terry looked intently at the woman whose eyes were so eloquently pleading. *Am I the good guy or the bad guy,* he wondered. *Maybe I'm a bad guy, but once, just once, maybe I'd like to do good.*

Slowly, maybe even reluctantly, he nodded his head. *Let us try to make men . . . or women . . . free.*

"All right," he told Ayanna. "We'll try."

"Let me make sure I understand what you want," the accountant said. Firelight from the barracks next door flickered off his face. "You want me to transfer all the money my chief has to you?"

"That's about right," Terry Welch answered. "For the privilege, I am authorized to let you have one percent of everything . . . recovered."

"Recovered" seemed like a better, more morally uplifting, word.

"One percent? Twenty *million* U.S. Dollars? That's a lot of money . . . but . . . I can't."

"The alternative . . . "

The accountant sighed. "Sir, no matter what you may do to me, I would rather that than take Gutaale's money and leave my family in his . . . care."

"Where is your family?" Terry asked.

"A few miles from here, in Nugaal."

"How many?"

"Forty-two."

"Forty-two?"

"I have three wives and one concubine. Plus my parents. And three brothers and their families. Forty-two."

Fuck. "Do you need any books?" Terry asked. "Any ledgers? Discs? Your laptop?"

The accountant shook his head and then tapped one finger to it. "It's all here."

Should I mention the couple of tons of gold in the basement? Dayid wondered. *Mmmm . . . maybe not. They came in, probably, by air; they will leave by air. Given the weight of some members of my family, telling them about the gold might get them left behind. And no matter what I may say, I do not want to be rigorously questioned. No, let Gutaale keep the gold. Maybe it will incline him to be more forgiving of the more distant members of my sept.*

D-Day, MV *Merciful*

"Terry reports 'mission accomplished,' boss," Waggoner said. "He lost one of his translators. Dead, no dustoff required. But . . . he's got a problem."

"Which is?" Stauer asked.

"Beyond the eleven men left in his own team, and the accountant, he needs transportation for seventy-one more people. He says, 'no argument, he needs it.' He says most of them are skinny and some are kids and that he can pack everybody on two helicopters. On the other hand, Buckwheat does need a dustoff."

★CHAPTER FORTY-NINE★

> The essential American soul is hard, isolate,
> stoic and a killer.
> —D. H. Lawrence

D-Day, two kilometers south of Bandar Qassim Airport, Ophir

Somewhere up on the ridge, Buckwheat and Fletcher traded shots with some locals who, by now, had become very reluctant to show their heads much. Rattus Hampson couldn't hear the outgoing shots. But he heard altogether too many incoming ones. Still, the ridge protected himself, his patient, and Wahab, even if it didn't do a lot for the snipers.

Buckwheat had trotted into the hide position, unceremoniously dumped Babcock-Moore on the hood of the Hummer, grabbed Fletcher and headed back to the ridge. Rattus had suspected that the man was simply too out of breath to give instructions.

Hampson and Wahab had gotten the black Brit to the ground without too much trouble. Now, with Wahab holding a flashlight, Rattus attempted to staunch some pretty severe bleeding.

"Will I ever dance again?" Vic asked, through gritted teeth.

"Sure you will," Rattus answered, cutting away torn cloth to get at the wound.

"Then I should be happy, because I never could before."

"You know how old a joke that is?"

"Don't you know how old we are?"

Gotta save this limey, Rattus thought. *Anybody who can crack jokes—even bad ones—with a bullet lodged in his femur is worth keeping.*

"You know," Rattus said, conversationally, as he probed for a lump of bronze-jacketed lead, "the last time I removed a bullet from a femur it was a goat's."

"Oh, fuck," Vic moaned, "I'm in the hands of a veterinarian."

D-Day, PZ Robin, formerly Beach Red, Ophir

In theory, the MI-17 could lift twenty-four combat equipped troops. In practice, if one were determined enough, and willing to pack men in like animals in a stock-yard, and didn't carry the potential extra fuel tanks, or machine gun or rocket pods, it could lift forty. Neither they nor the helicopter would enjoy it, but it could be done.

Moöo, Cruz thought, as the double lines of twenty former Marines on each side fed themselves into the cargo bay through the rear clamshell doors. He expected it, but laughed anyway, as the first of his passengers sounded off, loudly, "Mooo." Pretty soon the entire load, forty men, was *mooing*, too, and enthusiastically.

Cruz glanced to his right at his Russian copilot. Sure enough, the Russian understood perfectly well the joke and laughed right along.

"And awayyy we go," Cruz announced, as soon as his crew chief gave him the thumbs up. In his intercom he heard the Russian humming "Ride of the Valkyries" as the chopper lifted.

Ah, American culture, Cruz thought. *Such as it is*.

The three Hip helicopters started in line abreast. As they lifted, they shifted to a trail formation. Great clouds of sand swirled up around them as they left the beach, deserted, behind. They flew low. There was no sense in going high when the first stop, to drop off the mortars, was less than fifteen minutes away.

Cruz's Hip came down to a bouncy landing. *Got to expect that when you're this overloaded*. In the rear, the crew chief kicked open the clamshell doors and then got out of the way as six men unloaded, lugging a very heavy mortar with them. To the left and the right, other men, lugging other mortars, did the same. They dropped their chunks of steel and then queued up to receive the ammunition passed down to them, hand over hand, by the remaining men on the helicopter. This, twenty-two rounds only, didn't take that long.

Once again, at his crew chief's signal, Cruz pulled pitched and scooted away. He, followed by the other two, headed generally west. They had some time to burn, about fifteen minutes worth, to allow the mortars to set up to fire.

In the event, it took the mortars only about ten minutes before they called on the radio to announce they were ready to support. Cruz dialed in the frequency to the *Merciful* and said, "Send the air strike in now."

D-Day, MV *Merciful*

Luis had been trained to fire the machine gun mounted on the right side of the plane he had helped build. They even trained him to shoot wearing the funny goggles that let you see at night, *like the ones the* coyotes *sometimes used to slip you across the border.* But he'd never actually fired it from a moving aircraft. Still, how different could it be from firing off the side of the ship at a floating container?

On the other hand, taking off from the ship? Well, he'd also helped patch together one plane from the two that had been wrecked. And he'd gotten his hands pretty bloody from that salvage job, too. He was . . .

"*Señor,*" he said to the pilot, Harley, "I don't mind telling you I am scared shitless. I thought I was just getting into something harmless, like running drugs or maybe something like that. But this . . . " The Mexican sighed heavily.

"Too late now, *amigo,*" the pilot said, just as the signal was given for him to take off. The plane began to vibrate as he gave it the gas. In moments it was moving at an ever-increasing pace down the PSP flight deck.

Luis closed his eyes. He'd never liked flying and this

was worse than most. His stomach dropped as the plane lurched upward.

"Cheer up, Luis," the pilot shouted over the engine. "Nothing much to worry about now except the landing."

Looking to his left, Luis saw a bunch of boats tied up near the shore or pulled right up on the sand. Some of the bigger ones looked fast. He thought, maybe, too, they might be armed.

"I'll go in low," Harley said, "for this first pass. I'll expend the rockets on the big ones. You can try your luck with the little ones on shore. Got it?"

"*Si*, got it, *señor*."

"Good man," Harley said. "Now hang on to your balls, Luis, you're in for one fuckin' helluva ride."

D-Day, Bandar Qassim, Ophir

Gutaale looked west from the roof of his main residence in this, the largest city of his almost-country. Even at this distance, the light from the flames of fourteen burning aircraft was enough to notice.

Who would do *this to me?* the chief wondered. *Who could do this to me?*

An aide came to the roof and coughed politely.

"Yes, what is it?" Gutaale asked.

"It isn't just an attack on the airfield, Chief," the aide said. "Someone also seems to have stolen a boat from the naval warriors. Their leader has sent one of his faster boats in pursuit. Also . . . "

"Yes?" Gutaale asked, impatiently.

"Also the chief of the naval *mujahadin* says one of his boats went missing. Supposedly it, and the stolen boat, were in pursuit of a fat prize. The boat that was later stolen returned with engine trouble but the other continued on. It hasn't been heard from and does not respond to its radio."

That aide stood there, awaiting his leader's orders, when another one came up to the roof.

"Sir," said the second aide, "your brother has called. His village, Bandar Cisman, is under attack."

With a curse, Gutaale gave his orders. "Launch the entire fleet of naval *mujahadin*. Get my personal guard company in trucks and have them assemble here. And tell the armored force near Rako to mount up and go to my brother's aid.

"And I want a status report on *everything*, everywhere!"

D-Day, Suakin, Sudan

There was a guard not far away, standing in the light reflected off the waters from the prison on the mainland. The guard was pretty sure the boy wouldn't try to escape and, even if he did, that the blame would lie upon Labaan's head. For his part, the captive sat on the edge of the island, looking at the mainland wistfully, but also reminded by the prison's lights that things could have been much, much worse.

So many miles to the north, Adam had no idea that this day, rather this night, had any particular significance. All he knew was that it was somewhere around the fifth or sixth month of his captivity, and that that captivity had become, in many ways, altogether too comfortable. That, and that Makeda didn't approve of "parole."

On the other hand, the girl was realistic. Life had slapped her around far too much for her to be anything else. "Since you can't escape unless you're outside and you can't escape from outside if we're manacled together and since you had better not try to escape without me, since you gave me your word, too, I suppose we'll have to live with it. And, if your word to Labaan wasn't good, I suppose it wouldn't be any good to me, either."

He found himself, from time to time, comparing her with his old girlfriend, back in Boston, Maryam the Ethiopian. Those comparisons did not generally favor the latter.

What was Maryam, after all? Adam wondered. *Her father worked for the UN. She grew up among the people Labaan sometimes calls "tranzis." She was going to school on the UN ticket. She lived a sheltered life, an artificial life, with almost no idea of Africa as it was.*

Compare that with Makeda, who not only knows Africa as it is, but has experienced the very worst of it, first hand.

Maryam was dark and moody, despite her ignorance and sheltered life. Makeda is bright as the sun, despite her utterly shitty one. I would prefer day over night . . . and . . .

I wonder if, perhaps, Labaan didn't do me the biggest favor of all in taking me.

D-Day, Rako, Punt

"Speak up, dammit!" Major Muktar Maalin shouted into

his cell phone. Between the shouting, the massed shuffling of feet, the ascending roar of tank engines, and the cursing as some of those engines failed to roar, it was something besides easy to make out the frantic words of one of his uncle's, Gutaale's, minions.

Whoever was on the other end of the connection forced himself to calm down and enunciate. "Your uncle . . . the chief . . . wants . . . you to . . . take your . . . battalion . . . and go . . . to the aid . . . of your uncle . . . his brother . . . in Bandar Cisman. He is . . . under . . . attack."

Since the minion seemed to be having no trouble understanding Maalin's words, the major said, quickly, "Tell the chief I put my soldiers on alert when his brother called. We will be ready to roll within the hour."

"Hurry! Our chief's brother . . . urges all haste."

D-Day, Bandar Cisman

Instead of a flight helmet, he wore a padded wire set with headphones on each side and an adjustable boom mike. Air through the open window rushed through Luis' hair. The pilot wore the same. Both sets of headphones were connected by wire to a central box.

His gun was a fine weapon, Luis thought. His instructors had called it a PKB. It had spade grips he clutched to his chest, and fired, so they'd said, about eight hundred rounds a minute. *Who could count so fast*, Luis wondered. *No matter, it fires fast enough.*

The pilot, Harley, had lined up on his first target and begun firing rockets mounted on the wings. Harley had experience with these, apparently, because it took him only four shots before one struck the boat, blasting off one corner and setting the rest alight.

"I used to be better than this," the pilot cursed. "Curse of old age. Try your luck, Luis."

No, Luis found, *firing from a plane is different from firing from the ship*. He missed with his first several bursts completely. He was getting the range right, but the lead required was throwing him off. *Way* off.

"Next pass," Harley called, "start shooting *before* you think you're lined up on the target and let the plane walk it in for you." Harvey made a sweeping gesture taking in the stacks and stacks of ammunition crates. "It's not like we've got any shortage of machine gun ammo, *amigo*."

Luis nodded, "*Si, señor*."

Hovering two miles west of Bandar Cisman, Cruz watched the rockets go in, even as the CH-801's side-fired tracers drew bright lines in his NVGs, lines that faded only slowly. He glanced left and right. At the limits of vision, about a mile for objects of that size, he saw the other two Hips hovering as well.

"That works," he said. Passing the message on to the other two helicopters, he lifted his Hip's tail, applied power to the engines, and closed on the town.

"Move, Marines. MOVE!"

Cazz stood behind the clamshells, physically prodding the disembarking men into a semblance of order. Feet churning the gravel and sand, they snaked forward, in a reformed double line, around the sides of the helicopter.

Automatically, they stooped forward as they moved. Sure, the chopper's blades were high, *butcha nevah know*.

Ahead, five or six meters in front of the blades' reach, the platoon leader of Second Platoon, a 'youngster' of forty who'd retired from the Corps as a major, stood directing his squads into a platoon line. North and south, the other two platoons did the same. The only difference was that First Platoon, to the north, oriented to the southeast while Second, to the south, oriented northeast. The town was now boxed.

Cazz's RTO, another youngster of thirty-seven, tapped his shoulder with the handset of a radio. "Sir, I've got the mortars."

Taking the handset, Cazz said, "Slow fire, and I mean *slow*. Center of mass of the town. I want their attention and I want them *scared* . . . but not dead."

"Shot, over," came the reply, in mere seconds. In another forty or so, the Marines heard the freight train sound of a falling one-twenty, followed by a bright flash that silhouetted the one-story buildings of the place.

"That's the ticket," Cazz said. "Give 'em one every five minutes, no more, until further notice.

Ahead, at a range of three hundred to three hundred and fifty meters from the town, the Marine skirmish line went prone and began a slow, rattling fire on the buildings. "Scared," the man had said.

★ CHAPTER FIFTY ★

The dove, descending, breaks the air
With wings of incandescent terror.
—T.S. Eliot

D-Day, MV *Merciful*, northeast of Bandar Cisman

The occasional fall of mortar shells, to the southwest, was at best dimly perceptible, and then only if one was looking and knew what one was looking for. Nobody on the ship really was. They were much more concerned with reconfiguring, refueling, and arming the three Hips that bounced now on the flight deck.

Cruz saw Stauer standing to the left of his Hip, beckoning with one hand. He popped his door open, told his Russian copilot, "Your bird, but sit tight," unbuckled himself and stepped to the PSP deck.

"We've already made the arrangements," Stauer shouted over the roar of the choppers. "You'll—two of you—be outfitted with auxiliary fuel tanks and two rocket pods apiece. Then those two are going to Nugaal to pick up Welch, his team, the accountant, and a party of seventy-one civilians with not much more than the clothes on their backs. Your third bird will still support the Marines at Bandar Cisman."

"That's going to fuck up the pickup of Buckwheat's boys," Cruz objected, shaking his head doubtfully. "It's also going to interfere with striking Bandar Cisman before the Marines go in. I thought we planned on one Hip to pick up Welch's team and the accountant."

"Yeah," Stauer agreed. "But it got complicated. Doubly complicated. The accountant will cooperate, but only if his family—his *extended* family—is safe. And Terry liberated twenty-nine slaves. He says he won't leave them behind."

"Gonna cost us."

"Yeah. I'm worried about Buckwheat, not so much about the rest. I directed the birds dedicated to the strike on Bandar Qassim to continue to screen up the east coast to the town of Foar, engaging anything coming our way, then cut northwest toward Bandar Qassim Airport and extract Buckwheat. They should be able to do that, get back here, rearm and refuel, in time to go north again and hit anything coming our way. I've also directed Chin in *The Drunken Bastard* to move north ten miles and guard."

What are the risks? Cruz wondered. *I'd planned on the extra Hip at Bandar Cisman to be able to shift to help out Reilly if he couldn't handle the tanks. Maybe he can, maybe he can't. The ground up by Buckwheat is broken as hell. Sure, the CH-801s can lift on a short run, but they still need about three hundred feet. And*

*the Marines' mortars need more ammunition . . . but I
suppose Borsakov can take that.*

"Is Buckwheat at a place with at least three hundred
unobstructed feet clearance, and smooth enough?" Cruz
asked.

Stauer shook his head. "He—rather Rattus—says 'no,'
but there is such a place a couple of thousand meters
north."

"A couple of thousand meters . . . He's going to try to
take the airfield for extraction? No fucking way!"

"Relax," Stauer assured, "Rattus has a plan." *A fucked
up plan, but he has a plan.*

D-Day, seven miles west of Dhurbo, Ophir

"You have a plan for this, Eeyore?" Morales asked.

The enemy boat, which had started perhaps three
miles behind when they'd spotted it, had closed to within
a mile and a half. Soon enough, it would be in range. *And
then we're fucked,* Antoniewicz thought, *because we
haven't a thing to shoot back with good for more than
thirty or forty meters. And not super good at that.*

"No, no plan," he answered, "except to keep running
and hope for the best."

"We could head in to shore and crash the boat. Try to
lose them on land," Morales offered. "But . . ."

"Right. Simmons can't run."

"So what do we do?"

"Outrun them if we can."

"How do you outrun somebody who's faster than you?"

"Well," Eeyore said, "we *did* mine the boat."

Danger led to doubt. "We *hope* we mined the boat," Morales said.

"Yeah." It was a long way to the southern turn toward the ship. Eeyore looked wistfully to the southwest, and "home."

"Get to work on the boat's radio," he told Morales. "Maybe we can get some help before it's too late."

"That radio's a burned out piece of shit," Morales said. "But I'll try."

D-Day, midway between Faor and Bandar Qassim Airport

Approximately forty miles south of Antoniewicz and Morales, and completely unaware of their situation, or even their existence, Biggus Dickus Thornton, flying in the medevac plane, spoke to Rattus on the radio.

"How's your limey?" Thornton asked.

"He'll make it if you do," Rattus Hampson answered.

"We're about twenty minutes out."

"Load?"

"Two gunships, one dustoff. The gunships have one each side-firing machine gun, manned, two rocket pods and two machine gun pods each. Most we can carry is two men in the dustoff—that would be you and the Brit—plus one in each of the gunships . . . "

"Won't do, Biggus," Rattus answered. "Leaves us one short and we're not leaving anyone behind."

"I was about to say, one in each of the gunships plus one if we can expend all ammo."

D-Day, south of Bandar Qassim Airport

Rattus listened to the firing to the north and answered, "I don't think you're going to be short of targets, Biggus. Tell the pilots to go ahead and assume they'll expend all their load. Rattus, out."

They carefully laid Vic in the back of the Hummer, then Rattus carelessly tossed his aid bag in the passenger seat. Reaching into a different bag, Rattus pulled out two bungee cords. Taking a bungee cord, he began to affix their one remaining machine gun, the one he had carried, to the roll bar on top of the Hummer.

"You sure about this?" Wahab asked.

Rattus shook his head in the negative, saying, "No, I'm not. Are *you* willing to leave Buckwheat and Fletcher behind?"

Wahab snorted, thinking about good times in the not-so-distant past, camping out with Fulton, trading stories and lies, and spying. He remembered the American black saving, or at least trying to save, a young girl that he, Wahab, hadn't had and wouldn't have had either the foresight or the will or the courage to try to save. He remembered, too, his friend's—and, yes, Buckwheat *was* a friend, now—favorite saying: *Thank God my multi-great granddaddy got dragged onto that boat.*

"Not a chance," the African returned.

Rattus smiled broadly. "Thought not. After all, you're one of us, now."

Wahab felt a sudden warm rush of embarrassment on

his face, even as his heart felt warmed by the compliment and the acceptance.

D-Day, four and a half miles west of Dhurbo, Ophir

"I don't think this is going to work," Morales observed. "And, no, the fucking radio doesn't work for trans, though I can pick up BBC, if you're curious." He whistled a few bars of "Lillibullero," to make the point.

He could see the distant flashes of what was probably a machine gun on the pursuing boat. He rotated his monocular down and scanned for splashes. *Yep, about two hundred meters behind us and to port as we bear. On the plus side, they don't seem to be very good shots.* He said as much to Eeyore.

Antoniewicz had a sinking feeling in his stomach. "How good do they need to be? They'll close to point blank, eventually. Best bring Simmons forward and get him in a life vest."

"Aye, aye," Morales agreed.

D-Day, south of Bandar Qassim Airport

Even though he was firing subsonic ammunition, with a suppressor that would probably work with a One-o-Five, and did a pretty fair job of holding in the muzzle flash, too, every now and again Buckwheat got the feeling that somewhere, someone, out on the long slope below him, had his number. He got the feeling again when a long burst of machine gun fire pelted the rock behind which he covered, sending off shards in all the wrong directions. At times like those, he thought it wise to back up and find someplace else to shoot from.

Rifle cradled in the crook of his elbows, he backpeddled down the slope and out of the line of fire. This was, as it turned out, a very good thing as the next burst of fire didn't hit the rock; it hit precisely where he had been posted.

Maybe the suppressor is about done for, he thought, *They're only good for so many shots anyway. Flash might be leaking through. No, it's probably leaking through.*

He heard an engine's roar from behind him, coupled with the sound of gravel being tossed out by spinning tires.

The Hummer pulled up behind him. "Jump in and get on the machine gun," Rattus said. "Watch out you don't step on the Brit."

"*What?*"

"Jump in and get on the machine gun," the medic repeated. "We've got company coming, and I have a cunning plan. Ever hear of Joshua Chamberlain?"

"A cunning plan? Little Round Top?" Fulton rolled his eyes, saying, "Why don't I just blow my brains out now?"

"Just get in."

"What about Fletcher?" Fulton asked.

"Wahab's getting him."

Buckwheat bolted at a crouch for the Hummer. As he did, he heard the on-board radio say, "Rattus, Biggus; we're ninety seconds out. We can see the burning aircraft. We can also see what looks to be a loaded truck convoy leaving the city heading west. One of the gunships is going after the convoy; the other's yours. Where do you want it?"

★ ★ ★

Biggus practically strained his neck, twisting his head to keep an eye on everything that was going on in the air and on the ground, as the medevac bird loitered. For all practical purposes he was playing FAC, or forward air controller. He may have been a little rusty, but he did have some limited experience at it.

From the radio came Rattus's words, "We're just behind the topographical crest. The bad guys are mostly along the northern military crest. That's about seventeen or eighteen hundred meters south of the airfield."

Biggus put the mike to his lips and asked, "Can you give us a marker?"

"We'll give you lights for ten seconds, both vehicles, in thirty."

"That'll do. Then what?"

"You'll probably need more than one pass," Rattus said. "When you've expended your load, or as much as you need to, let me know. Then we're gonna charge, right over the top, all guns—such as they are—blazing. We'll meet you at the airstrip, west of the burning aircraft."

"Roger," Thornton said. It sounded pretty desperate to him but, then again, they did have the hurt limey. So . . .

Biggus gave orders to the other two. After hearing a couple of "Rogers," he shut up and watched.

As the armed aircraft to his north made its first pass, all he could say was, "Awesome."

The aircraft carried fourteen of what were called "S-8, 80mm" rockets, seven under each wing. The rockets were the mixed lot Victor Inning had provided; two per pod carried flechettes; three were high explosive; one was incendiary. The first one set to fire from each pod was illumination. One of these, from his right pod, the pilot to Biggus's north fired first.

Four seconds after the flash of the rocket's ignition could be seen, a two-megacandle flare blossomed over the truck convoy, slightly off center and to the north. In that four seconds the CH-801 had closed its range by two hundred and forty meters, give or take. In the next several seconds, the pilot let loose one entire pod, walking them up the road at and around the seven trucks. Most missed. In fact, all the high explosive and incendiary rounds missed. The flechette rockets, on the other hand, each of them spitting out two thousand thin, finned, steel darts, didn't have to be all *that* on target. Close was good enough where "close" was defined as two and a half truckloads of human flesh reduced to twitching, screaming, moaning, bleeding, gagging, puking, shitting lumps of meat . . . in a fraction of a second.

As the pilot turned away—safer that was than passing over a convoy of armed men, even if their drivers were jinking like mad—to line up for another run, his door gunner, Manuel, let loose with a long, two hundred round burst of machine gun fire. Manuel didn't hit much either. But his tracers did add to the overall ambience.

Buckwheat noticed that the fire snapping over the ridge slackened, indeed almost ceased, right after the northern sky lit up from the flare.

They're watching the fireworks, he thought. *That, and probably shitting their pants. Now's the time, now, for the other strike to go in.*

★ CHAPTER FIFTY-ONE ★

"A sword for the LORD and for Gideon!"
—Judges 7:20, the Bible, New International Version

D-Day, Rako-Dhuudo-Bandar Cisman highway, Ophir

Reilly listened to the reports from the scouts: "Scout Four . . . SitRep . . . fourteen tanks, moving east on the road . . . two groups . . . four tanks leading then ten more about four hundred meters after . . . dismounts riding on top . . . five or six, maybe seven, per." "Scout Two . . . same . . . just reaching the bend at Checkpoint Five." "Scout One, I make them at Checkpoint Four."

So far, so good, he thought. *Fourteen tanks with a gap of four hundred meters . . . mmm . . . call the column one point one klick long. That'll fit in the kill zone. Why only fourteen though? There were supposed to be up to twenty-four.* He called the TOC, back on the ship, to ask.

Boxer's voice answered, "When the UAV went over the lager there were ten still there, most with people working on them."

"Roger." *Okay then, ten down for maintenance. Par for the course.*

Then he heard, "This is Scout Two. Two more tanks, no dismounts on top. A klick and a half behind the others."

Shit! How did the UAVs miss that? Two tanks a kilometer and a half behind would put them out of the kill zone when he initiated the ambush. He didn't want to face *one* tank in a fair fight, let alone two. *There's a solution, but . . . man, that sucks.*

"Scout one, Alpha Six," Reilly sent.

"Scouts." Snyder's voice sounded worried. *Ah, he understands the problem, too.*

"When we initiate, I need you to engage the follow-on tanks."

There was a pause while Snyder formed a reply. That reply was, "Are you out of your fucking *mind*? We've got machine guns. That's *it*."

Reilly's voice stayed calm and firm. He understood perfectly well how Snyder felt. "I know. I don't expect you to kill anything. I just want you to button them up and make them think they're in the kill zone, too. And don't lose track of them when they roll off the road."

The answer to that was long enough in coming. "Wilco." *I will comply.*

D-Day, MV *Merciful*

Boxer burst into the TOC and said, "Shit! We missed two tanks."

"What are you talking about?" Stauer asked.

"The UAV passed over the tank column a few miles from the lager. It couldn't count the tanks in the column but counted ten in the camp. So we figured fourteen tanks Reilly would have to face and continued on to the town. On the flight back the pilot swung over the lager again and counted *eight*. So he followed the road for a while and found the other two, few enough he could count them, racing to join the rest."

"Will they catch up before Reilly's kill zone?"

"No. They'll still be out of it by the time Reilly has to engage."

"Ah . . . fuck. Get me Reilly on the horn."

D-Day, Rako-Dhuudo-Bandar Cisman highway, Ophir

"Yes, we identified the problem and I've got a handle on it, boss," Reilly answered. "Yes, it's a shitty, greasy, sloppy handle, but I've got a handle."

Man, I hate *being nagged.*

Sergeant Abdan reported in, "First tank entering the KZ."

Reilly finished up, "And I got to go now. Busy, doncha know. Send the dustoff our way, would you? We're probably going to need it."

The radio spouted, "Alpha Six, One-Six. First tank at Checkpoint Three . . . "

Lana, wearing NVGs, watched the long steel snake slither through the kill zone with a mix of eagerness and fear. Some of the fear was for her life and health, true.

More of it, though, was in the form of, *Lord, God, don't let me fail*.

In this she wasn't so very different from any of the others peering in at the sight of the massacre they hoped to make.

Though she didn't have to whisper—the tanks made more noise than she could hope to—still she did. "Gunner . . . eleven o'clock . . . gunner . . . ten o'clock . . . gunner . . . eleven o'clock."

With each command, Viljoen deftly spun the traversing wheel that also held his firing button. A certain tone crept into her voice, that same combination of fear for self and fear for self-image.

"Relax, Lana," Viljoen said. "It's . . . well, I won't say it's a piece of cake, but I will say you're as ready and as able as anyone I ever served with."

"Well, thanks a lot, lover," Dumisani piped in.

"I never served with you in combat, you black bastard. You were on the other side." Viljoen hesitated for a moment; he wasn't normally the maudlin sort. Then he added, "Dumi, if you were ever down range of my gun . . . I'm awfully glad I missed."

"What are you talking about?" the Zulu said. "You hit my tonsils every time."

"Asshole!"

"And sometimes that, too."

Lana couldn't help herself; she started to laugh.

Which was the point of the exchange, Viljoen thought. *As Dumi understood. As he understands damn near everything*.

★ ★ ★

Reilly felt his heart pounding with the sheer wicked joy of impending combat. It had been a long time, and every minute since the last had seemed like a pointless eternity. From behind the screen his driver and James had thrown up, as if through a veil, he watched the foremost approaching behemoth grow closer . . . and closer . . . four hundred meters . . . three hundred . . . two hundred.

"Guns up!" he sent over the general frequency. He couldn't see it but somehow he felt eight major antiarmor systems rising from the ground. A quick glance left and right showed Nagy's engineers manning machine guns and RPGs.

"One-six up . . . ATGMs up . . . Mortars, hanging."

One-fifty. One hundred.

"Company . . . FIRE!"

Major Maalin, riding in the fifth tank back, the one right after the gap, scanned left and right. He couldn't see a lot; the moonlight cast shadows on the low scrub and rocks that tended to conceal more than the moon illuminated.

Of course, if I could just have convinced uncle Gutaale that being able to see at night was at least as important as having a twenty-fourth tank . . . but, noooo, *he wanted the image more than the reality.*

Nominally, Maalin's command consisted of one large, very large tank company, and two infantry companies that were in theory going to get wheeled armored personnel carriers someday. For now, the company he had with him made do with riding on top of the tanks. Yes, it would sting if the tanks' guns fired.

The major had lost cellular communication with his uncle's office nearly an hour ago. There were broad patches of the country that the phone service simply couldn't reach. Indeed, if his cantonment hadn't been atop a hill, Maalin rather doubted he'd have any service at all. Certainly the town to the west and lower down, Rako, had no service at all.

And, of course, the tanks' radios didn't reach. *And didn't I complain about that, too?* "One less tank, uncle," I said. *"One less tank and we can get night vision devices, longer range radios, and even some more training ammunition." But, nooo, he didn't understand the importance of those things.*

And can he or his flunkies give me a spot of reconnaissance? A little intelligence on what lies ahead? No. That's why I have one tank platoon forward; maybe they can find out something at not too great a cost.

I swear . . .

Maalin's silent complaints stopped when he saw two bright flashes, perhaps two kilometers away, or maybe three—it was hard to tell at night and no one had ever taught him the flash-to-bang formula anyway.

For several seconds, he couldn't see anything related to those flashes. Then he saw something, two smaller ones that seemed to be nearing him. Those lights danced in bright circles. He was about to call for evasive action—a "Sagger Dance," western armies would have called it—when there was a much larger flash ahead, followed in just over a second by a substantial boom. Half a second after that something flew by his head, spitting small flames out the side.

What happened to that—*missile, it must have been*—

Maalin didn't know. He was too busy trying to make sense of the fire that seemed to come all at once, from everywhere. He heard sharp cracks all around his tank, and the sound of bronze ricocheting from steel, as the infantry he had boarded started to fall and crumple around the turret.

Shit, he thought.

Then another explosion, close by, went off by the side of the road. He saw the infantry on the tank ahead simply swept off, as if by a large broom. The tank commander, who had been riding unbuttoned, came apart in shreds of cloth and flesh. When Maalin heard the same kind of explosion behind him, he didn't even look. Since he was alive and some of his infantry still on his tank, he knew the one behind him had been similarly brushed off.

Directional antipersonnel mines. Those, too. Fuck.

While Dumi was still bringing the Eland up to hull down from turret down, Lana saw one of the missiles fired by Harvey's antitank section fly by a few hundred meters to her front before it buried itself in the rocks with a thunderous crash.

"Shitty Russian workmanship," she muttered, before breaking into the routine, "Gunner, HEAT, Tank, Eleven o'clock."

The gun crested the edge of the wadi, Viljoen made a minute correction to range and elevation, and then the road in front of her lit up with the strobelike muzzle flashes of her gun, and five others.

She was mesmerized by the display.

"Hit!" Viljoen said. There was no response. "Lana! HIT! Reload!"

"Wha . . .? What?"

"Reload, dammit."

"Ah, shit, sorry," she said. Automatically, she dropped her commander's seat a few inches, and bent to extract another round from the rack behind her. The few seconds she'd wasted meant she couldn't vacuum load but had to take the time to ram the shell all the way in.

"Up," Lana called, then stuck her head back out the commander's hatch just in time to see Viljoen smack another hollow charge shell into the engine compartment of the tank he'd first hit. The thing erupted in flames. Almost immediately thereafter, a great burst of fire emerged from all around the enemy turret, which sailed into the air like a rocket, fire blossoming all around and underneath it.

"That's a kill," Lana announced, as once again she stooped over to feed Viljoen's greedy gun.

She managed to get her head up again in time to see that at least four of the enemy tanks were burning. In the firelight, silhouetted, she saw dismounts racing toward her.

"Gunner! Machine Gun! Infantry!"

"I see them, Lana," Viljoen said, as his coaxial machine gun began to chatter. He spun his hand crank, sweeping fire across the line of dismounts sprinting for their position. In Mendes's field of view some of the infantry were bowled over while others dove for the dirt.

Something flew by overhead. Lana felt the wind of its passage and then the shockwave from behind as it exploded somewhere to her right rear. She looked and saw a tank making a minute adjustment. The muzzle of its smoking cannon looked to be a mile wide.

"Turret fucking down, Dumi!" she screamed. She felt the Eland shudder, then shift backwards in a hurry. She also felt herself being thrown face forward. And then she felt . . .

Like any good combat vehicle driver, and Dumi was by no means bad, the Zulu already had the gearshift in reverse and his foot on the brake. As soon as Lana called out, he slid his foot off the brake and mashed the gas. Gear and wheels shrieking, the Eland flew back at better than twenty miles an hour. On the wadi's sloping floor, it sank out of view of the surface.

Then Lana screamed, "Owww! Oh, shid! Muh fuggin' NODE. You addho', Dumi; you broke muh fuggin' NODE!"

Over Lana's pained shrieking, the crew heard Abdan say to the platoon leader, "Sir, time to charge."

"Lana?" Viljoen asked.

She shook her head. *God, that hurts.* "Fug id! Charge!"

The main gun was loaded and so didn't need her for now. Nose throbbing, Lana stood in the Eland's hatch, her shoulder pressed against the stock of the pintle-mounted machine gun. The gun's stock sank up and down with the movement of the Eland. At the same time and to the same cause, her blood rose and fell, raising and dropping the level of pain from her shattered nose. As bad, every thump of a wheel over a rock or over the lip of the wadi was transmitted instantly to the sundered cartilage, ruptured blood vessels, and pulverized bone.

With a double thump, and a barely suppressed groan

from Lana, the Eland emerged from the wadi into a scene of fire and smoke, fallen bodies and people running in confusion and terror. Along the road heavy vehicles sat, abandoned, or burned their souls away in the night breeze. Those were the obvious ones. Others, still alive and trying desperately to fight back, were less obvious.

In the few hidden moments in the wadi, the scene had changed in important ways. Targets and threats once seen had moved. New ones had appeared. Pain or not, Lana's eyes scanned for the tank that had driven her Eland down into the wadi for safety. She spotted it not far from where it had fired at her car. Screamed, "Gunner, HEAT, Tank!" into her microphone, she tugged the machine gun to line up on her enemy.

"*Where*, Lana?" Viljoen demanded.

"Ten o'clock . . . follow my tracers," she answered. Her finger stroked the trigger, sending a stream of lead, one in five with a glowing tail, in the general direction of the T-55. She hit nothing, not even the tank and certainly not the commander in its hatch with the terrified grimace across his face.

Viljoen couldn't see the tracers in his sight until he had spun the turret well to the left. The target was moving, even as its turret traversed to reacquire the old threat. Viljoen fired, missed, and cursed, "goddamittofuckinghell."

Lana let go the machine gun, dropping down once again to cram a round of 90mm into the gun. It was as well that she did. Moments later the target fired, missing high right through the space her body had occupied a split second before. She felt the muzzle blast and she felt the wind of the round's passage over her head.

Popping her head back up, Lana ordered, "Hard left, Dumi! Clode into it. Viljoen, can you spin dat t'ing faster dan he can traverde?"

"Betcher ass," the Boer replied, pride in self and determination in mission plain in his voice.

"I *am* bedding my add!"

The T-55's commander may not have seen or understood what Lana and her crew intended. The effect, however, was the same as if it did. While the Eland closed as quickly as Dumi could force it to, its turret swinging as fast as Viljoen could spin his gunner's wheel, the tank's turret likewise turned. If the tank's commander had been experienced and well-trained enough to order his driver into a hard pivot steer, or if the driver had understood on his own, the Eland and her crew might have lost the race. As it was, the car and the tank danced around each other, their turrets straining to line up for a killing shot.

The advantage the Eland had was Viljoen's strength and experience. The advantage the tank had was that its hydraulic traverse wouldn't tire as, eventually, the Boer must. There was only going to be one shot at it.

"Target!" Viljoen exulted, pressing the trigger. The Eland rocked sideways from the recoil of the 90mm. Mere meters ahead, the hollow charge shell impacted on the thinner side armor of the turret, just behind the commander's hatch. There was a flash as the shell exploded, a portion of its power forced into the metal cone at its nose. The cone collapsed, then transformed into a gas—more of a plasma, really—that shot forward, melting its way through the armor. The T-55 stopped dead in its tracks, smoke beginning to pour from every open orifice. Flames followed the smoke.

Lana popped up again, taking control of the machine gun. In her NVGs she saw the T-55's driver, scrambling out of his cramped hatch. She cut him down, then resumed her scanning. "Gunner, HEAT, Tank . . . "

Reilly didn't have a turret. He didn't even have a machine gun since James was on that, laughing his ass off while he bowled over Ophiri dismounts by the twos and threes.

Instead, he had eyes and a radio. With his eyes he counted nine burning tanks. An explosion and a burst of flame caused him to amend that to *No, ten of the mother-fuckers. Four to go. And who knows how many dismounts?*

Another dual flash, muzzle and target, almost made him add *Eleven and three.* A closer look told him that last wasn't a tank; it was one of his own infantry carriers coming apart at the seams.

How many did that cost me? Two anyway, machine gunner and driver. And maybe three or four. Shit. Hopefully Lana . . . Reilly just cut that thought off at the root.

"Is my fucking dustoff on the way yet?" he asked of the *Merciful*.

An RPG landed short, blowing up on the ground a couple of meters in front of Maalin's tank. The explosion rattled both the tank and the major. From whence it came, Maalin had no clue; the things seemed to come from everywhere and to land pretty much anywhere. He didn't have any night vision, though his panicky gunner did. The gunner simply gibbered when the major asked him to report.

At least the enemy seemed to have fired off all their

directional mines. Maalin wasn't sure how much difference that made; tracers from what seemed to him to be about a dozen or more machine guns lanced across the road from all directions. To add to the confusion, mortar shells—or maybe they were artillery; Maalin didn't have the experience to say—walked up and down the road, exploding in bright flashes followed by dark, evil smoke and sending their shards through flesh to rattle off armor.

Even without night vision, the major could see tanks burning both ahead of and behind him. By those flickering lights he saw bodies and parts of bodies. One, in particular, caught his attention, where a probably panicking tank had run over a certainly panicking infantryman, crushing the latter like a grape.

Moans and screams arose from every side. Maalin heard pleas for mercy and pity in his own tongue.

"Allah, have mercy," Major Maalin prayed. "Deliver me from this nightmare." He doubted that mercy would be forthcoming. This was the kind of nightmare he was also reasonably sure he wasn't going to awaken from.

He was getting no reports that made sense. As near as Maalin could determine from the radio, he had one platoon leader with no tanks but his own, two more tanks with no platoon leaders, a bunch of scattered, frightened-out-of-their-wits infantry more interested in getting out of what was now obviously a preplanned kill zone than in striking back, and a couple more tanks under his exec chasing some light vehicles somewhere to the west.

And now the enemy vehicles were in among his own, taking advantage of their maneuverability, size, and speed to move faster than his tanks' turrets could traverse.

There was one chance. It was hard to take it, but Maalin really couldn't see much choice. "Surrender," he sent out over the radio. "Get out of your vehicles and walk with your hands up." He said much the same to his own crew, then ripped off his tanker's helmet, a Russian job of pads and mesh with electronics running through it.

"Surrender!" he shouted to his own infantry. "Drop your arms and put up your hands. Surrender!"

In his NVGs Reilly saw the gesture. "Cease fire," he commanded. "Cease fire, I said, goddammit," he repeated when he also saw a machine gun from his own side chop down several Ophiris. The word passed from his radio to the others, and then by word of mouth. In a few minutes, the firing stopped. Only then did he see a much larger number of the enemy rise from the ground, putting up their hands. "Prisoner teams out."

"James, grab the radio. Follow me. Bring the translator."

Finding the senior officer remaining among the enemy's tanks wasn't particularly hard. It was just a matter of counting radio antennae, all pretty well lit by the fires of burning tanks. At least that's how Maalin assumed his foe found him.

"You are the commander?" the white enemy asked through an interpreter.

"I was," Major Maalin said.

"You have two tanks to the west, chasing a few of my vehicles. Order them here, and to surrender."

"And if I refuse?"

Reilly jerked a thumb over his shoulder to where his

own infantry were collecting up the beaten enemy and herding them out onto the main wadi floor. "Then all your men here go into a ditch and get shot, along with yourself. Then we'll hunt those tanks down and kill them anyway. But I don't have time to fuck around, so you get a chance to save their lives, and the others'."

It was a hard world, and a cruel one, Maalin knew. He didn't doubt this . . . *Well, American, I suppose he is, and if half the stories told of that vicious people are true, he'll carry out his threat. Murderers, it is said, the lot of them, whatever pious platitudes their government may put forth for public consumption.*

"One moment, please?" he asked, as he scrambled up the side of his tank, reached in, and took out a radio mike. What he said, Reilly didn't know, though it didn't seem to alarm the translator.

Then Reilly got a call from Snyder. "Alpha Six, Scout One. The enemy has reversed turrets and is rolling to your position. How did you do that?"

"Just good planning," Reilly answered, even while thinking, *Luck. Pure fucking luck. I was ready to trade you guys for a little time. Thank God, I didn't have to.*

A stretcher team trotted by, a moaning man bouncing on the stretcher. Reilly sighed. *It's never really been about killing the enemy,* he reminded himself. *It's always been about winning when that requires you to risk your life.*

He stood quietly for several minutes then, both his RTO and the enemy commander looking at him, intently in the one case, warily in the other.

"What's your name?" Reilly asked of the Ophiri.

"Maalin, Muktar. Major."

Reilly inclined his head toward the east, where Coffee had set up an ad hoc aid station that was rapidly filling.

"Major Maalin, have your men bring their wounded to my chief medic. We'll treat them as best we're able before we have to go."

"Yes, sir," Maalin answered. "Thank you, sir."

Reilly took the mike from James and broadcast, "By the way, all platoon leaders, this is Alpha Six. Do we have anybody who knows how to drive a T-55? I need . . . six of 'em."

"I kin dribe wun o' de pides o' shid," said a voice that sounded a lot like Lana's, but as if she were speaking with a clothespin over her nose.

Reilly ignored that for the moment, saying, "That's one. I need five more. And, Lana, if that was you, report to me, center of the kill zone. Other people who can drive a T-55 do the same. Infantry platoons and mortar section, I need two people from each of you to stand in a turret and look threatening."

He handed the mike back to James, who stuck it to his ear, listening intently. Suddenly, James smiled. "Dustoff, two minutes out," he announced. Turning to where Sergeant Coffee and the other two medics, under the lights of the medical Eland, fussed over seven wounded men, next to a line of five of their own dead, James pointed and repeated, "Dustoff, two minutes out!"

★ CHAPTER FIFTY-TWO ★

The bullet is a mad thing;
only the bayonet knows what it is about.
—Alexander Vasileyevich Suvarov, Count Rymnik

D-Day, Yemen

As hot as the day had been, and it had been nearly life threatening, despite the shade of the nets, the night was bitter. Konstantin shivered despite himself and despite the robes he wore over his battle dress. And the breeze didn't help. Unconsciously he pulled his headdress tighter to him, at the same time pressing on the earpiece *cum* microphone he wore, as did his men.

"Browned skin and contacts, fake beards or not, we're going to stand out like sore thumbs, you know," Galkin said, holding up his rifle for emphasis. This close, it was easy enough to see both, despite the dust laden breeze, blowing out of the northeast from Saudi Arabia's *Rub al Khali*, or Empty Quarter.

The Romans had called the place "Arabia Felix,"

Happy Arabia, this based on the income from harvesting and trading incense, as well as trade generally. Sadly, the bottom had nearly dropped out from the frankincense and myrrh markets many centuries past, while, conversely, the market in oil, which Yemen didn't have much of, had grown enormously in decades recent. Thus, while Saudis may have tooled around the desert in four-wheel drive Mercedes, it was more common to see Yemenis on dirt bikes doing the same. Or hear them.

Seeing but not hearing them would have been considered odd. That was one of the little weaknesses to the plan. Konstantin had accepted the weakness as necessary if he were going to be able to get to Yusuf's palace close enough, which meant quietly enough, to do the job in time to get picked up and brought home. His dirtbikes were as silent as the weapons his men carried.

Still, as long as the viewer was some distance away, then the procession of keffiyeh-covered, dishdasha-clothed men, with their robes hiked up around their waists, probably wouldn't invite much comment or attention.

And the arms they carried, that couldn't be hidden under robes?

"Oh, hell, this isn't Europe, or even Russia; *everybody* in Yemen who isn't a slave carries a rifle," Baluyev answered Galkin's objection. "Besides, it's dark."

"Even some of the slaves are armed," Konstantin said, "depending on how trusted they are."

"See? Even the slaves." Baluyev stopped for a moment, a curse on his lips. "Fuck; when did we get so used to using expressions like 'even the slaves'?"

Konstantin shrugged. Who knew, after all? It wasn't as

if the institution had ever gone out of style completely. Why, in the heyday of the Soviet Union virtually everyone in it or controlled by it had been a slave.

"Never mind," the major said. "We have this job to do, now. Maybe someday we can do something about some other problems. Maybe."

The shocks made more noise than the engines, squeaking in outraged protest as the dirtbikes slammed down onto the sand after skipping over the tops of dunes. The breeze had died down, though it left a great deal of dust hanging in the air. And it was still cold.

We look so much like Arabs, thought Konstantin, who loathed Islamics on general principle and had since Afghanistan, *that the only way we could look more Arabic is if I have everyone stop and fuck Galkin.*

I don't think that's necessary, though. Besides, even if it's a fair approximation of Islamics, it's unfair to Galkin.

That this might not have been fair to the Islamics, either, bothered the major not at all. He *really* didn't like, rather he utterly loathed, the religion and all its followers. Only solid self-discipline let him work with them at all. And he avoided that where possible. He hadn't, for example, taken the Arabic speaker Stauer had offered him.

Konstantin took one hand away from the handlebars and checked his wrist-mounted GPS. Yes, the old man had thoughtfully sent them receivers for GLONASS, the Russian system. *No, thank you, Chief. I'll use the Americans' system. They seem able to keep more than a dozen satellites operational at any one time, something we have signally failed at doing.*

Putting his hand back on the handlebars, Konstantin slowed, then slowed some more. He spotted the palace—and this was a *real* palace, large, imposing, and decorated to the point of tackiness and beyond—through the dust, some five kilometers distant. It was brightly lit. If the old man's reports were to be believed, and Konstantin had reasons to trust the old man's reports going back decades, it was quite well guarded.

Too brightly lit for them to be using night vision, Konstantin thought. *Not that they'd be likely to see us at this range, or even quite a bit closer, with the best night vision and no lights around the place. We continue.*

With that, he cut left, followed by the other five men in the team. One by one they entered a wadi that ran generally south, toward the sea, then followed it to where it ran rather close to the palace.

The Arabs had known for many centuries something that western optical science had only keyed into but recently; at night the human eye had a hell of a time making out pixels of a certain size and the colors didn't make all that much difference. In short, the checked keffiyehs worn by Konstantin and his men made superb camouflage.

This was all to the good as it was a five-hundred-meter belly crawl from the point of the wadi nearest the wall around Yusuf's palace to that wall. Outside the wall was little but sand and rocks and the very occasional bit of scrub . . . those, and a heavy layer of dust still floating on the air, courtesy of the late northeast wind blowing out of the *Rub al Khali*.

Konstantin lifted his head up and swept his gaze along the crenellated walls, both on the palace roof and the surrounding grounds wall, with his NVGs. The old man had provided Dutch manufacture for these, which was both more thoughtful and more practical than the GLONASS receivers that sat unused back with the helicopters. The palace was bright enough that he thought it better to leave the lens caps on, to gather light only through the peep holes in those caps. This worked surprisingly well. They'd already lain there through one changing of the guard. Ideally, they'd have waited through another to establish how long the shifts were, hence how long they'd have to operate before discovery. But there just wasn't enough time for that.

Besides, two hour shifts are the universal norm. And where did they go?

Guards? Guards?. . . Ah, there's one, the major observed, in both senses of the word. That guard, off by the right corner of the curtain wall, as Konstantin faced, held his rifle at the slope and tucked into the crook of one arm. He smoked a cigarette but, otherwise diligent, faced outward. *And if there's one there . . .* Konstantin looked left. *Uh, huh. There at the left corner.* That one was not particularly diligent, facing inward with his back against the wall. Of his rifle the Russian could see no sign. Of guards on the roof, likewise there was no sign.

And so we'll make our entrance where the guard is a slob. Konstantin used two fingers to beckon up Litvinov and Kravchenko. *But take care of the diligent one, first.*

"Yes, Comrade Major?" Kravchenko whispered.

Konstantin pointed at the more alert guard, to the right. "He's your job," he said. "On my signal."

Without another word, Kravchenko and Litvinov headed on their bellies in that direction. Baluyev was next up.

"Stay here and watch, *Praporschik*. Report. On my command, turn on the cellular jammer."

"Yes, Comrade Major."

Then, leading the remaining two, the major shifted the direction of his crawl about twenty degrees to the left.

There are at least nine different ways to kill a sentry, in theory, more or less quietly, and without the use of firearms. It's that "in theory" part, coupled with the "more or less" part, that so often prove problematic. People fight back, gouge, bite, scream . . . even the gushing of blood from a severed artery makes its quotient of sound. Moreover, no army really teaches even its special operations personnel to knife or strangle or bludgeon an enemy standing ten feet above them. It just doesn't work that way.

For those cases, there are quiet firearms. In this case, those firearms were a brace of PSS pistols, firing silent, subsonic, piston-driven SP-4 ammunition. Galkin, with Konstantin, held one. Kravchenko, with Litvinov, held another. All five men stood now, backs against the wall, waiting for a report from *Praporschik* Baluyev.

"Problem, Comrade Major," Baluyev said. All heard it in their earpieces. "I saw someone else walking the parapet. And the one above you is now facing out while the one at the other end is facing in."

"He's being blown, Comrade Major," Kravchenko whispered in the softest imaginable voice, though he couldn't quite hide the tremor of amusement contained therein. "We can hear him . . . err . . . them."

The major hadn't quite been expecting this. He thought frantically for a minute. *Shit. A third person and one we can't take out the same time as the others. No, this just can't be done. Can't. Shit, shit, shit.*

I wish I knew more about our contact. But the old man's always been cagey as hell about such things. "What you don't know you can't divulge."

But it has to be done; the old man wants it. But how? *Kill two guards at the same time? Okay; that we could do. Kill a third person, probably a woman—no, wait a minute. This is the Arabian Peninsula; there is no reason to assume the third person is female. In any case, kill someone that we can't see, before she—or he—screams? Not going to happen.*

Kill one and mount the wall, then go for the couple? Oh, God that doesn't exist, that's not going to . . .

Baluyev interrupted. "Comrade Major, the guard above you is turned away, watching the blow job. The pervert."

Maybe there is a God. And maybe we have to take a risk.

Konstantin squatted and pointed a single finger at Timer Musin. Once he was certain he had the sergeant's undivided attention, he made a throat cutting gesture, a quick flick of his index finger in the general direction of his own throat. Then the major directed both thumbs toward his own shoulders, at the same time sticking both index fingers up to indicate the direction of travel.

Musin raised an eyebrow, momentarily, then took half

a step on padded feet to place one foot on the major's shoulder, then both hands against the wall. He briefly took one hand away to loosen the restraining strap on his knife, then replaced it on the wall.

I am so glad you're not the huge sort, Sergeant Musin, Konstantin thought, *because I am frankly too old for this shit.*

Then Konstantin stood up, his back shrieking in protest.

Tim padded his hands lightly up the wall as the major raised him. As he felt himself nearing the summit of Konstantin's ability to propel him, he took his right hand off the wall and grasped his knife. His eyes cleared the edge of the wall and saw the distracted guard. His chin cleared, then his shoulders. He let his chest fall to the wall as he reached out with both hands.

Rather than a helmet, the guard was wearing a keffiyeh not dissimilar to the one adorning Musin's head. Strong fingers drove through the cloth to grip hair. An arm stronger still yanked backwards, even while the hand on the other, gripping its knife, took advantage of the exposed neck to drive the blade in to the hilt and then rip it all the way across the throat.

The guard's body went into a fair simulacrum of the funky chicken, shaking and twitching like a mad thing. Blood gushed; noisily, it seemed to Musin. It sailed upward, then sprinkled down, some of it landing on his keffiyeh. In an instant, Tim's legs and torso, using the late guard's body for balance, were on and over the wall. In the process, he lost his keffiyeh even as part of his false beard, scraping the wall, tore off. Ignoring the loss, still gripping his knife, Tim set his feet on the parapet and began a silent trot for the woman on her knees further down.

"Kill him, Krav."

Kravchenko took a quick but deep breath, let it out, then did both over again. Between his first and second breath he gave the ground another careful look to ensure that there were no obstacles. Then, pistol in both hands for a steady hold, he began to walk backwards. As soon as the guard's head came into view he aimed but . . .

"Shit, Comrade Major, two thirds of the bastard's head is covered by the crenellations. I haven't got a decent shot."

The girl was milky white, with midnight hair long in the back and cut in bangs across the front. She looked perhaps fourteen. Even her breasts, exposed where she'd opened her shirt, were small and budding like a young teen's. Her eyes were not closed, as Musin had expected. Rather, they were not only open, they saw him. And yet the woman did nothing except continue the business on which she'd been engaged. Then she held up one hand, palm out, stopping Musin in his tracks. He pressed his back against the parapet wall.

Removing her mouth from the guard, she began to rise from her knees, snake-like, slithering up the guard's body. Once she reached her full height of perhaps five feet, she took both the guard's hands and slid them under her shirt. Then she reached up to pull the guard's head down for a kiss. While they kissed, and while her left hand stroked the back of his neck, under his keffiyeh, she used her right to lift her skirt. Strapped to her thigh, the sergeant saw, was a long, thin stiletto. He watched, fascinated, as she silently drew it, rotated it, and then plunged it through the guard's chin and into his brain, spinning the thing like a mortar's pestle once it was well inside.

Pulling out the stiletto, she backed up slightly, and began easing her victim's body to the floor. Musin moved in to help. He had a very difficult time keeping his eyes off the breasts that looked so very young and tender.

Seeing that, she began to button her shirt against his gaze. She said, in good if highly annoyed Russian, and in a fully grown woman's voice, "Those are for business, rarely for pleasure. And, speaking of which, it's about time you assholes showed up. I've had to *entertain* these two every night for the last three weeks to make sure I would be here when you came, as the old man ordered."

"You . . . ummm . . . serve the motherland," Musin said, as if by way of acceptance of the woman's . . . job. Besides, she was altogether too pretty to judge.

She sighed, and at that moment she really did look fourteen. "In my own way," she said. "I'm Lada and, no, I'm *not* fourteen."

★CHAPTER FIFTY-THREE★

Don't let it end like this. Tell them I said something.
—Pancho Villa, Last words, 1923

D Day, Nugaal Highway, Ophir

Under its thin coat of dust, the limousine was brightly polished. It bounced and jarred over the potholed highway between the airfield and the town of Nugaal.

"And how many guards?" Welch asked Mr. Dayid, as the two sped up the highway. Terry rescrewed the suppressor onto the muzzle of his submachine gun as they rolled.

Pigfucker drove the limo. It was followed by the largest truck the parking lot in front of the palace had held, a more or less long-bed five ton. That was driven by Ryan, with Graft and Semmerlin in the back. All the men from Terry on down sported freshly touched up "Black-is-Beautiful." It wouldn't fool anybody for more than a second. That said, given the velocity of a bullet, even a subsonic one, a second was awfully long time to be laboring under an error.

The accountant shrugged, answering, "It varies

sometimes but never more than a dozen. Of those, not more than two or three are actually on duty at any given time."

"And the rest?" Welch asked.

"At this time of the morning? Asleep. Probably with one of the slave girls each."

Fuck. More slaves. I will not, not, NOT take on responsibility for liberating any more slaves.

"Your slaves?" Terry asked, a note of malice creeping into his voice.

"No," Jama Dayid said. "I follow the teachings of al-Nabhani, UHBP, that times have changed, that slavery is wrong, and that Allah intended that when times changed slavery would be seen as wrong. But . . . I am probably in the minority."

Terry just grunted. How did one answer that? *He tolerates? Am I as guilty because I've tolerated? I don't feel a twinge of regret about those Afghan men Stauer and his commandos killed; but what about the women and kids they carted off? I tolerated . . . and I have much to make up for.*

"How many slaves in the town?"

"Hundreds," Dayid said. "Too many. Mostly individually owned, and . . . maybe, too . . . maybe all not that unhappy."

In a way, the discussion of the plight of the slaves put Terry in the proper mood. Thus, even though he might have been able to force the guards on the gates to Dayid's house to surrender, the thought didn't even cross his mind. The limo rolled up; a guard came over, and Terry shot him down like a dog even as Pigfucker cut down the one on the other side.

Then Terry got out of the limo, shot first one then the other man again, to make sure. He opened the lift gate himself, then waved Hammell through. A few brisk steps brought him to the guardhouse, a small mud brick structure built against the wall. That half-sleeping guard he shot with a short burst, every round of four slamming the man's midsection.

"Go round up your family," He told Dayid. "Pigfucker, go with him."

As Dayid and Hammell walked off, Terry called out, "Semmerlin, come with me. Hey, Mr. Dayid, where's the guard barracks?"

While Mr. Dayid and Pigfucker, along with several men of Dayid's family, helped children and older people onto the back of the five-ton, Graft standing just behind the cab, with a machine gun, watched Welch and Semmerlin walk back from the barracks. Both Terry's submachine gun and Semmerlin's VSSK smoked from their muzzles. A half dozen veiled women walked behind the two. Some of the women wept, softly, half bent over, bodies shuddering with shock and fear. Still others skipped on dancing feet.

"You always were a soft touch, Terry." Graft shouted. "How the fuck you plan on fitting them all in two helicopters?"

"I don't fucking know. Have them all piss, shit, and puke first, maybe?"

D-Day, Bandar Cisman, Ophir

While bullets still occasionally snapped overhead, the shooting was rather desultory now, on both sides. That was fine, as far as Cazz was concerned. He wasn't expected to take the town on his own, anyway.

And fat chance I'd have doing it, with seven or eight hundred armed men in the buildings, and a hundred and twenty or so of us, and no heavy armor.

Besides, I'm only required to make sure everyone stays put until the Irish bastard gets back with the heavy shit and his captives.

Cazz hadn't yet had call to use either the one helicopter—*Fucking green beanies; I was supposed to have* two—or the two armed CH-801s to actually strike the town. The Hip was engaged in running ammunition, especially mortar ammunition—seven and a half tons of it—and small arms to his own men, while the two fixed wing jobs, having wrecked all the boats, circled counterclockwise above, keeping well outside of machine gun range, reporting whatever there was to be seen.

Another reason Cazz was perfectly happy to wait to assault was that the dustoff bird, carrying the colonel's lady, so he'd heard, was off somewhere to the west where Reilly had apparently executed the ambush he'd intended.

D-Day, Rako-Dhuudo-Bandar Cisman highway, Ophir

The CH-801 seemed to be straining to get back in the air, shuddering as its engine and propeller pushed almost enough air to lift it, then lost that air behind and below. The propeller also picked up smoke from the still-burning vehicles, sucking it in like a fan with cigarette smoke, and pushing it out behind, too.

"I could use some more morphine for my nine expectants," Coffee said to Phillie. "Expectant" was a code word for "expected to die." Since the Ophiris, who made up Coffee's entire population of expectants, were unlikely to speak English, it didn't really matter if they'd spoken freely. Still, old habits die hard.

"There are ninety one-hundred-milligram ampoules in the plane's kit," Phillie answered. "You can have half. I'll need the rest to sedate our own."

"Fair enough," Coffee agreed, turning for the plane.

Phillie, an ER nurse with several years experience of terribly hurt people behind her, couldn't quite figure out what was wrong with the scene. It wasn't the burning vehicles or the rent, burnt, crushed, and sundered bodies littering the road. It wasn't the smell. It wasn't the roar of armored vehicle engines as Reilly's first sergeant lined them up to push on. It wasn't . . .

Nobody's whining, she thought. *There's no "oh, my back," no "oh, the pain, the pain," no "I wanna lawyerrr!" They're stoic and tough. I didn't know people could be like this.*

Somebody did groan, though. Phillie looked over and, by the light of the burning tanks, saw someone being bounced on a stretcher.

"Gently, you assholes!" she shouted.

"Yes, ma'am," the two men at either end said, together. "We thought speed . . . "

"Speed won't do a fucking bit of good if you put him into shock."

"Yes, ma'am."

"It's a tough call, Phillie," Coffee said.

"Yeah, I know," she answered. *I'm a big girl. If I stay here, we can fit four of the worst wounded on the plane instead of three. They won't have any medical attention in flight, but the flight will only be about fifteen minutes. And they* are *tough men; they don't need me holding their hands, which is nearly all I could do in the cramped confines of the plane.*

And here *there's enough work to keep me busy for a while. And Coffee's got to move out with the main column . . . and . . .*

"Can you leave me one medic?" she asked. "And some guards?"

"I know Reilly," Coffee answered. "He won't give up able bodied troops for guards. Hell, he's taking some of the walking wounded with him. But . . . three or four of *our* wounded can still use a rifle. He's leaving them to guard prisoners. Will that do? And I can leave a medic. My junior one."

"It'll have to," Phillie said. "I'm staying. I'll go out with a later flight."

Coffee nodded and began to turn away. He turned back, suddenly, and said, "Phillie, I'm awful sorry for dumping you into the mud back in Brazil."

"Oh, shush," she answered, reaching out to spin him back around and send him on his way. "Don't sweat it; did me a world of good."

D Day, Bandar Qassim Airport, Ophir

As with the other strike, the one on the truck convoy, this

pilot led off with an illumination rocket. Having seen and heard what followed the previous such, the Ophiris dotted about the landscape of the ridge's northern slope—about half of them—dropped their crap and began to leg it for the north.

The rockets came fast after that: Flechette—which whined in with the drone of thousands of homicidal bees, high explosive, incendiary, high explosive, incendiary, flechette again, another flare, more flechette, and then three HE, interspersed with two incendiaries. They came in close enough together in time, if not in space, that the crest of the ridge lit up as if by strobe light.

Buckwheat doubted they hit much of anything—*well, except maybe for the flechette*—but that almost wasn't the point of an air strike, which was usually much more about frightening and disorganizing people than about killing them.

"All right, Rattus, you maniac," Buckwheat Fulton shouted, kicking the back of the medic's seat, "fucking charrrge!"

The engine was already running. Hampson slammed on the gas, causing the Hummer to lurch forward, spitting rocks and gravel out the back. Fulton barely hung on to the rollbar and the bungeed machine gun. Off to the left, they heard Fletcher howling with pure delight.

The Hummer crested the ridge, launching itself into the air for a moment before slamming back down. Buckwheat waited for it to settle a bit from the pounding, then opened up with the machine gun, spraying ball and tracer pretty much at random to the front. Below him, Rattus drove with his left hand, firing a rifle out the right side. If either of them hit anything, moving and bouncing like that, it was a miracle.

Still, they didn't have to. After the strike on the truck convoy, the second strike on themselves, and the totally unexpected charge of the light vehicles, most of the Ophiris who had pursued the snipers up the slope broke and ran. Neither Rattus nor Buckwheat tried to kill them. Rather, they fired more to encourage them in their flight.

"Shit," Fulton said. "We might just get away with this."

Sergeant Nurto Nuur, fiercely scar-faced, shook his head with disgust at the younger generation. So the bandits raiding them had called in a little air strike. So *what*? He'd faced worse, more than once, fighting Americans, Ethiopians, Malayans, Kenyans, his own former countrymen . . .

Bah. Fucking cowards.

Some of his own men had tried to run off, right after the light went off overhead. Nuur wasn't sure he could have restrained them except that the first real war rocket had killed the first man to get up and run, and done so faster and deader than a stomped mouse. That had made the rest listen to him, and crouch down behind his protecting rock.

Under the light of the overhead flare, Nuur counted six others, not all of them from his own squad. One of these had a machine gun, and had managed to retain his ammunition. That was to the good. Nuur gave the boy a terse commendation.

They almost bolted again when the bandits' vehicles topped the crest and charged, spitting bullets. Then, Nuur had had to put his rifle on his own men to hold them in position.

"Stay put, unless you want to die," he'd said, without reference to whether he meant die from the enemy's bullets, or from his own.

His judgment had been proved correct when the bullets that had been pinging off the great boulder to his front had stopped moments after they'd begun.

They can't control the machine gun from a moving vehicle, he thought. *They're doing well to keep them going generally to the north.*

"Give me your gun," Nuur then demanded of the machine gunner, holding his hands out to receive it. The gunner passed his machine gun over without demur. Nuur took it, gave it the most cursory inspection under the waning light of the overhead flare, and told the others, "Get behind me."

Then he took a prone firing position and waited. He didn't have to wait long.

Rattus heard Buckwheat's shout, "Shit, we might just get away with this," and laughed.

"Of course we . . . "

Hampson stopped speaking as a long stream of bullets, one in five a green-flaring tracer, passed around and— based on sound and feel—through his Hummer. They came from behind him, to his right. His windshield cracked, physically and audibly. He couldn't return fire.

"Buckwheat!" Rattus called, "get . . . "

He didn't bother continuing as Buckwheat had slumped forward onto his right shoulder. The medic's nose was assailed by the smell of blood and shit. Rattus aimed for the field and drove like a madman.

D-Day, Airfield, Five north-northeast of Nugaal, Ophir

Between Dayid's extended family, the liberated slaves, his own people, and the translator's body, Terry had eighty-nine people to shove, somehow, onto two helicopters.

He had one of his people, Graft, explaining through the remaining translator what they had to do. That wasn't a problem—"No water, no food, no baggage, no arms, no . . ." —until he got to the real stickler—"and get rid of any clothing that isn't absolutely essential to minimum modesty. That means shorts, ripped off skirts, and bras; no more."

When the people, other than the troops and the liberated slaves, began to rise in protest, Terry said, "Mr. Dayid, please go and explain to your relatives that they either do what they are told or they get left behind to the tender mercies of your clan chief while we do whatever it takes to extract the necessary information from you *despite* what will happen to them."

"Yes, sir," Dayid said, then hurried over to calm his people down. He must have been persuasive, because the men began removing trousers and robes as the women began to strip.

Venegas was on the radio to higher. Two of Terry's men had had to go and bring him in, but he could still run communications well enough.

"Two choppers inbound in five, Terry," Venegas said, his voice a study in nausea-induced weakness.

"Start splitting them into two groups," Welch ordered. "By *weight*, best you can judge it."

D-Day, Bandar Qassim Airport, Ophir

Hampson slammed on the brakes not far from where the medevac CH-801 had touched down. He didn't bother with lights; the entire field was still well lit by the hulks of burning aircraft.

As soon Hampson's feet were on the ground he was checking Fulton for vital signs. *Weak, fast pulse . . . but at least he's still alive.* A bullet cracked overhead, precluding any more careful diagnosis and all chance at treatment. He pulled the unconscious man out of the back, slung him over a shoulder, and began to race for the waiting plane.

Biggus Dickus met him halfway there. "Where's your wounded Brit?" he asked.

"Back of the Hummer," Rattus shouted, as the two passed by each other. As soon as Hampson was at the plane, he dropped the small ramp that made up the lower half of the tail and pulled out a low wheeled stretcher. He laid Buckwheat on it as carefully as possible, then pushed the stretcher in. He managed to lift the ramp and secure it by main force, then got into the plane himself and started digging frantically in its medical kit for an oxygen mask, a syringe, and drugs to keep blood pressure up. Bandages could come later.

Biggus came back and tossed Vic Babcock-Moore into the passenger seat next to the pilot. Vic groaned with the pain.

"Get the fuck out of here," Thornton shouted at the pilot, who nodded and began letting go the brake.

"What about you?" Hampson asked, as he affixed an oxygen mask over Buckwheat's comparatively pale face.

"I'm just an old ex-Corpsman. You're an SF medic. I'll get the next lift." Biggus slapped the side of the aircraft. "Just go."

Before Rattus could answer, the plane was surging down the runway, flanked by the burning wrecks of the Ophiri proto-Air Force. In moments, mere moments, it was airborne with the field and the wrecks rapidly receding below. Rattus looked behind the plane and saw some bright green streaks racing for heaven.

Already one of the gunships, covered by the other circling overhead, was landing to continue the pickup. It would follow the coast, to continue its original mission, while the dustoff risked its wings heading directly back to the ship at a speed that, strictly speaking, was not good for the plane.

About halfway back, with the coast visible in the distance, Buckwheat's body began to thrash uncontrollably. It went limp again as Rattus began applying CPR, though this was difficult in the closed and awkward confines of the plane. When Hampson finally gave up, and it was the radical drop in body temperature more than any other factor that made him decide it was hopeless, he said, with tears in his eyes, "We're all glad your multi-great granddaddy got dragged onto that boat, too, Master Sergeant Fulton."

★ CHAPTER FIFTY-FOUR ★

Mama, just killed a man.
Put my gun against his head
Pulled my trigger; now he's dead
—Freddy Mercury, Queen, *Bohemian Rhapsody*

D-Day, Yemen

Lada knew the way. More than that, she knew the best way to get from the wall into the house without being seen. That way led a short distance along the wall, to a set of concrete stairs leading to the ground. At the base of the stairs all was shadow, under the parapet. This they followed, Musin lugging one leaking corpse and Kravchenko the other, to a noisy heat pump under the wall. There they dropped the bodies. Galkin and Litvinov, holding the dead guards' rifles, were left behind, manning the wall to cover the eventual retreat.

Covered by the heat pump's *thrumm*, Lada explained the next step. "There, through that door," she pointed across a shadowy way, "is a long corridor that runs all the way through the house. Halfway there's a side branch to the right—"

"What's down there?" Konstantin asked.

"Servants' quarters," she said, then amended that to, "Slaves quarters. Storage. And some machinery. Two flights of stairs and an elevator. That's on the side branch. I don't have a key to the elevator."

"No guards?"

"Only if they're fucking one of the slaves. Yusuf is generous with his property that way."

"Right," Konstantin said. He considered, *Do we go slow up the corridor, listening at each door? No. what would be the point? If we don't hear anything it doesn't prove shit. And if we do, what do we do? Go in and kill the room's occupants? Too noisy.* "Go on," he told Lada.

"The far staircase," she continued, "goes all the way to the third floor. The nearer only goes directly to the second. We have to go to the far one, go up to the third floor, then come back and use the branch to get to the door to Yusuf's private quarters."

"Guard on the door?" Konstantin asked.

"Always. Two of them, sometimes three. And the door will be locked."

"How thick is this door?"

"Stout," she answered. "Very stout. Unless you use explosives the occupants of the room are unlikely to hear what's going on in the corridor."

"Occupants?" the major asked, emphasizing the plural.

She nodded her head. "Almost always. Sometimes one girl, sometimes two. Sometimes a little boy. Sometimes one of each. Sometimes all three. Or more."

"How did you—" He stopped his question. For the purposes of the mission it hardly mattered.

Lada shook her head and answered anyway. "I volunteered. For the Service if not for the mission. Through an intermediary, the old man arranged to have me sold directly to Yusuf." She shrugged. "I'm really twenty-four but I look fourteen. I claimed here to be sixteen. Yusuf figured I was a mature looking thirteen and enjoyed fucking me all the more for that."

"And once you volunteer for the service," Konstantin added, "you don't get a lot of choice about the missions. Where 'not a lot of' is defined as 'none.'"

"No, 'not a lot,'" she agreed. "Though I never imagined myself becoming a whore when I volunteered."

"You're not a whore," the major said. "You're just a soldier who uses a different set of weapons. Hang on to that; because it's *true*."

"Thank you, Major," she answered. She didn't sound convinced. "Questions?"

"How do we get through the door to Yusuf's quarters if it's so stout? I mean, we have explosives but . . . "

"There's a pad with a number control and a facial scan device." She smiled for the first time this night. "It knows me and I know the code."

"Works. Let's go."

People who had no business being there would have dashed across the open space between the wall and the ground floor door. People who belonged would have walked. Konstantin and his people *walked*. For added disguise, he pushed Lada's shoulder as she neared the door, causing her to stumble. It looked just as if she were going to be the main attraction at a gang bang somewhere inside.

So well did her discipline hold that she didn't even whisper, "Asshole!"

She thought it, though, even as she knew the major had done it only for effect.

The door squeaked, causing all of them but Lada to wince. "Relax," she said. "When something becomes routine, and I assure you that squeaking doors around here are the essence of normal and routine, people simply don't hear them anymore."

Konstantin knew that was true. Even so, he prodded everyone inside as quickly as possible without risking someone's tripping.

"It stinks down here," Musin observed, wrinkling his Tatar nose. "Stinks" was something of an understatement. "Reeks" would have been an understatement.

"What do you expect?" Lada answered. "Sixty-seven slaves, give or take, two toilets—Turkish type, and two showers that sometimes work and sometimes don't. And no laundry facilities except a utility sink. And the master wouldn't waste air conditioning on the slaves. His favorite camel? Sure. The slaves? Never. Of *course* it stinks."

"And you've put up with this for . . .?"

"About four months," she answered.

Musin nodded and said, respectfully, "Honey, you do serve the motherland."

Lada smiled for the second time that night.

The woman walked on bare feet. The footgear for the

men were boots, but soft ones more akin to very high topped sneakers. They made hardly a sound in the long corridor. Neither did they hear anything coming from the rooms, barring only some snoring.

Konstantin shot a questioning look at Lada.

"It's late," she replied, bitterly adding, "They're probably all done with their little boy bunging and little girl raping. Now hurry."

The stench of the slaves' quarters ended as soon as they'd shut the door behind them. Konstantin formed them in a Y, with Musin and Kravchenko up front, himself behind them, and Lada behind himself.

"You are the only way of getting into Yusuf's quarters quietly," he explained. "That won't matter if we run into somebody on the way, in a place we're not supposed to be, since massive shooting with unsuppressed firearms and quiet are pretty much mutually exclusive. But you may also be the only way of getting into the bastard's quarters at all, if the door is as stout as you've described."

"Fine," she agreed. "Two full flights up then. Pay no attention to the last flight; it only goes to the roof."

"Are there guards on the roof?" the major asked.

Lada chewed her lower lip for a moment, then answered, hesitatingly, "Routinely? I don't know. I've never been permitted up there. Helicopters sometimes land up there. I've seen guards go up there then."

The woman went first through the door that led from the staircase to the third floor. She walked down the corridor, with considerably more confidence than she, in fact, felt. Indeed, her heart was thumping against her chest enough for her to worry that the guards she knew she would meet when she entered the branch corridor would hear it or, at least, sense it.

For a second, she had to stop and force herself to calm. Konstantin's team, following close, barely stopped in time to prevent ramming her from behind.

A few deep breaths, a little act of will, and she nodded to herself, ready to proceed. A few feet ahead of the men, she turned the corner and uttered greetings to the guard, "Rashid, Abdul Rahman, *sabah inuur*." Then she stood in front of a small numeric pad and began to enter a code.

"The master sent for me," she told them, by way of explanation.

Konstantin heard the greetings to two men. *Fine*, he thought. *Just right*. He tapped Musin for attention, temporarily stuck his false beard back into place, then signaled for the Tatar to go first. In unconscious imitation of the girl, Musin forced himself to utter calm, then proceeded to walk down the corridor as if something on the very far end was his business, and nothing too close to where it branched off. His submachine gun was held with easy, practiced grace in both hands. True, if the inner guard looked they might well see that it was an unusual model. And the suppressor would surely seem strange, if they noticed the gun at all.

"*As-salama alaykum*." Tim said, waving casually with one hand as he crossed the open area. The other hand remained curled around the pistol grip. The guards waved back, giving in return, "*Wa alaykum essalamu*."

So the trick is, don't give them a lot of time to think about it. As soon as he reached the far edge of the branch corridor, and thus could be reasonably sure Krav and the major were waiting to pounce, Tim spun counterclockwise, firing instantly at the guard farthest to the left as he faced the door. Simultaneously, or near enough as made no difference, Kravchenko presented and fired at the guard to the right of the door as he faced.

Lada never heard a shot, so she never flinched from the keypad. While the bodies flopped to the floor, she hit "enter" and then stepped in front of a facial scanner.

"NVGs, on," Major Konstantin ordered.

At that moment, they heard a volley of fire coming from the yard, in the direction in which they'd left Galkin and Litvinov on guard. There came, too, the sound of a large and heavy door bolt being automatically thrown open.

"Ignore it," the major ordered. "Through the door. NOW!"

★CHAPTER FIFTY-FIVE★

PANDEMONIUM, n. Literally, the Place of
All the Demons. Most of them have escaped into
politics and finance, and the place is now used as a
lecture hall by the Audible Reformer. When disturbed
by his voice the ancient echoes clamor appropriate
responses most gratifying to his pride of distinction.
—Ambrose Bierce, *The Devil's Dictionary*

D-Day, MV *Merciful*

Unlike Stauer, whose most useful post was on the ship,
Sergeant Major Joshua didn't really have a most useful
post. Stauer didn't need him for what he was doing. The
operations staff was perfectly competent for their jobs and
would resent his butting in. Intel? *Shit, all I know about
intel is what I get asked to find out and how to read a
summary. And log? Forget log; Gordon's people have that
well in hand.*

He'd stood at a distance, ready to pounce if necessary,
for the boatload outward. He'd stood at a much farther
distance for the flight deck operations, *since I haven't clue*

618

one about that. He'd wandered the troop billets, mostly out of force of habit, to see if anyone was fucking off.

He'd completely skipped the mess since, other than Sergeant Island and a couple of Chinese women, the cooks were all off humping mortars with the grunts.

Admin? *Hmmm . . . if we decide to issue our own Combat Infantry Badges, note to self: CIBs for the cooks with the mortars and all the jarheads. But that's for later.*

Ultimately, the sergeant major had ended up down by sick bay. Fortuitously, he'd ended up there just before the order came down: "Incoming wounded."

He really hadn't a clue about the language that sounded vaguely Spanish, or the several slaps he heard after passing through the evac station.

"You stupid cunt, Tatiana," Elena said, delivering a series of slaps. "Not only is that the sergeant major, the next thing to *God*, but he's old enough to be your grand-father."

"If my grandfather had been half that much of a man," Tatiana answered, ducking the slaps as best she could, "I'd have fucked him, too."

"Bah!" Elena exclaimed in disgust. "You are a hopeless, useless, silly little tramp. You should have been left behind . . . "

"Incoming wounded," came over the loudspeakers, interrupting the senior Romanian girl's tirade. "Three stretcher cases inbound on a CH-801. Two minutes out."

"I'll beat you later, bitch," Elena said. "For now, get on a corner of a stretcher."

★ ★ ★

Sergeant Major Joshua was impressed. Whatever indiscipline had been behind the slapping and shouting he'd heard, it seemed to have disappeared as soon as the call came. He followed three amazingly young female stretcher teams out the hatch and onto the flight deck in time to see a light airplane touch down about midway from bow to superstructure. Under positive control from one of the flight deck crew, wearing a yellow jersey, the plane stopped. More yellow jerseyed men came out of the woodwork and turned it around by main strength. From somewhere a crewman in purple ran out a fuel line and began pumping fuel in.

All in all, considering it's nighttime, I'm kinda impressed, the sergeant major thought. *Not that I'd ever let that on to a bunch of squids.*

The Romanian girls and their gurneys, wheeled stretchers, in other words, lined up neatly beside and behind the plane, one after the other. One of them, Joshua didn't know her name, seemed to be in charge and, so far as he or anyone could tell, really was in charge.

The first man out was the one who'd come in sitting beside the pilot. He stepped off, took two steps, and promptly collapsed to the deck. One of the girls bent to the collapsed man. It was really too dark to make out her face. *Which is a pity,* the sergeant major thought, *as anytime somebody five-two and female tries to do a fireman's carry on someone six foot and male, she ought be commended for at least trying.* He went over to help, but did no more than required to get the man across the little female's shoulders. *Be a shame to take the glory away from her,* Joshua thought.

They also had trouble with two of the wounded, the two who'd had to sit up in the plane for lack of space. The other, the one lying down on the back ramp, took eight of them get onto the stretcher, which they'd collapsed, and still eight to lift the collapsed stretcher straight up. These were all big men and the girls were . . .

Well, they're little girls, Joshua thought. *Even so, they mostly make up in gentleness what they lack in physical strength. And their teamwork and coordination are good. Might be a wash. At least on the flat deck of a ship.*

The last of the seated men was the hardest. He screamed when they tried to pull him out. At that, the sergeant major went over to help. He was tall enough to get his hands under the wounded trooper's armpits, and strong enough to simply lift. The man still screamed, but this time the screaming was worthwhile.

One of the Romanian girls smiled something at him that Joshua hadn't seen in a very long time. He felt like the smile knocked twenty years of his age. *Twenty? Hah! Forty!"*

Then the girls were racing off, getting their charges to OR as quickly as anybody could expect. After a brief glance at the twitching posterior of the girl who'd smiled at him, the sergeant major looked up at the windows fronting the bridge. He could see Stauer's outline there and was pretty sure Stauer was watching him. Joshua pointed at himself, then at the plane. The figure in the window nodded. The sergeant major then jumped into the plane and began strapping himself in. In seconds, the CH-801 was roaring down the strip, heading out to pick up another load of the lamed and maimed.

D-Day, Bandar Qassim, Ophir

Gutaale, still on the roof of his main residence, stood alone, still staring at the flames to the east. The scope, the scale, and the sheer ferocity of the attack had him about convinced that he had not only come under the baleful gaze of the United States, but that, for some inexplicable reason, they'd decided the gloves were off.

Would they do this simply over the kidnapping of someone not even of their nation from their territory? That's hard to believe. But who else could do this kind of damage? My new air force; destroyed. My new armored force, bought so dearly from the Yemeni, Yusuf? Off of the air and probably destroyed. My palace by Nugaal; raided and burned, so the rumors say, and everyone in it killed. My personal guard ravaged just west of here.

No word from my parents in Rako and no way to get word to them or from them. My brother under siege in Bandar Cisman and, while him I can communicate with, his message is one of despair.

It's such an overreaction to a mere kidnapping that I just can't believe the Americans are behind it. But who else could be? Certainly no one here is capable of such monstrous mayhem.

One of the underlings of before came in bearing a radio transceiver.

"Chief," he said, "there are some problems at sea."

D-Day, MV *Merciful*

The two Hips carrying Terry Welch's much expanded party staggered in under an awful load. They touched down, and heavily, on the PSP flight deck. One landed about fifty meters shy of the bow and the other a similar distance from the superstructure. Cruz and the other pilot didn't even try to line them up with the ship before touching down. Rather, they waited only until they were centered, albeit crosswise, and then set them down as quickly as practical, causing the things to bounce on their landing gear even more than usual. The blades nearly touched the deck, so heavy was the landing.

The wide-eyed, standing, swaying, utterly terrified cargo didn't try to move inside the bouncing behemoths until they were ordered out. As they left, via the side troop doors, one of Terry's people was there to physically push their heads down out of the way of the rotors. Others were standing by to lead the lines toward the superstructure and then down into the mess deck, where they could be sorted before being billeted. Feeding would probably have to wait, though at least some water could be issued.

Welch had been first off. He walked to a point between the choppers and watched the people unload, then follow their guides sternward. One tall woman from one of the groups burst free of the line and ran to stand before him. It was Ayanna, the ex-slave.

"My . . . English," she began, "not . . . good. I try . . . tell. For freedom . . . anything."

Then she threw herself into a highly embarrassed Terry's arms, and kissed him on the cheek, just in case he didn't understand.

And I will not take advantage of that, he told himself, as she swayed away to rejoin the line. He sighed, *Although she's awfully pretty and I wouldn't mind a date . . . or something like that. Haven't had so much chance to date . . . for quite a while now, come to think of it.*

Welch forced the image of the girl—all *three* images, including the imaginary one, the one by firelight . . . without clothing—out of his mind and watched out for the accountant. As soon as he saw Mr. Dayid emerge from the Hip he walked briskly over and said, "Sir, you have a date with our *lawyer*."

Little by little, as portions of the force began filtering back to the ship or, at least, reporting that the hard parts were done, the almost unbearable stress and anxiety Stauer had been under began to lift. For this, he thanked both God and good subordinates. The news about Buckwheat Fulton was hard to take, but, *Mourn later.*

Still no word from Phillie, but the last word from Reilly was that she was doing fine and, "You know, boss, you oughta think about marrying that girl."

Which is pretty much a done deal. Note to self: One of these days, think about what changed you, or her, or the both of you, to finally make getting married seem like a good idea.

See Bridges about a prenuptual agreement? Nah. That's bullshit. If you're not sure about the person you're marrying, you shouldn't get married.

And I've come to be pretty sure about my Miss Potter.

Happily whistling the riff from "Lawyers, Guns, and Money," Bridges was already waiting by a two-station battery of computers, in a semi-lighted container on the deck just forward of the mess deck. He smiled and rubbed his hands together as soon as Terry brought Mr. Dayid in. Lox was there, as well, in case it proved necessary to bypass some IT security system or other.

"Sir," Bridges said, "it's a pleasure to meet you. Now, assuming Terry has explained . . . "

"One percent of everything I recover to me and mine, the rest to you," Dayid said. "I am amenable."

"I see that he has explained," Bridges said, smiling. "Very good. Now if you will have a seat and direct me to our first target . . . "

"We should do this by size and liquidity and work our way down," Dayid said. "If you agree, the largest single liquid account is with Hottinger's, in Nassau." As Bridges began to pull up the already bookmarked website for the bank, Dayid added, "The account number is ABZ305697. The password is 30127. And since you have another computer, I can begin working on other assets of the less liquid sort . . . "

Dayid stopped for a moment, then said, "I feel bad, you know, screwing my chief like this and leaving him vulnerable to the ravages of Khalid who is, I assure you, no saint either."

Bridges shrugged. "Don't worry about that overmuch. Khalid stiffed us in minor ways on the contract. He *thinks* he owns some assets that he is going to discover he doesn't."

★ CHAPTER FIFTY-SIX ★

Kill one; terrify a thousand.
—Sun Tzu, *The Art of War*

D-Day, Yemen

As the heaviest, Kravchenko tossed himself shoulder-first against the door, then fell to the floor, weapon aimed out, as the twin leaves burst open. Konstantin and Musin followed the slammed-open door, weapons to shoulders. Inside they found a large room, lavishly rugged and cushioned, with walls gilded in geometric shapes. Fully half a dozen doors opened onto the room, though all of them were closed. Whatever the layout of the place, it must have been well insulated as the sound of firing from outside almost completely disappeared once they were past the door.

Lada followed close behind, stepping over Kravchenko, pointing and shouting, "The bastard sleeps in there."

Following the woman's direction, the major and Musin ran to a closed door. Musin kicked it open while the major rushed in, aiming his submachine gun at Yusuf's head and saying, calm as you please, "Any excuse is a good one."

Musin followed Konstantin in, slinging his submachine gun, jumping on the bed, and rolling both of the girls flanking the Yemeni off the bed with his booted foot. He bent and flipped Yusuf onto his more than ample belly, then dropped down and pinned the man's hands behind him. Konstantin produced some sticky tape he'd gotten from the Americans on the ship and began to wrap Yusuf's hands together. Without a word, Lada went for a laptop lying on a marble table against one wall.

Meanwhile, Litvinov reported via short range radio, "Comrade Major, Galkin's down; dead I think. I'm pinned except that I can probably go over the wall. How far I'll get before they mount the wall and put one in my back I wouldn't bet on."

"Shit!" the major exclaimed, even as he continued wrapping Yusuf's hands. *Maybe Galkin was queer and maybe he wasn't. But by God, he was* our *queer and the fuckers are going to pay for that.*

From the open central bay, Kravchenko called, "Comrade Major, I have the wog's three sons in tow."

"Shoot them," Konstantin ordered. Immediately, the apartment was filled with a chorus of approximately post-pubescent male voices, screaming, and a cacophony of wailing female ones. "The old man wants this bastard *punished.*" Yusuf began to scream before Musin cuffed and punched him into silence. Of Litvinov, the major asked, "What the fuck happened, Lit?"

"Based on where the guards' bodies are, Comrade Major, I think Galkin saw someone coming for his position.

He never said a word, just opened fire. They must have seen him at about the same time—before they went down, anyway—because some of them got a few shots off, too. Right now, as I said, I'm pinned on the parapet."

"*Praporschik* Baluyev?" Konstantin called.

"Here, Comrade Major. Situation is nominal. I am in good position to cover Litvinov if he can run for it."

Konstantin switched radios. "Falcons?" he called.

"Here, Major," the senior of the helicopter pilots answered.

"Things have gotten complicated," Konstantin said. "A 'quiet' withdrawal is no longer an option. Come get us. I'll fill you in on the situation on the way."

"Roger. Ten minutes," the pilot answered. However surly a bastard he may have been before, once action had begun his voice and tone went entirely businesslike.

"So long?"

"Have to get the birds started and warmed up," the pilot said. "Remember, we didn't have, couldn't carry, enough fuel to both keep them running and make our rendezvous . . . not and carry all your equipment, all of you, and a minimum of our own ordnance."

"Understood. Please hurry."

"Wilco, Major."

"I've locked the women and very small children in one of the apartments—it actually looked more like a dungeon—Comrade Major," Kravchenko said, entering the room.

Lada followed. "It *was* a dungeon," she said. "Yusuf's sexual preferences were a bit . . . odd." She didn't elaborate.

Konstantin ignored the detail. In matters sexual he was very pedestrian, so much so that he really didn't like to even *think* about some of the strange turns human sexuality took. *Besides, I've got more important shit on my mind.*

He took his own pistol from a shoulder harness and started to toss it to Lada. He thought better of this, put the pistol away, then took Kravchenko's submachine gun and handed her that. "Can you use this?" he asked.

She examined it for all of a half second and answered, "Of course." She dropped the magazine with one hand, then jerked the bolt back and locked it to the rear. She lifted the weapon to inspect the chamber before replacing the magazine and releasing the bolt.

"Very good. Krav, put the wog on your shoulder. Sergeant Musin, lead."

"Where to, Comrade Major?" Tim asked.

"The roof. We're not getting out of the compound by ground and the roof's flat enough and big enough for the helicopter to come in."

In order—Musin, Konstantin, Kravchenko, and Lada—they lined up at the main door, better than half closed at the moment.

"Wait, Sergeant Musin," the major said. From a bag he took a grenade, pulled the pin, released the spoon, and bounced it through the slit between the door panels and off the far wall. The grenade flew from that wall to the covered area to the right of the branch corridor. Konstantin shifted position and aimed. Another one followed the first, this time bouncing to the left. There was heard another twin chorus of frightened shouts and screams before first one, then the other, exploded.

Hot on the heels of the blasts, Musin pushed the door

the rest of the way open and bounded forward. As he reached the end of the branch corridor he turned left and fired several bursts into the men, mostly lying and bleeding, though two were standing, swaying and stunned, in the long corridor to the left. Konstantin did the same, only to the right.

"SERGEANT MUSIN, LEAD!" Konstantin reminded. He had to shout. The grenades he had used, RDG-5s, had an unusually large explosive filler, nearly a quarter pound. But for the half closed door the blast would have deafened them all. As it was, except for those protected by earpieces, their eardrums throbbed while everything heard through them seemed to come from a great distance. Lacking a radio, and with one hand on the submachine gun and the other on Yusuf's laptop, both of Lada's ears hurt terribly.

"YES, SIR!"

People, more than a few, quartered in the rooms along the corridor, opened their doors. These were cut down instantly and without compunction. Most were men but two overly curious women died, too. Konstantin said a small prayer of thanks that no children had stuck their heads out. It was the kind of circumstance that really didn't permit a lot of time for close judgment calls.

At the door out which they'd come earlier, Musin stopped. "I CAN'T HEAR IF THERE'S ANYONE ON THE OTHER SIDE."

The major pushed him out of the way, then emptied a magazine through the door. He threw his own shoulder against it—*I am too fucking old for this!*—until it flew open. He briefly took out the earpiece and listened with his good ear. Yes, there was a commotion below. He replaced the earpiece and shouted, "GRENADE!" at Musin, pointing downward to indicate the direction.

While the major dropped and changed magazines, Musin nodded and pulled a single RGD-5 from his own bag. Arming it, he let it drop straight down the opening between the flights of steps. They didn't hear it hit bottom but they did hear and feel the blast. More screams followed that, one of which went on and on.

"UP!" Konstantin ordered, pointing.

"I DON'T KNOW WHAT'S UP THERE," Lada shouted.

"TARGETS!" Konstantin shouted back.

Musin, again, led the way. At the first landing, he ran into two keffiyeh-clad men, carrying rifles. Literally, ran into them. It was too close even to use a submachine gun. Instead, Musin threw himself into a tearing Tatar frenzy, a furball of slapping steel, punches, kicks, and headbutts. It seemed a long time, though it was probably less than two seconds, before Konstantin put his muzzle to one head and pulled the trigger, followed by another trigger pull for the other.

The two Yemeni guards, however, had had time enough to call out a warning. Before they reached the top of the steps, the air above was filled with a lead blizzard being poured in from outside.

"Shit," Konstantin muttered. Again switching radios he called, "Falcons, we need you fast."

"Five minutes, Major."

"In five minutes we might all be dead."

"I can't change the laws of physics, Comrade. Leave

that to the communists and the current American administration."

"Fuck the Americans and fuck the comm—"

Litvinov interrupted. "Comrade Major, Galkin is not dead. I'm not saying he'll live long but he's not dead." The radio also transmitted the sounds of bullets striking all around the transmitter, as well as the cracks of further misses, and the still more distant sound of rifle discharges.

"How do you know?"

"He called for me . . . for help."

"Okay, that's pretty much the definition of not dead. Can you get to him?"

"No. Not while I'm under this much fire."

"Tell him to hang on another five minutes."

"I'll try, but he seems to be rolling in and out of consciousness."

"Best you can do," Konstantin finished.

"And now?" Lada asked.

"And now we wait for support," the major answered. *And hope* those *fuckers don't have any grenades*.

"About two minutes out, Major. SITREP?"

Konstantin might have cursed the chopper pilots except *What would be the point? Besides, it never pays to curse out people you desperately need.*

"We're in three parties," the major said. "The largest of us, three of our men, one woman—don't ask—and one prisoner are trapped in a stairwell just below the roof. Two men, one of them wounded and not all that close to the other, are trapped and under fire on the eastern wall of the compound. One man is outside, to the east."

"I can't carry five of you on my own, Major. You've seen the passenger compartment. You just won't fit."

"The woman is tiny," Konstantin said. "As for the prisoner . . ."

So the old man wanted him for interrogation? So what? All he really needs is for the bastard to be dead. And I'm not leaving either one of my own, nor the woman, behind to satisfy an old man's desire for revenge. Let him be happy with the infliction of a shameful and painful death.

On a hunch, he asked, "Lada, what's on that laptop?"

"Everything, I think. Contacts, accounts, plans, assets. He never really lets it out of his sight."

Hmmm. Got the laptop, don't need the wog.

He took from a pouch a strand of piano wire, made to form a loop at one end. The loop he put around Yusuf's neck. The free end he tied off quickly on the stairs. Then he told Kravchenko, "Drop the fucker down to the next level."

With an indifferent shrug, Kravchenko walked down a couple of steps, then more or less tossed a screaming Yusuf through the opening. The screams cut off abruptly as the piano wire tightened. Yusuf swung violently and began to kick and dance, though the kicks grew weaker with each second his brain lacked fresh blood.

Tsk, thought the major. *That must hurt*. While Yusuf strangled, Konstantin took a pen and a notepad from one pocket and wrote on it, in Russian and English, "Pirate." He went down two steps and folded the note around the wire above the loop around Yusuf's neck. He couldn't tuck it between the wire and the neck because it had dug into the man's flesh at least half an inch. *Just in case anyone doubts why the swine was hanged.*

"Forget the prisoner," he told the senior pilot. "What I need is a rocket and gun attack on the roof to clear it off. The other bird needs to get a picture of what's pinning my two men on the wall and eliminate it."

"Wilco," the pilot answered simply.

"GRENADE," Konstantin shouted at Musin, once again, again signaling that he wanted it dropped. After it exploded below, he thought, *Ought to serve both to discourage pursuit* and *make absolutely sure the wog has enough time to finish strangling. Though that's probably overkill at this point.*

In mere moments, so it seemed, after the grenade went off, the roof began to shed dust and plaster as one rocket after another slammed into it. There was a lull, quickly followed by another salvo of rockets and what sounded like a series of very close together grenade explosions.

"The roof should be clear now, Major. My wingman is still hunting for whoever has your men pinned.

They emerged onto the roof cautiously, maintaining that caution until they were pretty certain that the MI-28 had done its job and left nothing alive. Then the four of them, including Lada, raced for the eastern edge of the thing.

Konstantin looked down and could see both Litvinov and Galkin, separated by nearly a hundred meters. He could also see flashes of fire coming from two places at ground level. *I can see why the helicopters are having trouble finding them.*

Rather than shout, Konstantin used the short range radio. "Krav?"

"Comrade Major?"

"Can you get a grenade close enough to those groups to matter?"

Kravchenko, too, looked over. "Sure. Easy."

"Do it, then." To the helicopters he said, "Watch for the grenade flash." Going back to short range radio, he told Litvinov, "The helicopters probably won't be able to kill the people who have you pinned. They might be able to drive them back for a while. Your choice if you want to try to retrieve Galkin."

Litvinov snorted. "Like that's a choice, Comrade Major. He may be a queer but he's still our queer."

"Good man," Konstantin said. "Exactly so."

Litvinov saw the grenades go off, then watched as the MI-28 rose above the wall and began to dance, its tail doing the *My girl's name is Señora* thing, its chin gun pelting first one section, then another, then back to the first. It expended all rounds quickly, then veered off to the east.

Gathering his courage, Litvinov got to his hands and feet and did a sort of sprinting crawl down to where Galkin's body lay. He was breathing, Litvinov saw, but also bleeding from more places than he cared to count. Picking the man up under his arms, Litvinov slung him over the parapet and then lowered him as far as he could down the wall. Then he let go. Galkin fell a few feet, then crumpled bonelessly to the ground.

Litvinov moved down a few feet from where he'd dropped Galkin. With an unvocalized prayer, he hopped his belly up to the crenellated wall, and swung his feet over. A couple of rounds struck the stuccoed mud brick below, where he'd been standing a moment before.

Slithering backwards, he lowered himself as far as he could, then also let go. When his feet hit the ground he did the very same parachute landing fall he'd learned many years ago at the airborne school at Ryazan. As he had there, more than once, he hit his head on something, hard.

Even as he cursed, he was moving to Galkin. Still cursing, he bent, got the other into a fireman's carry, and stood up. Then, as fast he as could, given the load, he began to sprint for Baluyev. It was an easy direction to hold because the *praporschik* was already firing at someone or something atop the wall, even as the other helicopter settled to the sand not far behind him.

The major watched Litvinov go. He also watched some of the guard force race to the wall once the helicopter had moved off. He and Kravchenko leaned over the side and pelted those guards with unexpected fire. They got some, *But not enough*.

"COME ON, KRAV," the major shouted, pushing the other in the direction of the helicopter, which had now landed on the roof. When they got to the door, they found Musin already buckled in, with Lada sitting more or less comfortably on his lap. Tim was trying very hard and somewhat unsuccessfully to hide a smile.

Ignoring the smile, Konstantin pushed Kravchenko in,

then followed, putting on the flight helmet even before seeing to his own buckling in.

"Get us the fuck out of here!"

The MI-28 lifted suddenly with the whine of rotors and jets, before nosing down and skimming out over the palace walls.

With the sun rising up out over the Indian Ocean, the pilot buzzed Konstantin. "Major," he said, "bad news. I'm sorry, but your man in the other helicopter died. There was nothing his mates could do."

★ CHAPTER FIFTY-SEVEN ★

Take pity of your town, and of your people,
Whiles yet my soldiers are in my command;
Whiles yet the cool and temperate wind of grace
O'erblows the filthy and contagious clouds
Of deadly murder, spoil, and villainy.
—Shakespeare, *Henry V*

D-Day, Rako, Ophir

The sun was a bare hint, not yet crept over the horizon but reflected still from scattered clouds. The reflection shone down on a column that appeared mostly made of dust, but was, in fact, four tanks, six gunned Elands, three Ferrets, and rather more than a dozen Elands without turrets—headquarters, infantry carriers of which there was now one fewer than there'd been, mortar and ammunition carriers, and an ambulance.

The company had begun the march west with six tanks. Two of those had fallen by the wayside—victims of poor maintenance or victims of drivers who, with the exception of swollen- and bent-nosed Lana, hadn't more than a clue what they were about. None of the newly captured tanks, given that their crews were nothing but a driver and a black or black-faced soldier standing in the turret to look intimidating, were truly combat capable.

But, Reilly *thought, when we show up at a town with better than two dozen combat vehicles I don't think we'll actually have to fight.*

Hope not, anyway. It would not only be bad for the town, we'd certainly end up killing a number of the people we intend to capture.

Reilly checked his map against his GPS. Then he glanced half to the right and said over the radio, "Scouts and antitank: That's the tank lager over there to your right. Go shoot it up . . . and have fun storming the castle, boys."

D-Day, East of Buro, Ophir

It had been said that a stern chase was a long chase. This chase must have seemed very long indeed to the pirates pursuing Eeyore and Morales.

Not long enough, though, thought Antoniewicz. *Not nearly long enough.*

Antoniewicz was crouched down almost under the ship's wheel. This didn't give a lot of cover, though it gave some. He steered by feel, mostly, supplemented with occasional risky glimpses forward.

Morales was crouched as well, though he was in the stern, holding one of the team's utterly inadequate underwater assault rifles. He was bleeding, the result of a side hit, not terribly serious in itself, from one of the bullets the pirates had been throwing their way infrequently and at random. The hit hurt, but, thought Morales, *probably not as much as a full day at BUDS.*

The pirates surprised the team, at first, by not firing continuously until the boat was a sinking colander. It took a while for Eeyore to guess the reason. *Fuckers don't want to damage the boat too badly. They're probably only shooting at all to try to entice us to surrender—like* that's *gonna happen—followed by a few deft throat slices and then over the side with our corpses. I'll turn and ram the bastards first. Try to, anyway. I'll be damned if . . .*

Eeyore's thought was cut off by a . . . well . . . if not an "Earth-shattering kaboom," at least a sea-shaking one.

"What the fuck?" he asked, risking a look up and a glance backwards.

What he saw when he looked to the stern was the boat that had been pursuing, on its side, taking in water, while pieces of the hull—crew, too, most likely—sailed up and up.

Morales started to laugh, the laughter bordering on hysteria. Eventually, he managed to get out, "I guess we mined that one, too, Eeyore."

Antoniewicz scratched his head, then rocked it side to side for a moment. "Five second fuses always last three," he said. "Maybe, on the other hand, twelve mile limpets always last for seventy-five. Or maybe it was a Friday afternoon limpet. Or—"

"Should we pick 'em up?" Morales interrupted.

Now it was Eeyore's turn to laugh. "Those bastards? Fuck 'em. The sharks can have 'em."

D-Day, Bandar Qassim, Ophir

Biggus had made sure Wahab and Fletcher boarded the other armed CH-801, before he got on the last one. By the time that was done, and everyone was airborne and approximately safe, the long night was pretty much over and Rosy-fingered Dawn, the child of Morning, was doing her thing.

She was doing it pretty well, in fact. The harbor was lit up brightly and was amazingly—

"Empty," Biggus announced. "The bitch is practically empty. They sortied every small and medium boat they had."

He used the radio to inform the *Merciful* just how much trouble he thought it, and everyone, was in.

"What have you got left?" asked the disembodied voice he thought he recognized as belonging to Waggoner.

"Just the machine guns," Thornton answered.

"Mmmm . . . that's not a lot," Waggoner observed. "And if they shipped shoulder-fired SAMs aboard any of the boats, they'll outrange you."

"Yeah, tell me something I don't know," Biggus answered.

"No," Waggoner said, "you tell me something I don't know, like what's your fuel status?"

The pilot answered that one. "We've got enough to get back. If you haven't moved too far south."

"Roger . . . hold a sec."

Biggus was pretty sure Waggoner was bent over a map,

protractor in hand, trying to figure out a way and a place to get all four armed birds onto the so-far-unseen pirate flotilla. Or extract everyone and head south before that flotilla showed up on the *Merciful*'s doorstep. Biggus was pretty sure that with two companies still on the ground, and probably two special operations teams, including the Russkis, none of that fancy shit was likely to work out.

"What's to work out?" he asked of Waggoner. "I know the map as well as you do. Most we can do is make a single pass and fuck with them a little. Assuming they don't fuck back worse."

"Mass is nice," Waggoner answered.

"Mass is nice when it's possible," Biggus countered. "Here and now, it ain't. Maybe later today it might be."

The voice on the other end changed from Waggoner to Stauer. "Biggus, forget fucking with them. I'd rather know how many they are, and their general layout, than have you bust caps on them to no good end and maybe lose two planes in the bargain. Stay out of potential SAM range. Swing by. Observe and report. Then come home."

With Stauer there was no arguing, not about operational matters, at least, and at least unless you could pin him between running a mission and his personal feelings.

"Roger, sir," Thornton answered.

"Won't argue with those orders," added the pilot.

D-Day, MV *Merciful*, off Bandar Cisman, Ophir

"Options, ops?" Stauer asked of Waggoner.

"We've got a few," the latter said. "One is, have the

Marine company assault Bandar Cisman, now, before Reilly and A Company can reinforce. Having the Ophiri chief's brother and his family on board might be enough to dissuade the flotilla from attacking."

Stauer made a quick mental calculation of the cost of that option, both in terms of his Marines and in terms of the likelihood of losing some of the captives he needed to the assault.

"No," he said. "Bad option."

Waggoner shrugged. "Didn't like that one, anyway. Second choice: Send Chin and *The Drunken Bastard* north."

"Death ride? Oooo . . . that's hard."

"Third choice: Kill the air support we've got going now, retrieve whatever we've got out there, refuel and rearm, convert the dustoff planes back to strikers, and hit them"—his finger traced a section of the eastern coast—"somewhere about here. But that's going to take a while to prep."

"Send Chin."

"Remind him that his crew's families are aboard?" Waggoner asked.

"He won't need the reminder."

D-Day, *The Drunken Bastard*

"Captain, call for you," said Chief Petty Officer Liu, he of the wife with the amazing skill with the gantry.

Chin stepped up from the charthouse to the bridge and took the radio's microphone.

"Chin here," he said.

"Captain, this is operations. We've got thirty-odd boats coming, we think, most smaller than yours and probably none as fast or as well-armed. Still, it's thirty or more. We need you to move north and stop them."

"One against thirty, eh? I like that," the Chinese skipper said. "Wilco." He handed the microphone back to Liu.

Liu took it, smiling, then said. "You style yourself a communist. Harrumph. You fool no one. You're no communist, Skipper; you're a *romantic*."

Chin didn't refute the charge. Instead, also smiling, he said, "Assemble the men, Chief." To himself, after Liu had begun shouting for the assembly, he whispered, "This is going to be *glorious*."

D-Day, fifty-four miles east of Bandar Qassim, Ophir

With having to concentrate on his flying, the pilot saw nothing. With the drone of his plane's motor, the pilot heard nothing. That is to say, he heard nothing until he heard Biggus Dickus Thornton begin to snicker in his headphones. The snicker became a laugh. The laugh a bellowing cacophony of sheer joy.

"They're alive!" Thornton shouted, lowering the binoculars he'd had pressed to his face. "They're alive!"

"Who? What?" the pilot asked.

"My team: Eeyore, Morales, Simmons. They're alive!"

"How do you know?"

"Look left," Thornton said, handing the binos forward before resuming his boisterous laugh.

The pilot took the field glasses, held them to his eyes, and did look. "What the fu . . . "

In his view, a large plume of wood and metal and bodies flew into the air, some distance out to sea. That was the first and obvious thing he saw. Rotating his head a few degrees to the left, he saw twenty or thirty boats. All of them stood stock still, no wakes, no bow waves, no white-churned water behind.

Even as he watched another boat disappeared in a flash of light, a cloud of smoke, and a deluge of spray.

"They *did* mine the fucking boats," Biggus said. "And if they mined them, and the boats went out anyway, it means the boats' crews hadn't a clue. If they hadn't a clue, it means my boys got away."

"Sounds reasonable," the pilot agreed. "But why are the boats still blowing up?"

"Fuck, I dunno," Biggus said. "Quality control at the factory, I imagine. Who cares, anyway? My boys are *alive*.

"Now let's go find 'em."

"As long as the fuel lasts, I'll try," the pilot concurred. "Don't expect a lot of circling."

Thornton took the radio, and sent his report to the *Merciful*. About halfway through, another voice, speaking English but with a Chinese accent, interrupted, saying, "You have no idea how this news distresses me."

D-Day, Rako, Ophir

In his hands, Reilly had the photos taken by Buckwheat Fulton and Wahab, weeks prior, showing who was to be taken from the town, once the people surrendered, or were crushed. He turned one over and muttered, "Circles and arrows, and paragraphs on the back of each one, telling what it's about."

The company surrounded the town, with a brace of tanks each to the northeast and southwest, infantry platoons northwest and southeast, and the gunned Elands interspersed by sections of two to the north, the east-southeast, and the west-southwest. Reilly's own personnel carrier stood on a small copse overlooking the town from the south. He spoke through his translator as his translator spoke through a set of loudspeakers attached to the Eland's sides.

"I'm not here to negotiate," Reilly said, the microphone picking up and echoing both his words and the translator's from the hills around the towns. Machine gun fire from the tank lager echoed, adding its own bit of punctuation.

"Whether you live or die matters not a bit to me.

"It should, however, matter to you. Surrender, then, all the people of this town, before I release my soldiers onto you.

"Or don't. And in the failing, watch your town burn. See your screaming daughters dragged out and raped before your eyes. Watch dishonor be heaped taller than a mountain upon your family names, forever. See your last little suckling baby tossed on the bayonets of my killers. Witness your stumbling old men and half blinded old women run down and pressed out like grapes to make a red wine of your dusty streets.

"You will not even be a memory, so completely will you and yours be erased.

"Come out now, all of you, toward me, and unarmed, or commend your souls to your god."

Never underestimate the benefits of a classical education, Reilly thought.

In one of the two T-55s to the northeast of the town of Rako, Lana Mendes sat in the driver's compartment. Behind her, in the turret, hands on a Russian .51 caliber machine gun, Schiebel—face painted black still, though the black was dusty and streaked now—watched the scene. He had a much better view than she did, though she could hear as well as he could.

"He dudn't mean id," she asked, through her smashed nose, "dud he?"

"No," the little grunt said, biting back a laugh. The poor girl sounded so funny, and her nose was such a mess, that not laughing was hard. "He's just saying it to frighten them into surrender. He wouldn't let any of those things happen. We wouldn't do any of them, even if he wanted us to." Schiebel hesitated, then added, "Well . . . except for destroying the town. We'd do that."

Even as he said it, hundreds of people, big and little, young and old, male and female, began to emerge from their shacks to trod, fearfully, to the south and Reilly.

★CHAPTER FIFTY-EIGHT★

We few, we happy few, we band of ruthless bastards!
—From "The Black Seal," *The Black Adder*

D-Day, Bandar Cisman, Ophir

"What the fuck?" Cazz asked of nobody in particular. "About time, but what the fuck?"

The spur to his question was the armored column, emerging from the dust, led three Ferrets followed by seven tanks he'd have taken for enemy, each of those tanks dragging another one by tow cables. Two of the dragged tanks, once they were close enough to really see, looked rather the worse for wear.

The tanks pulled into a row. Men, just one per, emerged from the turrets and began undoing the cables. The other vehicles began to split off into two columns, roughly evenly divided between turreted, gunned Elands and the unturreted ones packed with infantry. A third column, consisting of two more Ferret scout cars with some odd, boxy projections on top, and two obviously civilian trucks loaded down—packed to the rafters, really—with locals in their own dress, cut right and headed generally to the beach. A fourth, composed of three more turretless Elands, made straight for Cazz's own mortar platoon.

A single turretless Eland, with loudspeakers mounted to the sides, headed for Cazz. He saw Reilly riding in the empty turret well, one of his doggies manning the machine gun, the colonel's lady, Phillie, and his big, black sergeant major, Joshua. Also up there was one of the locals, an ancient type, what little hair he had gone steel gray.

"What's with the wrecks?" Cazz asked Reilly as the latter emerged from the Eland's side door.

"I'm a scrounge. Six of them we grabbed at the ambush, but two of those broke down. We picked up another three working ones at the lager, then I decided to tow the two that broke down and as many as looked like they might be repairable at the ambush site.

"I always wanted my very own tank platoon. Or company."

"He really wants his own division," Joshua said. "But he's a reasonable man and will settle for what he can get."

"Or division," Reilly admitted. "We'd have taken the rest but . . . they . . . ummm . . . weren't in the best shape. So, anyway, what wonderful entertainment have we got going here?"

"Nothing much since we penned them in. Oh, sure, we've traded shots back and forth and I lost two men, one dead, one wounded. Probably killed twenty or twenty-five of the locals, and I couldn't guess how many wounded. But basically, nothing much. Now that you're here with the heavy shit we can assault the place properly."

"Maybe not," Reilly said. "Maybe I've gotten a better idea."

"Really? What's that? I'm not even remotely averse to something that keeps any more of my boys from getting hurt."

Reilly pointed at the gray-fringed, mostly bald local. "The old man up there is the father of the chief of Ophir. He's also the father of the head of this town. I think he can talk his boy into surrendering. He seems very reasonable and very eager not to have done to any of his people what I promised would be done if I didn't get a surrender nice and quick."

Cazz raised an eyebrow. "Just out of curiosity, what did you promise?"

"Robbery, rape, murder, massacre, demolition, and extinction. Carthage, basically."

"Would you have . . . never mind, I don't want to know."

"Neither do I," Reilly admitted. "But having made the promise, and being, as I try to be, a man of my word . . .

"Anyway, I propose to send the old man—he goes by 'Zakariye,' by the way—under guard, to his son, to have a little chat."

"He'd have obliterated the place in no time flat," Joshua said. "Man of his word, after all." *Though I am a little miffed, still, that you both cost me fifty dollars to that son of a bitch, George, and are fucking a subordinate. Oh, well, I suppose every man has some failing. And, I admit, the girl is pretty. Or was, before turning her nose to mush. And noses can be fixed.*

★ ★ ★

All fire had ceased but ostentatiously armed helicopters, three of them now, and CH-801s, to the tune of four, circled the town menacingly overhead. Above those, and above all the witnesses, the sun beat down hot and fierce.

"If you try to harm either of these men, Son," Zakariye said, between the lines of occupied buildings and surrounding Marines and soldiers, his head inclining to one side, then the other, to indicate his grim-visaged guards, "or to free me, I have it on very good authority that this port will be obliterated, along with everyone in it."

The son, a man of no mean years himself, balked. His finger pointed at the circling aircraft as he said, "Gutaale will destroy those things in a moment."

"Jabir," the older man said, for this was his son's name, "Gutaale's precious new air force was destroyed on the ground. Why do you think his planes have not shown up yet?"

"His fleet—"

"No," Zakariye shook his head. "That lies on the bottom of the sea. And, before you mention the new tanks he purchased, stand for a moment."

Jabir stood and the father put one arm across his son's shoulders. "See there?" Zakariye said, pointing. "And there?" The point of aim shifted.

"Those *are* the tanks you were about to mention. No, son, your brother has nothing to send. You can fight, if you choose to, and you, your wives, my grandchildren, all will be killed."

"What choice, Father?" Jabir asked.

Zakariye sighed. "It seems that your brother seized someone he should not have. That's why these men came here. That's why they destroyed the airplanes, the boats and ships, the armored force. It was explained to me on the way here. They don't know where the man, more of a boy really, taken by Gutaale is. But they know where and who we are. They only want us to trade us."

"How do they know?" Jabir asked.

Zakariye laughed bitterly. "Do you recall an American 'journalist' who passed by here some months ago?"

Jabir thought for a moment, then shrugged and answered, "Al Ful-tan? He was just a scribbler, a maker of pictures and stories for magazines."

"Sadly," Zakariye corrected, "not. He was one of these men. They know exactly who we are. Or didn't you let al Ful-tan take a family portrait, and print you a copy?"

"Oh, shit. That was *dirty*."

"Yes, it was," the father agreed. "As to whether it was dirtier than kidnapping a free man from foreign soil and holding him as a hostage, I leave to Allah to determine. The question is now, as was also explained to me . . . quoted to me, "Will you yield and this avoid, or guilty, in defense, be thus destroyed?""

"Do you think Gutaale will trade?" Jabir asked. "If my brother will not, I'd rather die fighting."

"He'll trade," Zakariye said. "For he is no different from any of us; no different from Khalid, whose son was taken. Hilarious, is it not?" he asked.

D-Day, MV *Merciful*

Landing craft plied the waves, back and forth, bringing

both the prisoners from Rako and Bandar Cisman, as well as recovering the troops and armored vehicles. The latter set included over a dozen tanks, not all of them precisely pristine, that Reilly indicated he was willing to throw a serious tantrum over if he couldn't keep.

"We know where the boy is now," Boxer said. He could barely restrain the laughter in his voice. "Shortly after the attacks began, the Ophiri chief and his minions started burning up the air waves by radio and cell. We were able to monitor and record those calls, though it took us a little while to filter through them. A set of them went to Suakin. They wanted to know if the 'special prisoner' was still there and healthy. That's our boy."

"Suakin?" Waggoner asked. "As in, 'He cut our sentries up at?'"

"That's the place," Boxer agreed. "It's nothing now but ruins . . . correction, knowing where to look and having looked, some of those ruins were recently refurbished . . . on an island in the Red Sea connected by a causeway to Sudan.

"So the question is," Stauer said, "what do we do?"

"We've been running the helicopters hard," Cruz said. "Not just mine, but also the MI-28s that are due in shortly with Konstantin's people; both sets need a serious bout of maintenance before they'll be trustworthy for another operation. The CH-801s are in better shape—fixed wing is always easier to keep flying than rotary wing—but they're something less than ideal for the purpose."

"Of special operations people," Welch said, "we've got or will soon have nine of mine, ten counting me, including my remaining translator but not Venegas. Little Joe's not up to it and won't be for a while. Plus Biggus will have five, including himself, and assuming no losses. Then there's Rattus and Fletcher. And Konstantin is coming in with five, inclusive, assuming he's willing to go. That's twenty-one, plus a translator who's proven he won't run around like a chicken with his head cut off when the bullets start flying. We might profitably add in two engineers, maybe Nagy and Trim. Twenty-four heavily equipped men is a fair load on a Hip."

"How soon until we can get the ship into strike range?" Stauer asked Kosciusko.

"It's eleven hundred miles sailing to fair strike range," the ship's captain said. "At max speed, that's still sixty-one hours. That's a long time for word to get around about who did what, where, to whom."

"Yeah, boss," Boxer said. "Secrecy is probably an unattainable ideal at this point."

Chin gave a little cough. "Without getting into details I am sworn not to reveal, let it be noted that there is a *lot* of regular, old, gray paint stored in one of the containers below. Sprayers in another."

"That's true," Kosciusko said. "If we weren't in a terrible hurry and could head to sea, there's no pressing reason we couldn't repaint the ship underway and just sail up the Red Sea once the paint's at least tacky.

"We'd have to seriously reconfigure to hide everything," the skipper added, "given what's gone down the last twenty-four hours and all. Might even have to dump some shit. And we sure can't have the flight deck assembled, or the loading and unloading platforms."

Stauer clasped his hands behind his back and began to pace.

"The problem is," he said, "and Boxer, you'll agree, that Sudan is an altogether different kettle of fish from Ophir. It's a real country. Maybe a fucked up one but a real one. With a real military."

"Their navy's for shit," Boxer said. "Their air force, on the other hand, is impressive for numbers if only a *fifth* of them worked. And their ground forces could walk over us with a rock in each hand and still beat the shit out of us. Not that they'd use rocks, given their very large tank and artillery park.

"I don't think we want a war with Sudan."

"No," Stauer shook his head. "Here's what I think. Our best bet at this point is what we planned on, 'diplomacy.' Sorta. But that might not work. So here's what I want: Terry?"

"Sir."

"Collect your people, Biggus Dickus's pinnipeds, the Russians when they get here and assuming they agree to sign on, any other attachments you need, and Cruz. Waggoner, Boxer and Gordo, you go along, too. Plan an operation using nothing but helicopters and perhaps *The Drunken Bastard*, to go to Suakin, 'cut *their* sentries up,' and retrieve our boy. Kosciusko, as soon as we're finished loading take us out to sea and reconfigure us to look like a normal, innocent merchie. Do the camouflage thing as Captain Chin suggested."

Chin's chest swelled a bit. While he was always "the captain" to his own crew, it was rather warming for the Yankees to agree.

"Meanwhile," Stauer said, "I'm going to try the sweet light of reason. Cruz, get me a CH-801 ready to go before we take down the flight deck. And I need a volunteer pilot. Shouldn't need a translator. Gutaale allegedly speaks good English. And Boxer? I need a group portrait of all of our captives."

"Don't sweat the runway," Cruz said. "The two medevac birds are outfitted either for runway or water landings. We'll just have Mrs. Liu hoist one over the side when the time comes."

★CHAPTER FIFTY-NINE★

George Clemenceau made the remark that "War is too serious a business to trust to generals." Well, judging from the one he made at Versailles in 1919, peace is too serious a business to trust to statesmen.
—H. Beam Piper

D+1, Bandar Qassim, Ophir

The more he'd looked at it, the more his men had looked at it, the more Stauer thought that a hostage rescue at Suakin was a forlorn hope, to say nothing of an excessive risk to both his men's lives and his ultimate objective. He still had them planning it, back on the ship, even as Kosciusko's people repainted the hull and Mrs. Liu worked overtime to reconfigure the containers to look purely innocent.

Stauer mused, *If we'd known the boy was at Suakin, we could have done the job with a sixth of the manpower and at a tenth of the cost.* He smiled. *Damned good thing we didn't know.*

The pilot, McCaverty, now that the wounded were stabilized, tapped Stauer on the shoulder and pointed down at a port devoid of floating ships. There *were* a couple of larger ones—tied up, mind—but those were sunk.

Stauer could not help but laugh with pride at a job well done. *Be nice if we could get the fucking sub back, though,* he thought. *Hmmm . . . I wonder . . .*

"You sure they're willing to parley and not just string us up from the nearest lamppost?" McCaverty asked.

Stauer hesitated a moment before answering, "I'm sure they'd like to string us up from the nearest lampposts. But I'm even more sure that their chief doesn't want his entire family to feed the sharks. We should be safe enough. In any case, once I step off, you maneuver to a position from which you can do a quick takeoff. If they do grab me, just go. Fast."

That subject, safety, had led to a hell of a row with Phillie. *Hope we can make up,* he thought. *She'd be a hard girl to replace. What am I thinking? At my age she'd be an impossible girl to replace. Fortunately, I do have her example, insisting on getting on one of the medevac birds, to argue for me. I think it will work out.*

"I sincerely hope you're right," McCaverty said, as he circled the plane down to the now nearly vacant harbor. It touched down lightly, with only a minimal amount of splashing. He steered it for the docks where a small party of unarmed men, and a somewhat larger one of armed men, were waiting under a broad, fringed awning.

"I want to murder the filthy bastard," Gutaale said, quite despite the smile plastered across his face.

"You'll do no such thing," said Taban, standing beside him. Taban's tone carried the authority that came from speaking for the entire council of elders for the tribe. "I warned you months ago that the precedent you were setting might come back and bite us all in the ass. That has happened and it is *your* fault. It is going to take years to undo the damage you have caused us, if it can be undone. If you harm this man, his followers will then execute your entire family—which, I remind you, is also closely related to the rest of us—and then proceed to destroy the rest of us. In short, old friend, *no*."

"But he *robbed* me," Gutaale pleaded, his smile disappearing in a hate-filled grimace. "Virtually every cent I had to my, to our, name has been taken. All we have left is a couple of tons of melted gold bars under the ruins of the palace outside Nugaal. We are not only under the gun, we are now *poor*."

"There are other NGOs," Taban said. "Plenty of Europeans and Americans you can pick the pockets of. Plenty of roads to be badly built. Plenty of food aid and free medicine that can be taken and sold. And we can rebuild our fleet of naval *mujahadin,* in time. But for all that we must be alive. Harm this man and, based on what his group has done so far, we will no longer be alive. So forget it. And get a smile back on your face."

Stauer opened the door and was standing on the float even before McCaverty brought the plane to the edge of the dock. He made a little jump, trying hard not wince at the arthritis pains that shot across his knee, and landed well enough for a man in his fifties.

"I'm Wes Stauer," he introduced himself. "I am given to understand that you speak English. And I believe you have something that doesn't belong to you."

"How do I know," Gutaale asked, "that you will release my family if I give you the boy?"

Stauer shook his head. "You don't know. You can't know. But you can know that I've no personal reason for keeping them. And you can know, because I tell you so, that if you do not release the boy they will be turned over to Khalid. Khalid is much too personally involved in all this for you to expect the same kind of evenhanded, gentle treatment your family has received from me."

"And if I say that I will have the boy put through a wood chipper?"

Stauer sneered, snorted, and then shrugged with practiced indifference. "Then I say, so what? My contract was an either-or proposition. Either I get you to release the boy or I get Khalid the means of vast revenge. I get paid either way and, frankly, don't really care one way or the other."

"Speaking of pay, I want my accountant back and I want my money back," Gutaale said.

"No, and no. The money is now mine," which Stauer considered the truth. He then lied, diplomatically, "And your accountant, sadly, died under interrogation. You would be proud of the way he resisted us. Proud of the way he died with a blessing for your name on his lips and a plea for your forgiveness." The colonel's face grew icy and hard, "But it didn't stop him from shitting us everything you own. Several other members of his family, even more sadly, died, too." *My obligation to speak truthfully to an enemy is nonexistent until we make peace.*

Gutaale shivered. *This American bastard is even more vicious than the Arabs say they all are. Torturing to death a harmless accountant? Innocent family members?*

"You killed my people!" Gutaale shouted, mostly to cover his own fear.

Stauer smiled again, saying, "Yes, I did. Lots of them. If you think I regret that, you've been spending too much time surrounded by transnational progressives. What do I care how many I killed, or how, or even why? They stood in my way and they died. In droves."

I have been spending too much time surrounded by progressives, Gutaale silently agreed.

"I *told* you you've been spending too much time around the NGOs," Taban said in the local language, which he assumed, correctly, Stauer would not understand. "I mean, steal from them? Sure. That's all they're good for. But eventually you lose sight of the fact that they're freaks, off key notes in Allah's great orchestra, and that the world is absolutely nothing like the fantasy they portray and think they live in."

Stauer understood Taban's tone well enough, even if he didn't know the words. He consulted his watch, neither subtly nor ostentatiously. "Look," he said. "I really don't have a lot of time for this. You've got forty-eight hours to have the boy here, ready for pick up. At that time I'll have our captives in boats standing offshore. A single plane will come for the boy. If he's here, and gets on the plane safely, then the boats holding your people will drop them off somewhere within five miles of here, unharmed. If the boy is not here, however . . . but why go into detail? The boy *will* be here, *won't* he?"

"He will be here," Gutaale conceded, without a trace of good grace. "Unharmed."

D+1, Suakin, Sudan

Labaan found Makeda before he found Adam. The girl was washing clothing by hand in a tub. Bent over and concentrating, she didn't see him or hear him until he announced himself. "Woman, have you seen your man this morning?"

"He went for a walk," she replied, without bothering to look over her shoulder. "He does that a lot since he agreed to your 'parole.'" There was something in the keeper's voice that seemed to her to indicate a terrible upset. That, once she realized what it was, caused her to leave off her washing and turn around.

Yes, Labaan, for all his dark features, had gone pale.

"What is wrong?" she asked, immediately worried for both Adam and herself.

Labaan shook his head. "Nothing that need concern you." He shook it again, amending to, "Nothing that will cause either of you any harm. But finish up your chores as quickly as possible—no, just forget them and go pack. You and he are . . . moving. Today. As soon as possible."

"Moving?" she asked. "To where?"

"Bandar Qassim," he answered. "From there . . . well . . . to Adam's home, I suppose."

★ ★ ★

Since being captured, the only thing Makeda had ever been able to associate with automobiles was being carted off to market, or transferred from one owner to another. As such, she found the whole idea of riding in one most distressing. Indeed, it was distressing enough that she shook while standing next to the vehicle that had come for them, Adam's near presence notwithstanding.

"What's wrong, love?" he asked. When she told him, he said, "I could tell you that I understand. Perhaps in some way I even do. But the deeper part of the thing? No, that I would have to experience myself to tell you I honestly understood it. A captive I have been. A slave, never."

He grew quiet for a moment, before continuing, "And neither shall you be, from the moment we leave this place. I don't know how to free you legally, since the whole thing is extralegal everywhere I know of. I can tell you that you are free. You can come with me. You can stay here—"

"Not on your life," she said.

"I didn't think that was an option. Or you can come with me to my home and then go wherever you wish."

"What do you want?" she asked.

He sighed. "Me? I want you to stay with me."

Labaan, at the wheel of the car, overheard. *He is a good boy,* he thought. *And always was. If I had had a son . . .*

"Come," the old former captor insisted, pushing the thought away. "We must hurry or terrible things will happen. Come."

D+3, Bandar Qassim, Ophir

"I've never been in an airplane before, Adam," Makeda said. If the auto sojourn had visibly upset her, the prospect of actually leaving the Earth's surface looked to have her ready to vomit.

"It's fun," Adam assured her. "Really, I've done it many times."

"How many?" she asked.

"Ummm . . . twice," he admitted. "Not counting changing planes and brief stopovers. On my way to America to go to school and . . . ummm . . . on my way back to Africa. Ot maybe it was three times. But it will be fun."

"I would never personally describe flying as 'fun,'" Labaan said. "Though I know people who enjoy it. Some of them"—he immediately thought of Lance— "are idiots in my opinion. But it will not be so bad, girl. You'll be safe."

Makeda chewed her lower lip for a moment, then lifted her chin proudly and said, "If I knew for a fact that the thing was more than likely going to crash, and that chance was my only chance to be my own property again, I would *still* get on it."

Labaan and Adam exchanged glances. Labaan's glance translated as, "keeper." Adam's was more accurately described as accusatory: "And you *knew* I would find myself tied to this girl when you gave her to me. *Bastard*."

Labaan laughed and took Adam's hand. "You are a

good boy," he said, "and have every prospect of growing into a good man. Try to be a better one than my chief or yours."

"I will," the boy answered. "I promise." Taking the girl's hand, he led her to the airplane that floated to meet them at the dock.

The small floatplane came to the dock and twisted a bit. The engine's roar dropped off to a mild hum. Then the door popped open and a kindly faced man introduced himself. "I'm McCaverty," he said, "and I believe you people ordered a taxi."

"What if they take the boy, and that skinny slave he's acquired, and then *don't* release our people?" Gutaale fretted.

Taban shook his head. "You've not only been spending too much time with the bleeding hearts, chief, you've been listening too much to your own conniving heart. There is no reason, *none*, for the American not to give you back your people once he has what he came for. Besides," he pointed to sea, "there are the boats bringing them."

Past the landing craft and their escorting patrol boat that Taban had pointed to, the big boat, the one that had launched the others, had its crane over the side. A slack line ran into the water. Nobody on shore had the faintest idea why.

"Now show some manners and wave your former guest goodbye."

★EPILOGUE★

Kosciusko had left the bridge under his XO's command. Now he, like all the other company commanders, the staff, the sergeant major, and pretty much everyone else who could be fitted into the chapel _cum_ recreation _cum_ planning area, sat or, in many cases, stood, to hear what Stauer had to say. Only a few key players, notably the mess sergeant, were not in attendance. Neither was Wahab, as he had to go drop off Adam and Makeda and then retrieve his wife and family before Khalid discovered some things were not quite what he thought they were. The chaplain, Wilson, had just finished the memorial service for the slain, every one of whom was laying in a refrigerated container somewhere forward. They'd be buried later, somewhere to be determined.

Payments, rather _large_ payments, were already en route to the next of kin of the dead the force had suffered, carried by the two retired general officers who had had a place in planning the operation, back in San Antonio, but were too old, and knew it, for taking a more active role. In Galkin's case, for his next of kin—his mother, living in Saint Petersburg—the money had been sent through Father Pavel, in Paldiski, along with a small contribution to his church. Sure, Galkin hadn't really been part of the force, had never signed an enlistment contract, but, Stauer thought, *Let's be big about this. What's a little piece of paper with a signature, anyway?*

"Gentlemen, ladies, couple of things," Stauer began. "First off, to announce a wedding: Chaplain Wilson will be officiating over a marriage between Miss Potter and myself in three days. You're all invited—Lana Mendes and the Romanian nurses' aides are *required*—to attend. Ladies, I am informed that the bride will be perfectly happy to have you serve as her bridesmaids in the same attire she'll be wearing, battle dress.

"Gordo, you have the logistics down on that?"

Harry Gordon looked up from a clipboard. "Yes, sir. There's still half a container of booze we stashed away for the victory celebration. Even these reprobates couldn't kill it all off. And, while Sergeant Island says that the 1910 Manual for Army Cooks doesn't have anything specifically about weddings, he can improvise. He also says that, since the manual does not cover the subject matter, perhaps it's a bad idea. However, you being the boss and the manual giving great deference to command, he says he'll play along."

The sergeant major harrumphed. "Sergeant Island is a wise man, sir, and I think you should give his counsel serious weight."

That earned him a dirty look from Phillie until she

realized he was smiling—*What? Joshua never smiles!* Though, of course, he sometimes did—and wasn't remotely serious.

"And," Gordo continued, "Phillie doesn't have to wear battle dress. It seems that Doctor Lin not only sews guts, she sews as a hobby. Or maybe it was a necessity in China. Dunno. Anyway, there is enough white material in sick bay that she is sure she and her own people can come up with a proper dress. Silk, no. White, yes."

Reilly cast a sidewise glance at Lana. *Should I ask about a second dress? Nah, I haven't even asked* her. *And besides, she'll want her poor nose fixed before she consents to having her picture taken. And she'll want pictures. If she agrees. Which, of course, she might not.*

"It'll still be battle dress for the bridesmaids, though." Gordo looked personally affronted that he didn't have a solution to that minor problem.

"Fair enough," Stauer agreed. "That work for you, Phillie?"

She nodded, speechless. The whole idea that Wes was actually going to follow through, especially after the fight they'd had . . . *Thank you, God. Will You forgive me if I don't have any more sexual sins to confess, since none of the deliciously wet and sloppy stuff I intend to indulge in to excess will be a sin anymore?*

"Speaking more generally, and toward the future," Stauer added, "We really need to do some thinking, some planning, and some talking.

"How many of you guys have any idea of how much money we have?" Stauer looked around. *No, from the faces only a few do.*

"All right." He pointed at a thin middle aged Ophiri, standing against the rear bulkhead, and said, "Courtesy of the 'late' Mr. Dayid, also late of Gutaale's accounting service, we have . . . billions. A couple, anyway. Not counting the assets we got from this job. If you check your enlistment contracts, you'll note that *I* get to control and dispose of any property seized. Sorry, Reilly, that means I own those tanks you filched.

"What *that* means, though, is that we can afford to stay together, doing what we do best, until we're finally just too old to walk anymore." Stauer looked around at the small sea of mostly gray-headed men, with weather- and care-worn faces, and added, "In other words, until some-time next year, anyway."

That drew a hearty and good-natured laugh from the company.

"Or, we can split up the money and each of you will be a millionaire. For about ten minutes until the tax bite hits. And good luck explaining to the IRS where the money came from.

"Before I ask you to decide, I want Boxer to talk to you about life, the universe, and everything. Ralph?" Stauer stepped off center as Ralph took his place.

"Lights. Camera," said Boxer. Immediately the lights dimmed to nothing, to be partially replaced by a somewhat blurry rectangle projected against the wall behind him.

"He wasn't joking, you know," Boxer said, conversationally. "I mean about that tax bite. For the American majority among us, the top marginal rate—and we'll all be in it—is now forty-two percent, and the Social Security and Medicare rate—which is flat—comes in at a little over eighteen percent. And with the cap lifted, you'll pay that on every dollar. The Euro's will pay even more. If you come from a state like California, New York, Illinois, or one or the New England states, you can add anything up to twelve percent to that. And there's no guarantee that that won't go up, even retroactively, because the rates are driving people to flee both high tax states, and the high tax United States, for better climes, rather than being driven into the lower class by being taxed on behalf of the lower class.

"Unfortunately, in the long run, there *are* no better climes. First slide."

A map of the world appreared, showing sea lanes interrupted by markers of explosions off the coast of Somalia, both coasts of Panama, the Straits of Mallaca, and some few other places.

"Those markers you see," Boxer explained, "were piratical attacks on shipping ten years ago. Next slide." The map remained, but the number of markers dropped roughly in half. "That's this year's. Looks better, no? Well . . . as a matter of fact . . . *no*. Because . . . next slide." The map disappeared, to be replaced by a chart showing the number of merchant vessels actually in operation carrying goods, and their average tonnage. More precisely, it showed the severe drop in both.

"That's right," Boxer said. "There are fewer piratical attacks only because the volume of international trade by sea has dropped through the floor. Next slide."

The map returned, this time showing explosive markers on land. There were a lot of them. Everywhere. "That's terrorist incidents, ten years ago. Next slide.

"That's last year's. Note how many fewer there were. Good thing, right?

"Wrong. Most of the areas that don't have any terrorism now—Afhanistan, Iraq, Egypt, for example—don't have it because they've fallen to Sharia law, and a) the imans and mullahs don't put up with that shit while b) why engage in terror; they've got what they want. In places that haven't yet fallen—Europe, notably, but also Africa, Latin America, and Asia—and which have large Moslem minorites, terrorist incidents are way up. Moreover, ethnically, culturally, or religiously motivated crimes—robbery, rape, arson, murder—have been going up at an average increase of six percent a year for the last ten years. As far as crime goes, sometimes the Moslems are the culprits, sometimes the victims, and sometimes they've got nothing to do with it at all. It's not altogether clear that *anybody*, or any group, respects law much anymore.

"Terrrorism, by the way, would certainly have gone up even more except that money is tight. Why is money tight? Next slide."

Boxer went silent for a moment, giving his audience the chance to digest the information. This one concerned the price of oil. On the face of it, the information was good. Oil had been dropping irregularly but generally for ten years.

"This is why money is tight and part of why terrorism is down. The oil states, and especially Arab and other Islamic oil states, don't have any to give away. Their governments are barely hanging on, and to do so they're having to liquidate assets held in other countries to keep up their massive welfare systems and the security forces that try to keep a lid on things. In the long run, of course, this is death to them. It's only a matter of time before there's armed revolution in the streets of Riyadh and Kuwait City of a size and power they can't put down.

"No bad thing, you think. Fuck 'em, you think. But why is the price of oil down? Next slide."

This one showed industrial output from Europe, Asia, and the Americas. It was all bad news. All of it.

"Next."

That one showed the growth in budgets of various trans- and supranational organizations, ranging from the United Way to the European Union to the United Nations.

"Interesting, isn't it, how while everything else is sinking into the sewer, the budgets of the transnational progressive organizations, fed by 'contributions' from the developed world, and various frauds like 'cap and trade' keep rising? As domestic taxes keep rising? As the governments of the world prove ever less capable of 'soaking the rich' and ever more adept at soaking the working class under the guise of soaking the rich? I'd suggest that that's not entirely a coincidence.

"No more slides," Boxer said. "But remember, those were just a taste of what's going on. Remember, too, that all the really measurable things aren't very important, and all the really important things aren't very measurable. Worse than all that material shit is this: people in our civilization don't have any hope any more. They don't have any faith. They've stopped believing things can be fixed.

"Some years ago, a German attempted to list all the reasons for the collapse of the Western Roman Empire. He stopped when he reached two hundred. There were probably more. I imagine that, in our more complex world, we could come up with five hundred, or a thousand. No matter. We don't need to. The pattern is clear, as clear as anything has ever been. To quote a wise old man of my acquaintance, 'Civilization is on the ropes.' And that's even without a plague or new ice age. And I wouldn't bet against those, either."

Boxer went silent and looked over at Stauer. Stauer nodded, and began to walk to center stage, as Boxer walked off to the side. "Lights," Stauer called, and once again the bay was brightly lit. That is, it was brightly lit except for the dark looks on hundreds of faces following Boxer's little briefing.

"So what are we going to do about it?" Stauer asked. "More pointedly, what *can* we do about it?"

He let the men and women, and the few girls, think about that in silence for a moment, then said, "We can *fight* it! It's probably the only thing we're good for, but by *God*, we *are* good at it. Old and decrepit as we may be, we are still goddamned good at it.

"I don't know about you, but for me, I don't want my grandchildren—maybe my great-great-great grandchildren, someday, sitting in the burned out, washed out, crumbling ruins of my civilization—to say, 'Oh, if only old man Wes had had the balls to fight it, back when it could still be fought.' No, sir. I'll fight it."

He looked over at Reilly, who had an unaccountable smile on his face. "Something funny?" Stauer asked.

"Not funny, exactly," Reilly answered. "But it made me remember something I had to memorize when I was in high school:

'Old age hath yet his honour and his toil;
Death closes all: but something ere the end,
Some work of noble note, may yet be done,
Not unbecoming men that strove with Gods.'

"Odd, the things one remembers," Reilly finished.

"Maybe not so odd," Stauer replied. "Maybe just right."

"Maybe," Reilly half agreed. "So what have you got in mind, boss?"

"I've been thinking that the best way to do that just might be to open a military school somewhere. Nothing else is going to give us the excuse to have a base and be armed to the teeth on that base."

"Back to Brazil, sir?" Cazz asked.

"No," Stauer shook his head, "I don't think so. The Brazilians couldn't, or at least wouldn't, pay well enough for having their troops attend a school to keep it running on its own. That takes Oil Arabs, America, or Europe . . . or Japan, I suppose. And, being properly patriotic sorts, the Brazilians are unlikely to simply acquiesce in our flying in a new foreign infantry battalion, regiment, or brigade once a month so that we can train them. They've also got some issues with arms in private hands. I figure they'll *really* balk at tanks. Not to mention what an awkward position we'd be in if they ever discovered what we prepared to do while in their country."

"We'll keep that Rhode Island sized chunk of land that Khalid *thought* he owned, mind you. But we'll keep it as an investment, nothing more, and we'll be extracting what we left behind as we can."

"You're thinking a new jungle school, Colonel?" Joshua asked. The U. S. Army had closed its jungle school, the Jungle Operations Training Center, at Fort Sherman, Panama, many years before. "Sure be nice to spend my sunset years kicking tail in Panama."

"Ah, yes, I almost forgot; you used to be a lane walker there at JOTC, weren't you? Anyway, Sherman's an option, Sergeant Major, yes," Stauer agreed. "It's even for sale, most of it, and has all the facilities we'd need, to include an airstrip, bunkerage, barracks, married housing— some anyway, offices, ranges, an impact area, and dock space for the landing craft and the *Bastard*. It's also on the Canal which would make slipping a unit out at need and discretely fairly easy. But, Bridges has checked; it is *not* going cheap."

"Does this include us?" Konstantin asked. He knew about the payment being sent to Galkin's mother and thought, *Now this is a group with a great Russian kind of heart, the kind of group we could be proud to be in.*

"If you and your men wish it to, Major, yes. Your pilots and ground crew, too, since, while we own the helicopters, we can't fly them. The other non-Americans, too, naturally."

"If we stay," Konstantin thought about Yusuf's laptop, and again of a payment sent to the mother of one of his men, "we may have a contribution to make worth having. And, you understand, it is *our* civilization, too, that is falling."

"I understand," Stauer said, thought he really didn't. And the way the Russian had said "contribution" didn't sound like he meant their own mortal selves.

"Ummm . . . Sir, if I may?" Gary Trim interrupted, his words distinguished by quite a pleasant British accent.

"Go ahead, sapper."

"Sergeant Babcock-Moore and I discovered that Guyana actually has some . . . pretty suitable land. For . . . well, for dirt, sir. Couple of dollars an acre, or less."

"Facilities?"

"No," Trim admitted, shaking his head. "No, those we'd have to build ourselves or have built. Still, just doing that, providing jobs, would probably endear us to the locals. And I am, after all, an engineer and, arguably, so is that Hun, Nagy."

"I found that chunk when we were first looking," Gordon added. "It's got potential."

Seated in a wheelchair, one leg up and cast, Vic Babcock-Moore thought, *And there is one local, anyway, I wouldn't mind being 'endeared' to. And, this time, I've gotten her number.*

"It's an option to consider," Stauer said. "Great tracts of land, eh?"

This last caused Vic to startle. *How the hell did he know what I was thinking?*

Stauer rubbed his hands together. "Now, not that I'll consider myself bound by it, but let me get a feeling for who would like us to stay together and who would like us to set up a school. Also who would like us to stay in this business? For the first, show of hands."

Stauer didn't bother to count. Some people probably hadn't raised their hands. Most had.

"And for the second?" This told much the same story, as did the third poll.

"Resolved then," Stauer said, in his most formal voice, "that this organization, name to be designated, shall find a place to establish a base, and set up a school to train First World armies in operating in Third World places, and that all present shall have a place at that school, salaries and other benefits to be determined. Further resolved, that said organization shall retain the ability to conduct such operations as it has in the past, and to conduct them, as and when appropriate, to save our civilization, if we can, but at least to fight for it."

★ACKNOWLEDGEMENTS★

Special thanks to my wife, Yoli,
and editrix, Toni Weisskopf.
And to the barflies, friends, and general helpers:
Rob Hampson, Charlie Prael, Barry Sentinel,
Victor Sargent, the Forgotten Soldiers Bike Club,
Roger Ross, Mo Kirby, Sue Kerr, Peter Gold,
Steve St. Onge, Ori Pomerantz, Neil Frandsen,
Dick Evans, Tom Wallis, Francis Turner,
Mickey zvi Maor, Tim Arthur, Bill Swears, Steve Yee,
Alen Ostanek, Chris French, Justin Watson,
Chris Nuttall, Av'andira, Harry Russell,
Keith Robertsson, Thomas Price, Lahela Corrigan,
Scott Connors, Paul Howard, John Cristiano,
and all the rest of the friends and 'flies who've helped
with the planning, execution, and test reading. If I've
forgotten anyone, chalk it up to premature senility.

The Following is an excerpt from:

A DESERT CALLED PEACE:
THE AMAZON
▦◉▦ LEGION ▦◉▦

TOM KRATMAN

Available from Baen Books
April 2011
Hardcover

WHAT HAS GONE BEFORE
(5,000,000 BC THROUGH ANNO CONDITA (AC) 472):

Long ago, long before the appearance of man, came to Earth the aliens known to us only as the "Noahs." About them, as a species, nothing is known. Their very existence can only be surmised by the project they left behind. Somewhat like the biblical Noah, these aliens transported from Earth to another planet samples of virtually every species existing in the time period approximately five hundred thousand to five million years ago. There is considerable controversy about these dates as species are found that are believed to have appeared on Old Earth less than half a million years ago, as well as some believed to have gone extinct more than five million years ago. The common explanation for these anomalies is that the species believed to have been extinct were, in fact, not, while other species evolved from those brought by the Noahs.

Whatever the case, having transported these species, and having left behind various other, typically genengineered species, some of them apparently to inhibit the development of intelligent life on the new world, the Noahs disappeared, leaving no other trace beyond a few incomprehensible and inert artifacts, and possibly the rift through which they moved between Earth and the new world.

In the Old Earth year 2037 AD a robotic interstellar probe, the *Cristobal Colon*, driven by lightsail, disappeared en route to Alpha Centauri. Three years later it returned, under automated guidance, through the same rift in space into which it had disappeared. The *Colon* brought with it wonderful news of another Earth-like planet, orbiting another star. (Note, here, that not only is the other star not Alpha Centauri, it's not so far been proved that it is even in the same galaxy, or universe for that matter, as ours.) Moreover, implicit in its disappearance and return was the news that here, finally, was a relatively cheap means to colonize another planet.

The first colonization effort was an utter disaster, with the ship, the *Cheng Ho*, breaking down into ethnic and religious strife that annihilated almost every crewman and colonist aboard her. Thereafter, rather than risk further bloodshed by mixing colonies, the colonization effort would be run by regional supranationals such as NAFTA, the European Union, the Organization of African Unity, MERCOSUR, the Russian Empire and the Chinese Hegemony. Each of these groups were given colonization rights to specific areas on the new world, which was named—with a stunning lack of originality—"Terra Nova," or something in another tongue that meant the same thing. Most groups elected to establish national colonies within their respective mandates, some of them under United Nations' "guidance."

With the removal from Earth of substantial numbers of the most difficult and intransigent portions of the populations of Earth's various nations, the power and influence of trans- and supranational organizations such as the UN and EU increased dramatically. With the increase of transnational power, often enough expressed in corruption, even more of Earth's more difficult, ethnocentric, and traditionalist population volunteered to leave. Still others were deported forcibly. Within not much more than a century and a quarter, and much less in many cases, nations had ceased to have much meaning or importance on Earth. On the other hand, and over about the same time scale, nations had become pre-eminent on Terra Nova. Moreover, because of the way the surface of the new world had been divided, these nations tended to reflect—if only generally—the nations of Old Earth.

Warfare was endemic, beginning with the wars of liberation by many of the weaker colonies to throw off the yoke of Earth's United Nations and continuing, most recently, with a terrorist and counter-terrorist war between the *Salafi Ikhwan*, an Islamic terrorist group, various states that supported them, and—surreptitiously— the United Earth Peace Fleet, on the one hand, and a coalition led by the Federated States of Columbia, on the other.

This eleven year bloodletting began in earnest with the destruction of several buildings in the Federated States of Columbia and ended in fire with the nuclear destruction of the city of Hajar in the unofficially terrorist-sponsoring state of Yithrab.

Prominent in that war, and single-handedly responsible for the destruction of Hajar, was Patrick Hennessey, more commonly known as Patricio Carrera, and the rather large and effective force of Spanish-speaking mercenaries he personally raised, the *Legion del Cid*, based in and recruiting largely from *la Republica de Balboa*, a small nation straddling the isthmus between Southern Columbia and *Colombia del Norte*.

Balboa's geographic position, well-suited not only to dominate trade north and south but also, because of the Balboa Transitway, an above-sea-level canal linking Terra Nova's Shimmering Sea and *Mar Furioso*, key to commerce across the globe, was in many ways ideal. It *should* have been a happy state, peaceful and prosperous.

It was also, unfortunately, ideal as a conduit for Terra Nova's international drug trade. Worse, its political history, barring only a short stint as a truly representative republic following the war of liberation against United Earth, some centuries prior, was one of unmixed oligarchy, said oligarchy being venal, lawless, and competent only in corruption. Perhaps still worse, during the war against the terrorists, the security needs of the country had been filled by the introduction of troops from the Tauran Union to secure the Transitway and its immediate surrounds.

Carrera had learned well from the *Salafi Ikhwan*, however. The drug trade through Balboa was ended by war and terroristic reprisal to a degree that left the surviving drug lords quaking in their beds at night. The oligarchy was beaten through the electoral process and the final nails driven into its coffin—and into the heels of the oligarchs—when it attempted to stage a comeback in the form of a coup against the elected government and Carrera, its firm supporter. Carrera's second wife, Lourdes—Balboan as had been his first, Linda, murdered with her children by the *Salafi Ikhwan*—figured prominently in the suppression of the coup.

The problem of the Tauran Union's control of the Transitway remains, as does the problem of the nuclear armed United Earth Peace Fleet, orbiting above the planet. The Taurans will not leave, and the Balboans—a proud people, with much recent success in war—will not tolerate that they should remain.

And yet, with one hundred times the population and three or four hundred times the wealth, the Tauran Union outclasses little Balboa in almost every way, even without the support of Old Earth. Sadly, they have that support. Everything, everyone, will have to be used to finish the job of freeing the country and, if possible, the planet. The children must fight. The old must serve, too. And the women?

This is their story, the story of Balboa's *Tercio Amazona*, the Amazon Regiment.

▦ CHAPTER ONE ▦

> . . . a failure, but not a waste.
> —LTC (Ret.) John Baynes, *Morale*

A phone was ringing somewhere. People—women and children mostly—screamed. Others, men and women, both, shouted. Their voices were distant, as if they came from the mouth of a tunnel. Runaway freight trains, having jumped their tracks and taken off into low ballistic flight, crashed into scrap metal yards, one after another. Over that was the sound of jet engines straining and helicopter rotors beating at the air.

With a barely suppressed shriek of her own, Maria Fuentes sat bolt upright in her trembling bed, her hand going automatically to her mouth to stifle the sound. As her eyes adjusted to the small light streaming in through her bedroom window, she realized that she wasn't asleep any longer.

"It was a . . ." she began to say. She stopped, mid-sentence, when she realized that she could still hear the trains, the crashes, the screams.

"*Mierda!*" she exclaimed, as she threw off the light covers. "Not a nightmare. Shit. Oh, *shit.*" Maria felt nausea rising, mostly fed by sudden unexpected fear.

The phone, which had stopped ringing, began again as Maria raced for her baby's—Alma's—room. She stopped and picked it up.

"Sergeant Fuentes."

"Maria? Cristina." Centurion Cristina Zamora was Maria's reserve platoon leader. "Alert posture Henrique. No drill." Zamora's voice was strained, nervous. Maria couldn't remember ever having heard Cristina's voice as anything but perfectly calm before. Not ever. She felt a fluttering in the pit of her stomach. *Zamora's upset? We're so fucked.*

"*Not* a drill?" she asked, pointlessly.

"No, Maria, not a drill. Alert posture Henrique."

"Henrique? Okay, I understand." *'Henrique.' Call up all the reservists, but only those militia who can be quickly and conveniently assembled.* "I guess time's more important than numbers, huh?"

"They don't tell me these things, Maria. Later."

The phone's tone changed, telling Maria that Zamora had hung up.

Maria's phone was already programmed with the necessary numbers to conduct an alert. She scanned through until she found the number for her assistant, Marta Bugatti. She pressed that button, then the button for 'speaker.' She placed the phone on her bed and, while the phone was ringing, pulled out her Legion-issue foot locker. A couple of flicks of the retainers and the top popped open. She was pulling her tiger-striped, pixilated battle dress trousers on when the ringing stopped and a deep voice—deep for a woman, anyway—answered, "Bugatti here, Maria."

"Marta. Alert. 'Henrique.' No shit."

"Oh, *really*? I would never have guessed!"

Unseen by Maria, a mile and a half from Maria's small apartment, Bugatti shook her head in general disgust and then held her own telephone receiver towards the nearest window. On her own end, Maria could easily make out the sound of chattering machine guns.

Marta's voice returned in a moment. "So what fucking else is fucking new? I'll take care of it. I'll . . . " Marta's phone went dead.

"Marta? *Marta*?" Maria pounded her own phone on the foot locker's plastic edge in frustration mixed with fear. "Shit. Dead." She closed the cell and tossed it on the bed. She thought, *OK, Marta. You're a bitch . . . sometimes. But you're a lovable bitch and you're my bitch besides. I'll trust you.*

Maria pulled on her boots, green nylon and black leather, tucked her trousers into them, and then speed laced them shut. She wound the ends of the laces around her legs and tied them to hold the trousers in place. From her locker she took her battle dress jacket. She was buttoning this as she started for her daughter's bedroom.

She started, then stopped short at Alma's door. *My God, I am going to have to leave her, then fight; maybe die, too, and leave her forever.*

Suddenly Maria felt even more ill. *How can I leave my baby?* Just as suddenly, she felt even worse. *How can I abandon my friends, my sisters, my troops?*

Bad mother; bad friend. Responsible parent; irresponsible soldier? Hero? Coward? None of those words mean a damn thing. Whatever I do, it's going to be because I'm more afraid of not doing it than of not doing the other. I'm going to be a coward in some way, no matter what.

Had she been a different person, *any* different person, she might just have stood there, indecisive, until it was all over. But Maria wasn't just *anybody*. The powers that be had selected her very carefully, then trained her more carefully still. They had even organized her unit very carefully, paying more than usual attention to the needs of single military mothers. With or without Maria, Alma would be all right. She knew that. But without her, her troops—her friends—might not. She had no choice, really. She'd made the decision years before.

I have to go.

Alma was still sleeping soundly in her little bed when her mother entered. Maria smiled as her sight took in her daughter's few dozen pounds and few little feet of soft lines, dark lashes and curly hair. Maria marveled that not only was Alma hers, but that the baby wasn't awake and screaming.

I could never hope to sleep with artillery flying anywhere nearby, not even in training. What makes it so easy for a kid?

Maria looked out the window from Alma's bedroom. She couldn't see much but the street they lived on, and not all of that. Streetlights illuminated the scene. So far as she could see none of Terra Nova's moons had any noticeable part in that. Then the streetlights began to flicker out, leaving nothing but the moons' light.

Below the apartment, people were running in the streets, most of them tugging on uniforms. Just about everybody was carrying a rifle, machine gun, or rocket launcher. A number of those who weren't armed seemed to be trying to hold back someone who was. Somebody's mother, wife, or maybe girlfriend was crying for him to come back. Maria couldn't see where anyone did turn back though.

Returning to her own room, Maria continued pulling gear from the locker. Out came load bearing equipment, her helmet, her silk and liquid-metal *lorica*, the Legion's standard body armor. Her centurion's baton she picked up for a moment, then replaced it in the locker. Last came her modified F-26 "Zion" rifle.

She held the rifle in her hands for a moment, drawing some small comfort from its heft and weight. Then she slapped a drum magazine in, turned the key on the back to put pressure on the spring, and jacked a round home.

I hope Alma stays asleep. She hates to see me in helmet and body armor.

Fully clothed and armed, Maria slung her rifle across her back, walked back to the baby's bedroom, then picked her up in her arms.

Alma almost woke up then, sucking air in with three gasping "uh . . . uh . . . uhs." The mother waited a minute or two, holding her, stroking her hair and saying, "Don't worry, baby. Everything will be all right, baby. Don't worry, love. Mama's here." The child snuggled her soft hair into an armored shoulder and fell back, sound asleep.

Once Alma had fallen asleep again, it was out the door and down three flights of stairs. Maria didn't bother with locking the door behind her; crime hadn't been much of a problem in this part of the city for some time; current invasion excepted, of course.

▨▨▨

—end excerpt—
from *The Amazon Legion*
available in hardcover,
April 2011, from Baen Books

Epic Urban Adventure by a New Star of Fantasy

DRAW ONE IN THE DARK

by Sarah A. Hoyt

Every one of us has a beast inside. But for Kyrie Smith, the beast is no metaphor. Thrust into an ever-changing world of shifters, where shape-shifting dragons, giant cats and other beasts wage a secret war behind humanity's back, Kyrie tries to control her inner animal and remain human as best she can....

"Analytically, it's a tour de force: logical, built from assumptions, with no contradictions, which is astonishing given the subject matter. It's also gripping enough that I finished it in one day."

—Jerry Pournelle

1-4165-2092-9 • $25.00